angels with engine failure

an Arabian cyberpunk tale cycle

Bradley VanDeventer

Angels With Engine Failure, First Edition.

Copyright © Bradley VanDeventer (2018). All rights reserved.

ISBN: 978-1-7320282-7-2

Publisher: Flying Knee Press

Cover design: David Provolo

For inquiries regarding this book, contact: bradleylvan@outlook.com

TABLE OF CONTENTS

THE OUTERNATIONALIST

*In the Name of Allah, the All-Merciful, the Compassionate,
the Omniscient, I will tell a tale of a tale.*

t his will be the story of a story that refused to be told
with such fervor, that, when it finally was told, it unleashed a chain reaction that devastated many things in
its wake. The story itself was not poisonous. It was a
story that moved so deftly within the hierarchies of fiction that it
pierced through the fabric of reality and made a mess of the whole
deal. Since I lack the expertise of the narratrix, I have decided to
include a preamble to her telling of it. I therefore write verbatim:

"The truth and the fiction were equal, because both led up
to the present. It was not the fault of the fiction that it had never
happened; but it was the truth's fault that it could not prove that
it itself had happened. What mattered was that both of the two
traced a route to Now, and each could make a claim to being
its parent. In this way, the history of the world could be remade,
and nothing would matter; the world would proceed in the same
manner. So long as the fiction could account for things like scars
and earned wisdom as well as the agreed-upon past could,
everything claiming to be the present would still be in order."

I was one of a kind. Really, I was. There was no one quite like me. Not even close. Look, it wasn't even to my liking. I had no pride in the matter. Yes, all people are unique in their own ways. I get that. But I was a societal one-off. I wished it were otherwise, but it was not to be so.

As if to drive that point home, the state goons referred to me in my repatriation dossier as The Outernationalist. It sounded more like an epithet than a commendation of my nature or abilities. A better lot would have to be a mere bastard. My lack of belonging was now so thorough that I couldn't refer to either country, Venice or Aswadistan, as my fatherland.

I was a sort-of prodigal son. I was directed to return to Aswadistan, my country of birth, in order to assist in a political transition, the likes and implications of which the world had never before seen.

It all came as a shock. I knew I was an orphan, but I thought I was a Venetian orphan, born in Cannaregio and raised by the pudgy, warm arms of La Serenissima. The breeze off the Grand Canal felt at home on my skin. The brackish brine from the water opened my pores and transfused with my Italianate blood like a genetic cocktail that made all the sense in the world. But no. Unrecorded by memory, I had been raised for my first two years by the Aswadistani Child Services, in the capital city, Aswadibad, before being sent into orbit like a space dog. Aswadistan must have paid Venice the entire time? And now I was legally responsible to help usher in an era of peace and prosperity for my country of birth. It was the bill I had to foot, for sure, but like any other working-class adult, I would earn my living. What the fuck.

I was still not fully buffered. The remaining fifteen percent of me sat at the boarding gate, leafing through a nature magazine.

The attaché who had accompanied me from my apartment to the airport in a black limousine leaned into me and asked, "May I have my pen back?"

I was offended, not because he leaned into me, nor because he wanted his pen back. I was offended because…I just was. I didn't know why. I'm sure, though, it was for a good reason. On some astral plane or other, this guy had likely not done me a great wrong, but a minor slight that injured my sensibility. I handed him the pen. He put it in his suit pocket and set his black briefcase on his meaty lap.

"These papers," he said, patting the briefcase forcefully, "shall do for now. Upon arrival, you will need to fill out more. Many more."

"What were all of those for then?" I asked, rubbing my left wrist. I had signed my signature at least forty times.

"Did you not pay attention the entire time?" the attaché pleaded. "Form C-324 states that you relinquish your right to ambassadorial asylum once you are in the protection of the former sultan's state apparatus. C-18 is a query stating that you wish to apply for the right to apply for audience with the former sultan." He held his palms up, in synchronicity to his raised eyebrows.

"I-92 is your requesting a panel to determine that you are not a threat to state security, including but not limited to the desire to spread seditious propaganda, licentious gossip, jokes in bad taste, limericks concerning fornication and/or cronyism, haiku about the former sultan's halitosis, which does not exist, bawdy tales of palace tomfoolery, or inclinations to Socialism— excuse me while I fight back the urge to sneeze, me being allergic to such abominations as Socialism, which our prophet, may God's mercy be upon him, loathed in the extreme."

"Where in the Qur'an does it state Mohammed's hatred of a

political system that didn't yet exist?" I couldn't help myself.

He leaned in again. "Sir, are you a Socialist?"

"N-no."

"Sir," came a voice over the intercom, "Can you please raise your seat for take-off?"

"Form 318," the attaché continued, "is a sworn statement that you will present a threat of none of these things to the panel hearing. Form Z-23 is a petition to—"

"Hold up, man," I interrupted, "what's the reason for that last form if I'm to attend a panel hearing determining whether or not I'm a threat?" I tossed the nature magazine onto the glass end table, fed up with pages of any kind, and the printed word thereon.

"Do you not recall just signing Form 317, stating your willingness to sign the form?"

"What form?"

"Form 318. Have you not been listening the whole time? Perhaps, if you'll excuse the generalization, you psychonauts spread your brains over the cosmos a tad too thinly at times?" Ooh. In some universe, perhaps not this one, I would get my revenge for that remark.

"Thank you, sir," continued the intercom. "After reaching elevation, you may unbuckle your seat belt and recline at your leisure."

"Granted," continued the attaché, "our protocol is intricate, but you will find it is for a reason. Though at first appearance tedious, it will show itself to possess a surprising efficiency, and to be a perfect example of the system it represents." His tone was now apologetic. As thanks, I let the matter rest. I smiled. My brief acquaintance with the immediate future knew he would smile back, which of course he did.

Dealing with the attaché was annoying, especially while high, but at least it chiseled away at the anxiety of waiting to board the plane. I immediately envied all birds their wings. The drug then dramatically tapered off. It always resulted in a full buffering and a supernova of immediate mental clarity. I had run a mental obstacle course, to be sure, but nothing to ruin my wrists over. What was the alternative? Sobriety?

A company called GnosisNet hired me as a shaman to teach the coders the initiatory steps to properly navigating the Salviasphere. How they were to transduce such intricate sensibilities into algorithms that would allow for a person's political malleability and grasp of perfect citizenship was anyone's guess. Aswadistan's citizenry itself need not undergo this tutelage since their state-run cortical rations would include the correct sequence of psychedelic conditioning. A curious resurgence in Hellenistic philosophy among the Aswadistani technocracy determined the program's prefix. I had been expecting something nationalistically Arabic, but no: GnosisNet it was.

Compounding all of this was the fact that the first election would be a plebiscite between a software-run government and a democracy. Should the latter prevail, a bevy of candidates were clamoring for the spot.

Mehmet Al-Raschid had recently stepped down as sultan to run as a legitimate democratic reformer. He had even vacated his royal palace, which in the long term was to be converted into a museum of a bygone authoritarian age, but presently served as GnosisNet headquarters.

The amount of paperwork I had dealt with to even interview for the job was ludicrous: I filled out forms to obtain forms in order to gain audience with someone who knew someone who knew the former sultan. I then had signed statements saying I had not talked to such-and-such, and had to file a two-page form saying I hadn't signed such a disclaimer. I got it: Aswadistan was in a political transition, and the last thing they wanted to deal with was litigation and publicity black eyes. I had told the attaché that I was the least litigious person on earth—whereupon he produced a three-page sworn affidavit for me to sign, stating that this was true. I just wanted the Outernationalist gig, and a free trip out of Venice. Just as important, though: I was in future love.

I was fully buffered by the time we landed at Salahuddin Airport. Once the attaché and I exited the international terminal with our luggage, I launched my personal profile on Eros. Within a two-mile radius, I got a meager one response. One response! I made a beeline for this person, who appeared to be on the ground level of the same terminal, perhaps still behind customs. I was going to have to wait. It would be worth it, of course, because the signal registered as a 97 on a 100-point scale. She was attractive, down to pound, and more importantly, available within the hour. I looked over at the attaché, planning my escape from his and his country's tyranny. "It's nice out," I said.

"Indeed," he said, smiling around a cigarette. "Fresh air." He blew out smoke and tossed the cigarette onto the concrete, exterminating it with his right wing-tip. I wouldn't be able to bumble around the airport for another hour, so consciously trying to not let my eyes squint in concentration, which would give me away, I signed into my autorama and made a reservation at a nearby four-star establishment with free proxy apostasy and a pool. I could give seven fucks about the proxy apostasy, but the pool was essential. Alcohol would be a plus—not for me, since I didn't drink, but it appeared that my match enjoyed margaritas with sea salt and polka-dotted umbrellas.

"Sir," I said, "it seems that I need to use the bathroom." I called his bladder's bluff: "Would you care to join me?"

He mulled over a conundrum of the need to urinate and his trust or lack thereof in me, and the potential calories needed to burn in accompanying his charge. "No," he dismissed me with a hand wave. "I'm fine. You go ahead."

Great. No ultra-violence necessary.

The hotel was closer to the airport than I thought. I didn't run my GPS, since the new fad dictated that checking in on social media (read surveillance) was passé. Sometimes these trends got it right.

Having already made my perfect match, I doubled down on privacy by putting up my firewall on Eros, on the miniscule chance that the attaché liked swarthy expats such as myself and would use that conduit to hone in on me. I was virtually grid-free. I did, though, have to let Eros run for a minute or two in order to interface with the hotel concierge and his database.

I was no longer in future love. I was in love.

Eternal ecstasy of emeralds unfolded. When we met at the pool, she had on a morphochrome bikini, which went through a sequence of white, purple, black, blue, and silver, according to her mood and according to the outside lighting. There was an option on the Eros system that rewired your cerebral circuitry so that you and your match held the profile and past of a torrid relationship in your head, but I didn't go for that fake authenticity. Neither did she, which made her even more perfect. I could describe her physical attributes, but that would diminish her. She was everything I ever wanted. It was so beautiful that it hurt. She was my physical ideal of a woman, and she would stop at nothing to sate my every desire, with a mix of complacency and rebellion that sent my head reeling. I didn't swig any salvia divinorum tincture the entire time. I was in the throes of an amorous paradise. The pool, the palm trees, the margaritas with sea salt and polka-dotted umbrellas, the whispered passages from Khalil Gibran, the grenade kisses in my ears, the intricate entwinement of limbs and satin bed sheets, the long tresses of her black hair flailing everywhere—over her eyes, into the sky, across the floor, into the beyond . . .

She took my sanity hostage. It became too much. I stored the experience as snapshots of ridiculous happiness I could turn to in times of duress. I just couldn't take it anymore. I promised I would see her again. She pleaded with me not to go, but I told her, without being too specific, that I had to report to work. We would indeed see each other again. She could not possibly begrudge the perfect man for her. I was relieved to be away from such joy.

I had to report to the Venetian consulate. More paperwork, and lots of it. My Eros romp was discouraging to Aswadistan's bureaucrats. I don't know what the attaché said about my transgression, and I was sure he absolved himself of any responsibility in having lost me, but I had to assume that someone somewhere inferred that one of the drawbacks to employing a salvia head to help install the patches in GnosisNet was that being under the sway of the Divine Shepardess meant a minor detour or two. Really, I committed no crime; I merely looked like a jackass—the ensuing freedom of which I recommend to everyone.

I tried convincing the bureaucrats that, as long as they took their time, everything would be just fine. Hurriedness was to be blamed for all the troubles in the world. Missteps, misplacements, misunderstandings, etc. All runners eventually tripped. It's why I didn't believe in physical exercise. Mental decathletes were just as bad—juggling movie scripts, Boolean algebra equations, ways to scheme and scam, learning Esperanto. You'll get your mind threads all knotted up into a ball of Velcro. One thought at a time, one step at a time. Don't reinvent the wheel, don't run. Any need to do these things means you've already messed up.

The world could learn a lot from my current state, I insisted. Every fiber of my physical self maneuvered with a leisurely pace that lacked any displeasure with the way the world already was. There was a certain obscenity to ambition and having goals, a neurosis to not reconciling oneself with entropy, a stubbornness in insisting that what will be wrought in the future will be better than what already was.

Look, man, I was no cheerleader for conformity; calculated recalcitrance was the key, slow-motion rebellion was what it was all about. It may have been the salvia divinorum talking, I don't know.

This time, instead of a single bureaucrat, I got three. These guys were enormous. They scooped clean tubs of human growth hormone hummus and swung 70-pound kettle bells for dessert. They were nice, actually. I got the sense that, though my endeavor had been a pain in the ass, my services were still very much needed and hence appreciated. The state could not have been any more dead-on in selecting these three red-tape apes to strike me with the perfect note of intimidation and respect. I was overly cordial, even solicitous. I asked them about Aswadistan, about the general zeitgeist of the citizenry, about its hopes for the coming transition, and the eventual election.

"Change is in the air," said the first.

"The people and its leaders are brimming with hope," said the second.

"My left triceps is killing me," said the third.

"There may be an ultimate futility," I said, "in finding the perfect form of governance. An optimist may say that a just government may be a precursor to such technological advancements that will lead to immortality—a state which may itself not mean eternal happiness. I'm telling you, man, we need brand-new neurons. The ones we have are set up to oscillate us back and forth with enough fervor to make an erogenous yo-yo blush. We also need an entirely different set of physics. This muck that passes for Newtonian thermodynamics sucks. Grinding away toward perfection in a closed system, only to find that the outer, "open" system is itself closed when looked upon at a bigger scale, means that no matter what you do, matter will be done unto you. My advice to you fellas is to take more drugs."

No way would I fill out the forms sober. Since salvia divinorum, illegal in all countries but Turkey, Japan, and Aswadistan, had no real stigma to it, I shamelessly plopped a few droplets of the tincture under my tongue. I offered some to the red-tape apes.

"No, thank you, sir," said the first.

"That's very kind of you, but I'm agonist free," said the second.

"You don't work out, do you?" muttered the third.

I stabbed away at the knee-high stack of paperwork like a Teutonic Knight impaling a supine Saracen. Only thirty percent of me, though, actually was doing that; the other seventy percent of me smeared itself across the sheets of paper like a dissipating amoeba of black ink and legalese; in Modern Standard Arabic, mind you, a language I was not fluent in, but which my translation software took care of nigh accurately. This time, though, I not only knew the language, but acted as its letters. I started out as the letter shin, reveling in its exuberance from right to left. I had the most kinship with ya', and didn't take up well with the other consonants. My nemesis, of course, was sin. Alif, the prima donna of all of us, turned out to be a real pushover, despite her omnipresence. I loved the interconnectedness of being part of words, enjoyed the communalism of it all, so it always hurt to have to roll my right leg up into a fancy trough whenever I found myself at the end of a word. The thankless job of the caboose.

After an hour or so of these dances across the paper, to the sound of the three goons addressing the other thirty percent of me, I was able to congeal back into the Outernationalist, sitting in a fold-out chair, facing my interlocutors, massaging my aching right wrist. The tincture had done its job: compressed an otherwise excruciating signing session into not only what seemed to be a shorter time frame, but into an orthographical romp through the jungles of written Arabic. It was a bigger success than the last time I had dissociated myself, when I had become a coat of beige semi gloss enamel paint for the waiting room of an urgent care clinic when Mamma had sliced her hand while cutting away at a red onion. This time there was no doting mother, this time I did not fall in love with a wall clock with a minute hand to die for and an hour hand that sent my hormones into hyper-drive.

"Sir," said the first bureaucrat, "I would like to be able to tell you that we are finished, and that you may report to the lab for duty, but it seems that we are one form short."

"Uh…what?" said I.

"A most unfortunate turn of events," said the second one. "We ran the packet through the database to determine your immediate work eligibility and your temporary resident status, and it did not give approval. It says we are one form short." He portrayed small-ness with a thumb and index finger, and smirked and squinted behind it. "Just one form!"

"Sir," said the third one, "stay away from our sweet treats

during your stay here. Despite overwhelming evidence that the consumption of sugar leads to not only obesity and heart disease, but even cancer, the populace keeps indulging in these nefarious sugar bombs."

"Not even baklava?" I asked.

"Especially not baklava," he replied. He folded his enormous arms, as if guarding me from the wooden entrance of a seedy dive that plied in such radioactive desserts.

"Sir," continued the first one, "we ran the packet through the database again, to see whether there was perhaps an error, and there was. Here, then, is the form." He handed it to me. "Please sign it and you'll be all set to freely move about our wonderful nation." I did so.

"It is our pleasure," said the second, "to make your stay not only productive for the country as a whole, which I'm quite sure it will be, but pleasurable for yourself. One may even say fulfilling. Inshallah."

"Still hurts," said the third one, unfolding his arms and massaging his right triceps.

Son of a bitch.

If indeed Aswadistan ended up with the perfect form of government and rendered career politicians and autocratic heads of state obsolete, there was nothing in the proposal put forth by the Ulema detailing the mechanisms that would render red tape obsolete as well. You might even say that the increasing workload dumped onto GnosisNet would result in more and more forms being spat out, to be filled out for every little thing. So I got to wondering: if someone were to decide to go off-grid, or even just burst through his or her allotted state-subsidized and state-regulated hallucinogenic haze and raise the smallest rebellion, who would put that person back in line? I'd yet to hear whether or not a police force was to remain, or if everyone had such utopian confidence in the launching of the system that there would be no law enforcement. The only thing to scare the shit out of me more than a heavy-handed state would be no state at all. The three muscle-bound bureaucrats were in the process of running the packet through the scanner, even giving it a few preemptory kicks, when the solemn echo of a muezzin called everyone to midday prayers. In unison, they about-faced, dropped to their knees, and went into a modified child's pose. I knelt and prayed as well before deciding it was time to bounce.

I walked the streets of Aswadistan for some time, trying to find a reason to live. I came upon an outdoor discotheque that took up an entire city block. A vast night simulator hung over the entire affair, blocking out all sunlight and reflecting Day-Glo wires, strobes, and pinwheel lights. I maneuvered onto new platforms, rising and falling, avoiding offers to dance with girls I wouldn't hesitate to indulge on some other occasion. It was at times like these that I felt the rectilinear agreeability of my face become more a bane than an asset. My hollow head ached with meaninglessness. To the northeast, off in the distance, beyond the night simulator, I could see the former sultan's palace. Its bulbous onion domes towered over all the surrounding executive buildings and mosques. I crept closer and closer. I was a stone's slingshot away, but bureaucratically so far. I could see lights on in the north turret. Fuck it. I kept walking.

Then the Death Module came into view. Though it was there all along—indeed, it towered over all the onion domes and turrets—it waited for just the right blend of discotheque lights to shine on it as if in order to be revealed with the requisite terror.

In Al-Raschid's mechanized garden of state-run surveillance, the
Death Module was the centerpiece. This bat-winged contraption
was not exactly a radar, which it resembled and therefore caused,
perhaps to its benefit, everyone to think it to be. It was either a
wind turbine used to power the data-mining servers way below in
the three-storied basement of the palace, or, as the more fanciful
tended to believe, a sort of wind anemometer that tracked the gos-
sips and goings-on of Aswadibad, and clustered them into packets
that could thereafter be presented as entertainment, or as evidence
in court, if not both. Tariq Shareef, Al-Raschid's technology vizier,
went on record to say that it was one of many devices necessary
for the GnosisNet software, an undersized one at that, and that
it should be seen as no more than a symbol for freedom, if not a
beacon for impending utopia.

In all media outlets, it had taken on a fetishistic significance
for both Najwa, the court storyteller, and her former boss. Their
relationship to it made for a weird ménage-à-trois between a king,
his courtesan, and a dirty device that got them both off. Citizens
wondered if they engaged in wild coitus after a compelling story
had been told by one and listened to by the other—the spinning
Death Module, seen through the minaret window, flashing bright
with the lightning strikes, interposing itself between kisses and
shifting of limbs, getting in on the carnal act, speeding up its spin
in time to the accelerating thrusts and pants, and coming to a near-
dead halt once climax had been achieved. They said demoted djinn
and lesser ifrits hung about its edges, not coming into contact with
it as that would banish them from this world, but lapping up the
stray remnants of prayers and desires and confessions, engorging
themselves on the sordid details of the citizenry's transgressions
and trysts.

"Would the *sharqeen* like a bit of Haoma?" came a voice in my left ear.

When I turned around, I found a striking Nubian waitress in a silver Mylar halter top holding up to my nose a tray, upon which sat a black tumbler.

And finally, the fifteen percent of my buffering brain caught up to the rest of me and in an osmotic rush seethed back into my being like so much prodigal putty. I felt whole again. In other words, I felt like shit. The black tumbler of Haoma was off-limits. My refractory periods were sacred. "*Shukran jazeelan,*" I told the waitress, "*mamnuah*."

"That is not true," said the Nubian gem. The corners of her luscious mouth wrenched downward. "The Grand Ayatollah has not only sanctioned this initiatory potion, but has himself taken on the mantle of Grand Shaman In administering this brew for facilitated understanding of the Qur'an and a deeper communion with Allah, the All-Compassionate. You are, of course, free to refuse this ever-effective tool in your journey toward righteousness, as you are free to do anything else in Aswadistan, as are we all, given either the impending democratic reforms or the launching of the software, I recommending the former, what with the experience and record of Sultan Al-Raschid, Steward of Mohammed, upon whose head rests the blessed hand of Allah, the All-Compassionate, since it is ludicrous to think that a program can replace the inspired reason of a professional head of state, let alone the sanctioned righteousness and understanding of a tried and true sultan who is benevolent to his people, that is, us, to, as a goodwill gesture, forsake that which was righteously his, namely, the Sultanate and that wondrous and splendid palace to which it is obvious that you are headed toward, with what seems to be a not entirely innocuous purpose, if you'll excuse me in my recriminations, since it is neither my place as a waitress to question your political affiliation or to hold in doubt your business with the sultan's palace, since clearly you are not here to party, as you have refused with no small snootiness the advances of not a few aesthetically pleasing houris, who in no possible way belong to the state apparatus but are mere-ly looking to immerse themselves in a little harmless communion with Allah, He who is most Merciful and Just, through their nubile persons and not-yet-quite-developed cortical networks."

Someone was remotely typing this dialogue for her, but I need-ed to play it cool. I picked up the black tumbler to buy time and contemplate my next move. I gazed down into the sloshing brew. The Haoma may have been actually sanctioned by the Grand Aya-tollah, and even taken by the Ulema itself. But I had never taken the drug, and as I had stated in my dissertation, it is irresponsible to partake of entheogens without understanding their nature and capabilities, and without the proper set and setting. Plus, I had just become whole again, and it only seemed proper to withhold send-ing my sanity packing and out the door immediately thereafter, much as I loathed sobriety.

I clicked my GPS on as I set the black tumbler down on the waitress's platter. The Ulema would cast their net immediately. To further tangle up the waitress and her remote puppet-mas-ter, I launched my Eros profile right at her. She went weak at the knees and confusion stirred in her eyes. She was interested in my advance, but she appeared to be scanning some invective on her autoramic readout that forbade her to engage. I cupped her lovely chin in my hand and tumesced in seconds. "You're the most beau-tiful girl here," I said, placing my other hand on her tawny shoul-der. I became granite. "It's too bad you're working."

I doubt the puppet-master, likely an anti-GnosisNet stooge for Mehmet Al-Raschid and his viziers, bought my story. He or she may still divine my intentions of entering the palace, where I was to begin my work with GnosisNet, but the sudden erogenous intrigue seemed to make the person behind the scenes pull his or her hands away from the keyboard. The waitress just stood there. What could she possibly do? Not only was she on the clock, but she was at the mercy of whoever was typing her dialogue.

Holy-moly, that didn't stop her.

She blended into me and planted her mouth onto mine. Her free hand clutched at my waist. Was she being commanded to do this or was she acting on her own volition? Did the discotheque allow for employee/patron fraternization, and if so, was the employer in cahoots with Al-Raschid's campaign team and in on the whole jig? Either way, it was clear that the puppet-master got turned on and in a voyeuristic fit dropped his or her duties.

This was not unheard of where I came from. It had even become a craze, and for those at the business end of it, a form of employment. Total strangers would meet in St. Mark's square. The attraction and compatibility may be authentic, but they were in the employ of remote voyeurs who were either incapacitated, unprepossessing, or simply too busy to make a good match themselves. The couple left St. Mark's as sexual marionettes, muttering inane dialogue from their autoramic readouts. The proprietors on each side either ceded control to the couple or dictated the action, according to an agreement. They never really met each other, which, if they did, would make for a strange tetrarchy of non-Euclidean pornography. This phenomenon rendered pre-recorded videos obsolete. No need to have your genitals subjected to ridiculous dialogue or ineffective camera angles or positions. Sure, a great meet-up could be stored for further viewing, but why not jump back into a live scenario once you're fully charged? There were no more porn stars. Some marionettes would be more coveted for their expertise, but they were not to be viewed by millions. And if only two more people whom you'd never meet knew about your dirty deeds, there was no stigma.

I had never been down that path. If I knew the waitress had logged off from her puppet-master, then I might think otherwise. That person in control was not just an innocent sponsor; not with that overtly biased monologue.

I nibbled behind her ear. "What is to guarantee that Al-Raschid will be true to his word? Sure, he has been a progressive sultan, but a sultan nonetheless."

"I like you," she whispered in my ear. "Where are you staying? I get off in five minutes." Unlikely, that. It was 4:03 in the afternoon.

"I don't think Haoma is the answer. It's on the wrong side."

"You are right, butterfly," she huffed. She started to grind against me.

"Though the sultan is a steaming column of jackal feces, with the Russian flag plugged in on top. Plus, he has bad breath."

"Enough politics," she continued. "There must be a secluded spot we can go to in this place."

"I'm afraid not," I said, breaking free. I was excited, but I remembered my perfect match at the hotel by the airport. True love could wait. "Okay, then, where's the women's room?"

"We will look for it." She smirked. Any savvy puppet-master would have allowed the waitress, who would clearly know where the facilities were, to give an appropriate response. This person was impatient. It could have been a callow campaign intern losing her cool at the keyboard, figuring if she's not being paid, she can at least get her proxy shag on. It could have been a middle-aged gentleman as well, hired to shadow me and prevent me from reporting to work.

"Sir?" came a voice from over the waitress's shoulder. Standing there was a tall, gangly man in a white turban, grey beard, and a caftan of indeterminate color. He held a rolled up prayer rug under his left armpit.

I feigned familiarity. "It's been so long," I said, holding my arms out for a hug.

"Stop!" the waitress belted out—either at the materialization of my savior or in frustration at the suddenly overwhelming task at hand.

The tall mullah glided over to her, bent down sideways, and looked up at her face with avuncular concern. "Girl, are you fine? Is there something bothering you? If so, just tell me." I walked behind him to inconspicuously see if he had been sent with any help, and to assess possible obstacles and exit points.

"The Venetian here," muttered the waitress, "and I, were discussing politics, and arguing about the legality of Haoma, which, for dubious reasons, he had decided to forgo. Now, obviously, it is not required by law of him to imbibe of the undeniably beneficial brew, sanctioned by the Ulema, stewards of the faith of Allah, the All-Merciful and the Compassionate, but his steadfast refusal to do so raises a red flag as to his intentions, which may or may not be seditious, given his criticism of Al-Raschid's track record and policy, an entirely progressive and benign one considering that sultans of the past, sanctioned by Allah, the All-Knowing, and holding the direct lineage of the first sultan, Mohammed, Allah's mercy be upon him as he is the One and Only Prophet, have been more severe when taken into historical context."

Pity registered on the mullah's face, which spoke of many years on earth, but had retained a youthful vigor through diet and mental conditioning. He looked up at me. "Sir, is all of this true?"

"The part concerning me is true. Of the former sultan, not so much." What the hell. The mullah must have trusted my wits on this, or he was playing the white knight. "I was merely on my way to work," I continued, "to the palace, when she began harassing me." I passed the ball back. "What are you doing here, Nawaz?"

The mullah, hands on her shoulders, staring into her eyes, didn't even wince at the invented name. "I, too, am on my way to the palace. Girl, what have you against the launching of Gnosis-Net? Don't you trust in its ability to administer peace throughout the land without the flawed meddling of politicians?"

I looked around furtively for new enemies. No one. Everyone kept dancing. I even saw a few people take down tumblers of Haoma, wiping feral mouths on sleeves. If the mullah were to whisk me away to safety, he was dragging the procedure out painfully slowly. I was getting restless.

"It is not tantamount to truth," responded the waitress, "that the software should succeed in its endeavor to dole out good governance, a chimerical proposition if ever there was one, what with the imperfection of mankind and what will be inevitable glitches in the software, seeing that human input means an all-too-human element, which should make itself manifest once the software has been implemented and everyone plugged in and everyone's entheogenic ration handed out, as if those two things should make for a concoction of perfect citizenry, a lofty state that cannot be achieved by each citizen, who instead of doing his or her civic duty, is told to render his or herself docile with drugs and simply sit back and let a mere program do what, for a thousand-and-a-half years, sultans throughout the ages have been doing not only remarkably well, but under the aegis and sanction of Allah, whose prophet is Mohammed, upon whose head be the blessed Hand of Allah, inshallah." The waitress blinked.

The mullah nodded his head to all of this. "What will happen if the gentleman refuses the Haoma?"

"He would be doing himself a huge disservice."

"So you yourself propose to administer docility in the form of a psychedelic substance, when you have clearly stated that a combination of drugs and technology is not the solution to the world's woes?"

The waitress's beautiful Nubian face, placid through manipulation, didn't bother considering anything contrary to the script. A single tear plopped out from the corner of her right eye and raced down to her lovely mouth. She was beginning to break. Her lips started trembling. Sensing this, the mullah stood up tall and straight and with one hand undid the ruby brooch at his neck. The caftan of indeterminate color came undone. Underneath he wore linen of the purest white. "Let us end your misery, girl. Sir, come close to me."

I had never met the guy, but I wasn't about to argue. I ran up to him. He flung the caftan high into the air, like a Neapolitan chef flings a circle of pizza dough. It hung way up there for quite some time, swaying under the strobe lights, running the full light spectrum as if mirroring the limited abilities of the physical world. Everyone—the mullah, myself, the waitress, the dancers, other waiters and waitresses—agreed to set aside political differences, even possible death-dealing, to watch the caftan scintillate in and out of existence.

The caftan froze in midair, then plummeted earthward. The mullah clutched me to himself. I closed my eyes.

Gasps of all shapes and sizes punctured the thumping music. I opened my eyes to see a waitress far off faint to the floor, her tray and drinks crashing to the ground and rolling off a rising platform. I looked over to the Nubian waitress. Instead of staring directly ahead, which is where the mullah and I remained, she looked around, perhaps not in search of us so much as in a desperate plea to find sympathizers with whom to form a consensual reality. I could still see the mullah, and he me. He held a forefinger up to his lips and smirked. Then, he quietly took the prayer rug he had tucked under his armpit and with a snap unrolled it on the discotheque floor. He motioned me to step onto it.

"Abracadabra!" he belted out. The patrons of the discotheque jumped in fright at the disembodied command. I myself was scared shitless by the fact that the rug had begun to raise us up over everyone's heads.

The mullah slowly slid his caftan off from us as we rose, taking special care in smoothing it free of creases. He seemed to have done all of this before. I remembered having turned my GPS on, so I clicked it off. "Up there!" yelled out a boy in a yellow jumpsuit, pointing up at us. I began to shake. I was no acrophobe; I just have never been on a flying rug before. Its edges didn't curl up to guard one from falling over. I wasn't familiar with its propulsion properties nor its tactile responsiveness to passengers. If you tipped over, it may or may not adjust and dip down and save you.

I gulped. "Is this thing conscious?"

"Of course not, sir," he said, clasping the caftan at his neck with the ruby brooch. "But I myself am."

I sought the absolute center of the rug. "Neural network woven through the fibers, and linked into your account."

"Very good," he said, furrowing his brow.

I looked down at the gathered crowd. A forest of fingers pointed up at us. The Nubian waitress drank the Haoma in one desperate gulp, wiped her mouth on her sleeve, and with stunning accuracy threw the empty black tumbler up at us. I caught it. "Ha ha! How's that for your stupid sultan! Putana!"

"Sir," said the mullah. "Most unprofessional." We had achieved the necessary altitude, so now he guided it forward with an admonishing jerk. I grasped at an edge for dear life. "Be nice," he said. "The poor girl was in a terrible spot." I looked down and saw her shaking a fist at us. She screamed in frustration and stomped on the ground.

And we were off. The magic carpet went vertical in order to dodge the highest discotheque platform, which was in the process of lowering itself with three or four dancers who had, due to their elevation, been oblivious to our caper.

The palace was a block away, but we didn't directly go there. The mullah, who insisted I call him Jafar, gave me a tour of Aswadibad. The capital city, the biggest in Inner Asia, was the center of a labyrinthine Buddhist mandala, with bleached-concrete freeways stretching for miles before tangling themselves into gnarled connections, with oases of palm trees and rock gardens inside the on-ramp and off-ramp loops. Mosques the colors of sapphire and topaz bedecked the flat landscape like so many sparkling jewels. Vehicle traffic seemed to move without much gridlock. Children in uniforms played soccer on rectangles of neon green artificial turf. Sunlight ricocheted off the skyscrapers. To the north, clusters of shantytowns smeared across the foothills of the mountains.

Jafar said he was screening the palace the entire time for renegades. He said that Bedouins from the interminable stretches of mustard-yellow desert to the east were harassing palace employees with propaganda and laser guns.

"Why?"

"Anarchists."

"They are not proponents of GnosisNet?"

"Not at all. They fear losing their indigenous territory to the wind turbines that have already encroached upon the desert. If only they knew that GnosisNet would take care of them in full. Once installed and implemented, it would bestow countless benefits upon the citizens of Aswadibad."

He cleared his throat. "Mehmet Al-Raschid tended to leave them alone, save the installation of the wind turbines. Everyone knows he was a moderate, despite his extravagance for the arts, which some had bemoaned. Philistines. When he abandoned the palace for his townhouse, and they got wind that the palace became GnosisNet headquarters, they made it their ground zero. They won't hesitate to shoot you, if they think that you are an integral piece of the software launch. Other than their use of magic carpets and laser guns, they detest technology. Which makes our tracking of them easy. Once we detect that they have cleared away from the premises, we will go there."

"But what if I wish to leave the premises once there?" They couldn't be rounded up and shot, of course, as that would run counter to everything the reforms stood for. I told him that I was in love, and what if I couldn't leave the palace when Esmeralda was available, or get back in once I was out on the street?

"We will equip you with a tracker so that you can monitor them yourself. You will be surprised, even disappointed, when you realize how easy it is and how oblivious they are."

"Besides that, because of my profession, I tend to get sidetracked. Even at times lost."

"Sir, where is your guardian angel?"

"I've never had one."

"That is a great mistake."

It made sense that the majority of Aswadistan's population would be touting around those applications that kept them out of big trouble, considering the importance of the drug-induced harmony that would be phased in once GnosisNet launched. Hell, the app could be patched into the platform itself. Not only did the guardian angel crack down on crime, but it kept you from getting into bad situations. The facial readouts of strangers, the loose boards of a stairwell, the faulty chains in a high-rise elevator, the erratic dodo weaving in and out of freeway lanes—all of these things were detected by a molecular-thermal projection and thrown together to give a probability readout of potential catastrophe.

The guardian angel's female voice announced hotspots and routes of escape. (What does the perpetual female automated voice say about our supposedly patriarchal societies?) It sure took the edge off of social interaction. If you never went down the dark alley where the fishnet-stocking-sporting trannies with chrome switchblades liked to hang out, you might not run into the Valkyrie who could hitch your hormones to a shooting star.

Not for me. The younger generation back in Venice used the guardian angels, though the Laguna's breakwaters were annually retrofitted and a single Hun hadn't been seen in the area for over seventeen-hundred years.

Besides, I couldn't afford a guardian angel. Since the funds from my last consulting job I did for a Giudecca pleasure den were about to dry up, I wasn't going to pay to be told how to live anytime soon.

Jafar said that he would see that I be provided with one once I got to work in the palace. "What if I don't like her?" I asked.

"Why will you not? She will keep you safe."

"Is it compulsory?"

"Of course not. Nothing is going to be ever again, save being a good citizen. Will you at least try it for a day?"

"I'm poor. Is there a shareware version?"

It was twilight when we began to head toward the palace. It had got quite cold up in the air. Colonies of LED lights popped into existence like fluorescent barnacles on the darkness below. Air traffic lights atop the skyscrapers and taller downtown mosques helped us to avoid colliding into surprise black walls. I could see

Jafar's silhouette against the backdrop of the starlight. Occasionally, I caught a glimpse of his eyes. Despite our hour-long carpet ride, he did not look fatigued.

He said that the anarchists almost always returned to the desert once the sun went down. "Look." His silhouetted arm extended behind him at an angle, pointing out to the north, to the mountains. Three massive V-formations flocked eastward. There must have been about fifty of them, all turbaned, each one on a magic carpet. "Are they Shia?"

"For the most part, yes. They mean well."

Jafar had the bone structure of a freethinker. But I was beginning to find his commitment to GnosisNet troubling. Dogmas turned my stomach. Believing that a software program could solve all of the world's woes demanded that you chug at least a gallon or two of that acrid gullibility juice. And where there was dogma, there also lurked enforcement mechanisms to make sure it became and remained the status quo.

I scoured my autorama for research on the GnosisNet paradigm; found out that one of the Aswadistani ambassador's selling points to the world was the absence of a constabulary force. This account-ed for the importance of the drug rations. But how long could this lotus-eating go on before the buildings began to crumble and the harvests went untended and everyone was too stoned to take out the trash? If the programmers of GnosisNet thought that the Divine Shepardess —salvia's pet name—was going to let them fully function, then they were already doomed . I was a black belt at navigating the Salviasphere and even I couldn't tie my own shoes hours after chewing a quid.

A muezzin's call to prayer boomed across the night sky. Jafar steered the magic carpet straight up, then, once he felt we had enough elevation, about-faced and knelt in prayer. We began a slow, downward waft. I about-faced as well, and beseeched Allah that the earth still be some ways away by the time the prayer was over with.

We entered through the window of a brightly-lit minaret. Sandalwood incense smoke wafted all around. I had to massage my eyes, and as Jafar rolled up his carpet, stretch my limbs. "If you can't tell me how far off we are from downloading glucosamine chondroitin straight into our joints, don't go on about utopia and shit," I said.

As soon as Jafar disappeared to see to my guardian angel, two women and a man with foldout seats and a towering stack of forms emerged from the sandalwood haze. I reached for my salvia tincture inside my jacket pocket when one of the women stayed my hand. "Not yet, dear. There are three forms you must sign before partaking."

"I must have been mistaken," I said, "in thinking Aswadistan a free country, with civil liberties and nonsense like that."

"Not mistaken at all," she said. "The country is so free that people and entities can own private property, which is what this palace technically is."

"I thought the sultan gave it up for a townhouse," I murmured.

"You are correct," she said, "but the Ulema now holds the title. These forms merely absolve them of any responsibility should something amiss result from your journeys through, I believe you refer to it as, the Salviasphere?"

"I do. And it is not just a hypothetical place. Others and I have been mapping it out through the years."

"So consider these forms as your passport to go back and forth from here and there as freely as you please."

I tolerated concrete reality like a soldier, signing away, not bothering to translate or care.

Al-Raschid's harem was still intact. With him gone, it took over the palace. A fleshpot of varying colors and nationalities lounged and chirped throughout, no room or stairwell too hidden or forbidden for the leisurely scheming and gossiping of nubile twenty-somethings who, cut off from state funding, relied upon the magnanimity of the Ulema to ply their trade to bashful programmers, systems administrators, and GnosisNet executives . . . eyelashes fluttering among the humming servers, veils torn away to reveal apricot lips ready to wreak havoc in a minaret by the light of the moon after an unrelenting day of carpal-tunnel-syndrome-inducing coding.

After one week in the palace, my Eros account had lapsed. I had not received a single alert from the countless concubines peppering the palace, so I logged into my account and sure enough found that it had been cancelled for lack of payment. Son of a bitch. I haggled to no avail with customer service, gesticulating with such violence that not a few of the palace ladies probably withdrew any growing interest. Using my tracker to see the coast was clear from the Bedouin anarchists outside the palace, I went ahead and visited Esmeralda as scheduled, feeling that she was either wonderful enough to withstand a deviation from our love's curriculum, which was precisely calibrated to keep the romance alive.

She didn't protest. I told you she was perfect.

A few days later, my Eros account was reactivated. Not only had my outburst not driven away potential matches, but I found that an effeminate programmer with a too-well-manicured beard and a magenta Mohawk took a liking to me. His ogling didn't bother me; at least he had a soul, unlike those who had bought into taking de-sex meds. I'd been a de-sex med holdout, never understanding why someone would not want to be in love, not want to undergo the pyrotechnical display of emotions. Yes, love could be painful.

But I wasn't convinced that its total absence equaled instant equanimity. I believed in the usefulness of passion. What would life be without it? I didn't buy into the idea of self-sufficiency. So many people nowadays wished to turn into rocks.

Oh, the obsolescence of falling in love. I guess Esmeralda and I hadn't experienced that gradual escalation in emotions with the crescendo that is consummation. We were in bed together before we knew each other. But I fell in love with her post-coitus. And it was a love without the insomnia-inducing acidic fear that it would go unrequited. That patina of hate for the object of love who may not pull through for you did not exist. It was therefore immaculate.

My first order of business was to act as shaman for a focus group culled from various demographics—curmudgeonly mullahs loyal to the former sultan, teenagers naïve enough to believe in utopia and actually want it, clueless housewives whose sole purpose in life was to eliminate their husbands' other wives, a few palace concubines thrown in for amusement, and a couple of anarchist prospects.

I gathered them into a brightly-lit physical therapy room and seated them in a circle on the floor. Each person was given a bottle of water and an oversized pillow for comfort and/or consolation. I was about to request my preferred space music but found the calm chamber music piping through the entire palace to be soothing and, more importantly, non-threatening to over-activated imaginations. I started with ten micrograms of salvia divinorum tincture under each person's tongue. The first reaction was from a pretty forty-something who removed her headscarf, claiming the air molecules were chewing away at her body. I leaned her back onto her pillow and told her to relax, patting her hair. She said I was the molecules' overlord, and that I was to blame. She relaxed a bit, but bucked at the hips.

She bifurcated, one part of her struggling with the new world she found herself in while the other part knew she was in a room with other people, undergoing a test. I told her to ride it out.

After the three-minute mark, assuming everyone had calmed down, I would unleash the political questionnaire.

But salvia makes time dilate like the bellows of an accordion: seconds become the backdrops of revelations, inner dialogues, cerebral-cortical concerti; minutes transmogrify into revolutions.

Freki and Geri, two Scandinavian concubines, consoled each other with their long limbs, weeping with their heads pressed together. "I have to make sure that they make it," Freki said.

I walked over to them. "That who makes it?"

"My friends, who are hiding behind zippers embedded in the air. You don't see them? There's one right there. He just zipped himself up and disappeared." She pointed right in front of her, where I happened to be standing. The idea of zippers in space was a salvia staple. "Whom are they hiding from?" I asked.

"From life itself," Freki muttered. "They don't deserve it."

"What don't they deserve?" I asked.

"Life, which is after them. It is not fair." She tucked a lock of dirty-blond hair behind her ear and wiped away a tear. "They're chased by stress demons."

"What are these demons made of?" I asked, on my haunches in front of her.

"Events. Consequences."

"Bubbles," added Geri.

"How do we save them?"

"Pause time and let them situate themselves before pressing play again. They just need a break."

"Fizzy frolicking," added Geri, "like a champagne ghost crunching down on me."

"Can you unzip one and show one to me?"

Freki looked up at me angrily, reddened eyes. "That would be so rude. How dare you." She sniffled and kissed the part in Geri's brown hair.

"You!" someone shouted behind me. I about-faced. A portly mullah in white, called Wahid, stood pointing at me. "Apostate. You have done contrary to Allah's will."

Before I could point out that he had volunteered for the experiment, another mullah, Sifr, dressed in black and with a well-groomed white beard and piercing hazel eyes, fired back, "It is not for you to claim what is or isn't Allah's will. This young man is working on behalf of the future, which with Allah's will, will be free once and for all of Shaitan's political minions."

"Blasphemer!" yelled Wahid at Sifr, hurling optical thunderbolts. He turned to the middle-aged woman who was defending herself against the world's molecules. "You, too!" He clearly intended to gobble up everyone with his religio-fascist righteousness. I ran up to him and screamed into his face. He stumbled backwards before folding down to the floor to clutch his pillow. Dilemma: a security detail or even constable would have solved the problem of this killjoy, but that would require a penal system. I wondered what the anarchists thought of it all. Shit, why not ask? One of them had been watching us.

I crouched down next to him. "Dubayb," I whispered into his ear, "what would have been the proper course of action in dealing with that psycho mullah?" I meant to field that question with everyone later.

I could see the salvinorin A coursing through the circuitry of his bloodshot eyes.

"You should have made him shake hands with the five-sided demure demon who keeps spreading his flesh out among us and smells like sandalwood."

The only person to harbor an emotional response to the drug was Tariq, a teenager who fell madly in love with a corner. No joke. He was at that age where hormones were a volcanic stew. I asked him to point to the corner. With a coy, stealthy glance, he nodded up at the corner directly behind me. I was about to turn around when he tugged at my sleeve . He wanted my discretion , so I sat next to him and gradually faced toward the juncture of two walls, the bottom at which sat a fruit-patterned water cooler. I slowly drew my sight upward. Nothing remarkable : a simple beige-painted corner of two walls and a ceiling.

I leaned my head into his. "Do you see a pretty girl's face there?"

"Shh! Why does there need to be a face?" he protested.

"A nice girly figure?"

"No!" He hung his head and sighed. "No."

I looked up again at the corner. It was just a corner. "Is it a girl?"

"Of course not, sir. That would be ridiculous."

"Do you like girls?" I asked.

"Of course."

"And do you like corners?"

"Stop it." I had drawn him into a logic trap, and he didn't like it.

"Is the corner pretty?"

"Very much," he said, fixing his hair.

Nikola Tesla had fallen in love with a pigeon. An uncle of mine had fallen in love with a goldfish name Filomeno, through the drug datura. He eventually begrudged the fish his ichthyophilia, and would be moved in a crime of passion to flush Filomeno down the toilet. A corner, though? I placed a hand on Tariq's shoulder. "My worst incident was when I became a coat of paint on all five sides of my bedroom. And not only was I helplessly plastered to the walls and ceiling, but I was trapped behind the alpha-coat—that is, the newer coat of paint that pinned me against the wall forever and pressed against the grimy, older coat of paint, which was periwinkle."

From a few feet away, Dubayb, the young anarchist, rocked back and forth on his side. He told me that he had become one with the maroon carpet. "I don't appreciate everyone stepping on me."

"What do you propose to do about it?" I called out. He was physically incapable of retaliation, and didn't approve of a constabulary force. Which left him nothing.

"Ride it out," he murmured.

"Good boy." I shoved his pillow into his arms to render him more three-dimensional.

Some major distraction was In order, because everyone was too into navigating his or her own newfound reality. Wahid and Sifr, the white mullah and the black mullah, renewed their hostility toward each other in a volubility that threatened everyone else's trip. I imagined it became apparent to the Ulema, who were monitoring the whole focus group, that wily salvia was not an ideal drug for the conditioning of model citizenry. It didn't make the user more malleable in consensual reality—it restructured reality altogether. How one interacted with so-called objective reality was reworked to the point of dysfunction and even paralysis. Moving through space and interacting with one's own molecules could become problematic—forget about performing civic duty.

But I needed to remain on the payroll. If the citizens could not benefit from a daily ration of salvia divinorum, then maybe the administrators of GnosisNet could. I curtailed the political questionnaire and let everyone go on his or her merry way. They waddled back onto the tundra of reality like penguins with hangovers.

The daily state readout appeared across my autorama. "Someday, any day now, illumination will be instantaneous. Cortical algorithms proscribed by the Ulema, sub-contracted to brain-app firms, will wire everyone into a telepathic grid of empathy and disdain for privacy. Cameras are already being phased out, bested by optical files that can be firewalled from other citizens but not withheld from the Ulema, which claims network jurisdiction and cites the importance of total transparency in order for GnosisNet to adequately do its job. One's dirty little secrets will not be allowed to hijack the system for everyone else. If you desire privacy, you shirk your patriotic duty."

The most suitable of administrators for GnosisNet were to be the Ishraqiyun. Like Plato's philosopher-kings, this group's lack of desire for power made them not only qualified, but necessarily eligible. Problem was, mystics forced to engage in the most non-mystical of endeavors, i.e. politics, would simply up the metaphysical ante by committing self-annihilation or take civil disobedience to new levels. The irony of coercing the best and brightest into the greatest stewards of coercion should have been lost on no one, but goddamn it was.

In what must have been a garden of earthly delights set up and run by the Ulema, prospects of an austere nature were being groomed for selfless statesmanship at an illumination farm a hundred miles to the east of Aswadibad, out in the desert. The two seminal texts in their literary syllabus were Plato's *The Republic* and Suhrawardi's *Hiqmat al-Ishraq*, or *Philosophy of Illumination*.

The latter scribe, a twelfth-century mystic from northern Iran, met an untimely death at the hands of Saladin for having turned his son into a light-worshipping pansy. Suhrawardi courted controversy wherever he went, walking a high-wire act between the Peripatetics, the Sufis, and the Zoroastrians, dishing out disdain for all of them one time or another while touting a light-infused interpretation of Allah's beneficence. He claimed that to become illuminated one must let oneself become bathed in the light of all things, which are of Allah to begin with, and to achieve *nur al-anwar*, or light of lights. Of course, this hagiophilia took a lifetime. Yet, for the latter part of the twentieth century and the first half of the twenty-first, European hermeneutics professors touted the Ishraqi torch before passing it to the progressive Shia sects, who thereafter took it to the Great Reform at Mecca, where it was wholeheartedly accepted.

The Great Reform at Mecca not only answered epistemological and cultural questions pertaining to sharia, but debated on proper governance and even codified allowable systems, provided they not be autocratic, or even theocratic; too many popular uprisings and coups de état by disaffected viziers meant that a heavy-handed rule over the people would no longer be tolerated.

Other forms of mollification were required. Democracy was a centuries-old but workable solution, though most Islamic cultures were not used to the civic burden that such a system placed on its individuals. Syria, Lebanon, and Jordan all went through the growing pains of that transition, and came out on the other side with economic growth and increased tourism. The Saudi Families, having once been a kingdom before all of their oil got used up, devolved decades ago into factions of pajama-wearing warlords bickering over sand dunes and promising their followers better bandwidth over the rival tribes. Israel continued in its secular democracy, though it remained embroiled in its conflict with Palestine, which had traded the Gaza Strip for a twenty-mile corridor connecting the Golan Heights to the West Bank, which, in a land grab from the Jordanian Civil War, wrapped itself entirely around the Dead Sea. The canker sore continued, of course, to be Jerusalem. Israel, with a large portion of its budget being funneled in from the West, had no interest in Qur'anic Illuminationism, much less a paradigm like GnosisNet.

Jafar entered the conference room and quickly approached me. I did nothing as he slammed his strong, sinewy hands onto my shoulders and pressed his forehead against mine.

I recalled falling. Not physically falling. It was like my identity fell. It collapsed under its own weight, down into the black, echoing shaft that was my physical self, which must have remained standing. And then a pain arrived, as I continued to fall. Streaks of liquid chrome rained down upon me faster than I fell, dowsing me in a torrent of molecule-tightening burns, making sentient beings out of every cell of my body, rendering me a colony—a metropolis—of screaming organisms that launched into an orchestra of precision-conducted excruciation. I was being punished for thinking I could walk with my psychonaut's cocksureness. I would give up anything to stop the pain, even life itself. I would take back any insult hurled at even the deserving. I would do Allah's bidding until the end of my days, beg alms out on the street, pray five times a day, fly to Mecca, grow my beard, stop the entheogens. I would forsake Esmeralda.

The gratuitous joys of life were nothing compared to the absence of pain. My eyes were too busy squinting from the pain to emit tears. What a farce a life could really be, no matter how charmed. How all pleasures were wiped out from the torments of impending death. As the never-ending pain began to turn time itself into a brane whose dimensions resembled less and less those of chronological passing, and expanded outward in all directions to become so all-encompassing as to be outside of time, a veritable dark aspect of Allah, I began to reconcile myself to the idea of dying, provided it seal shut the roar of the universe that administered the torture.

I was not dead yet. The pain because so unbearable even to my legs, and I collapsed into a nose-breaking downward dog. The impact caused me to relapse back into the real world. I could faintly hear Jafar speaking somewhere out beyond the black-walled universe of my nuclear reactor of a brain. I tried to log off but could not. All of the ports were too busy with incoming packets of data to shut off. I saw a sopping pool of blood down on the carpeted floor. I became so infused with the pain that I became the pain. It started out in filaments and ended in all-consuming darkness.

NARRATRIX

i never knew I blacked out until I had the color of consciousness to compare it to. Sunlight blasted down upon me from a minaret window. A wild-haired head eclipsed the light, and, seeing me favoring the intercession, settled there for good. A cool hand caressed my forehead. That minor instigator of endorphins immediately let open the floodgates of delight. The pain I had felt, so thorough in its intention, so black in its entirety, was gone. Not a bruise, not a singed brain neuron. A banner of hot-pink text exploded across my eyes , blotting out the wild-haired head. "DIGI-DJINN. Brought to you by CORE-CORP." An update bar emerged at the lower -left side. My head had apparently rebooted while unconscious, and I had woken up during the finishing stages. Core-Corp was a Swiss firm that had been a brain-app powerhouse in Europe for the last fifteen years. They had recently cracked the Middle East mar-ket. I liked their products. Besides Eros, I would on occasion use their ZenIt, an app that eased you through ordeals —gridlock, an acetaminophen-immune migraine, a baby shower —by dispensing koans and tidbits of wisdom ripped from the Dhammapada.

The update bar at the lower left corner gave way to *installation complete.*

I thought I was being forced through a walk-through ad. A Hague court ruling upheld a class-action lawsuit against Core-Corp, who up until then bombarded their app customers with pop-ups and labyrinthine walk-through ads that cluttered your bandwidth and even caused it to seize up. Core-Corp could now only run banners and pop-ups on their free apps, and warnings had to be given for the walk-throughs, which everyone always clicked out of.

"Mister," said the person holding my head, in a warm mezzo-soprano. "Can you hear me?"

"I can," I replied.

"Can you hear me thoroughly?"

"Yes."

"Very well," she said, and began to tell me the tale of:

The Plaid Assassin

In the sixth century, Hagira time, twelfth century to the infidel, there lived a wily old Nizari sheik named Hassan-I-Sabbah, known also as the Old Man of the Mountain. From his elaborate garden fortress of Alamut, in the Alborz Mountains of northern Iran, he delegated the deaths of Seljuq viziers and Christian generals. He was a proponent of the Fatimid Caliph in Egypt.

Young *fida'i* in search of meaning sought his tutelage . In order to return to the promised virgin-filled paradise that he had initially tantalized them with , they would smoke hashish before leaving Alamut to do his bloody bidding , hence they became known as the hashisheen, from which comes the word " assassin ."Most of these assassinations were carried out with daggers . Hemlock poisoning would also work. The hashisheen were patient. They would fully integrate themselves into society and wait for years, even, to make their move. They would even have families, only to forsake them once the deed was done. Politics are done with dirty hands and even dirtier minds. One of the hashisheen even managed to infiltrate Saladin's tent and pin a note to a pillow next to his head with a dagger, suggesting a truce. This was known as a "pointed and weighty argument." It could be very persuasive. The Kurdish general had been harassing Nizari strongholds. It cost him little to broker a peace deal with the Nizaris. He even had a new tax source.

Now, pretend that half of everything I have just told you is false. You need not pretend, really, because its half-falsity is true. This is how the story goes in the West, and how it has been regurgitated back to the East, all because Marco Polo and Christian Crusaders, and even Sunnis, have spun and re-spun this yard in like manner, both for the sake of convenience and as a way to demean the Nizari sect by claiming them to be drug-addled sycophants to a rickety, syphilitic sexagenarian with a grudge against the Turks. I may as well tell you about Ferdinand Magellan's overthrow of the Aztec empire and Hernan Cortez's discovery of Hispaniola. Names and places and the incorrect permutations thereof are not irresponsible if they are possible. Who's to say what really happened in the past, when even the effervescence of the present is hard enough for us to grasp with any sort of consensus? If history is written by the winners, as Bonaparte supposedly said, then it can be erased by the losers, which are the rest of us. But never mind.

The Old Man of the Mountain now exists somewhere in your head, never to be taken out until old age or cerebral trauma or illness begins to wreak havoc on your data storage. I have already implanted the Old Man of the Mountain in your mind, whether he be called Hassan-I-Sabbah or Raschid Dinan, a successor of his. I won't go too much into the details that will supposedly correct the story, since for me details are jewels used to encrust the crown of a narrative, and do not determine whether or not that crown fits your head.

Now, the Nizaris did really exist, supposedly. Everything must be supposed, including you and me here—me talking and you listening. I suppose I shall continue then. Hassan-I-Sabbah was the first leader of this hashisheen sect. He would have successors, and they would all embroil themselves in territorial and spiritual squabbles with the Seljuqs, the Christians, and even the Fatim-ids, whom they initially supported. The *fida'i*, or *fedayeen*, did commit assassinations at their leaders' behest, though whether or not they partook of hashish beforehand is debatable. Even more doubtful is whether they frolicked with houris in paradisiacal gar - dens in dream -states so astounding that dangerous missions were worth taking in order to return. As difficult as it would be for the Old Man of the Mountain to haul up all the junk into the moun - tains — potable water , lush gardens, serviceable virgins—it is easy for me to fling them into the inextricable webbing of your brain.

Hassan-I-Sabbah was a true mystic. He knew the Qur'an word for word, had been to Egypt, Syria, and Iraq to converse on meta-physical matters, astronomy, and mathematics. He adopted an Is-mailism that was at odds with the ruling Seljuq Sunnism. Resourc-es are one thing. Territory another. States of mind yet another. In a perfect world everyone will have water, bandwidth, and land. In a perfect world everyone thinks alike. That's why I feel imperfec-tion to be perfect and perfection to be an imp. There must be no sharing of paradises.

Among the *fedayeen* was a girl named Nur. Some say she was the only female to become an assassin. Others say she was not as- tute enough to perform Dinan's dangerous assignments. Some say she stayed behind and read Greek philosophy texts to an increas - ingly -blind Dinan and in so doing became a mystic herself. Others say she became the best assassin of all. What's almost consensual was her fondness for dogs and her preference for plaid.

At the age of ten, she encountered a handsome Crusader from Scotland who had got lost from his march to Hattin. He was parched to the point of near-death. In exchange for a decanter of water, he gave her a puppy dog and a swatch of plaid. It goes, because nothing is totally consensual, that she was of half-Scottish descent, a creature of forced miscegenation from one of the battles at Ascalon. It also goes that she had no preference for plaid, and that she had merely been rolled up in a carpet of plaid presented to Farrukh Shah on behalf of Baldwin IV, the leper king. She lay waiting, the poisoned tip of her dagger perilously close to her own neck. The roll of carpet was of an average size—not large enough to encompass the floor of a waiting room, yet not small enough to serve as a prayer rug. She herself was not of average size. Some accounts detail her being of a dainty proportion, small enough to ride her dog, now grown up, as one rides a horse. Other accounts claim her being of a more corpulent size, too ungainly to be a stealthy assassin, let alone be an houri back up in Alamut. What's almost agreed on, though not entirely so, is that when a messenger presented the roll of plaid carpet to Farrukh Shah, the military leader commanded the roll be opened at his feet, and out popped Nur, veil-mouthed and kohl-eyed, twirling in a trance-inducing death dance toward her target, and plunging her dagger into Farrukh Shah's chest.

As I told you before, the hashisheen were great infiltrators. A security guard who had been in Farrukh Shah's employ for three years was one of Dinan's best assassins. By the time all the ministers and soldiers attended to the dying Shah, this assassin had snatched Nur, dainty or not, by the wrist, and made a getaway with an Arabian stallion waiting outside.

Obviously, Baldwin the IV was not responsible. It was the Old Man of the Mountain. Perhaps Farrukh Shah, Saladin's nephew, had reneged on the truce. Nevertheless, Nur was the assassin, and she would strike again. Her calling card was plaid, whether it be a roll of carpet, a banner flown from her horse, or a seemingly innocuous bracelet worn around the wrist of an unsuspecting soldier who accepted it as a gift from a local girl. She would disguise herself among the design, and at the right time materialize from the material, regardless of its size. Saladin banned plaid from the kingdom, on pain of death. Like any other pattern out among the dusty sands of Syria, though, it was not hard to hide.

Al-Amir, the new Fatimid caliph, was of the Mustali clan of Ismailis. A rift had occurred between them and Dinan's Nizaris, whom Al-Amir derisively referred to as the hashishiyah, which means not partakers of hashish, but "uneducated rabble." If the enemy of your enemy is your friend, then it follows that the enemy of the enemy of your enemy is also your enemy. The hashishiyah were Shia, sure, but they were belligerents unto the Christians and were on workable terms with Saladin, who would later wrest control from the Fatimids and thereby become Sultan of Syria and Egypt.

Smear campaigns date back to time immemorial. What the Ulema are doing to Al-Raschid nowadays is nothing new. We all besmirch each other's names and deride each other with insults and the questioning of our mothers' honor. Once Saladin heard that Al-Amir had referred to the Nizaris so disparagingly, he lifted the ban on plaid. He let the Old Man of the Mountain know that he had done so. This was a clear green light for Dinan to go after the Fatimids back in Egypt.

In Cairo, among his harem's diaphanous curtains and the restless curvatures of mouth-veiled, kohl-eyed girls, Al-Amir whiled away entire days under the influence of Diviner's Sage, which he could not have brought back from Al-Meksik, given the date. Perhaps the plant can be found in the Atlas Mountains in Al-Maghreb.

He could feel his grip on the caliphate begin to weaken. Saladin was making a name for himself out in Syria, the Christians were gaining and losing and regaining city-states, and the Nizaris were a nuisance. Intoxication was an easy escape.

Some say the harem girls complained of a newcomer among them, an outlandish and ungainly girl dressed in plaid—plaid top, plaid bottom, plaid veil—who belly-danced and cavorted with guests as if her limbs were creepers and here kohl-rimmed eyes temptations from Shaitan himself. She was defiant toward the other girls when provoked, and even hostile when it came to her dog, which she had bribed the palace guards into keeping and would feed on the sly.

Others say there existed no such girl dressed in plaid, and that Nur, the Old Man of the Mountain's very best assassin, of dainty proportion, followed Al-Amir for two years, tucked there in his hallucinations, embedded in the two-dimensional folds of his shaky consciousness, waiting for the right moment to strike. And strike, she did. On the Island of Roda, in the middle of the River Nile, Al-Amir, struggling to retain interest in whatever matter of state had called him away from his palace, partook of Diviner's Sage. Nur, dormant on days that Al-Amir was sober, expanded that day outward from the caliph's plaid hallucination, and killed him. There was to be found no poisoned dagger beside his pillow, no note dictated by the Old Man of the Mountain, no puncture wound. There were, however, two plaid impressions of either side of his lifeless neck.

"I assure you," I chirped, head still in her lap, "I am not an assassin."

This was my first encounter with Najwa, the Lebanese narratrix who would entangle me in a web of truths, half-truths, fictions, and semi-fictions. She cut a healthy figure at that time, olive of skin, luscious of lips, soft in all the proper places . . . no bones showing like later, when a disdain for sustenance would complement her vision quests taken in pursuit less of enlightenment than of an unrequited love.

She had that wild hairdo that made her out to be something between a pop diva and a drug-addled street urchin. It was her natural dark brown tone, with three red tresses shooting off here and there, like generous flecks of blood that was not hers. Two long parallel slashes of black mascara ran diagonally across her face, continuing down her neck. She wore camouflage fatigues, boots and all, affecting the militant look from two decades ago. Assassin's eyeliner.

By the time I gathered the energy to sit up and run the story back through my tinny skull, she had disappeared and come back with coffee. The caffeine jolted me immediately, thankfully.

I was about to introduce myself when my autorama screen flashed, *Markaz al-Mahal Presents: Brain Brawlers 34! Muharram Ti-sa'tasher! The very best in MMMA (Mental Mixed Martial Arts)! Tune in to watch the world's best remote mind fighters slug it out in thirty-minute bouts to see who is the deadliest cerebral savage of them all! True warriors fight behind the front lines! Even truer warriors don't leave their homes to fight! See who reigns supreme atop the mountain of motherfuckers who can telekinetically kick your ass in this tournament of tournaments! Fuck chess! Fuck football! Fuck golf! Fuck checkers! Fuck camel racing! Fuck table tennis! Fuck tennis! Fuck football again! Fuck MMA. And most of all: Fuck You! Don't delay! Purchase now. Eighty dirahim.*

Up popped a scrawny kid straining himself with his eyes closed as he sat in an ergonomic recliner. Facing him was a red hologram in which his cyborg avatar and that of his opponent engaged in striking, grappling, and transitioning with telemetric precision. There was no getting around the adware that came with my shareware Digi-Djinn, which was why it was free. It vexed me that the Ulema couldn't afford me a premium guardian angel.

I'd almost rather take my chances getting mauled by a terrestrial vehicle or shaken down by one of Aswadibad's mind mafia thugs—the notorious head hackers—than be pestered by inane ads that blasted your eyeballs and distracted you from the real world.

Despite the ad's violation of my brain, I was intrigued by the MMMA. I purchased the Brain Brawlers tournament and went into my calendar to set up a reminder when the date arrived. Suddenly, vivid images of four different beings began flashing in my head. Not on my autorama, but in my actual head—like something between memories and closed-eye visuals. They were turbaned, long-bearded mullahs. They hovered over the ground wraithlike and zoomed dangerously in and out, scowling as they approached, faceless as they receded. Three were dressed in black and one in white.

"Is there any way of getting rid of the adware?" I asked Najwa.

"I couldn't tell you," she said.

I perused the FAQ page and learned that I could uninstall the guardian angel after a thirty-day trial; until then, I was stuck.

I texted my hacker friend Sawdust, a Tashkent native whom I'd never met in person. He was in Syria, and wouldn't be available until next week, but that he would indeed help me as soon as possible. I had no choice but to accept the Digi-Djinn. Fucking Jafar. I wondered if he got a commission, or if he genuinely thought that I needed it to stay out of trouble.

"I detest the idea of a guardian angel," Najwa said, sipping her coffee. "I've an almost unhealthy disdain for the impending GnosisNet paradigm. It behooves one to mistrust all things put out by Core-Corp, a Shaitanic abomination of a company if there ever was one."

As a rule, I didn't date women taller than me. Nevertheless, I tried a straight-search of her on Eros: nothing. She must have had a firewall up on her interlocutor-assessor readout, because I couldn't tell whether or not she found me a dangerous liability. She appeared to be off-grid, which was illegal. I'd have Sawdust probe her.

She had those green eyes that make a mockery of everything, the kind of Bollywood starlet green eyes that hover over a city skyline and pity every lost, downtrodden soul on route to Hell and oblivion. They certainly helped with her storytelling.

Unlike the vast majority of Aswadibad's street storytellers, she didn't use holograms in her storytelling. You could go into any opium den and sit on a sprawling carpet along with everyone else at the feet of the most revered yarn-pullers and be disappointed if they didn't shoot out images of Nur al-Din, Zenki, Othman, T. E. Lawrence, and Sayed Al-Hussari.

The anarchists who hovered outside the palace walls, citing model citizenship and personal restraint as the cornerstones for self-governance, employed holograms to harass her. Since she was off-grid, as were they, their efforts to localize their three-dimensional graffiti were in vain. She dissipated them with a Sig Sauer Ionizer Wand that she kept strapped to her right thigh, but every now and then, because they would blindly send out loads of them, she would happen upon a copulating couple or a geriatric pervert exposing himself. She did on occasion call upon the robot chamber ensemble to strike up a soothing background while she launched into a tale. The robots were so perfect in their renditions that it would have behooved the mechanic to lay off a bit on the oiling, to add a touch of human imperfection to their playing. They were equipped with thermal sensors that told them when humans were approaching. I've heard on two occasions that their auto-play setting programs them to practice etudes of unimaginable complexity when no human ear is around. I wished to catch them in the act. "The mechanic comes by once a week," Najwa told me. "If he finds that they have been practicing alone for too long, he shuts them off. Occasionally, because of over-heating, any given musician will be down for days as it waits for incoming replacement parts."

During midday, while Najwa and I knelt toward Mecca, to praise He who is Lord over All, I saw out the corner of my eye that the musicians, down the hall in their parlor, were praying as well. I thought they may have been spies for Al-Raschid, until the time Suha, one of the former sultan's concubines, threw a decanter of rose water against the oud player, whose left arm broke off, exposing wiring and circuitry.

When I was in Najwa's presence and she did not speak, she marveled me with anti-stories, or anti-narratives, which were non-events and possibilities never given the chance in the real world, or even in the imaginary world. These ideas were the shadows of her told tales, the negative impressions of transpired events. They were the marble-veined networks of probability, the avenues left neglected by occurrences that chose distinct courses and left everything else to the land of *never-happened*. I liked to spend loads of time in these areas, in these enchanted lands of *what-if*.

No matter how fantastic one of Najwa's tales might be, its stubborn absoluteness paled in comparison to the splendor of everything else that was not the tale, that is, all non-events and outcomes left behind. These things convinced me that stories, and even lives lived, were the most tragic of things, since they could not extend outside the boundaries of their own selves. A life, no matter how charmed and charged with good fortune, was just another exercise in despair, since its exclusivity left no room for variation. Julius Caesar never made it to Parthia. There was a particularly well-endowed Nubian slave whom the Queen of Sheba never quite got around to knowing.

It was this kind of thinking that always denied me the joy of looking back on my past with fondness. The past was so stale in its inability to budge from what it was that it depressed me. It was why mysteries were so precious and why man's need to know everything, especially how to flout death, would be his downfall.

Najwa had at her disposal two devices for mining from reality the prima materia to be twisted and molded into stories. The first of these was Rose, whom I grew to detest.

Rose got on my nerves early on. She was a pest, blindsiding me in the head or getting all up in my face for no reason. She was Najwa's milquetoast, which I guess was the point. I had never seen such groveling enacted by a human or even a dog. Rose went to the utmost lengths to appease her master, either by betraying others or being a nuisance in the hopes that her master was watching and would approve.

Rose was Najwa's pet butterfly. Kept in a gilded cage and subsisting on a diet of nectar, Rose would be unleashed from captivity to float among palace rooms and corridors, and even into the city, to eavesdrop on tantalizing goings-on, to gather up gossip, to witness the trading of illicit substances, to survey politicians' failures to pray five times a day, to report on torrid affairs, hushed-up murders, copious consumption of alcohol, whispered blasphemies, shouted apostasies, mudslinging, the disrespecting of parents, the mises-en-scène of strewn-about undergarments that added up to more than those of two people.

Sometimes, Rose would be out on reconnaissance for days on end. If Najwa happened to be in the middle of a tale, with a dozen or so listeners at her feet, and the butterfly entered the room, it would ceremoniously alight on her hand, which she kept hennaed for that purpose, or it would obediently enter its cage to feed. It was when the narratrix held the butterfly up to her right ear, and appeared to be listening with undivided attention, that I suspected Rose to be a robot.

The second device for collecting story-worthy tidbits of reality was the Death Module. The radar. The spinning radar. The spinning radar atop the palace. The spinning radar that spun atop the palace on a pole twice as tall as the palace minarets. It seemed that every time that I ventured outside the palace and caught a glimpse of the radar, the weather was full-on thunder and rain. There it spun among the flashes of lightning and torrents of sky water, in defiance of the inclement weather or as its chief cause, spinning with enough intent to churn the heavens into a raging downpour.

For five years, Najwa had been Al-Raschid's personal storyteller. The former sultan, a patron of the arts, had a fascination for stories since childhood. Najwa's one request when accepting the position of court narratrix was the installation of a device that could gather up the secrets and imprecations of the populace. This only suited Al-Raschid, who designed his digital power apparatus with a panopticon tied into social media networks already in place. Under the auspices of the controversial Eastern Hemisphere Only Trade Agreement, Middle Eastern electronics firms that bought the government contracts for cameras cut bargain deals with Chinese die-cut factories and Russian lens crafters. A veritable tsunami of eyes crashed onshore and spilled across the land. Crime went down; and directly proportional to that, privacy. Whenever questioned about the omnipresent cameras by someone with a modicum of civic understanding, Al-Raschid would hug the interlocutor, find a lens (they were everywhere you turned), cite the latest decline in crime statistics and purported nonexistence of recidivism, and smile.

Al-Raschid also loved to bring up the phasing out of drones. He did actually deserve credit for that sweeping measure. You'd be hard pressed to find an unmanned police bird prowling the skies nowadays. The sky belonged to Allah and his fowl; it served as a mantle to sheath us from the harmful effects of the sun and to enliven our days. To make sure the technology was never used against the citizens, only the smaller retail drones were permitted. The restaurant copters hovering shawarma straight down into your hands, or department store flyover models dropping off parachute-equipped boxes of shoes or cricket bats, had to be under ten kilos in weight. On top of that, at the Great Reform, the mullahs had ruled incineration to be un-Islamic. This gave the Middle East a huge moral advantage over the West, where drones were still employed in warfare, not to mention in the surveillance of its own citizens. The mullahs' decree fit right in with Al-Raschid's grand dream of a paradisiacal panopticon. No need to cook a wrongdoer when you could snare him in a web of his own publicized iniquity.

The only story ever officially credited to Najwa had been used by the government to stir the people into outrage against drone technology. It even became an animated short, airing both on children and adult channels.

There once lived a family of drones. There was Daddy Drone, Mommy Drone, and Baby Drone. They lived in the heart of Dronibad. Like all drone families, they had their problems. But they were happy. Daddy Drone was a national hero because he had gone above and beyond in incinerating so many vermin insurgents throughout the land. Mommy Drone was an exemplary eye-in-the-sky for the surveillance of miscreants and lawbreakers. Baby

Drone was being groomed to issue traffic reports and even put out brush fires up in the mountains. He would grow up to do the work of the people, and not the dark deeds of his parents. This was known as progress. But Baby Drone didn't want to do the work of the people. For what mattered the people to a splendid specimen such as a drone? Of what significance was an anthill to a human, if not a nuisance? So Baby Drone flew away from home. He went missing for weeks. He had been hanging out with misfit drones who blew away villages for recreation and for laughs peeked in on the private depravities of politicians. The fun was nonstop, until maintenance issues came up. The lead rebel drone, Spike, thought to have been the toughest of street drones, began to experience turbine failure. The other drones patched him up the best they could. Spike was tough, however, and he continued to lead raids. But after a while Spike began hacking up orders to the point of unintelligibility. No one wants to be led by an invalid, so there was a power struggle within the group. Baby Drone, known now as Smash, made his case. What better way to come off as alpha drone that to propose turning against Dronibad itself? Smash issued a directive for all rebel drones to unleash simultaneous hellfire on their respective sectors of the city. Leading by example, as that would earn him the desired respect, Smash himself would bomb the heart of Dronibad. The rush of love for his parents didn't overtake his heart until he had already let loose his payload. He recognized his house only seconds before it was blown to smithereens. He gave out a great wail. By the time he called off the raid, the other drones had already unburdened themselves of their ordnance. Dronibad was no more. The infrastructure was leveled flat. Not a bridge stood erect. Not a street light pole could be seen standing among the smoke. Drone parts were strewn about among the wreckage. Once-green parks were flooded with lakes of gasoline and engine oil. Knowing that the other rebel drones had heard his laments and would probably take them for weakness, Smash fled into the desert, where fuel was scarce and unrefined, and where nary another drone could be said to exist. To this day, if you use the coordinates given by the defense minister, you can happen upon a dune of sand that refuses to move with all of the others, regardless of the wind, a rusted rudder jutting out from its crest.

Moral of the story: technology was great until it turned against itself. And that was when the world learned of and subsequently hated the Lebanese narratrix who warmed the sultan's imagination and quite possibly his bed. His ex-wife, Qamar, immediately became the darling whom everyone felt sorry for and therefore loved. Scandal was unleashed like a plague of frogs. It became common knowledge that the spinning radar atop the palace was the narratrix's evil contraption used to spy on the people and to maintain control over the sultan.

Superstition flooded the palace once Al-Raschid had vacated it, almost as a spiteful response to the Oxford-educated son of a neurosurgeon whose hobbies included deciphering French Deconstructionists in the original and Sudoku. No one would venture up to repair the Death Module, not even the palace mechanics. So Najwa herself learned to service it.

The mullah wraiths appeared in my mind again, the four of them taking turns in zooming up to me in a premeditated permutation that always kept me guessing. I couldn't stop flinching each time because they kept the disrupting rhythm of a boxer who has mastered the feint. I could think them away, but only with difficulty. I had to become engrossed in something else; then, like memories or pending pots on the stove burners of thought, they would be gone.

"What is your current relationship to the former sultan?" I asked Najwa.

We stood at the parapet, gazing out at the city skyline, with nothing to do. I then realized I had been lulled into inactivity by this languid woman. She ignored me as if either I wasn't there, or she hadn't heard me. "They say that the key to discredit a scandal is to lose it in a tangle of other feigned transgressions," I said. "Say that Al-Raschid groped an intern. Well, that's not so bad compared to his fondling of two of his nieces. So I don't know what to believe now."

"How about nothing," she replied. "Al-Raschid's running opponent, Hafez, has never been accused of corruption, therefore it is entirely possible that he is guilty of that."

I laughed.

She elaborated. "Everything observed and recorded becomes even more suspect once it is discovered that the opposition could very well have used computer-graphic imaging to film scenarios of someone in compromising positions or acts. Now the flowing vein of reality becomes lost within the marbled slab of truth and untruth. If the panopticon cuts down on crime because it permits everything to be observed, then it also cuts down on the just punishment of any crime because it permits everything to be both believed and disbelieved.

"There is then a hierarchy of realities that has to be sorted out in order to get to the bottom of what is real or what has real -ly happened . To wit: There is reality . Whatever that means . Then there is real reality ; then really real reality ; then unreal reality ; then really unreal reality ; then unreality ; then real unreality; and finally, really real unreality."

A Ukrainian company began issuing "reality tags," personalized chips that were collected in a database, which then detected reality forgeries and form a true narrative of the wearer's life, preserving one's credibility, and more importantly, honor. "Marvel at nothing," Najwa told me, "for nothing is marvelous." There at the parapet, overlooking the city skyline, my knees buckled from the dizzying implications of that hierarchy of realities. It was like I was experiencing the reality -shaking effects of salvia divinorum without even having taken it. My week -long abstinence from the Divine Shepardess was made tolerable by this other stewardess of unreality, who would take drawn -out puffs from her hookah and blow into my eyes a djinn of smoke that transmogrified at her command. Once back inside the minaret, she told me the tale of:

A Plague of Mirrors

There are mirrors that reflect with faith, and mirrors that reflect with mendacity. There are mirrors of love and mirrors of hate. The former foster warmth, the latter a viscous iciness. There are specialty mirrors that unreflect the reflections of others, and thereby reflect accurately, though not at all truthfully. There are double-dealing mirrors that unreflect unreflections and therefore reflect what was intended by the twice-removed mirrors.

I know what you are thinking: that I am toying with the definition of what a mirror truly is. Well, know then that a real mirror does not show you truth. Rather, it gives a backward image, a reversed two-dimensional portrait. Even the background is reversed. It toys with reality because it lies. The foreground is false as is the background. Entirely false. So close to reality, but not. There are no degrees of reality. Either a thing is real or it is not. And a reflection is not real. It projects a very similar scenario but it is entirely false. It merely suggests. It gives a close estimate of what is going on. It confirms, in real-time, what we think is the case. But it lies. Not only does it fail to take into account the third dimension, but it offers up a two-dimensional lie, which is the directional reversal that it calls its reflection. That we look to it for confirmation is more than just vanity. It is recklessness.

If you hold up a mirror to a mirror, do not think that you are finally beholding reality. It is still a lie. The photons have gathered in the promise of informing you, but they have, upon reflection, conspired to deceive you. The directional reversal is itself reversed, sure, but it is still wrong. For at the core of the second reflection is the first reflection's lie. And a temple of truth cannot be constructed atop a foundation of lies.

This is why it is forbidden to portray His prophet Mohammed, upon whom be peace. If you have tried to encapsulate the truth of the Messenger with whatever tools are at your disposal, then you have already failed. You have come up short, and therefore lied. There are truths in this world that are so all-encompassing that they must be left to themselves, and are not to be held in the palm of a trickster's hand for the masses to behold.

Permit me to introduce you to Ardashir. Not the Sassanid king, but the ominilingual playboy of Ctesiphon. Geometry agreed with his face, it has been said, but not with his soul. Handsome and honey-tongued though he was, he tended to snag his soul onto the world's jagged edges that the rest of us would effortlessly glide past. Some attributed this to his bargain with Shaitan for the talents that his vocation demanded, others to the possibility to his having been an ifrit who had hijacked a human because it had become bored with mischief. Either way, he found himself in trouble nearly every day, and had spiritual crises with a regularity matched only by his meals. This was during *Jahiliyah*, the time of ignorance, before Allah made his dispensation to Muhammed, upon whom be peace.

Ardashir, when not translating texts, was given to wander in the empty desert, where he would converse with dust devils. Only there could he find respite, for the dust evils either respected the status of his ifrit soul or felt sorry for him. He had grown proficient in the language of wind, and would keep them abreast of the goings-on of the empire, in exchange for their wind poetry, which soothed his soul.

In effect, Ardashir and the dust devils were plagiarizing each other. It is easy to mock a mirror for its tendency to plagiarize reality, but really no one or no thing is original. Everyone and everything apes everything and everyone else. Allah, as you know, is the fountainhead of all.

Now Ctesiphon had its share of competent storytellers. Purple-lipped, white-bearded raconteurs in extravagant turbans and jangling, effeminate jewelry plied their trade with the same lascivious relish that opium dealers dish out their inky supplies of somnolence. Ardashir had run through the inventories of the best storytellers and was wanting for new material. He was near despair when a vaunted storyteller from Alexandria, named El-Misri, arrived in town for unknown reasons. Notoriety followed this old man, and Ardashir was determined to be among the first to hear what were hopefully new stories, and well-told ones at that. Ardashir spoke Egyptian fluently, Greek even better. So the chances of understanding the old man were high. Venturing into the crowded city, however, meant subjecting his soul to cuts and bruises, but there was no way around it. One must invest in one's equanimity.

El-Misri's inaugural storytelling session was to be held on the second story of a dusty tenement near the Fire Pillar. The housing was held in the monument's shadow for a good part of the day, it being summer, when the sun arched in perfect linearity and only bestowed light with the diffusion of spilling across the horizon before it set. El-Misri chose than venue because his narrative pyrotechnics fared best in the shade. Many said that it was because he was of the cult of Set. Others, that he was a high-ranking vampyr.

Attendance was beyond capacity, with people snaking up and down the staircases and cramming into the hall. Ardashir was ready to enter the storytelling room when he heard a young lady's voice shout his name. He gazed down over the balcony to find staring up at him an exceptionally beautiful Nabataean whore by the name of Azam. Rumor was that she was deficient in the ways of the mind. Some say, though, that this was a ruse. "Translator," she said, "Descend from there. You are in danger, no more than always, but in danger still." Word must have gotten around about his sensitive soul.

"I will not descend," he said, "as I am about to hear a tale told by El-Misri."

"I, too, tell tales," Azam shouted up. "Yet El-Misri is not as fetching as I. And my endings are the envy of all of Baalbek."

So he descended. He won twice over. For though he was fortunate to hear a tale told with such clarity and élan, he was blessed to possess her. This took place at a nearby inn, where she had been staying. She was far from deficient. She told him the story of Al-Din and the Plague of Mirrors. It was not imparted by verbal account, but by an extravagant display of carnal prowess.

They lay entangled afterward, he tracing his forefinger up her spine. "I've heard that you subsist on nothing but river water and butterflies."

"That is partly true," she said, gazing over her shoulder at him. "I only eat butterflies after they have feasted on nectar. It is good for the humors and it keeps the djinn at bay. But I also like bread." She would smash the gathered butterflies into a smeary paste and eat it up rather unbecomingly.

Ardashir's soul had been hitherto untouched that day, until

he disentangled himself from Azam and went to survey himself in a mirror.

Think about why we refer to our consultations with mirrors with the preposition "in," instead of, say, "at." This is not an error. For though a mirror is nothing but surface, much like a black hole, its energy is to be measured two-dimensionally. It is a hologram awaiting decoding. You are now one of the very few in the world to know this dark and dangerous secret. If you love someone, do not apprise her or him of this ever.

Azam's tale to Ardashir went thus:

In the court of Al-Din, there was a gilt-framed mirror that replicated like a virus, spread like a wildfire, wreaked havoc with the king's idea of reality, reflection, and correspondence.

"There is an artifice to music," spoke Al-Din's wife, estranged from him since back before his memory served. "It lies in the pleasing propagation of sound. There is an analogous play involving mirrors. It is far from pleasing, and even malignant, but no less artful. The beatitude of the blood. One is convinced that it is wine coursing through one's veins."

"You shut up," demanded the king.

"It may seem self-evident that a mirror cannot lie," said the queen, "but this is misleading. A reflection is neither a lie nor truth. The endless variations between a lie and a truth comprise the vast terrain where a mirror plague does its damage. There is only one yazata, or angel, for every ten mirrors in the world, yet a demon for each."

"Shut. Up."

Long before the queen became the king's bride, when very young, and a commoner, she had an eye for a tall, handsome mage, who, though a criminal, knew how to respect a girl's honor. This mage vowed to return for her when she became of age. She never forgot him, even after she became queen. Three years into her marriage to the king, she began receiving messages from the mage through her gilt-framed mirror. The mage, who had been dismembered by brigands on his way to Antioch, had been converted to a demon, not because of his intentions, for he never harmed a soul, but because Allah disapproved of his spells and wares.

In the morning upon waking, and at night before going to bed, Al-Din began to hear his wife murmur imprecations of love as she combed her hair while gazing into the mirror on the far side of the bedchamber. Tending to herself in such a way was new, because she usually relied on her chambermaids to prepare her for the day or night. She used the very reflection to see him approaching from behind, way on the other side of the room where sat the bed, whereupon she would cease her sordid whisperings and conspiratorial cooing. Al-Din became suspicious of this, and he was determined to find out what she was saying. Manhandling her into confessing would not work. And for whatever reason, she would never consult the mirror when alone, as slaves he had hidden in the bedchamber would attest to. She only spoke into the mirror when he was present.

He sought the help of one of his viziers, who was of the same stature as he. This vizier was to hide out under the royal bed, readily dressed in the same pajamas as the king, and, at night, when the queen became engrossed with her mirror, would emerge from under the bed and linger in the background of the queen's reflection, posing as the king, as Al-Din himself would have taken his position inside an large hamper a few paces away from the mirror, and listen.

The ruse worked perfectly, and Al-Din immediately wished that it had not.

"I care not if he knows, my darling," came a guttural voice from the wall. "I will be able to wipe out his whole army once I am ready, which is nigh."

"You know that I am ready to give whatever you may ask of me," murmured the queen. "I will defile myself for you with objects of iron, of bronze, and of stone."

"He will have to be present," replied the guttural voice. "Only then will it work. You will need to be bold, as you will be performing for me while he is present."

"Then you will have to be quick," said the queen, unleashing a lascivious moan, as if clutching herself.

"I do everything quickly," said the voice, "as you shall see."

Ardashir removed his forefinger from the narrating whore's spine and approached the mirror on the other side of the room. In vain he searched for his reflection in the glass. Azam, who still sat on the bed directly behind him, wore a mischievous smile. "Do not worry," she said. "No harm will come to you. I only hold your soul ransom in exchange for your services."

"How did you snatch up my soul?" he asked, still searching for it by touching his body.

"It was out in the open like no other," she said, smile gone. "It could be grasped like a banner from a pole. Do not worry. I have it stored inside this here." And she produced a wooden box from a drawer beside the bed. "People say that you speak the language of the wind, and are proficient in its poetry. I imagine the job would be simple for you."

Ardashir, upset that pretty Azam had not told him the story out of attraction, but as blackmail, controlled his temper. "I could produce a translation within minutes," he said calmly. "But what's to stop me from wresting my soul from you and strangling you?"

Azam chuckled. "You can take this box by force, and even

open it up, but you know not the spell to apply it to your person. Not only am I willing to give it back to you, but I will also tighten up its seams so that it does not get into further trouble."

Ardashir gazed back at the mirror. Her reflection ran fingers through its hair. He had nothing to lose. "Very well," he said, whereupon her reflection left the bed naked and went to fetch a clay jar. He produced a pen and a parchment from his satchel.

Azam asked that it be translated into Syriac. The work, though simple, was drawn out, as wind words consist of very many syllables. It was near dusk when he finished. "Now," she said, neatly setting his pen and parchment onto the table, "we continue the story." And she led him back to bed.

Rare is the cuckolded man, let alone a king used to having his way in all matters, who will not act rashly when presented with the guilty party. Al-Din, boiling with rage, emerged from the hamper. He commanded his vizier to seize the queen and toss her into the dungeon, while he went to exact revenge from the mirror. "Stygian dog!" he howled, reaching for the shadowy image beyond the glass surface.

The mage, who could not be reached, for the king's claws only met the hard mirror, moved his lips in an invocation. The spell began near inaudibly, but increased in volume, until it became a roar. Al-Din could not understand a word, and seeing that attacking the shadowy figure before him was futile, rammed his fist into the middle of the mirror, shattering it.

The invocation continued, and Al-Din, now terrified, began to back away. He meant to run from the scene, but the reflection of one of the various shards of the now-broken mirror followed him. He exited the bedchamber and turned down a hall. Looking back, he found that the light from the reflection had bent. He attacked his reflection, and fell into the world of the mirror.

The Egyptian mage had cursed him with a mirror plague. If you hold a hand-held mirror up to large mirror on the wall, you will see a reflection of a reflection, into infinity. Each reflection begets another, which begets another, diminishing beyond the sight of human capability, sure, but truly never ending. All of this is performed with a straight trajectory. Now imagine how this grows more complex once you are able to bend light. This terror is the first order of the mage's mirror plague.

If a mirror image is a two-dimensional reflection of its three-dimensional cause, then a mirror plague's second order is to reverse this—so that reality as it has been known becomes a mere analogue; and what was once a reflection becomes a portal onto a tactile reality. The reflection in this case is the conjunction of all the space-time trajectories, all the multiversal vectors leading up to it. It subjects the victim, in this case a king, to a multiplicity of existences, fading in and out of various pasts and presents, future providing the illusion of hope.

We know that a single existence can oftentimes be unbearable. Now imagine having to cope with innumerable realities, wherein each one you are condemned to do your best as a king. He might achieve progress in one of the innumerable cross-sections, only to split into innumerable others. The mirror plague took on the crenellated aspect of barnacles on a hull. Or a deck of cards being shuffled. In some lives he was murdered by ambitious viziers or relatives. In others, the Rum invaded from the west. In some, the mage forced himself on the queen while the king was compelled to watch. In others, the king successfully choked the mage to death. Like a poisoned thread, the king traveled across that vast multiverse, vowing to exterminate the "real" mage. In one cross-section, the king succeeded in blinding himself with hot irons. A mirror need not be observed to reflect light, much like a black hole. Each cross-section bore an oppressive loneliness, sealed off forever from all other versions of himself, though inextricably linked in the plague of self-replication propagated by the bending light. He took to shouting as a futile exercise in communicating with the other versions of himself, in vain trying to piece together a manageable life that retained a modicum of linearity. Al-Din's only hope was to happen upon a reversing spell. In one of the millions upon millions of cross-sections of the multiverse, he discovered hidden in an earthenware jar a scroll written in an unknown language, and in that same cross-section, he searched for a translator.

"The true horror of the Stygian mage's spell on Al-Din," Azam's body continued to narrate, "is not that it threw the king into an ontological paradox, but that it forced him to see reality as it truly is. Know, then, that there is a version of you that has indeed strangled a version of me for having pilfered your soul. In vain, of course. There is also a version of you that has proposed marriage to a version of me that has agreed to be your faithful wife, to renounce her vocation and to tell her stories solely for the amusement of her husband. And though I subsist only on river water, bread, and butterflies, I would gladly learn the ways of the kitchen for you."

"Since you have agreed to restore my soul to me," Ardashir said, "and in good order, and are becoming to me as no other girl has ever been, and are adept in the ways of the bedroom and can spin a good yarn by means of those ways, I have decided to ask for your hand in marriage. My only demand is that you no longer deceive me."

Azam bit her lip. She appeared to bandy about a great thought in her head. "Very well, translator. I consent to marry you, and to be faithful to you. I beg for your forgiveness. I only deceived you because my uncle, desperate for help, asked me to have the scroll translated, and you are the only one throughout the world (for I have searched far and wide) who speaks the language of the wind, which can bend and unbend light."

Ardashir emerged from the bed and approached the mirror. Seeing this, Azam popped open the wooden box. She swayed seductively on the bed, coaxing forth his soul, which spoke fluently the florid language of her body, and thereby did her bidding. Ardashir saw his reflection slowly emerge before him.

"My uncle has suffered long enough," she spoke. "Will you accompany me to Nabataea? He will regain his sanity, reestablish his kingdom, kill the queen, banish the mage to a world of torment, and lavish gifts on us."

Upon their return to Ctesiphon, Ardashir took his new wife to the desert. Though no longer in need of solace, for his soul had been stitched up tightly, he wished to express gratitude to the winds. A dust devil had plucked the notorious raconteur El-Misri from the tenement, mid-story, and to the horror of his listeners, whipped him to death. Winds hate to be coaxed into performing dark deeds. They are not meant to bend light. Everyone knows that that domain belongs to gravity.

Najwa's telling of the mirror plague became a reverse-Matryoshka doll of narration and intent. The multiversal deceits of the Egyptian mage's curse manifested themselves analogously to my attentions. I found myself, like Al-Din, in a sprawling multidimension, where perception itself pried open doors and sealed off nascent universes for good. And much like those of the pretty Nabataean, Najwa's stories no longer possessed the characteristics of a linear narrative, lacking the staccato delivery of sentences. She seemed to narrate vertically as well as horizontally, on an x-y axis. I felt to have assimilated the story vector by an induction rather than by the hard, sensory input of listening. No, I did not possess her then; of course, I wish I had. She did verbalize the whole story, though I couldn't recall hearing it. It was as if she had surreptitiously implanted the engrams comprising the narrative into my brain. Perhaps she possessed a brain-app for this, despite her claiming to be entirely off-grid.

Either way, she sealed the story up by producing a little wooden box, out from which she plucked a small, jagged chip of glass, which she then tossed onto the floor.

The light reflected did not bend. I did not feel myself get sucked into the world of the reflection once I hovered over the shard and gazed directly down. I did, though, dwell on the tenuous nature of truth, and what being present at a given time and a given place truly meant.

The story was her way of absolving Al-Raschid of whatever dubious or even plain horrendous activities he may been guilty of. It would certainly be more difficult to judge someone of his past misdeeds if he were not even the same cross-section of what came to be known as the present Al-Raschid. If you could muddle up your sordid past with the filth of the present perpetrated by others, could you emerge unsullied? Who was to say that the molecular remnants of your crimes clung behind you like a dusty comet's tail when you made your path to the present? Maybe every single second of your life was a fresh start, only because it was a fresh you. I found these reactionary implications of hers amusing, and worthy of consideration, but I also found them to be desperate.

It was good old-fashioned disinformation through entertainment. She unfurled narrative tape like a Turing machine of untruth. No, truth was not stranger than fiction. Whoever went along with that was an amateur at disbelief suspension. Fiction had the handicap of not mattering as much, but it also had the freedom to breathe, to flex and wrap around reality like a cancer. The confused braiding of truth and fiction to a susceptible audience was the best ruse of all.

Al-Raschid used to ravish Najwa all up and down the palace. He did it out in the open. In front of friends, family, and visiting heads of state, who on occasion joined in, holding up red cards.

No, actually, he didn't. He did it behind closed doors, where only guards could hear the moaning coming from the bedchamber. And only he did, by himself.

No, that is not true either. He ravished her in front of his ex-wife, and she did or didn't get off on that.

Wait, no, that is not true either. Mehmet Al-Raschid, the former sultan of Aswadistan, never ravished Najwa. It never happened. There existed no records—no audio or video recordings, no cortical readout logs, no true memories from either party—that it ever took place. In fact, the universe stood as witness that the two never engaged in coitus. The current atomic structure was such that it never relinquished enough atoms to make up what would be the conjoining of the sultan's and the narratrix's genitalia. All butterfly-effect back-entries pointed to that never happening.

But it has happened in your mind because I have implanted that image in there. Both of us, teller and listener, are complicit in launching a very real cross-section of these two into a sweating, panting configuration—well-toned, depilated sultan tearing up that musky Old Testament desert snatch, bronze limbs of hers beckoning.

There are records of that in your mind. It is a very real imprint of something that has happened. Notice how your imagination takes over from there, as if requiring almost no volitional input from you, as if your mind has tapped into a superhighway of the universe upon which another cross-section of reality is hellbent on heading toward the future, barreling through the present, ultimately unable to escape its past . No data mining is necessary to confirm that. We can degauss the analog past with the digital present to create a supra-digital future where truth and fiction are the lizard's tail that gets knocked off by hard reality and grows back the way we want it to.

I woke up the next morning with the intension to free myself from her filibustering of my duties. It would take a good amount of effort, like assembling furniture through a hangover. I clumsily scaled down the scaffolding of hierarchical realities she had propped up, and once standing upon what I assumed was basement reality, summoned my Uzbek friend Sawdust to the palace.

He got a bit roughed up by the anarchists outside, but shook it off. He came in through a turret window by way of a jet pack, which doubled as a hookah. He was one of Inner Asia's foremost experts on thought decryption. He espoused the use of many firewalls—veils upon veils of deceits and false flags, fake political affiliations (or perhaps not!), matters of taste convoluted to the point of incomprehensibility, pheromonal red herrings, honey-pot goals to throw off interceptors, dead-end assessments of friends and enemies who could be one in the same. He was a staunch proponent of the q-cloud, where one could store away one's own engrams to the point of untraceability. No technology yet existed that could fish someone else's data out of the q-ether and decode it.

It was the first time I saw him in person. He was obese but fast-twitchy. He had a neatly trimmed beard and a full mujahideen getup. I embraced him and immediately learned the pertinence of his nickname.

"So," he said, "where is she, dog?" He always called me that.

I shushed him.

"What?" He smirked. "Who cares." A beep went off, and he took a drag from his hookah tube, which looped over his right shoulder; blew out smoke.

The original reason for his visit was to see if he could uninstall my guardian angel. But I also wanted to see if he could plumb the depths of Najwa's mind and find damning images of her and Al-Raschid. "You'll stick her with the scopolamine pen, then I'll head-hack her and search for caliph tags," he whispered. "Two-pronged approach. The scopolamine blend also has an amnesiac add-on. So she won't even remember the ninety minutes proceeding the injection."

A capital scheme.

Najwa emerged, affecting a Rajasthani queen: red sari with brocaded gold, nose ring, mauve lipstick, bindi—the works. I pricked her on the right shoulder and she collapsed into my arms. The tray of coffee pot and cups dashed loudly to the floor, causing a mess of shattered porcelain and steaming, dark liquid. I lay her out on the divan, propping a pillow under her head.

Sawdust reclined on a bean bag chair and tilted his head back, eyes closed. He stayed like that for some time. His years of experience working for Core-Corps wasn't paying off. He was having problems with the cookies, which replicated upon attempts at removal. Pop-ups cluttered my readout, reminding me of poor Al-Din's inescapable affliction. I was ready to rip the whole cortical modem out from my frontal lobe and let the traumatic chips fall where they may.

"What is it that you wish to be rid of?" panted Sawdust, swinging an overhand right at me and nailing my chest. "The actual angel or the adware?"

"Both," I said. He must have been so high that he was

forgetting his original purpose of being there.

"Hey!" he erupted. "Who. Is. This? Ess . . . Ess . . .Essmer . . . all . . ."

"Knock it off," I muttered, sitting up and looking over at him. He stared up at the ceiling, elated, mouth nearing drool mode. He had opened up some folders from my Eros account and chanced upon a still shot of my perfect match in her morphochrome bikini. "So violent, dog," Sawdust sneered. "So many bad vibes. You could use a puff or two of this Berber strain. Need to chill the fuck out. Speaking of which__" He tugged on the tube with his teeth and took a generous drag, blowing the smoke over the sleeping Najwa. The extracurricular drag didn't stop him from taking the scheduled dose when his alert sounded a minute later. I wondered if the *hasheesh* compromised his hacking abilities. He sat back and after ten minutes was able to rid me of the actual guardian angel, but Core-Corps's adware had its claws in my brain deep.

"How many days left for the trial to end?" he asked.

"Twenty-one," I said.

"Three weeks. You'll be fine. Just keep your cursor pre-hovered over the 'X'." He sat up and gazed over at Najwa, ready to plumb the depths of her mind. He was drenched in sweat by the time he cried, "I can't find a thing, man. I'm deep in. Packet sniffing, IP spoofing, nothing works."

She began swaying her head, eyelids fluttering. "I told you that she was off-grid," I said.

"Yes, I know. But there still should be trace drivers and other files. Assuming she had a modem at one point." He shook his head in dismay. "But I can't find a damn thing. There's nothing. Firewall detection yields nothing either." He took a toke from his hookah tube, as if that would help.

"Keep looking. Find the former sultan. Not caliph." We had

some solid minutes left. I wanted to go over and pat her head. Her eyelids stopped fluttering. "Fuck," he muttered, then said some slur in untranslatable Pashtun. "I can't find a single thing. No proxy servers, no IP addresses, no cookies, no registries, nothing." He blew out smoke and shook his head.

"Well there must be something," I pleaded. "She's got a damn library in there."

"No," he said. "There's nothing. She's really, really off-grid. Like she's never had any brain-apps installed at all. Ever. There's nothing. Nothing. I can't even detect drivers for a Core-Corps cortical modem, which are supposed to be open source and out in the open. Port scan, nothing. Believe it or not, she's a true analog."

Her breathing settled into a purr. "Shit," I said.

THE PERENNIAL MUSIC

Once upon a time, I woke up one day and gave a shit. That sense of purpose terrified me, so the very next day, I cleared away the mental cobwebs of concern with drugs. This is why I couldn't recommend them enough.

Everything was easy again. Political persuasions and religious affiliations were matters of cultural upbringing, and never wrong turns through life's labyrinth. The brackish laguna water back in Venice was not meant to be slurped up, and like every other Venetian who went about his day, I avoided it. It was an easy thing to do, merely requiring not going through the intricate effort to actually ingest it. It seemed, anyway, that to cause trouble in the world involved an immense amount of calorie-burning that could only be attributed to boredom. To be a nuisance unto the world seemed tedious.

Maladjusted, sexually frustrated, intellectually stifled, vertically challenged, phallically deficient, malnourished, disenfranchised, under-appreciated, fiscally stifled—all were symptoms of the egocentric Age of Aquarius, before we learned to make the electron our bitch. Nano-tech had resolved a lot of these issues. Insurgents, instead of attending sausage parties out in the desert with monkey

bars and mud runs, got their whey protein and felt good enough
to build a school; droughts were alleviated with water desalination
wells and evaporation-condensation derricks; bod-mod booths and
sex-change express wagons in large part gave way to the compatibility paradigms like Eros, and its German beta version, Conjuga.

Now the political squabbles were over bandwidth. Now the
front line was in our heads. Somewhere along the line, geopolitics
stopped caring about natural resources and began concerning itself
with the perfect neurotransmitter cocktail, and the legality thereof.
Had Odysseus lent a closer ear to the Lotus Eaters, he would have
learned of a thousand Trojan Wars waged upon the battlefields
of innerspace.

Which was why analogs like Najwa were looked upon with deep
suspicion. More than because of a simple retro sensibility, there had
to be a good reason why they held out on the paradise between the
ears. Her unloading so much narrative junk onto me meant there
was something sordid lurking in her mind that she was deflecting
me from. Such cerebral rebellion betokened a kind of selfishness
when it was everyone's civic duty to forgo mental sovereignty.

Since Sawdust proved to be no help in divining her thoughts, I
would up unreality's ante by plunging myself into the Salviasphere.

I, Simurgh, traversed the plains of wraiths . . . wraiths upon
wraiths, upon more wraiths, and then some more, then more. There
were way more than four now. Most were dressed in black turbans,
black caftans, black beards. But a select few donned white. I fend-
ed them off by taking flight in my tincture-induced vision quest.
They had established a beachhead within the Salviasphere via the
Core-Corps guardian angel, but they still had a ton to learn. I had
only to stay steps ahead.

When they talked of different strains of cannabis, or different blends of coca or opium, they talked of gradations of quality and effect. Not so with salvia divinorum. Don't believe the lies. Like two or more black holes of matching density being identical, so are strains of salvia. The algorithm is immutable, as are its effects. When I felt the presence of the Shepardess, it was always the same feeling. The takeaway, however, was always different. How my mind interacted within the Salviasphere was where the real mystery lay. The flower of resourcefulness I sought came into view and blossomed forth with petals of logic.

I needed to gain entry into the mysteries of the yarn-spinner brotherhood.

I would seek out the opium-den district to hunt down Najwa's history. I had left while she still lay unconscious, lest she shackle me again to lethargy with a tale. Upon leaving the palace I learned that the anarchists outside, with their antique, jet-powered flying carpets and laser guns, did not harass people upon leaving the premises. They only had issues with those entering.

I was a few miles from the palace when an ad popped up and actually piqued my interest:

Come sign up for flying carpet lessons now! Don't delay! Already have a kilim you'd like to customize? Or do you want the latest in trend-setting models and weaves? Either way, leave with your own flying carpet upon graduation! Don't despair! You'll be zipping through the skies like Aladdin in no time! Sign up for our crash course today! Limited spots available.

The neural networking to navigate a magic carpet was regulated by Aswadibad's transportation board, and the amount of paperwork involved would likely be ridiculous. So I decided to keep walking. Much of Aswadibad's pedestrian infrastructure was equipped with foot conveyors, making for surprisingly fast commuting.

Not only had the narratrix's yarns been keeping me from my

hired duties, but they had been leaving my head cluttered with unanswered correspondence. Dangerous, that.

I was fidgeting with lunch at a shawarma stand when I was served with a court summons. Apparently, I had been invited to an identity-swap party a week ago. The head organizer was threatening litigation for damages lost. I had supposedly consented to attendance. I recalled no such thing. The invitation, along with the subsequent citations, was sent to my old IP address. I sat down on a bench and logged into the court hearing. The *qadi* proved lenient, though he berated me for not having my e-mail protocol up to date. The whole litigious nature of a neural gathering that was supposed to be progressive and egalitarian left a bad taste in my mouth. The shawarma vendor had placed my meal beside me on the bench while I was busy with the hearing. I picked it up and took a generous bite. It was horrible. Clearly one's palate was not ethnically determined. My Venetian tastes would take a lifetime to overhaul. A taste-bud acclimation app would be a capital idea. I skyhooked the shawarma into a garbage bin. The vendor scowled.

I had been to an identity-swap party before in Giudecca, and I didn't like it. The idea was to become inebriated on quick spurts of others' personalities. Just one maladjusted ideologue could ruin the whole thing.

What started as a great compliment—others wanting to microdose on your personality and thought patterns—became a liability: you couldn't think outside of yourself, which is a very human trait. The other participants held you accountable for being you—as advertised, anyway—and any deviation therefrom was tantamount to malfeasance. A dickhead dentist from Mestre had given me a hard time for not being on salvia. In return, I had asked him for a fluoride strip, which he had failed to produce.

I arrived at the storytelling district in Laylabad surprisingly fast, passing the ongoing open-air platform discotheque where Jafar had rescued me from trouble with his invisibility cloak. Sunlight became scarcer as I got closer to downtown. The alleys smelled of stray cat urine and fakir shit. Children played on the fire escapes and up on Spanish-tiled roofs, flying carpet traffic overhead threatening decapitation. The storytelling tenements were like jewelry bazaars, where each person from his allotted space plied his trade with a competitiveness that came from having to vie for a fickle public's attention, though a certain solidarity was required to keep the establishment as a whole afloat. As I walked down a hall, I heard snippets of swashbuckling dovetail with psychosexual espionage, only to crash against strolls through galactic gardens and scenes of celestial mayhem. Baritones boomed forth from acoustically enhanced echo chambers while sibilant whispers wafted about rooms deadened by foam walls. There were styles and stories for everyone. Various soothing aromas emanated from all rooms.

I was standing in line, waiting with many others to be herded into a parlor like so many narration-deprived cattle, when I checked with my bank and realized that the weekly dirhams were still being wired into my account. Here I was on a self-indulgent odyssey to find out what I could about Najwa, whose inscrutable personality had captivated me, and the Ulema was still paying me my stipend. The salvia seminar I had conducted was fruitless. If the Great Launch was to proceed apace, assuming everything was in order from a software and politics standpoint, then why were my shamanic services needed? The only scenario I could conceive of was this: since I was on retainer, then I might be needed to conduct sessions at a later point, as part of a contingency plan. It was beginning to look like the civilian drug was to be the narcotic qat.

Society was halfway there to political docility. Half the people in attendance were either mulching on bright green quids of the stuff or sipping its tea extract. This was normal for listening to the traditional storytellers spin their yarns, though much of the older folk preferred opium, sucking up serenity through an underground network that rivaled the plumbing. I vowed to stay sober.

The violent, chauvinistic, gratuitous stories they told down in Laylabad's streets and alleys were good. But they were the rejected step-siblings of Najwa's refined narrations. They involved magic-carpet jaunts across princesses' windows, and the filthy treatment of said princesses. They concerned potions and sweetmeats that induced satyriasis and lycanthropy. One story reported the gender reassignment of Richard Coeur de Leon, who fell in love with his erstwhile third-crusade rival Saladin. And the Horns of Hattin was not a decisive battle in Palestine, but a set of yak remains encrusted with amethyst and used in deflowering ceremonies upon the sacking of the remaining Christian cities. I could not fancy a young Najwa sharpening her skills among such riffraff without her having to pay some exacting toll that compromised her honor.

My favorite story that day was clean but no less disturbing. It was pure chance that I should be privy so quickly to the blast that would open a Pandora's Box of narrative, unraveling the mystery that was Najwa. It was told by one Zenki, an old man with a withered left hand and a long, white, flowing beard above which presided two piercing hazel eyes that lent his tale special credence. I was the only one sitting on the flea-ridden carpet, facing him as he sat opposite me on a red-painted plywood platform.

The Deaf Harpist and the Tree of Evil

"Somewhere among the ruins and dunes carved over the ages by the wind and the sun, there was an oasis of refreshing springs and lush verdure. Clutters of date palms kept most of the area all but covered from the heat and grateful therefore was the lucky sojourner happening upon the place. In the middle of the copse of palms, however, was a wide clearing, and in its center stood a tree of an uncertain variety. Its singularity was only further marked by the fact that it towered over all the palms. Upon closer inspection, one learned that, though considerably taller than all the other trees, its supremacy was aided by its being perched on a little mound.

"Now upon the mound, sidled up to the tree, could be found a woman of indeterminate age. Some say she was young, while others contend she was quite old, while yet others claim that her countenance betrayed a strange amalgam of having been somehow both. How this can be possible is only for Allah to determine, but what is certain is that she was always seen plucking away at an imposing harp, her gaunt arms harnessing the gilt device like creepers. She was also deaf. This disability made her other senses all the more acute, not least of which was her sense of sight, for she could spot a child two leagues away if the horizon would allow her it, if dunes and mirage waves did not stand in the way.

"Yes, I have heard that she had no eye for adults, saying, 'The only grown-up I need tolerate in this here life is myself, Allah forefend that I should have to tolerate another.' She knew all the songs that children held in their hearts, all the ones they held in their heads, and all the ones they held in the pit of their stomachs. She specialized in all three: favored and preferred songs, songs just learned, and songs unknown and therefore feared.

"The tree that she leaned herself against possessed a big knot-hole not a meter above the ground, and some say she would place her lips up against it and murmur, as if talking to the tree. Indeed, it seemed to be her only companion there at the oasis. 'I haven't stepped out onto the sand in years. And I say, you should not have to suffer your little footsies to do so either, so come here my child, come here.' She gave a few strums to her instrument and muttered a popular melody about the letters of the alphabet or plant-eating animals.

"The tree was lush in a very manifold way, in that some branches hung down like those of weeping willows, while others jutted straight up like Italian cypresses. It bore pine cones on one end but sprouted blossoms on the other. Even its bark was variegated when one made a trip around its trunk. It also had maple leaves of orange, yellow and brown. "The tree of evil, goaded by the harp-playing of the deaf woman, sucked the souls out of children once they had placed their heads against the knothole. All of the leaves were the number of souls take by the tree.

"This large orange leaf that I hold in my hand," finished the storyteller, indeed twirling it playfully by its stem, "is the soul of an orange-haired Azerbaijani boy who ventured off away from a negligent father on a hunting trip."

Not ten seconds after this Zenki ended his tale, an espresso copter lowered into the space between him and me and buzzed in place like an oversized hummingbird. He reached out with his good hand and accepted the caffeinated cargo to let the craft zip up and back to its hub. Zenki catapulted the cup's hot contents against the back wall of his throat and convulsed, lowering his aching head into his hands. He straightened up and peeled open his hypnotic eyes. He smiled.

I shouted up to him in broken Arabic, "I am looking for a woman storyteller who works off-grid."

He immediately DM'd me with: *No, you are not. You know where to find her. You should erase your GPS history if you wish to be more mysterious.*

I smiled. He smiled back.

I turned my translator on before continuing. "Then I am searching for her past."

"Then you have come to the wrong place, young man. If you cannot ask her about her own past, then your intentions must be dubious. What do you intend to do with such information, if not blackmail or outright incriminate her?"

He was sharp for a septuagenarian.

"I am merely in love with her," I said. "And I wish to win over her heart."

Zenki's hazel eyes marinated the brains behind them.

I elaborated, "Because she is off-grid, and I don't know what moves her, I must use old-fashioned means of guesswork to woo her." I immediately firewalled my Eros profile, lest he find Esmeralda.

We both turned at the sound of footfalls echoing from the parlor entrance. A slender figure emerged from the shadows. It was a girl dressed in a green mylar burqa. She ceremoniously removed the article to reveal a nakedness that was more surprising for its transgender aspect than its vitiligo. I looked back to the old storyteller, withholding judgment. He defied me with his eyes, stroking his long white beard.

"Can you help me?" I pleaded.

He took the opportunity to wave away the transgender with his withered left hand. "We don't abet those who set themselves against one of our own. That you have come here to find out how to win her heart is laughable. She is not one of our own. And you seem lost. Like you don't belong in this city. Or even this country, though your complexion is thoroughly native. Where are you from, young man?"

"The Republic of Venice," I proudly declared. "I am an outernationalist. Native Aswadistani, transplant at two."

"Those people have gone back to having doges, no?"

"Yes, indeed. The world community has deemed it archaic, but it is in fact a quite just form of governance, and it suits our size well. It would not work, say, with even a country the size of Sopra-Po."

"The Great Launch has taken some ideas from the intricate methods of old doge selection procedures," offered Zenki.

I did not know that. Suddenly, another espresso copter zipped in, this time dropping off a cup to Zenki then moving on to offer me one. I grabbed it and immediately took a sip. It was rather good. "To La Serenissima," Zenki said, holding his cup out to me. "To Sopra-Po. To Apulia. To Toscana. And to what was once Italia."

"Cin-cin," I said, and tossed back the espresso.

"I have a tale of Venetian vampires that I have been toying with," he said. "It concerns two sisters, three vaporetti, one viridian sex toy made of Murano glass, and revenge crafted from the mandrake root."

"I would like to hear it sometime."

Zenki downed the espresso like he did the first time, running through the whole ritual of shivering and head-clutching. He primly sat back up straight. "I could call on you upon its completion."

"I would like that." I wiped my mouth on my sleeve. "Sir, do all of your stories have allegorical implications? Would the Venetian vampires stand for something, or would it just be a story told for amusement?"

"Both. Stories, young man, are meant for entertainment. Overt political grandstanding or moral posturing do the listener a disservice. However, elements of these can add to the listener's edification if done properly. As of yet, the Venetian vampire story would have no political or moral import, since I have never been there, and have nothing novel to say about the situation. Though that could change upon the story's completion."

"What about soul-eating trees and deaf, harp-strumming witches?" I bluntly asked.

His hazel eyes squinted, and a sly smile slashed across his face. He stroked his beard. "Young man, if you provide me with impressions of your home that are not to be found online due to your republic's protectionism, then I will help you with cracking the nut that is Najwa." He let go of the orange leaf. It slowly wafted to the plywood platform.

"Na'am," I muttered.

I apprised him of the Venetian public's disillusionment with Sopra-Po, which had been the first republic to break off from Italia, setting in motion a chain reaction that did away with the widespread corruption of the old politicos who dragged the peninsula through a recession and consequent alienation with the stronger European Union powers who had to foot the bill and call for austerity measures in exchange. In general, Italians were accustomed—some would say even expected—to live outside their means in order to cut *la bella figura*. They resented the pinch and took to rioting. It continued in Milan, that smog-draped smokestack of a city. No one reported to work. The fashion and textile industries quickly atrophied. Business didn't pick up until the central government in Rome ceded control to the provinces. Crony capitalism had basically turned against itself. Palm-greasing CEOs learned that selling an honest, quality product was just as lucrative as a swindle job. Italian society basically fucked itself into sustainability. Tricolore nationalism took a hit, sure—but La Repubblica had in reality only lasted less than three-hundred years. Venice's break with Sopra-Po came with a mutual understanding that tax collecting and representation was more of a headache than the central government was willing to deal with, what with Venice's intricate tourism and cultural bureaucracy.

Zenki smiled at all of this, stroking his beard. It wasn't the information he seemed to relish, as much as the ideas that simmered forth because of the information. "Tell me about your childhood. Also, do you love Italia, or just Venice? Is pederasty prominent there? What's it like to ride a vaporetto? What dialect do you speak, if any? Is the Doge's Palace as captivating as they say? Does it not look like an Ottoman mosque? What are your impressions of Turks? Is infidelity frowned upon or encouraged? Are the breakwaters dependable? Is Lido as run down as they say? What is an *enoteca*? Is mid-air traffic restricted to the mainland? Describe Cannaregio to me. Explain Mestre's train system. Are there still cheap knockoffs of carnevale masks? What's the local impression of Giacomo Casanova? How do my espressi compare? Do you know a decryption expert who can get me into Venice's virtual private network? Do you approve of the Doge?"

"He's a douchey doge," I snapped.

"Why?" Zenki asked.

"He's just arrogant. He administers well enough, I guess, but he acts like he's the last Coca Cola in the desert."

"Is he young and handsome?" Zenki asked.

"Yes and yes," I replied.

"So you are jealous of him," Zenki said, smiling.

"An enoteca is a wine bar," I explained, "usually facing the promenade. A bunch of sixty-somethings in bifocals and cold-colored windbreakers burn through their inheritances by out-drinking each other. They denounce tourists as Huns, yet fail to realize that Venice's main import is its past."

"What about mid-air traffic?"

"There isn't any," I said. "Aside from the motoscafi, vaporetti, and gondole—bicycles and feet are the main modes of transport."

"What about the mainland?" Zenki asked. His head had slowly been creeping closer to me. He was absolutely engaged in soaking up information. I hoped he proved as adept in dispensing it.

"Automobiles and trains. There are no magic carpets, I'm afraid." He mulled this over for some time. I was impressed in the lack of national pride that he evinced. Any patriotic dupe would have gloated over this like caramel over an apple.

I continued answering questions and giving impressions. I felt like Marco Polo in front of Kublai Khan.

When he finally began to speak of Najwa, his voice, usually calm and measured for narrative purposes, carried to it a wistfulness, almost as if he were speaking of someone dead. His black-draped monologue seemed more a eulogy than an indictment. The espresso copter visited us three more times. He turned down the drinks, though I accepted upon the last visit. He snapped out of his melancholy when called upon by Hamid, a fellow storyteller, who soon after entered the salon. He was relieved to pass the narrative baton onto our visitor.

Hamid was a mountain of a young man, as fat as Zenki was slender. Bald of head and billowy at all points, the protégé deferred to the elder master with an endearing touch. Zenki hung around, out of a concern that I receive as many answers as I had earlier received questions, but also in order to add asides to Hamid's impressions.

I began to hear a low hum as the backdrop of the narration: djinns of iniquity slowly gnawing at the narratrix's reputation. What story of hers could undo the disaster I was compiling? The consensus was that she was gifted but had abused her abilities for the notoriety of the court. No guttersnipe sisterhood had come to her rescue. Self-made only because self-obsessed, she bedecked herself with jewel-encrusted anecdotes in order to mask a despicable reality. Allusions to an escape from a state orphanage to the abandonment of a four-year-old son came up as often as did old accusations of menages-à-trois with Al-Raschid and Qamar, the former sultan's now-ex-wife. Hamid told me to seek out an oud player, a former storyteller apprentice who had been a rejected suitor of Najwa's. They did not know his name, though they did know that he was first oudist for the Perennial Music being played at the Red Mosque (Al-Masjid Al-Ahmar) a few blocks from downtown.

They were incredulous that I had never heard, much less heard of, the Perennial Music. They willfully changed subjects to tell me all about it.

The Perennial Music was a composition that was being played just as I was learning of it. It was playing when they first learned of it themselves, and will be playing well after a lot of people are dead. They couldn't accurately describe it for the single fact that it was always changing. It was a symphony, which was inaccurate, since the composition had and could lapse into instrumental solos or chamber ensembles at any moment.

I waved hands at Zenki and Hamid, as if to say, *Enough, I get it.* It's an allegory. It's a fable depicting the great composition that is the world itself, with the entire gamut of emotions and eventualities. *No, no,* they admonished with shaking heads and wagging indices. *It is all-too real.* The Perennial Music is a composition that can be heard at the Al-Masjid Al-Ahmar auditorium. It has been going on for twenty-some years now, with no sign of wrapping itself up.

The world's classical musical composers deemed it a monstrosity. They labored away for months on end to produce a twenty-minute-long string quartet, when there was at the center of Aswadibad a beast of an opus that threatened to last all time. Which raised the question: who was the composer? Or better yet: who were the composers? Some held it to be the work of a super-genius. I myself didn't; there would simply be way, way too much to compose. Since the music hadn't stopped for over twenty years, then the composer simply mustn't stop composing. He would have to compose, say, ten seconds' worth of music for over fifty instruments—and have only ten seconds to do so. I therefore believed that there was a group of composers. The composition was all over the place in terms of style and pathos.

Zenki held that a committee funding the Perennial Music had been set up by old Jehangir Al-Raschid, that heavy-handed former neurosurgeon, before ceding the sultanate to his son, Mehmet. It made sense. Jehangir loved public works, was a patron of the arts, and therefore led a less-tight economy than his offspring. The fervent nationalism that was in full effect had not yet spread. The West was still welcomed to trade, and Aswadistan had only dreams of self-reliance, a status realized by Mehmet Al-Raschid's reactionary protectionism.

I decided to seek out the oud player. Hamid wished to tag along. "I haven't been downtown in over two years. I've been making mad money spinning yarns here, and I have everything I need coming to me. Qat, women, food, men."

Zenki also wanted to go. A master storyteller like himself needed to continually mine the real world for material. He was certainly not above a jaunt to the auditorium with me as a canary in a coal mine. "There will be a lull in client traffic here for a good three hours," he said.

I arranged it so that Maryam, a clickbait reporter friend of mine with Associated Press credentials, would pose as a paparazzi looking for a lead on Al-Raschid's love life. She would then present me as a cub reporter. The two storytellers would meantime sit in the audience to watch and hear the orchestra in action.

On our flyway downtown, Zenki told me that the musicians refrained from conducting interviews. Part of their training, along with the attainment of a virtuosic musical skill, consisted of a rigorous set of bylaws, pertaining both to conduct within the orchestra and public relations matters. So instead of a reporter I would profess to be a pollster, and of a decidedly rightist bent. It worked. In fact, an exiting dumbek player had an apoplectic fit when I accosted him with a clipboard, railing against the former sultan. Maryam's eyes shifted nervously over her veil as she struggled to refrain from defending her political favorite. She joined Zenki and Hamid inside to hear the music.

"Is the entire percussion section in favor of the Great Launch?" I asked. "I know the strings are very conservative. Most especially the oud players. Maybe because it's a traditional instrument."

The dumbek player, not yet in his thirties, said that the strings' political leanings were fostered from a perspective of privilege, as opposed to the more manual, and therefore working-class, background like those of the percussionists or even the middling woodwinds.

"Nuri and his lot," he griped, "wouldn't know what to do with a callus below their fingertips. They're no better than the sheet-shifters, if you ask me." I ran a search on Nuri, oud, Perennial Music, Najwa, storyteller. I got pages of results, which I saved before excusing myself, lest our interview draw attention from disapproving fellow musicians. I entered the dimly-lit auditorium and found my three companions seated in a back row.

I also ran a search on 'sheet-shifters.' Among the rotating shifts of musicians and conductors on the payroll, were the curious, white-robed sheet-shifters, to which the dumbek player had just alluded. To these busybodies was assigned the sole but demanding task of making sure the proper booklet and page of music was set before incoming, present, and outgoing musicians. They hurriedly moved about, racing up and down the aisles of musicians. They were the epitome of economical motion. They briskly appeared from either side of the stage, sometimes employing hand-trucks to wheel in stacks of sheet music, which got parsed out among the others with no wasted effort. Things would get especially hectic during the changing of shifts, when musicians had to be absolutely certain they were performing the correct pieces.

I found that approaching these entities was much harder than doing so with the musicians. They lacked the haughtiness of the performers; but they simply didn't speak. They evinced no emotion, but simply gazed back at me, the whites of their eyes blazing through the darkness caused by their cowls.

Unlike the musicians, who were dressed in black-tie, the sheet-shifters wore the purest white. Their frenzied presence was the embodiment of the fickle and restless music, which shifted in and out of varying modes, never staying still, always on the go. Responsible for bringing in and taking out the actual physical segments of the Perennial Music, they were its stewards; they were the stevedores of song.

They retrieved the pertinent pieces of music from what some contested to be a vault, others a gallery. I found it troubling that there should be a vault—or gallery—of yet-to-be-played music, and not a mirroring one storing that which had already been performed. I imagined the composer had the stacks and stacks carted back to his workshop, having to make his way among the labyrinth of his own musings, tripping over and bumping into the sounds of the past.

The Perennial Music was fifteen minutes into an avant-garde percussion arrangement, sprinkled with string pizzicati, when a story war played itself out in my brain.

Out of etiquette, I consented to the cortical entry of my two companions: we wanted to continue communication, but not at the expense of the fellow audience members, of which there were a good fifty. Hamid shifted his rotund form in the seat next to me before unpacking a yarn concerning the composition before us.

"A man of unknown extraction, and even less-known age, resides in an unpainted cedar shack in a green grass valley somewhere in the Anti-Lebanon Mountains. Two ever-youthful women, who were once his foot soldiers before he gave up his warlordship, and are now his loving servants, go about unveiled while tending to his needs—fetching him water and fish from a nearby stream, making his bed, providing him with ink and paper, and clipping the toenails of his right foot."

"What about his left foot?" I asked.

Hamid heaved a great sigh. My blunder may as well have been worse than America befriending the House of Saud. We sat listening a bit to the percolations of snare drum, wind chimes, cowbell, and cello body-pounding. A few people ushered into the auditorium to sit in front of us, just as people arbitrarily stood up and left. I got the feeling that people wandered off from the street and decided to listen to bits of the composition as if getting their meditative fix—much like someone would enter a basilica back at home in order to get in some good spiritual housekeeping time. Hamid cleared his throat and continued.

"If you stretched out and tied together the large and small intestines of the people whose deaths he was personally responsible for, you could draw a straight line from Beirut to Baghdad. And if you stretched out and tied together the large and small intestines of the people whose deaths he was not responsible for, you could draw a straight line from the center of the earth to the center of the sun, on perihelion day. Repentance unto Allah is done in numerous ways. Some perform the Hajj while others give alms to the poor. Some do both while some do none. Some absolve themselves of sin by dying while others live and perform acts of mercy. Some twist words and concepts in order to trick others, and some do the same in order to trick themselves. What never changes, though, is Allah's willingness to forgive.

"When this man placed his first foot onto the narrower-than-narrow bridge of Sirat, he heard the screams for mercy shooting up from both sides of the hellfire down below. He has been walking the bridge for more than twenty years, and the screams have not stopped, nor has his effort to drown them out. Tight-roping your way across a scorching abyss is thirsty business, so it is good that one of his women servants brings him water while he places pen to inkwell then pen to paper, taking breaks only to pray toward Mecca, tend towards nature, trim his left toenails, or sleep.

As if on cue, the entire orchestra exploded into an allegro molto, with the brass section duking it out with the woodwinds, and ultimately winning.

"He still wears his camouflage," continued Hamid, "as if the enemy might catch sight of him out in the valley, in his cedar shack, and take him out. He sleeps in camouflage, composes in camouflage. Even his music sounds like camouflage, if you listen closely. There are blotches of earthy tones that blend into each other and evoke natural belonging. Notice there is never anything technological or artificial about the composition."

For starters, I noticed that there were no synthesizers of any sort, analog or digital. Aside from the microphones and PA speakers that transduced the sounds, everything comprising the orchestra had been culled from nature.

"What did one of the warlord composer's servant girls tell the other, about disenfranchisement? This:

"'What do you do with a black screw, a green screw, and a white screw, on a patch of blue velvet?'

"'I know not,' said the second girl, folding the composer's laundry. 'What?'

"'And what were Constantine XI's last words,' asked the first girl, 'as he leaped into the fray during the fall of Istanbul, and into the tender arms of history? And what is seventy-two plus seventeen? I know the answer to two of these questions at any given time, but not all three at once.'

"'Explain,' said the other girl. And they thought they heard the composer's quill pause over the paper.

'Explain,' she said again.

"And the first girl did. She said that there was something almost digital to the answers to those three questions that prohibited them from being known all at once. As if one of the millions of zeros and ones of one question conflicted with the zeros and ones of another. Only a memory erasure of any one of those three allowed the third one to be known, whichever one it may be. There was a glitch in the human mind—anyone's human mind— that prohibited knowledge of all three at once. And this was the case with only those three questions . Even the slightest change in one of the questions , such as changing the patch of velvet from blue to ochre, would allow for the mental capacity of all three.

"This phenomenon is well known in musicology. It is called harmonic distortion. When you play certain chords on a piano, you will find that the sound of certain notes on the diatonic scale are drowned out by others. It is merely acoustics at work, and therefore nothing to balk at. But who would think the mind works likewise? But check this out." Hamid shifted his outsized form in his seat, harmonically distorting the entire row of seats into a tremor. "The note that has been drowned out has been engulfed by the others. It is no longer there. If you look at its sine wave on an oscilloscope, you will see it has been perturbed, or clipped. It is not merely inaudible to the human ear: it is gone. Perhaps—and this is the warlord composer's very own theory—man will evolve to the point of being capable of perceiving that note, only by inference brought forth from a deep understanding of distortion itself. Imagine the implications. And perhaps man will eventually be able as well to know the answers to all three of those questions at once."

"Seventy-two plus seventeen is eighty-nine," I responded.

"Okay," Hamid conceded. "Now I will ask you the first question, and you will answer."

"But I don't know the answer," I said.

"Don't worry," he said. "I will tell it to you. Look, the context of the three questions is immaterial. 'What do you do with a black screw, a green screw, and a white screw, on a patch of blue velvet?' Anyone can do whatever the hell he or she wants to with those four objects. You may answer, 'Put them in your pocket', or, as is necessary to illustrate the phenomenon, 'You build an Islamic empire over the ocean.' Okay, so I will ask you one more time, whereupon you must give the proper response for the phenomenon to function. Here goes. 'What do you do with a black screw, a green screw, and a white screw, on a patch of blue velvet?'"

I scanned my cache for the transcript and responded immediately, "You build an Islamic empire over the ocean." The symbolism of the screws having the three colors of the pan-Arabic flag was not lost on me. Nor the velvet representing the ocean. Aswadistan had indeed harnessed desalination technology and helped solve earth's potable water problems, and in the process become an economic powerhouse on the world stage.

"Okay," continued Hamid. "What were Constantine XI's last words as he leaped into the fray during the siege of Istanbul, and into the tender arms of history?"

"How do I know?" I went. "You have yet to tell me yourself."

Hamid gave a supercilious chuckle. "He was purported to say, 'I will defend this city to the last drop of my blood.'"

"What if I knew the answer in the original Greek?" I asked.

"It would not matter," Hamid explained. "It's the essence of the answer that does. For instance, you being able to respond in your Italian, and me responding in Arabic, as we are both communicating each in his own tongue now, with each other, matters not."

"Fine," I said.

"Here goes, then," Hamid said, and cleared his throat. "What do you do with a black screw, a green screw, and a white screw, on a patch of blue velvet?"

"You build an Islamic empire over the ocean," I quickly responded. I looked at Hamid and shrugged. He smiled.

"And what were Constantine XI's last words before dying in battle?"

"'I will defend my city to the last drop of my blood.'"

Immediately, he asked, "What is seventy-two plus seventeen?"

And I drew a blank. Not only could I not recall the number, which my short-term memory should have culled from a clipboard I may as well be holding in my hand, but I couldn't even lay out the two numbers on a mental notepad and do the grade-school summation. It was the strangest thing. I felt as if I had been pulled down into the Salviasphere, where the mathematics of reality break down for no reason other than to impishly confound. I sat there listening to the music, focusing on a pair of crash cymbals, spiraling away at the brass striations every time the cymbalist mashed his cargo together.

Then, it occurred to me to call up the transcript, opening a dedicated word-processing window on the right side of my autorama. "Okay, Hamid. Ask me again, but in a different order."

"Fine," Hamid said. And he saved the Constantine question for last.

And I couldn't find it on my word processor. The lines of text where the answer should have been had literally been deleted. I perused the page-long transcript a few more times. Nothing. "Well?" Hamid urged, elbowing me in the left ribs.

"Don't do that," I told him.

"I can understand why you're upset," he muttered aloud. "It confounds everyone. But you mustn't be disappointed in yourself. It happens to everyone. And only with those three questions."

I scanned the document yet again. There was the question. But there was no written answer. Either the dictation software failed to type out that part of the transcript of Hamid and me communicating, or it had indeed typed it out, only to have it be subsequently erased by an unknown agency. My old-fashioned cerebral neurology was cloudy when I posed the question to myself. Who was Constantine XI? What about his other ten namesakes? Supposedly, he besieged a historical city?

I needed a break from the mental plyometrics. Hamid humored me, allowing me to enjoy some of the music, which had devolved into a maudlin oud solo. I wondered if that was Nuri, whom I was to accost at some given point. The solo then erupted into complicated passages of sick virtuosity and multi-fingered picking trills that resonated throughout the auditorium. The forty or so other musicians sat motionless, facing forward in semi-darkness. Even the room at left stage, whence issued the sheet-shifters, had its lights dimmed, nary a silhouette to be seen through the large glass window. The solo did not sound improvisational; a diminished scale seemed to recur, along with a secondary bass theme perpetrated by the oud player's thumb. Perhaps, the warlord composer had taken a long sip of water while composing this or trimmed his left toenails.

I opened the transcript back up. Okay: Constantine XI said (and I was astounded by the fact that moments ago I had completely forgotten that he was the last Byzantine emperor, and had leapt into battle against Mehmet the Conqueror, at the fall of Constantinople , now Istanbul), "I will defend my city to the last drop of my blood." And seventy-two plus seventeen is eighty-nine . And . . .and . . . I scanned the transcript.

Fuck.

If the warlord composer had been slaving away at a decades-long musical composition as he waited for higher man to usher in a new age, he had best remain plugging away. He would die yanking pathos from the celestial spheres by the handful before finding his *übermensh*. I knew I sure as fuck wasn't it. I felt dumb - er than a sack of potatoes.

I didn't ascertain whether or not Hamid had taken on a triumphant aspect with his narrative strangulation of a helpless Venetian. Zenki had come to the rescue with a counterstrike that was less confounding than his protégé's triple-heliced riddle/paradox, but no less fanciful.

"Yeah, some may contend Hell to be a fiery furnace, or a torture garden tended to for the express whims of sadistic demons. Both of these may be close to the truth, I daresay, but the most anguishing aspect of Jahannam, or Hell, would not be the curriculum therein. I contend, then, that Hell is in one's head, and is therefore of the utmost grotesque aspect. I say, then, that Hell is self-referential, self-reflexive. Yea, Hell is a sphere—agony enclosed upon itself, with nary a chance at escape, nightmarish not because of monstrous inhabitants or situations, though these may indeed be present, but because it's inescapable, a spheroid prison."

I was about to break the most cardinal of listener rules, that of interruption, but Zenki forced my agape mouth shut by continuing. "In the demonic dimension, each and every soul floats by within a transparent bubble. This bubble is the person's subconscious, after having departed our world. Each person in his bubble cannot see beyond the wall of that bubble, though the demons can gaze in.

"Whatever bubble a demon chooses to burst, for whatever reason, is the cause of this Perennial Music that you now hear and deem pleasing to the ears. The composition is but a desultory continuum of random sufferings, strung together by chance. Is that a serene harp solo you hear? It represents a prepubescent girl who has committed suicide with spoonfuls of cinnamon because she has besmirched her family's name. A clarinet quintet percolates like a flock of grounded geese pecking at bread? Five innocent people have perished in a water heater explosion."

The panic of the music coming from the stage and the dark cosmology the old storyteller was divulging sent my head reeling in sensory overload. I sought out a visible sign of serenity—no matter how trivial—and settled on the mysterious figures who scurried among the musicians. "Those sheet-shifters," I asked. "What of them?"

"Those seemingly pure entities in their white linen?" Zenki continued. "They are the very agents of evil. The cloth they sport is spun of the self-same material as the notes transposed onto the sheet music they tout around. This happens on a lower plane than the bubbles, much closer to our own realm. Some say you can actually see it, if you manage to penetrate the brotherhood and gaze upon the insides of their linen. Actual music will emanate and cause fluctuations in the air. The self-composing music is merely a transposition of the dead's suffering, semaphored by the sheet-shifters, who are the avatars of evil bursting the bubbles on the higher plane."

I looked over to Hamid, who concurred with a shrug.

"I need to talk to a few of them, then," I said.

Zenki chuckled. "You will snare an extraterrestrial before you get your hands on a sheet-shifter. Unlike the musicians—or any citizen, for that matter—they have no profiles. A proximity scan will yield nothing. They offer no bandwidth interference. They are will-o'-the-wisps. They never speak, never cock their heads in interest or upon the dropping of eaves; never shake their heads yea or nay; emit no smell. You can grasp a hand's worth of linen, though it be deadly, smeared with the neurotoxin extracted from a Portuguese man-o'-war." And he held up his withered, decrepit left hand.

"That Hamid presents the composition as not only a humanist exercise in evolution, but as a creative praise of Allah, is tantamount to blasphemy," he continued. "It is a fiendish affair, a devilish concoction, an impish opus, and a mischievous. The most complicit agents of this Shaitanic symphony are in fact the sheet-shifters, those wraiths of wrath." There was flange on the old man's voice, which meant he spoke to me in private. All of Hamid's story had taken place between the three of us. This one-on-one addendum with me meant that Zenki was willing to forgo impressing his protégé/opponent, and was possibly setting up some mental jiu-jitsu against his reckless student. Hamid immediately packet-sniffed my head, and Zenki, sensing this, went three-way before continuing.

"Do you deny that the music is beautiful?" I asked.

"I deny its benevolence," said Zenki. "We may as well imagine Michael asphyxiating Raphael with the entrails of Gabriel. Through no fault of theirs, the musicians are made to tune their instruments to the pre-crucifixion scars on Issa's back."

Hamid shifted his corpulence in the seat next to me, cleared his throat, and countered: "Each convoluted, baroque bar of composition is the stochastic interpretation of a drop of opium spilt on the floor as some demon sultan self-medicates his way to recovery from having been vanquished by Allah. Therefore, the Perennial Music is diabolical in nature, and the listening of it should be forbidden. Though it may fall under certain statutes pertaining to proxy apostasy." That was a blatant disregard for his mentor's narrative. It appeared that the mentor-protégé arrangement had been supplanted by a one-on-one slobberknocker.

I wasn't sure how long Maryam had been seated at my right. Either I had been too intrigued by the narrative fight to notice her return, or she was that slick. She DM'd me: *I got you an interview with the oud player. How on earth did you manage that?* I typed.

Look over at me. I did. She slowly lowered the veil from her face, smiled a burgundy smile, batted eyelids, and tapped her top row of teeth with the tip of her tongue. You may as well call that look The Vow-Breaker. I blocked out Zenki and Hamid, just in case.

"He finishes his shift in two hours," she said, raising the veil back over face. The stew that were my hormones boiled hot. I thought of whatever Nuri anticipated with Maryam; of Najwa, whose past I was intrigued by only because her present self remained as much a mystery; and of Esmeralda, whom I was meant to visit later that day at a new locale of assignation that Eros deemed integral to keep the flame of perfect love lit.

What was narrative itself if not foreplay? Without a storyline or situational lead-up, the lovemaking was just animal copulation. That was the whole impetus behind a revenge fuck, a grudge fuck, or a seduction months in the making. The plots spooled forth into the future, dragging us toward our target of desire, and did not stop at the barrier that was the flesh. Therewith continued the story. The confluence of events ended at the intertwining of bodies, attaining resolution. The very best story one could ever be entertained by was the one where he ended up being its own hero. That's why rapists have horrible imaginations.

If I missed my appointment with Esmeralda, the perfect love could be ruined beyond repair. It would be remiss of me to go outside of Eros and plead with her, since the endorphin matches were nigh-infallible and made our pairing perfect in the first place. Should her level drop beyond mine, it would be difficult to ramp back up. My absence could make her clamor for me all the more, though that itself would have been suggested by Eros. It even prohibited still shots of each other for certain spans of time, in order that desire remain active, and it be heightened upon our seeing each other in person. I tried to access jpegs of her, only to receive temporary suspension notifications. Since we hadn't seen each other in a while, the app's proposed duration of absence had probably reached its limit before either of us would break into disinterest.

I wondered what these storytellers did for love. One was old and withered, the other awkward and unbecoming. There was no reason to think that these two yarn jockeys could not and did not invent elaborate tales of abducted seraglio virgins and nubile princesses in distress, and insert themselves as shredded, swashbuckling bandits to the rescue.

Both of them came knocking on my head's door, wanting back in. I let them link up, but because they found Maryam in there with me, neither of them continued his narration. Either their stories had ended on their own volition, or they found the female presence stultifying. I imagined that their parlors had been often visited by young women (for I recalled seeing not a few on the balcony that led to all the rooms), and that they knew how to keep the flow going in their presence. Maybe they just despised journalists. The reporter versus bullshitter bout would go on until the Judgment Day.

The orchestra broke off into two separate pieces of music play-ing simultaneously. The left side—with its own section of strings, brass, woodwinds, and percussion—launched into a jazzy 1970s crime soundtrack affair with muted trumpets, disruptive and ob-noxious saxophone wails, and dissonant strings; while the right side—two oudists, a sitarist, two tabla players, and a tambour player—meandered around a rhythm of an evening raga. This bifurcation of the composition may as well have been staged for my purpose, what with two storytellers invading my head with their distinct takes. To Hamid's credit, he didn't copy Zenki, and as an act of reverence steered clear of resorting to the old man's bag of tricks, choosing instead to hone his own craft. Like all good students, he had a rebellious streak in him.

Annoyingly, though, he kept DMing me with narrative asides to which neither Zenki or Maryam were privy. I found these nudg-es uncomfortable and slimy, like tentacles groping my imagina-tion. I was an innocent bystander amidst a story war, with my at-tention focused on something else. I launched a disappearance pass his way. He would assume I was scanning through mail or looking something up. I eventually looked askance at him. He sat staring at the musicians onstage, though probably gazing at notes on his autorama. His retroussé nose gave him a haughty aspect, and he told stories with that attitude. Hamid made what at first appeared to be a sensible move, in that he incorporated some of his mentor's elements into his own story, making Zenki's entire version out to be nothing more than a subplot. But instead of it being clever, it ended up being a desperate ploy to avoid what should have been a true tête-à-tête to determine the more interesting, more viable, and therefore more real history of the composition.

I had trouble following some of the developments, what with Maryam poking me with incoming tidbits pertaining to Nuri. The music onstage then took a curious turn: the two disparate sides dovetailed into each other, then went into an allegretto before collapsing into an oud chamber piece. I surveyed the six oud players. Maryam blatantly pointed him out to me in analog: a narrow-shouldered, tousle-haired, boyish virtuoso who likely came—as the dumbek player outside had hinted—from the privileged class, growing up in the northwest quarter of the greater Aswadibad metropolis, known as Ash-Shams, a sun-drenched collection of security-gated, terracotta-roofed mini-mansions with synthetic lawns peppered with cryptozoological topiaries, tossed against the southern foothills two decades ago by tech upstarts fleeing the contagion of rust emitted by the city's still-ubiquitous shanties.

All of a sudden, I felt something flutter at my left ear. I swatted at it with my right hand, hitting nothing. I turned my head and saw a bug of some sort flap into the darkness.

Hamid poked Maryam, who immediately laser-locked her large green eyes onto me, embarrassed. I sensed self-esteem issues with the youth, but he was in a daring mood. Due to either kindness or curiosity, she linked up. He let me link up as well.

Hamid's new narrative tack called for listener participation. The second-person narrative, though gimmicky, had me on the edge of my seat. You would normally lend more credence to a story that happened elsewhere in the world than in your own direct sphere of influence, simply because you were not there to negate its happening. Hamid tangled us up in his threads, whipping us around that way and this.

"Allow me to propose to you a scenario," he said, directly at Maryam.

Intriguing music of the highest caliber was being played in front of us. These storyteller types didn't know how to keep their mouths shut. "The red wind had stopped," he muttered. "So he formatted her head. The end."

I looked over at Maryam. Maryam looked over at me.

Hamid cleared his throat. He was done.

"Excuse me?" Maryam pleaded.

"The end," Hamid stated, staring straight ahead. He had the profile of a capybara, arrogant as all hell.

"The end of what?" Maryam pleaded again. I meant to stay out of it.

"The red wind had stopped. So he formatted her head. The. End."

"What wind?" Maryam asked. Shushes issued from people seated three rows in front of us. "And why is the wind red?" she whispered.

"No," Hamid said.

What are you talking about? she DM'd him.

"No," Hamid confirmed aloud. "No."

Maryam sat silent for a while, then asked, "Where is the red wind located?"

"No," Hamid continued.

"Is this a story?" Maryam pleaded.

"Yes," Hamid confirmed.

A moment of silence elapsed before Maryam tested the narrative waters once more. "Was he wishing for the red wind?"

"Yes."

"Why?"

Silence, not even a no.

"Was it supposed to benefit him in some way?" Maryam asked.

"Yes," Hamid confirmed. His answers were meant to be monosyllabic. She was to provide the details herself, and he was merely a binary responder.

"Was it supposed to come to him?"

"No."

"He was supposed to go to it?"

"Yes."

"Does this whole thing involve the Perennial Music?" Maryam asked.

I hoped for a no, as a yes would entail at least a few hundred questions before this reverse narrative played itself out to a satisfactory dénouement. "Yes," Hamid chirped.

"Are the ifrits involved?"

"Yes."

"Do they create the wind?"

"No."

Maryam got resourceful. "Was there something he wanted within or beyond the red wind? Or is the desired result of it having blown on him what he is after?"

"Yes. Yes."

Fuck.

I reached for my salvia tincture inside my vest pocket, but desisted. I wanted to find out if there was room for one more in this reverse-engineered story. I asked Hamid, "Is the female whose head was formatted someone real?"

Hamid did not answer. I had committed two fouls: I interloped in what was meant to be a manipulative interaction with

Maryam, and maybe worse, I brought into focus the fact that his story may be in the end just a story, thereby damaging any suspension of disbelief. But the young lad, wanting to appear gracious in front of Maryam, ended up answering, "Yes."

"Is love involved?" Maryam asked. That was a great question, as its answer would guide all subsequent questions, thereby eliminating a great many that might yield roundabout clues.

"Does the man love the woman?" she asked. "And does she love him?"

"Yes," Hamid stated. "Yes."

"Does he wish for her to forget him?"

"Yes."

"Because he did not achieve what he set out to achieve?"

"Yes."

I found that I had been tensely hunched over out of undivided interest, eyes peeled, because an attack on the brass section from the orchestra startled the hell out of me. I remembered I was inside an auditorium. I looked over at Zenki. The old man sat still, eyes closed, hands calmly clasped in his lap, mumbling, nodding to the Perennial Music. I figured I would work the love interest portion of the story and let Maryam stay busy with the red wind; that way we could meet in the middle and get on with interviewing Nuri after his shift ended. "Is she willing to undergo the formatting?"

Hamid sat silent before answering. "No."

Oh, shit. Drama. "Does she wish for him to obtain the prize from the red wind?"

"Yes."

Maryam, "Does the red wind blow at a particular place?"

"Yes," answered Hamid.

"Is she married to him?" I asked.

"Is the particular place in Aswadistan?" Maryam asked.

"No. No."

"Does he feel inadequate before her because there was no red wind?" she asked immediately, wishing for the rapid-fire pace to continue. She glanced at me. "Is undergoing the red wind a test? Is there a physical object to be obtained from it, or beyond it?"

Hamid appeared fine with the pace as well. "Yes. Yes. Yes."

My turn. "Is she aware of the test? The red wind?"

"Did the red wind unexpectedly stop?"

"Yes. Yes." Hamid nodded.

"Is his passage of this test, or rite, necessary for their happi - ness?" I asked.

"Is the red wind in the Middle East?" Maryam followed.

"Yes. No."

"Financial happiness?"

"In Europe?"

"Yes. No."

"Is there something scandalous about their relationship?"

"In the Americas?"

"Yes. No."

"Africa? Australia?"

"Asia? Antarctica?"

"No. No. No. No."

"Was he hoping for a promotion of some sort?"

"In outer space?"

"Yes. No."

There was a pause in the development. I imagined various re-lationship scenarios in which a promotion was of a paramount importance for the relationship to continue, at least with dignity; while Maryam, as well as I, couldn't imagine where the hell this red wind was if not on one of the seven continents. I hoped she didn't begin island hopping.

"Is the red wind on an island?"

"No."

"On Earth?" she asked.

Hamid hesitated, then said, "No."

"On another plane?" Maryam wondered.

"Yes," Hamid was quick to say, a tinge of disappointment in his voice.

I pounced like a leopard. "Is he a Sufi? An Ishraqi?"

"No. Yes." The young plot-jockey knew the difference. And he had his story's details hashed out. I had to give him credit. I looked over at his mentor, who had now fallen asleep.

I did a search on Illuminationist cosmology and came up with three cities: Jabalqa, Jabarsa, and Hurqalya. These locales, though not on our physical plane, were very much real. They were imaginal, not imaginary; and existed on a plane of consensual reality constructed by Ishraqis throughout the ages. They could be approached only through years of spiritual austerity and meditation on Allah's light. The keys to their gates were bestowed upon those who obtained *nur al-anwar*, or light of lights. I shot the three names over to Maryam, so that she could ask Hamid herself if the red wind was to be found therein.

"No," muttered Hamid to her. "No. No."

She messaged me that I should do the asking, since she would be busy for a few minutes with research on those three cities.

"Is she a princess?" I asked. "Is that why he needs the promotion?"

"No. No."

"Is their relationship a secret?"

"Yes," Hamid confirmed.

"Is there a child?"

"Yes."

Holy shit. "Girl?"

"No."

"The boy belongs to the two of them?"

"Yes."

"Is the boy alive?"

No answer.

"Is he dead?"

No answer.

"Is it uncertain?"

"Yes."

All of a sudden, an alert went off in my head. It wasn't my anti-virus software, which I had tailored to give a green flash at the bottom left corner. Something or someone was trying to seize me up, wanting to brute-force my head. A white flash eclipsed my autorama three times before disappearing. I had never experienced that before. I checked my inbox: nothing.

Maryam messaged me emojis of delight. She had found something. She asked, "Is the red wind on Mountain Qaf?"

Hamid, impressed, wistfully, "Yes."

"Does the red wind blow upon those scaling the mountain?"

"Yes."

"And it has stopped blowing?"

"Yes."

"Does someone have anything to do with it?"

"Yes."

"Other Ishraqis?"

"No."

"The ifrits? Have the ifrits stopped the wind?"

"Yes."

"Did Allah create the red wind?" I asked.

"Yes."

"But the ifrits stopped it?"

"Yes."

Ever the reporter, Maryam asked, "Did they stop it because they realized that the red wind was producing Illuminated Ones?"

Hamid, barely masking his being impressed, answered, "Yes!"

She took over. "Is there a reason why the wind is red?"

"Yes."

"Does it have to do with blood?"

"Yes."

"The blood of damned souls?"

"No."

"The blood of those who went before?"

"Yes."

"Up the Mountain Qaf?"

"Yes."

"Does the child compromise his ability to scale Mountain Qaf?"

"Yes."

"Because of issue? Because of the impurity of having issue?"

"Yes."

"Was he depending on scaling Mountain Qaf through the red wind in order to raise the child, which prevented him from effectively scaling?"

Hamid did not answer. She needed to be more succinct.

"Was there financial gain in reaching the top of Mountain Qaf?"

"Yes."

"Is an illumination farm involved?"

Hesitation. "Yes."

So an Ishraqi man needed to achieve enlightenment not for spiritual reasons, but for pecuniary reasons—in order to raise a child he had with a woman whose head was to be formatted. That meant that he was to be part of GnosisNet. Not quite the selfless endeavor that proponents of the Great Launch claimed it to be. He would achieve illumination for materialistic purposes. Fair enough. Who the fuck were we kidding, anyway? We all wanted something and would do what we needed to get it. Maybe he'd become a great soul in the process. At least he wouldn't be a deadbeat like my foster father.

I relieved Maryam. "Did she end up being formatted?"

"Yes."

"So all her registry files were erased?"

"Yes."

"Because his ability to support the child fell through?"

"Yes."

"Did this result in the child being taken away?"

"Yes?"

I looked over at Maryam, who grew glum.

"By the State?"

"No."

"Is the Perennial Music related to the stopping or diverting of the red wind?"

"Yes."

"Did the stoppage of the red wind happen when the Perennial Music was initiated?"

"No."

"Later?"

"Yes."

"Much later?"

"Yes."

"Was the red wind's stoppage in the last few years or more recent than that?"

"Yes."

"Is there still an insurgent in a valley somewhere in the Anti-Lebanon Mountains composing like mad, while two women tend to his needs?

"Yes."

"Does he channel the pathos of the torturing ifrits?"

"Yes."

"Some sort of ifrit rebellion?"

"Yes."

"Because they realized they were doing Allah's work?"

"Yes."

"Would the ceasing of the Perennial Music mean the restarting of the red wind?"

Hesitation. "Yes."

"Is that why the music is a diabolical diversion, and to be avoided?"

"Yes."

"Is the Ishraqi at an illumination farm?"

No answer, which always meant maybe. Again, three white flashes eclipsed my autorama. I shook my head, thinking my cortical modem needed a tune-up, or just may be loose, since I hadn't been to the data doctor in over a year. I checked my inbox. There was a message: *This is Sawdust! I just hyper-encrypted your system and set you up with a cloud server linked to my own VPN. Those flashes were me. Look, someone nearby is packet sniffing you like crazy! And that person has a decryption device that is way better than your shitty symmetrical encryption. Get out of there now before it figures it out and cracks open your files like a coconut! And log the fuck off! Get out of downtown! Ask for me tomorrow at the Oasis of Kisses. Hate those head-hacking mafia fucks.*

MODEMECTOMY

I regretted not being able to speak to Nuri the oud player. I came clean with Maryam as to why I couldn't stick around. As for the two storytellers, I told them that a business meeting was waiting for me. Despite Sawdust's request that I not dare log on, I sent out what is known in Eros-speak as an Ad-Lib(ido). A still shot of me gazing down at my crotch while showering that morning was sent off to my Esmeralda, who had agreed by sending me one back. She also sent me two words. "Al-Hindabad" and "Fottami." This was the entire gist of Satyros, the sexting app also put out by Core-Corps. It was Eros's smutty kid brother. I tumesced immediately.

Eros allowed you one Ad-Lib(ido) per billing cycle. It was an aberration from the packaged curriculum, so it must not be abused. Sure, you could break from the scheduling and do what you want, if you and your partner felt you were going to outsmart the app's biofeedback software and live happily ever after on endorphin dumps alone. But Eros was clever enough to work with one Ad-Lib(ido) per month. There had been much blowback by Eros coders and algorithm admin when Core-Corps announced that Satyros would become an embedded adjunct. But a job was a job.

I just couldn't wait until midnight, which was what Eros scheduled for us. Esmeralda and I could meet up through Ad Lib(ido), but we were not to overstay the allotted time of forty-five minutes. Sometimes, only oral contact was allowed, and Eros would use the mounting desire for penetration to reschedule meetings, thereby keeping the coals lit. But an unauthorized session of coitus could dump a bucket of water on the flame and extinguish it for good. I wouldn't find out what I was allowed to do with her, or unto her, until we saw each other and Eros performed its neurotransmitter assessment scans. I had a glimmer of hope that it would reassess us to the point of green-lighting full-on coitus there and then. I wanted her long-term because I loved her, but because I loved her , I wanted her short-term in her entirety.

I fought to forgo the Ad Lib(ido) and logged off. I accosted a magic carpet pilot and asked to be taken to the nearest illumination farm, mentioning the word "Ishraqiyun." He said something, but I couldn't understand him, as I didn't speak Arabic. I mentioned the word "Ishraqiyun" again and still he vehemently refused to take me there. This went on for some time. I stuck my tongue into the vast void of my Arabic lexicon, lapping up nothingness, slurping up dark matter, and regurgitated it into an intricate bauble worthy of a Murano glassblower. I said, "Al-Hindabad."

I took a heroic swig from my salvia tincture. I would not be going to the illumination farm. I asked the pilot to fly me to meet Esmeralda.

Whenever I got hyper-faded on salvia divinorum, I came into contact with a sultry, arm-swaying, bangle-shimmering gamelan dancer. She leads the lotus-eating charge into apolitical Armageddon. She applauds us for surrendering. She commends us for setting down our machines. She oversees the aftermaths, but never intervenes. She is the impenetrable firewall, the cheerleader rattling her pom-poms as we spiral down that tie-dyed abyss, the goddess of the Salviasphere.

I loved technology, but I found being logged off liberating. With everything networked into everything else, autonomy seemed scarce. Yet technology was just a utility belt slung around the Neanderthal's rickety hips, and those who despised technology did so with brain patterns wrought from same.

Drugs are technology. But our brains interact with them on a different grid, one as of yet unreachable by the coruscating neural networks of Core-Corps and Tru-Tech. I was beginning to more and more understand people's growing disillusionment with the digital plague of lidless eyes and tireless threshold monitoring. The Salviasphere that I navigated was on a frequency that may as well be tucked deep into the endless folds of the eleven dimensions proposed by the string theorists. Its cartography was left to me and a few others.

I grew nervous as we soared toward the Al-Hindabad hotel. The pilot, ever so deft with the command of his craft, took me beyond the main entrance and down into the courtyard, right in front of the automatic glass doors that gave onto the concierge desk. I approached the woman, a middle-aged harpy with an overbite and mascara'd eyes that could pop the lid off a monk's celibacy. She reached out and clutched my wrist in order to stamp it with the invisible barcode key. Esmeralda had logged us in as Mr. and Mrs. Fottami, which turned me on further. I began buffering as the elevator shot me up.

The salvia, instead of curbing my libido, turbocharged it. I couldn't wait to feel her naked body against mine. If frottage was all that Eros permitted, so be it; I would ejaculate through my pores, impregnate her with my sweat. I reached the room and swiped my imprinted wrist across the lock. The lights were off and the curtains were closed. "Fottami," hissed a voice from the far side of the room.

I found myself arguing with my own atoms. They relented and I won. Then the vast majority of the universe's molecules converged in the room. A swollen, oversized hand pushed me deeper into the folds of darkness toward the voice. I reached out with arms that until then had been given the sole task of holding up light that shot across space and time. Now there was no light. Now my arms could play and be free. They reached out and caught a voice. The voice squealed in my arms. I tightened my arms toward my own body, and the voice squealed more.

All of Aswadibad begin to attack me. The malevolence was so intense, I became convinced that I was deserving of it. I was the anomaly that had committed the heinous crime of merely existing. My being there was inexcusable. My consciousness, torn away from the hive mind of the capital city about to undergo a pilot project of computerized governance, perpetrated the crime of thinking for itself. If my stream of thought became like a shaft of miscreant light roaring through the vast darkness, then I would truly feel what a force light could be when it collapsed upon me like a white dwarf star imploding into a black hole. And the voice, the "fottami," kept erupting all over the darkness.

I no longer knew libido. The harmless, entirely selfish act of coitus had been zipped up and away into another dimensional fold, somewhere wherefrom it could not be retrieved. They quarantined my crotch files, they deleted the sex drivers necessary to act upon what was not long ago an untamable erotic urge. For simply wanting to get my ashes hauled, I was ground zero for what was becoming a black hole of untold amounts of information, compressed onto a two-dimensional hard disk. All subsequent waves of light crashed into the collection of data—"fottami" its war cry.

There was always room for more information, more data, more light. Bits chirped among each other, like little informational vermin, saying there was always room for one more. And there was. Everything rushed together, called forth by necessity, away from the abomination that was separation. There would be no motive once assembled, just like a killing machine has no real will: it simply must be; another agent was needed to operate it.

I was no longer convinced I was there for eternity when the pressure began to alleviate, and light became something I began to see rather than feel. It stung my eyes. I grew confident that I was alive, then I was grateful. "Fottami" had been replaced by rhythmic invectives of Castilian Spanish. A few fists made their ways to my face, ushering forth sheets of light behind them, like so many comet tails. I didn't know what to do but cover up with my forearms once I hauled up my pants from around my ankles and buttoned them up. I had every reason to be upset with this unfavorable turn of events involving Esmeralda, my perfect Eros match, but I was happy to be alive and not having the universe crashing right down upon me. I could bear the weight of this capriccio interaction between two lovers suddenly at odds with one another; it was the apocalyptic black symphony that was intolerable. The vox angelica of the diminishing salvia trip could make anything acceptable, honestly.

Esmeralda relented in her assault only to step into her silver panties and sling on her matching bra. She kept spitting forth rapid-fire Spanish. Her hair was in an unkempt Gorgon's cut. Sweat percolated on her lovely brow. I couldn't translate, since I was logged off. The room was a mess. I was about to log on, open up Eros, and run a neurotransmitter assessment test on us, to see if our situation was salvageable, but her autorama would immediately alert her of my linking in. Being off-grid was more tiresome

than the romantics liked to admit. One problem with liberty was
that it was tedious. She crammed the rest of her outfit in her purse,
wrapped herself up in a teal chador, and left the room, not bothering with the door.

I was still drifting along with the salvia's vox angelica, sleep-
ward, my neurons tickled by the three-dimensional world. I would
grow morose later. I had to remain off-grid while finding Sawdust
and have him secure my system for intruders.

Though it was in fact a crime to be off-grid, all you had to
say upon questioning was that your system was shut down for re-
pairs—virus removal, defragmentation, OS upgrades, brain surgery, etc. For them to deduce your history of logging off by re-
viewing timestamps was legal, but hardly worth the time. The head
cops, the only section of the disbanded police force to remain intact, had been the bottom of the barrel, and still commanded little
respect. Known as much for their incompetence in understanding
data collection protocol as their substandard computer skills, they
chose to stay out of real trouble and justified their state-funded
salaries by going after upstart spammers and pop-up vandals. Who
you really had to fear were private sector detectives the government
would hire to head hack you with the latest password-crackers and
proxy-server DOS attacks that made you desperate then vulnerable. You'd confess every analog session you ever had just to get
them out. This made Najwa's proximity to the court all the more
curious. Tariq Shareef, the spindly former minister of media,
now Al-Raschid's campaign advisor, grew defensive when asked
of the narratrix's curious immunity to the law. Since he was in
effect top cop, he should have been the first to, if not arrest her
outright , at least force her to comply with the minimum
state cortical modem requirements to link up with the rest of

the citizenry. This could have been a decisive blow to Al-Raschid's campaign if she had not been seen more as a cheap paramour to be despised than a velvet-tongued flouter of the law.

The anarchists' raison d'être was the "sovereignty of the senses." No matter how utopian or just a form of governance may be, it could not be abided if it were compulsory. "Better to have shit for brains," their hologram graffiti across palace walls declared, "than to have a constable between the ears." I was impressed by their ability to work off-grid, communicating with each other via anachronistic private workstations that used to be held in one's palm. Many of the holograms that regularly harassed Najwa at the palace showed off those devices, which looked about the size of a deck of cards.

I was beginning to find the Aswadistani conformity to convenience sickening. As long as a qat-riddled citizen could order up instantaneous orgasm or identity swap with a convicted murderer, he would willingly relinquish his privacy to the state. I was used to at least a little privacy. Unlike in Venice, where transparency worked both ways and even the color of the doge's undergarments was public knowledge, the Ulema was immune to public probing, with its VPNs and legions of IT troglodytes, hummus-breathed script kiddies, and gray-hat hackers with dubious resumes and over-stamped passports.

I was bothered awake by something fluttering at my mouth. I hated bugs. I hated that I had to touch them in order to kill them. I failed, and the nuisance was nowhere to be seen.

I went to the Oasis of Kisses, a three-story joyshack that served as a brothel, a criminal-mind arcade, and an extreme-sports simulation ranch. Among the sundry fads to overrun the hipster set a few years back was that of proxy apostasy. An otherwise good

Muslim tapped into the autorama of a criminal and networked with his endorphin profile. Allah could not and would not forgive mortal sins such as murder, false witnessing, and the eating of cloven-hoofed animals—but to see the world through a transgressor's eyes and feel his rush of adrenaline was permissible—commendable, in fact, for it took a certain bravery to see the horrors of a psychopath. To observe firsthand a despicable act committed by someone else was an expending of negative energy as well as a way to gain a hand up in empathy.

At the extreme-sports simulation ranch, on the open-air third floor, gym members were pushing the VO 2 Max threshold with unregulated supplements containing taurine, beta-alanine, cordyceps mushrooms, and beet extract. People ran three-minute miles on treadmills, scaled a virtual Mt. Everest without supplementary oxygen, and took up fifteen-minute crash courses in apnea training to free-dive VR Marianas Trenches.

The supplement company Up and Away was selling their products at a booth. They started out with dopamine outsourcing, their trailers known as 'happy houses' camped out in front of yoga studios offered up instantaneous transfusions to those who couldn't afford serotonin booster accounts. They also held classes in guided pranayama masturbation—of which there came into being world-famous autorama celebrities who led groups into synchronized climax then peddled their sponsors' products post-orgasm, i.e. the Klaw for men and the Kucumber for women. Just like with proxy apostasy, the refractory period became the new penance. It was more important than the prior indulgence. It served not so much as a time to recharge and cool the ejaculatory jets, but as a time to meditate upon that which was most important: equanimity, stillness, and quiet. It didn't matter how you got to Allah; it mattered only that you got there.

The lower two floors of the franchise-operated joyshack catered more to the forty-and-up crowd. For the twenty- and thirty-something set, establishments like the Oasis of Kisses were on the wane. Of all things, narrative was the new notoriety: what others thought of you mattered most, though everyone else was too busy impressing others to be impressed by same. Of course, this didn't stop anyone from playing this over-inflated pretend. Now in demand was the need for tailor-made personal histories—unearned battle wounds, feigned avuncular molestations, instantaneous trauma, phantom natural disasters, and trumped-up tragedies.

Tru-Tech's monopoly on the Middle East's nickel mines secured the conglomerate a stronghold on 3D printing, a technology that seemed promising and paradigm-shifting, but fizzled out as soon as objects began taking a back seat to ideas. Core-Corps beat Tru-Tech in the scramble for bandwidth and perception tech. Lie-peddlers that they were, Core-Corp's brain apps and résumé-enhancement firms were no worse than a cosmetics company. Alluring meant alluring either way. You are lying to me, as I am lying to you. Regardless, let's hook up. Or at least say we did.

The entire history of trends and fads had the erotic urge as its motor. Now that panting, sweating machine had turned against itself. Boy didn't have to bed girl now that all the boy had to do was claim that he did so. There was too much calorie-burning involved in actual dating. The prize itself could be simulated—though it often as not wasn't, because an asexual proclivity due to de-sex meds would kick in, or it was on to impressing someone new. Something odd was happening to the twenty-something DNA sequence, and it sure as hell wasn't evolution. I found the hip, morose anahedonia nauseating. So it was comforting to see patrons, mostly men, indulging in activities that made them happy.

Sawdust detested exercise, but he had the cardiovascular endurance of a bon vivant and didn't give a Frenchman's fuck what others thought of him. When he wasn't zipping about in his jet-pack that doubled as a hookah, he was gracelessness incarnate with his jerky gait. All I had to do once inside the joyshack was look for a wide patch of earth tones in the cold-colored array of patrons. I trusted that he would be looking out for me through a travel-edition heat-signature monitor that he could have placed near the front entrance, by the double doors that resembled the Ishtar Gate. Since I was logged off, there was no way he could track me otherwise.

I grew exhausted in asking random employees for a dusty Uzbek. There was a kiosk selling B12 shots and questionable cures for satyriasis. I could use an energy boost. I had no hard currency, alas, and couldn't access my bank account. This freedom business was growing more inconvenient by the minute. A big cloud of hasheesh parted at the back of my head and billowed back at my face. Annoyance gave way to elation.

"Dog, I just got done tying up and gagging an Afghani family of six. I was about to ravish the mother and eldest daughter, but went after the father instead, just because. Just. Because. I set the mud-brick house on fire. I regretted gagging them, because there was no screaming. What a chicken-shit murderer. Rip-off." I craned my neck over my left shoulder. The Inner Asian Oscar Wilde.

Standing next to him was a beautiful woman in a black bob haircut. This was Dune Buggy, the most important woman off-roader to ever exist, having single-handedly ushered in the sport to the Middle East twenty years ago. She had just transitioned back to a she; her short stint as a man comprised a less-than-stellar career as co-pilot. Not content to sit in the passenger seat and navigate, she re-unequipped and went back to tearing up the desert circuit. She wore a magenta sports bra that showed a scalding-hot midriff and wide, athletic shoulders. An onyx stone was set between her eyebrows.

Sawdust introduced us. She acknowledged me with a blink. Their newest hobby was that of vintage networking. She therefore found my case interesting once Sawdust explained it. They touted a curious mixture of hi-tech and lo-tech. Hence Sawdust's state-of-the-art jetpack, yet his preference for old-school hasheesh instead of the de rigueur serotonin booster kit.

"Who has been spying upon me?" I asked him.

A volcanic eruption of smoke, blacker than usual, headed toward me. I heard his voice from behind it. "Everyone is spying on everyone, dog."

"Why the cause for alarm, then?"

"Someone found a way to overwrite your autorama's source code. And not even really overwrite it. More like gobble it up. They may as well have chewed into your brain, dog."

"Am I in bad shape, then?"

"Virtually, yes. You couldn't, for instance, have had an effective proxy apostasy as I just had, because the necessary drivers for the surrogate endorphin rush was missing . You would only have the visual and audio recordings. I've been preaching to you about the q-cloud, dog."

The main drawback of having everything in the q-cloud was the time it took to stream down whatever you needed. Sure, IT specialists swore by it, citing not only its security but its ability to boost processing power due to less clutter. It became a problem if you found yourself in a bandwidth dead zone that even a digitized metropolis like Aswadibad was not immune to. It had been nearly fifteen years since the dream of infinite storage and bandwidth had come to a screeching halt by the sliding-scale technology of quantum computing.

I looked over at Dune Buggy. She nodded assent.

More words came from the smoke. "I grew alarmed when I found that I couldn't message you. See, I'm running a different OS. Black Tar. Whoever hacked you had taken out the protocol needed for you to handshake with a Black Tar user. So they must have been using Core-Corps OS, and had figured that closing all communicative escape shafts, as it were, would keep you hemmed in. Or they may have scanned your handshake history and seen that someone running Black Tar had been present when we left that plot-jockey unconscious back at the palace."

"She is off-grid," I asserted, defensively.

"But is the palace?" continued the smoke. "She may be an analog, but whoever's keeping an eye on her surely isn't. You'd be crazy to think so. The Ulema, the GnosisNet admins, Al-Raschid's clan. Who knows?"

"How about the anarchists?"

"No, dog."

"No? Why not?"

The smoke had dissipated, and I could finally see Sawdust. "Not only do they lack the capacity, but they're too idealistic. The liberty of the brain is sacred to them. They wouldn't violate that high-mindedness in order to, no disrespect, inconvenience a small-time shaman like you."

"So what do you suggest?" I was at one of those points in my life where you couldn't foresee what the next earth-shattering five minutes entailed, let alone the long vapor trail that is the rest of your life.

"We'll format the fuck out of you, dog," Sawdust said, and tugged off his hookah pipe. Dune Buggy nodded assent. "But first we have more fun."

Within Aswadistan's new system, it would not be incarceration that served as punishment for unlawful transgressions; it would be inconvenience . Nothing of the jail cell's coziness would be found among a tireless barrage of character assassination, slander, mudslinging, and instantaneous litigation with ad hoc *qadis*, or judges. You could deny all charges with long-winded rebuttals in the comment sections of news posts or profile pokes, but good luck with that. Plus, since there were no victimless crimes, you may have very well done something wrong to someone in order to elicit an identity attack from the offended party or parties. It was public shaming by everyone upon everyone—a back-and-forth barrage of red-hot accusations and instant depositions . The public gobbled it up more out of voyeurism than civic duty. Case closed. I had to log on to have fun of Sawdust proportions. I immediately became the focus of a two-pronged attack by an ad hoc court system. Two *qadis*—contrasting with each other in character but not in severity—got to legally rummage through my head, leaving out and arbitrarily inserting various details of the two indictments as if by roulette. The case presented by the identity-swap-party organizer was pending, and a backlog of addenda choked up my autorama once Sawdust and Dune Buggy rebooted it to prepare for formatting.

Too—and it hurts my solar plexus to say it—Esmeralda was suing me for "romantic distress." I recalled almost nothing of our contretemps, save for the darkness-enshrouded salvia trip that made me both oblivious and unresponsive to my erstwhile perfect match. I couldn't blame Eros's handling of the Ad Lib(ido), much as I wished to. The fault was mine, and I could have attributed it as much to my off-grid existence as to an amateurish, unshamanic jaunt through the Salviasphere. The ensuing porn-laced litigation became a Kama Sutra-esque cavalcade of disputed sexual positions and contested pet names. Various promises that I had made were played back from Esmeralda's POV in typed out transcripts. Humiliating for me. Perhaps I should have countersued. The two *qadis* may as well have reached down under their judiciary caftans to quickly uncork themselves in order to achieve the necessary impartiality . I wasn't entirely familiar with Aswadistan's penal practices , so I wasn't sure if I would be monetarily responsible , or if the stigma was a blackened reputation as a lover and a lifetime ban from Eros.

Aswadistanis hardly settled on au naturel. Though my hair is naturally black, I wore it a Cisalpine platinum blond; but I found the multi-limbed jungle of purple, orange, and blue skin within the Oasis of Kisses almost too hot.

I tempered my libido with a single drop of salvia tincture, lest I fly apart at the most inopportune of times. I crawled through the carnal cave unscathed. I didn't possess the necessary neurons, cerebral or otherwise, to make any of the acts of libertinage worthwhile. Some of it was upbringing, some of it was from missing the necessary drivers for the transgressions to register. My autorama was too busy rebooting its compromised version of itself to make use of so much bootleg nectar. Some cloud storage facility may be harboring those missing files. I was too incomplete in the head to even have fun.

Dune Buggy suggested setting up a honey pot. This was a properly placed decoy to lure potential cyber-intruders into a trap, both in order to decipher their identities, and to keep them off my real digital trail while I underwent the modem removal. My total disloyalty to anyone or any cause made it simple to set up this honey pot. We threw out clues alluding to the unwholesome proclivities of GnosisNet ITs or the possible alliance between the anarchist Bedouin and the Ulema. And just to mix in a bit of Najwa, we linked her name up with the miscreant son of Tru-Tech's CEO, who had been fighting pedophilia charges for the last ten minutes.

They had me under ether, so I didn't see the executive decision get made. While Sawdust fine-tooth-combed through my directory files, Dune Buggy tried to write in the missing source code. But to no avail.

The Tru-Tech cortical modem fought its extraction like an octopus being pulled from a face. I woke up with not only no autorama, but no software. It was beyond disorienting. My head ached and I struggled to remember the details of my current predicament. Analog sight was blurry, and when I went to enhance my hearing ability, there was no graphic at the top left allowing me to choose between directional and omni-directional. I grew morose.

Sawdust printed out a still shot of Esmeralda in her morpho-chrome bikini. He flipped it over to show me it. I shuttered. The most impressive part was the bikini. Instead of the wasp-wasted, athletic señorita I had hung all my ideals on, standing in a desperate seduction pose was a somewhat pear-shaped girl of smallish stature. She still had that golden hue I marveled at during love, and her face was pleasant; but she was not the God-chiseled volleyball-player Valkyrie I had fallen for. Sawdust whispered into Dune Buggy's ear. My heart sank. I felt miserable not for the daunting disparity between what I had perceived through my autorama and what reality was, but because I felt sorry for Esmeralda. I wanted her to look magnificent more for her own sake, more for her own self-worth, then for mine. There was a tragic sadness to an unattractive woman. This girl was not ugly, but she still possessed some of that sadness. Then I remembered that she was in the process of suing me for romantic distress. I gazed into the eyes in the photo: maybe not the nervous eyes of a sociopath, but surely the dead black eyes of a litigious shark willing to devour me entrails first.

While Dune Buggy disappeared to go about the dual task of setting up a heat signature descrambler and a blackout box to wipe out the local bandwidth for one minute, I said my gratitude and goodbye to Sawdust.

"Meet me here in eight days' time, dog. And I will have for you a whole new identity. Look for purple hair. See this as a spiritual sabbatical, and go find you peace."

There were two flashes. The first was a quick blink of the lights within the Oasis of Kisses. The second was a darkening of everything that sent a wave of concern throughout the establishment. As always with these blackout boxes, the initial apocalyptic worry gave way to the recognition of some nearby deadbeat needing to get off-grid like a miscreant kid needed to leave the sandbox because the other children had forced him out.

OUT AT THE ILLUMINATION FARM

i took a long magic carpet ride out to the desert. The wind howled delightfully across my skin. There was too much drama in procuring a tickling of the erogenous zones when the largest organ of your body was waiting there to be blasted into bliss.

Towering wind turbines spun in mindless unison—white sentinels milking the sky for man's increasing energy demands. Wind became a recurring theme out in the desert: the wind from the magic carpet ride in, the turbines, and that which I was in search of—the red wind that Hamid the young storyteller spoke of. There was a cleansing property to wind: as the pilot expertly dodged the roaring turbine blades, I felt their push atomize the patina of smut that had accumulated on me from the Oasis of Kisses.

By undergoing the modemectomy, I didn't so much as have a veil torn away from my eyes as have a filter of conformity plucked from my skull. My sight had gone from an initial blurry to quite acute.

I watched the pilot neural-network his aircraft with the calm expertise the gondolieri used to navigate the canals back home, insulting each other's football teams upon passing. I could assemble a portrait by various physical clues. Whereas before there was just an orgy of neon, I saw now before me a warm-colored avatar of health. His turban and scarf matched his carpet in its brown-auburn arabesque pattern. The wind-carved crow's feet at the corners of his eyes denoted a wisdom attainable only through the sky, from which everything down below appeared as insignificant as a colony of scurrying red ants.

More and more wind turbines. And then more. And then, among a cluster of date-palmed oases set at safe distances from the turbines and from monster sand dunes capable of engulfing entire villages, were the anarchists. Finally seeing their base of operations was not due to the clarity of being modem-less, but to the effort of having a modicum of guts to leave the metropolis.

"Can they see us?" I asked the magic carpet pilot.

He slowly craned his head up at me, eyes searing all doubt. He focused on the trip. We still weren't halfway there.

Ten years back, Tru-Tech launched three models of self-propelled magic carpets. The small- and medium-sized models were protested against and boycotted by the pilots' union, which won a class-action lawsuit—the only explanation for the surprising decision being that there must have been *qadis* who had relatives or friends who were pilots, because the overpaid thread jockeys weren't exactly known for tact, and didn't exactly tug on citizens' heartstrings.

It was a black eye for the engineering conglomerate, which pooled its efforts into the third model. Where the first catered to the individual who could convert his prayer rug into a mode of transport, and the second suited a maximum of five people, the third and largest caught on as the nation's new mode of mass transit. A person embarking upon the outsized magic carpet, big enough to double as a centerpiece to a Saudi prince's foyer, docked his autorama into a hub located at the center of the weave. He could thereby signal his debarkation point. I had never ridden those community carpets before.

They had more detractors than proponents. Most people cited that they always ran late, and that no one was present to monitor efficient debarkations or rein in contentious or indecisive passengers. Others said the carpets trapped in the odors of all the city's demographics and reeked in a stew of socialist funk. Yet others cited the lack of safety from a mechanical standpoint: tragic crashes happened often, resulting in further carnage down on the ground. And from a criminal standpoint: black-clad brigands known as the Trapeze Mafia swung in on nifty rappelling cables and shook down passengers for dirhams or harassed them with a serotonin-sabotage known as "mind jacking." A more daring fellow of the bunch might harness himself and crawl under the carpet to scrawl obscenities and gang tags in Kufic script for the terrestrial folk below. Therefore, the small- and medium-sized magic carpets were brought back. The pilots didn't lose their jobs as a consequence; there simply became less of them. There were always people who couldn't afford or chose not to fly themselves.

Halfway through the trip, my brain had begun to twitch on its own accord with no outside influences—much like a bodybuilder's pectoral muscle that has been exercised to the point of maneuverability. I could bat around an idea, have it ricochet like a pinball, and not worry about a retort from the rest of the world. There were no more pop-ups from the failed guardian angel installation, no more brain-app drivers or even cookies, not even an operating system with a crude shell of an autorama known as a desktop to navigate whatever else might have still been there. I was literally off-grid. The informational biofeedback loop had been sealed off.

According to Aswadistan's tech-sponsored demagoguery,

choosing to not have your ideas vetted to ensure they weren't moronic before acting upon them was tantamount to intellectual sedition. I grew jittery from peering over the precipice down into the yawning abyss of free thought. I may as well have crawled over the edge of the magic carpet and plummeted headfirst into the desert sands. Yet my newfound cerebral sovereignty did not guarantee full invisibility.

For insidious elements insinuated easily enough. In that dead zone of bandwidth, that dearth of information exchange—where memes and engrams were swapped back and forth in an archaic semaphore of grunts and crude gestures—there was still a tiny presence of the panopticon. Something stirred on my left shoulder. My chin swatted it off as I turned to look, and I found darting about in the air a cherry-red butterfly. Rose fluttered away into the vast sky.

The pilot held out a parachute. He pointed down and shook his head. He refused to land. I took it and worked my arms through the shoulder straps. Before jumping, I would swig some salvia tincture.

Seconds later, the mullah wraiths appeared. They zoomed in and out, unleashing silent, snaggle-toothed screams as they drew near. They didn't travel through the GnosisNet bandwidth. They had dug trenches in the Salviasphere and could roam free with impunity. They didn't seem fully capable of attacking, however. I looked over to the pilot, who did not see them.

I jumped. I tunneled through the air, whipping the whole ensemble of atoms into superposition. The salvia kicked in, and now donning the bridal dress of singularity, I struggled to find the ripcord. My molecules slithered beyond the barrier, my entire body passing through a sieve. The illumination farm itself was in the real world, a hundred miles east of where the Bedouin had their outposts. The student Ishraqiyun maneuvered, though, in and out of the imaginal realm, not to be confused with imaginary. Sympathetic to the Salviasphere, the imaginal realm was a real physical locale, tucked in a dimensional valley accessible only from the seismic result of believing and knowing where to look for its coordinates. Though not contiguous with the terrain that I had been surveying for four years, it shared its ontological frequency. It was hard to imagine the state apparatus tapping into the dimension without some kind of trans-dimensional telemetry, which wouldn't materialize until quantum computing was in full swing. I was blinded by my billowing parachute upon landing. Once I swatted it down into submission, the world before my eyes was knocked up to a vibration as brilliant as a pastel landscape painting. It was at an oasis, no less. I lay there not ten seconds before a wave of heat engulfed me, knocking me out.

The plaster of time flaked away from infinity in sheaths large and small.

I awoke with my head in a lap, which hummed whenever he spoke. He was Murad, the illumination farm's star Ishraqi. "It took me years to learn the language with which to chastise the wind," he said. "To begin, I had to unlearn the hatefulness inherent to my native tongue. I had to learn oneness with redness. I can't recall how many years that took. Sixteen? Forget the obvious pigmentation of blood, for I have become proficient at bleeding into the sky, and now have blueness in my veins."

All the community blood particles hung in the air, too small to be visible, but numbering in the trillions. I could feel their presence, a colony of rejected offspring ready to turn on their parents. They were sustained by the humming of the servers, which were everywhere. Murad had his back against the galvanized casing of an end unit to a row that shot back across the entire oasis, ending half-buried in a sand dune. A strap from my buried parachute poked out from the sand.

He held out a date to my mouth with a warmness I found discomforting. His batting eyelashes hurled vexation at my refusal. Somewhere, I know not where, a woman's sleek thighs moved beneath a bed sheet. All at once, his effeminacy unfurled like a rose that had been granted permission to bloom. He smelled of frankincense. His baggy white pantaloons were low-slung at his hips like a concubine was wont to wear them. His painted toenails matched his pantaloons. And he swayed his arms with a courtesan's grace.

Everything was saturated with estrogen. Maybe that was evolution, the blunting of man's serrated edge. There was a feminine aspect even to the servers. Aside from their collective hum, they gave off a maternal warmth, like that of a womb. I knew not what purpose they served here, other than as mechanical furniture or as facilitators to deep meditation. For sure they didn't power GnosisNet back in Aswadibad, as that system had its own legions of servers choking up city blocks and clogging up the former sultan's palace.

The oversexed atmosphere was disorienting. I expected white-robed acolytes who scoffed at music and spat at calligraphy. Every sexually charged impulse was acted upon, only to be stifled at the threshold. There was plenty of groping and frottage. There was never any kissing, though many a set of plump lips parted in anticipation, in full engagement mode, only to clam up at the proximity to flesh. Everything was powered by this ability to pull back from the very precipice of consummation. Maybe an innocent soul from the future would recognize it as an advanced form of communal affection. All counterparts of that most luscious of acts were there, but never to be paired up: a thin layer of a yellow muslin veil stretching across a girl's voluptuous mons veneris was as diaphanous as the material extending across the throbbing member of a suffering initiate a few feet away.

It was as if every object at the illumination farm was gearing up to harness the intrinsic erotic energy of the world and amass it for some unknown offensive. The salvia was stirring up a hurricane of paradigm-shifting consciousness by rendering everything a joke. Just imagine: materialistic earnestness being overrun by earth-shattering frivolousness. The jester was about to kick the blowhard monarch off his throne and, what the hell, pop a seat.

Murad had a bad left eye. It must have been due to a childhood accident. He was above average in height, with a slender build that gave his profile a wraith-like allure that a woman might take to. He had fine bone structure and, despite the wispy onset of a beard, a favorable jaw line that, matched with his one good hazel eye, gave him a leading man's air. He wore his hair quite long, tying it up in a knot. His voice betrayed an alarming femininity—a bane most easily dispensed with through the muttering of decidedly masculine tropes and Ishraqi aphorisms no worldly woman would be caught dead dealing in. His slender hands were calloused from climbing rugged Mount Qaf and steering his motorcycle.

It was fascinating to watch the women tempt him—rubbing exposed patches of flesh up against him in dud attempts at seduction. He had probably grown weary of the fairer sex's attentions and had found it a tedious charade, especially when compared to more invigorating activities, like the contemplation of light.

I have never considered myself malicious. But to see someone like Murad traverse back and forth between the worldliness of possessing good genetics and being a darling ascetic (at which he certainly excelled) irked me to no end. It bothered me that Najwa at one point pined for him enough to have his child. It bothered me even more that he shrugged the responsibility off and donned white to spout forth about *nur al-anwar*. I wished to sully his reputation every chance I got.

I wished to drown him to death—to dowse his Illuminationist ambition into nonexistence, to extinguish the fires that composed his hierarchy of light. I wished to besot the gorgeous, flowing chestnut locks on his head when he loosened his hair. My hostility toward him alarmed me.

It was not all just sensual deprogramming that went on at the illumination farm. There was a rigorous curriculum comprising Ishraqi life: whirling like dervishes without music, following the five pillars, engaging in grueling physical exercise and meditation, and unlearning Aristotelian ethics. Curious were the art detestation courses. More curious were the epithets hurled at Abd' al-Malik, Islam's Paul. They felt that this caliph strayed too far from the Prophet's original teachings.

The greatest object of their derision was the rainbow. This hatred of the light spectrum stemmed from the Ishraqi principle of light. Though there was a hierarchy of lights—the pinnacle being *nur al-anwar* (light of lights)—there was no place in Illuminationist theology for diffuse light, or color. Pigments and all objects of beauty were the djinn of distraction. The lone exception to this was the revered Al-Khidr, the Green One, an Arthurian-legend-type figure who popped up throughout history, even going as far back as having befriended and abetted Alexander the Great. Al-Khidr was the exemplar of virtue, both spiritual and political (some Ishraqiyun scoffed at my distinction of the two).

It was the woman named Tamra who told me of Murad's relationship with Najwa. "There should be no secrets, Eetahlee," she said, christening me with my nationality. "Information is key to assessing the world. Nothing shall be withheld." I needn't stroke her ego or hit on her to open the floodgates of gossip, for she divulged it all on her own. I found it hard to focus, since she was stunning, and certainly no prude. Tamra used to be a palace courtesan back in Aswadibad. She had been banished from the city for some harem transgression whose intricacy I could not grasp as she told it to me. It was like she had tossed me a set of fiddlesticks and all I had left in my hands were two, the rest strewn about on the floor. Out in the desert, she used to comfort weary, woman-starved travelers. She came to Illuminationism on accident. She moved with a slow, opium-charged rhythm, with the somnolent efficiency of one whose body held the imprints of a thousand-and-one men, a lover's palimpsest. Across her skin crawled terabytes of information awaiting decompression—most of it invaluable, all of it lurid.

"I have no dog in this fight, Eetahlee. They both betrayed each other. He and she. They are both strong-willed, so no one was really hurt. The child, I'm afraid, may be a different story."

Najwa never alluded to her son. In Aswadistani culture it was extremely remiss for a mother not to be there while her child grew up. Her decision to live off-grid was likely a way of disposing of a past fraught with mistakes and irresponsibility.

Murad rarely visited this son, who supposedly lived in the pearl city of Jabarsa, in the care of three sisters who had illicit affairs with thunder. The boy's name was Jameel, Arabic for 'beautiful.' "Perhaps, in another time, in another place, in another dimension ," Tamra said, shifting gears, "I would send you to paradise with my thighs."

She then screamed. A handful of Ishraqiyun were given to screaming. It was the only way they could hear themselves over the omnipresent hum of the servers, and to reassure themselves of being alive. Life did feel tenuous at the illumination farm. The scenery never changed. What changed was how you interacted with that scenery. This was rudimentary Salviasphere navigating.

That an army of spiritual soldiers trained to contemplate the otherworldly should be the stewards of a program to perfectly govern the citizens of a worldly nation was beyond contemptible. These lotus eaters didn't even know how to do their own laundry. Some would say that their lack of experience in mundane matters was exactly what made them qualified, like a civilian prime minister—or doge—in charge of the military. Checks and balances, and all that shit. Fair enough. But I couldn't imagine the implications of one of those empty shells becoming a politician. The only thing worse than a politician with no scruples would be one with no soul.

But why would they care about the real world when they could remain blissed out at the farm?

Tamra told me how to arrive at the amethyst city of Jabalqa. "I would tell you everything if I knew more than anything," she said. "But I know one thing only, and this one thing I have already told you. Go to Jabalqa and listen carefully, for nothing is ever repeated in Jabalqa."

This place was fully situated in the imaginal realm. I would attest to its verity a thousand times over. I got there by riding a vibrational wave that shot off from the Salviasphere, veering east. The streets were carved of amethyst. All structures, residences and places of gathering, were made too of amethyst. The citizens conducted their affairs in whispers, as if not to divulge the location of their beautiful city to extra-dimensional rabble like myself. There was a complicity, too, to their whispering, as if they knew they were being ontologically sneaky.

I approached a short, stocky figure in a blue burnoose and asked what he knew of Najwa. I realized then that I never knew her surname. "I know what everyone else here knows, which is everything," he whispered. "I know neither more nor less, but the exact same thing, which is, as I said, everything."

"Everything pertaining to Najwa?"

"No," whispered the man with his dark, pudgy face. "Everything of everything. Though you must listen carefully, for I will not repeat it. One, because I haven't the time. And two, because it will have changed completely, at which point it will be something else entirely different, which I will know in its entirety, but which will very well overwrite that which I had meant to tell you at the beginning."

"So tell me," I began, voice low. "Do you not fear to be accused of gossip-mongering?"

"It is not gossip if it is true, and I swear everything I know is not untrue. And as for truth-mongering, I am afraid I am guilty."

"What is Najwa's relationship to the former sultan of Aswadistan, Mehmet Al-Raschid?"

"She is nothing to him now but a political supporter."

How a citizen of Jabalqa could stay abreast of the real world's current events would be anyone's guess. I didn't see any signal towers among the amethyst structures. "What did she used to be unto him?"

"She used to be his chief storyteller, for the sultan enjoyed stories. She then became his lover. That is not surprising, since she was already a concubine within his harem. She also bore him a child."

I rattled my head back and forth. "Did she not bear Murad a child?"

"She did not. She bore the sultan a child, though Murad took custody of the boy."

"What is the boy's name?" I asked, to see whether or not he was full of shit.

"I can't tell you now," he whispered.

"I thought you knew everything?" I asked contemptuously.

"I know all things, yet not at all times."

I was about to fish for a known fact to test him when a tall woman in a pink burnoose approached him as if I weren't even there. She bent down to feed him a wafer, which he greedily ate. She then departed.

"The boy's name is Jameel. You found that out earlier from Tamra back at the farm. He lives in Jabarsa with three women who are sisters of each other, were sired by a human man and a virtual woman, and are currently vying for the affections of a bolt of lightning that has ionized into nothingness but will reform soon and crack against the Jabarsa sky in a few days' time. They become neglectful of the boy whenever this happens. I know not your intentions, for that is not a thing. But if you are looking to abduct him, that would be your opportunity."

"Where are your scruples, man?" I asked.

"Knowledge makes no room for any. Plus, you will do what you will do. Everything that I know is nothing that will dissuade you."

"Thank you," I whispered.

"That is not necessary," he said, "since I would have told anyone anything, since there shall be no secrets, and you are no one special."

"Now that I know," I shouted, and went on my way. The entire amethyst city of Jabalqa shushed me.

The illumination farm was not the hub of the imaginal realm; it was, like countless other centers of spiritual earnestness, a tributary that fed into the consensual reality of Jabarsa, Jabalqa, and Hurqalya. Only Mountain Qaf could be said to be at the center.

The way up to its summit was treacherously steep, serrated, and fraught with nightmarish happenings, such as having to traverse paths of chopped-up mirrors that not only snagged away deeply at the traveler's flesh but threw back reflections of his inner ugliness. There were also the legendary red winds, those that Hamid said had stopped. They whipped the flesh of those going up. Most of the rare souls who made it to the top were skeletonized versions of themselves. There was peril even to turn away, since the sheer face would not guarantee safe descent. A fabled monk who inhabited a cave only feet away from the summit was said to possess a patina of skin clinging to a rickety frame, having been seared by the red winds . They said his reason for stopping just short of the summit was to keep the mystery of his quest alive. He feared that reaching his goal would kill off the impetus to live.

Aiding those in the ascent of Mountain Qaf was the practiced loathing of all arts. All works of art were to be derided not only for their distracting nature, but for their inability to encompass all things, which can only be the province of Allah. Works of art told lies of omission by not including all things, by carving away everything deemed extraneous. But how much beauty and truth does a bas-relief discard? Why toss so much of Allah's creation? Works of art peddled in shade, in exclusivity, in gradation, in the chiaroscuro of maybe and maybe not; whereas *nur al-anwar* shone light upon all things.

But after a few years, after reaching the summit of Mountain Qaf, musical pieces, Sufi poems, and sculptures were introduced back into a monk's life. They were to be appreciated not exactly for what they were, but for what they were not—meaning, that which was not the objet d'art was to be meditated upon. For example, a story was nothing but what it purported to tell. It left out so much of the world and called itself the truth. An Ishraqi learned to listen around a musical piece, look around a sculpture, and hear around a story. Similarly, Najwa had conditioned me to where she used anti-stories to drive me mad.

Underneath Murad's diaphanous white muslin lurked a layer of black attire that creaked every time he moved. It may as well have been an exoskeleton. He traveled between the three cities of Jabalqa, Jabarsa, and Hurqalya on an old Harley Davidson motorcycle, and the apparel was black leather meant to protect him from the ferocious wind. It was especially useful for going to Hurqalya, that high-elevation city literally constructed by wind, which its outskirts emitted in hurricane proportions as a deterrent to the unwelcome.

I didn't know what Murad did on his tours of the cities. Perhaps he liquidated demons of unreason, or gave press junkets on how to be magnificent. Whatever it was, it seemed of paramount importance.

As much as I initially detested him, he showed me much consideration. I wasn't sure if he divined the purpose for my visit, but he supported what he mistook to be my esoteric efforts. His tips and advice went in one ear and came out the other, but I did take one thing he proposed to heart: there would be a moment, perhaps not far off, perhaps still years in the future, when everything would . . . f l i p. Otherness, so long associated with the esoteric state sought after, would become the norm, and the real world, at least the one lived in by the majority, became anomalous, and in effect newly wondrous. Perpetual astonishment became the order of the day, and the minutiae of mortality became a non-factor. This was the Great Work that the students at the illumination farm had sworn to take up, for the benefit of the citizens of Aswadistan.

I asked him about Najwah. "I couldn't help but notice her

thoroughgoing abstinence from all psychedelics, even from neu-rotransmitter aids. Was she ever a prospect for the Ishraqiyun?"

Murad unleashed a worldly cackle, wherein lay derision that a thousand years of asceticism would not vanquish. "Like all hat-ers of technology, she is a hypocrite, and retains a sanctimonious stance on technology by being years behind the curve. Though not a single backwards society in the history of the world would shun a hammer."

"Which is technology," I said.

"Which is technology," he agreed. "The detractors of technol-ogy may hate that gadgets, programmable blood, and self-repli-cating nanobots will threaten their way of life, but they hate their own ignorance of how to use these things even more. They use technology to lash out against it, for instance. Communication is technology."

"Information is technology," I offered.

"A rhyming stanza is technology," he said.

"Drugs are technology." I loved to say that.

"Yes," he said, "they are." And I heard a metallic click, where-upon he withdrew from under his diaphanous white muslin, from one of the countless pockets on his black leathered person, a switchblade with a gold-inlaid handle. He stabbed at the air, and caught right in the thorax a cherry-red butterfly that had been snooping about. The thing fluttered twice and went limp. "Most hypocrisy," he said, introducing the kill to his lips, "is borne of frustration." He began munching. "Rather than from a dissonance between belief and action. There are certain paradigms of technol-ogy that a troglodyte would find just suitable."

It got chilly at night. Off in the distance, beyond a chain of sand dunes, a group of jackals howled. "Where do they come from?" I asked. "Who brought them here?"

"No one brought them here," he said, wiping his mouth on his sleeve. "They belong here."

"Is this just another cross-section of the multiverse?"

"Yes," he replied. Maybe I detested him because he knew so much. It was not out of envy of his abilities, but out of a fear of what a better version of me would be faced with should I emulate him in the least by seeking self-improvement.

The servers continued to hum, and in vain I fought off sleepiness. I let my head fall in his lap. I let him pet my head.

"Tell me about the boy," I asked upon waking. It was early morning. I had been lying on my side. He had wrapped me in sheep's wool and placed a pillow beneath my head. There was no sign he had slept. He straddled his motorcycle, splendid and skinny in his black leather gear. He wrapped a black turban around his head and stretched and tied a black veil over his mouth. "There are winds I must beat back. I am sorry there is no breakfast. We have grown unaccustomed to eating around here. There are sweetmeats and yoghurt in Hurqalya, should you become desperate. Just pay a visit to any of the travelers stopped in their tents." He kick-started the motorcycle. "Jameel was sired by the sultan. I took the boy into my care because someone had to. He will become a monster, I am afraid."

"I don't think I have what it takes to journey to Hurqalya," I said. I was officially starving.

"You have no choice," he said. "It is the only way out. Traveling west across the desert will only bring you back here if the sandstorms and jackals don't get you first. So will traveling east, for that matter. I apologize for leaving you so abruptly. After fighting the winds back, I will be called on to give a seminar on scoffing at French Deconstructionism and the potential hermeneutics of sushi arrangements. Ma' as-salaamah."

Ever since having my cortical modem extracted, I thought that my return to Aswadibad would be to undergo an assault of the senses. It was a veritable lull compared to the neural torture I endured on my way to Hurqalya. That city, which was made up of wind, was a citizenless city. That was a contradiction in terms, until you figured in the nomadic presence of ifrits and djinn—the malevolent spirits who used Hurqalya as a stopover point for long journeys between realms and as a hub wherein to get in extracurricular harassment time on journeying souls like my own.

Hamid, like all storytellers, proved to be a liar. The howling red winds were very much present. They ripped at my flesh. They tasted of copper. It meant people on the same path in front of me were being bled as they proceeded. But there was no way but forward.

I had asked Murad how to get there the night before, and how to reach the desert which led back to Aswadibad.

"Simply follow the path of most resistance. Don't worry about the rest. Do that which you most wish not to."

I only briefly considered his motorcycle to be a cheating maneuver to navigate the winds; it likely made their bite worse.

I didn't know how many days it took to arrive at and pass through Hurqalya. I recalled abatements of the wind where I would search for my salvia tincture in vain. At some point, it had been blown out of my inside vest pocket. Dotting the terrain were threadbare tents, from which issued groans. I took naps during these soft zones, and would be blasted awake by the winds, which forced me to my feet. Onward. I had not eaten my whole time in the imaginal realm. I seemed to have lost the ability to clot, as my countless wounds issued forth rivulets of blood that would be whipped into a red haze whenever the winds kicked up.

I lost track of the sun's course through the sky, and also that of the moon, by whose generous light I traveled at night. The loss of blood, lack of sleep, and absence of food converged upon me in a rush of numbness. I no longer hurt. I was sliding toward death, calmly. I grew emotionally desperate, wanting to see my foster mamma back in Venice, and wanting to confront Najwa with my own incriminating narrative. I didn't know if it was a mirage, but I thought I saw the imposing, white base of a wind turbine not far off. My eyes were too dry to cry tears of joy.

What was it about my head that made people want to put it in their laps? I awoke to look up at a pretty face smiling down at me. "Jafar," said Maryam, "ready your carpet. He is alive."

The imaginal realm had expulsed me like a deadbeat kangaroo parent evicts a babe from its pouch. It zipped shut and kicked waves of sand into my face for good measure. A trans-dimensional hangover set to work on my body. They hauled me onto the magic carpet.

Jafar's hi-tech craft was a refreshing fuck-you to the rustic, heat-choked desert. I wanted my autorama back like never before. I wanted a guardian angel too, asinine pop-ups and all. I wanted cables to bind me to the interfaces of the world. I wanted my genitalia docked into the orgasmatronic hive. A curse on silence and contemplation. I preferred the transparency of the panopticon to that of the insipid vellum of Illuminationism. I preferred the variegated lights of LED, neon, and glitter—and the whores who came with those—to the bleakness of the light of lights that shone upon everything and bathed it in its boredom.

"Sir," said Jafar, facing forward, minding potential air traffic, "this reconnaissance of ours would have been easier if you had been on-grid." Maryam felt above my right ear for the cortical modem plug, grossly fingering the empty socket.

Jafar took us well above the turbines. I rested in my reporter friend's lap, my body sucking through bag after bag of portable IV drips she had plugged into the crook of my arm.

We flew over the anarchist oases unmolested. This was due more to their eschewing of honing tech than to Jafar's high-altitude path. Maryam yanked out the IV needle from my arm and flattened the empty bag out on top of the others, on the carpet. They resembled juice packs given to sugar junkie kids on a hot day. Jafar cast a disapproving glance at Maryam, who snagged the stack of empty IV bags up from his exquisite weave and crammed them into her purse. We made it to Aswadibad.

The vertical hulks of office buildings and apartments, along with the preachy digital billboards, set in motion a sensory car -nival that my time in the imaginal realm had made all the more gratuitous.

"Dear," I said to Maryam, "I am so hungry."

"Very well," she said, and adopted the blank stare of one engrossed in her autorama. A minute later, a shawarma copter sidled up to her. Jafar, initially startled by the visit, shook his head to turn down the snack and as a sign of disapproval.

I devoured two shawarmas. Maryam's chewing face looked down at me and smiled. We shared a joy not brought on by financial success, or religious ecstasy, or even by fame, but by that most communal of things: delicious food.

Sawdust and Dune Buggy had formatted my head and removed my cortical modem , yet there were unaccounted -for neural pathways that made up a meta-network. I was more than ever that archetype of non-belonging: the Outernationalist . A left-over truth prompt kicked around in my thoughts , whose designs were never meant to be my own, but were now just parts of the package set up by my employers via the guardian angel installation. *Najwa was a virus that needed to be extracted.* She was jeopardizing the entire Great Launch. Her spinning radar kept the GnosisNet programmers from beta-testing their brainchild with the needed fidelity, since peoples' deepest desires and imprecations gathered up by that device would often override their docility for neurotransmitter regulation. I didn't understand how this could be the case. It seemed like so much bro-science. Salvia was not meant to be the drug administered to the populace. Not even close. It was all a ruse. Maybe I was, after all, the Plaid Assassin. Every move I made could very well have been a line in a calculated stream of code written in order for me to ingratiate myself with her, and ultimately take her out. I had a paranoia attack. All of a sudden, I felt knotted up in a tangle of ulterior motives. If, as Sawdust had alluded to, I had been head-hacked by the Mafia or by the Ulema —assuming they weren't in cahoots, if not one and the same —I couldn't even trust my own judgment. I hoped the truth prompt was just a remnant left over from the modemectomy and formatting, and not a Trojan Horse ready to blossom me into a government-run goon.

Suddenly there appeared in midair a wildly gesticulating Mehmet Al-Raschid. Like all charlatans who couldn't convince people by the merit of reason, he used his trademark rollercoaster voice and overactive hands to drive home his point. At first, I thought Jafar had turned on a news hologram, but the high-rises kept cutting off the image as we drew closer. Other billboards lit up. Most were various ads of the former sultan, the rest of his chief rival, the reactionary throwback Yusuf Ar-Rahman, who some people thought was in Al-Raschid's employ, and was running as an arch-conservative in order to credit Al-Raschid as a progressive and no-brainer alternative to GnosisNet. Ar-Rahman's ads consisted of string music-drenched montages of minarets against sunsets, legions of devout Muslims circumambulating the Ka'aba, golden-age enactments of the Ummayids laying down the law—then a professorial Ar-Rahman (cardiologist by trade) in glasses, a stethoscope draped around his neck, a sphygmomanometer in his left hand, and the Holy Qur'an is his right. The guy didn't stand a chance. Any political dummy knew that Al-Raschid had invented a special brand of technophilia, just the right amount of progressivism to capture the young vote, and an edition of Sharia law that, while lax when it came to the more severe cultural mores, was staunchly conservative in matters like marriage, finance, and halal.

Both of the opponents' ads ended with testimonials from once-disenfranchised citizens with trumped-up sob stories, then by endorsements either from Tru-Tech or Core-Corps. The latter company's stake in the voting software raised questions of possible fraud. "You will be our string-theory jihadi," Jafar said. "If Spain had its fifth column, we will have our eleventh. Who knows? Aside from the pecuniary compensation owed you, you may glean some bonus activities. You are now, after all, an analog just like her." For someone who claimed the upper hand in the scruples department, he sure could make a present lady uncomfortable. Maryam's eyes deflected the chauvinism at me before rolling.

I hated how the term 'string theory' got thrown around.

Jafar was my one and only contact with the Ulema. I suspected he might be an actual member, much like the twentieth-century politburo bosses who ousted the experts and took over entire industries—their version of getting their hands dirty; though dirt should not be confused with bullshit.

I wiped chicken juice from my mouth with my tattered, red-wind-stained sleeve. "Whatever you say, big boy." Back in Venice, I had submitted my resume to the Ulema for my shamanic services. The stacks of paperwork that awaited me was the least of my worries now. They had their claws in so damn deep. The psyche-delic scene back home was underground, but here it was becoming the frontlines of geopolitical warfare.

The naïveté of having any aspirations—or plans, grand schemes, or lofty goals—was that one assumed the world would proceed apace without eruption of apocalypse, or the unleashing of violence. I thought of all the things I was going to do after shut-ting down the Death Module, and look good doing them (short of donning a cape, which I would do were it socially permissible). I never considered that a laser beam would blast a hole in the middle of Jafar's magic carpet and take a toe off of Maryam's right foot.

I bolted up. Maryam, poor girl, howled in pain. The anar-chists were upon us. Usually content to buzz around the palace, harassing those coming and going, they detected our approach. Their magic carpets were black, gold-embroidered stealth models capable of scrambling both Jafar's and Maryam's guardian angels. Three of the anarchists, black clad, approached us head on, toting ray guns. Two more sidled up to us from below, tauntingly mim-icking our drunken, slow descent. All five circled us like cowboys corralling a stray calf. They pointed their guns at us, not shooting.

One of them laced a grappling cable into our carpet and began to tug. Jafar would have none of it; he pulled out from under his invisibility cloak a nondescript lamp.

"Rub, by Allah!" he commanded me after tossing it into my lap. He steered our craft with enough resistance to buy us time while I did what I was told. I rubbed. I ridiculously rubbed. We were in grave danger, and I was stroking a lamp with an innate autoerotic fervor that, hopefully, caused our potential captors to hesitate a bit and have a chuckle. It must have worked, for, pour-ing out and up from the spigot of the dirty, burnished lamp was a tower of stardust that blinded everyone.

A basso profundo roar that could only originate from Hell emanated from a large swirl of particles. The mass began to congeal into a hulking humanoid figure that seemed upset at having been summoned. It stretched while taking shape, sinews shifting into place like time-lapsed sand dunes under wind. Even Jafar, usually cool as a cucumber, did a few double takes while he tried to keep us from tail-spinning.

Shit got hectic. A drone medic with a red crescent emblem, ordered either by Jafar or Maryam, alighted ten or so feet above us, assessing the situation before committing to the patient. The face of a salt-and-pepper-haired-and-bearded doctor appeared on the drone screen, asking in unintelligible Arabic what was the matter. Maryam belted out something while craning up her left leg. The drone steadily zoomed down to her injury. Two of the drone's robotic arms cauterized then sutured the wound, all while the other two had been unfurling a long bandage, which they then wrapped tightly over the foot as the onscreen doctor muttered soothing words and prescribed an exogenous pain med, which one of the arms then fished out from the pharmo-kit slung on its posterior.

The medic sped away into the air, then disintegrated at the impact of one of anarchist's laser beams. Regardless of their anti-government ideals, they were little better than the militant Islamists of yore who destroyed centuries-old antiquities. It meant they were growing desperate, or deemed the current catch worth it. Surely this wasn't one of their standard-procedure harassments.

A magic carpet dogfight broke out. I didn't know how versatile the utility mist was, but Jafar had decided to render out of it a duplicate of our own high-tech mode of conveyance, and a pistol laser, which he shot at the enemy. A hole the size of a bowling ball punched through one of the anarchist's chest. The poor bastard slumped over and his craft rolled him up into a neat deathly bundle, which plummeted to the ground, causing untold damage below. "Sir, the carpet at our left. That is yours. Commandeer it, please."

"If you come with us, Eetahlee," came a megaphoned voice from behind me, echoing off the skyscrapers, "we promise not to kill you." I looked back. It was Tamra from the illumination farm, wrapped in a black chador, veil and all. "Whatever I know," I shouted back, "of what use is it to you?" My magic carpet seemed to operate not by my volition, but by repelling itself from that of my pursuer. I was having close calls up against office windows, almost ate it from the anemometer of a weather station, and almost got impaled by a crescent moon atop a mosque.

"Your cause is wrongheaded," belted Tamra. "You'd be better to join us. We could use your talents. Land your craft and we'll discuss it in detail." Shit. I'd play the diplomacy card once I got backed into a corner, or began to free fall. Until then, I allowed the weave to zip me about the Aswadibad skyline. Tamra continued to tail me but didn't seem to gain any ground.

Salvia liked to teach me to not fear death, since life was just a rough-draft cross-section of an infinitely thick stack of multitudinous realities. Still, I wasn't yet ready to die. Though stone sober, I began to have a kind of fun. I started blowing kisses back at my pursuer , causing her to gesture angrily . Just then , another of those stealth carpets appeared at four o'clock. My magic carpet's repellent did not work against multiple pursuers.

"Eetahlee," came Tamra upon my starboard, "Just listen a bit to something." She sidled up close enough to me to enter the carpet's magnetic field, then bounced away. Her lurid eyes squinted in anger over her black veil.

She shot out a grappling hook, which punched through the

front of my carpet. The other anarchist, at port side now, steadied his craft, then shot out his own projectile, which latched onto the back. They were good. The grappling hook at the front held still while the one at the rear began yanking me violently up, causing the carpet to tightly roll over me. I couldn't breathe. I was about to die.

It was the funniest moment of my life.

I was rolled up like a dope, no better than Shah Mohammed wound up in his rug and trampled by Tartar horses in order to avoid the unclean act of shedding Muslim blood. And these aerial Mongols spun me, tightly wound carpet and all, toward I know not where.

All five senses shut down. The world punched out. The universe closed up shop.

BETA TESTING

i hit a floor. The momentum unfurled the magic carpet to expose me to a brightly-lit room. A giant woman picked me up gingerly by the back collar with thumb and forefinger, and plopped me down onto the dry, jasmine-scented palm of her other hand. She drew me up to her window-sized green eyes. Najwa on a 10x scale. I lay on my side, gazing up at her scarlet smile stretching wider than my length. Go ahead: chew me up.

Something was broken or out of joint on my right side. Sacroiliac, maybe. Lumbar two, perhaps. It burned. The pain was way less funny than what I thought was to be my death.

She spoke.

"It is within my capacity to crush you, but not within my heart. Everything that you have experienced ever since we last saw each other is the addendum to the last narrative I had related to you. You could figure it out on your own and then decide which side of this war you belong on. Do you remember how I told you to pay much attention to the story I had been telling, and even more attention to what was to follow? You can now stop paying attention and begin the decipherment of these last few days."

"I just had a modemectomy," I slurred, "so I'm not exactly in a position of playing oracle at Delphi."

"Good," she said, "you have done the right thing, and believe it or not should now be more perceptive than ever. All that online clutter is gone now. Everything, crystalline."

"Not clear at all. I've been in the Salviasphere half the time." With much pain, I propped myself up on my elbow. "Have I even left this place?"

She held me up to her eyes. "You must decide for yourself." Her lips were the size of divans, the bottom one plush and inviting.

"I can't decide, because I don't know. I thought I went to a joyshack and had my cortical modem removed . I also thought I visited the illumination farm out in the desert and met Murad . I. Don't. Know. Do you? I thought I was brought back by agents of the Ulema and came close to being killed by the anarchists outside . I was rolled up into a carpet and , à la Cleopatra, flung into the turret window."

"There is an unfurled Turkish carpet down over there," she said, pointing with her green eyes.

"That doesn't mean anything," I said.

"No," she said.

I had an idea of her mechanics of deception, but could never manage to put a finger on the techniques, for as soon as I thought I had it figured out, she had dodged predictability and veered off into a different approach. Her stories were full of traps and ambushes. She would narrate me halfway across the world to a strange country, and I would shake myself from my attentive listening to find myself in an unknown alley, or at an aquarium, wondering what I was doing there and how I got there.

She had me walking the plank of her imagination. She shuttled me to precarious heights, where the air of her inventions, always fictitious but ever so deadly, was rarefied. I teetered on a balance beam of enchantment. Every time I did fall, she cradled me in the arms of yet another story, cushioning my swoons with the throw pillows of tales that always began benignly enough.

A wiser man would have sought retribution for having had his brain so toyed with. I shook my head. Junk she had stowed away between my ever-open ears clanked. My head became a warehouse to her tireless musings, a mausoleum where dwelt the phantasms of her tales, dead once told. I quit catalogueing her inventions and just let them dovetail with reality. It was all a giant mess.

We came across a two-piped hookah. Whenever she partook of hasheesh, her stories took on a freakish turn. Already stoned out of my own gourd on salvia, I could never manage a fight. I had to deal with transvestite ifrits and kaleidoscopic djinns; philosophical dragons with severe cases of acrophobia; a pair of Siamese twin dwarves who finished each other's sentences; and a translucent black mamba who told jokes every time a person fed her a rusty nail. Bloodthirsty tyrants dined with angels, mechanical birds fought over Faerie entrails.

A real social handicap showed up in her stories like ugly growths on otherwise beautiful sketches. Her ignorance of the modern male psyche, for instance, appeared in biographies of men way too chivalrous for today. And women, whether abducted from seraglios, or poisoning lovers by whom they have been jilted, were always too hopeful in finding the ideal gentleman to court. Her heroes and heroines lacked the jadedness that any fully functioning adult attained by the age of thirty.

These faults, however, did not serve to undermine the integrity of her inventions; they only reminded me that they were cross-sections of the great Truth, which was the world in its entirety; the stories were therefore lies of omission. For you told a lie of the world simply by telling the tiny truth of a tale. Our consciences lied to us all day simply because we didn't know everything. You only had to mine the multiverse to learn that fiction was but a filtered version of the Truth.

She lied to me about her own identity by not saying a thing about herself. It created a mystique at first, but then it became desperate and pathetic. I had filled in gaps by roaming about the city and hobnobbing with sleaze-ball raconteurs and wind-torn ascetics. It was as if the dispersed carnage of who she was had been littered about the city, investing its smoke-filled alleys and rain-slicked streets with her soul, its ashen aftertaste mingling with sighs and shakings of heads.

The legendary narratrix Scheherazade spun tales to save lives. This one in my presence was concocting fictions to end mine. But so long as I could get back online after a time and broadcast my story, I feared not death. I meantime meant to exhaust her memory bank and tongue, to where her telling as much as my listening would sap her of all her life. She could go ahead and commit narrative suicide with the same blow that would kill me.

She asked me accompany her up to the Death Module. I never offered to fix it by myself. I could not stand to be up there alone with that radar, in a silent, windless night in which only its constant spinning could be heard. It curdled my blood. I could feel it threatening Aswadibad and its inhabitants below with a monstrous promise to reduce all and everything to gossip. It was the metal hybrid of a vampire and a voyeur. I waited for the anarchists with their magic carpets and ray guns to succeed in its destruction, wondering why it proved so difficult a task. Najwa would harness us with ground wire before climbing up, since the invisible Faraday cage covered only the outer eighty percent of the Death Module.

I thought of Rose, her spook of a red butterfly. I thought I had seen Murad stab it with a switchblade before devouring it. But now I wasn't even certain I had ever even been in the imaginal realm. That was the dilemma of working within the Salviasphere: it allowed me to peer beyond the distracting veneers of peoples' autorama-enhanced auras, but I had trouble figuring out what ultimately did or did not happen. Being a multi-dimensionalist carried the bane of sometimes not knowing in what dimension things mattered anymore. Lotus-eating here, withering away there. But who said there mattered more than here? And from which side were they saying it from?

The GnosisNet beta-testing was a week away. One thing was now clear: I had not been brought in by the Ulema to lead citizens down an irretrievable path inside the Salviasphere. Thing was, it turned out that the Ulema, as a body composed of real persons, could hardly be said to exist. There were agents—the wizard Jafar, the journalist Maryam—but there existed no secret group of finger-wagging curmudgeons calling the shots. GnosisNet had been open-source from the start. The religious authorities were long dead. It was enough to be a good Muslim.

It was therefore my newfound task to eliminate the gray goo that filtered through the Salviasphere architecture. With the help of a half-dozen willing GnosisNet IT specialists assigned to the EntheoGenerator division, I set up a ghost infra-structure where the miscreant bots could frenzy their ways into Boolean dead ends and become sealed off from the original protocol. In order for the eventual decay of that entire dummy structure to not become too obvious too soon, a cover-up tapestry also had to be put in place. Since everyone during the test run would be zoned out on salvia instead of the originally proscribed psilocybin, not a voter worth his salt would detect the discrepancies found in the IP addresses.

I also had to convince voters that GnosisNet was a psychedelic utopia. This was beyond easy; it was pure fun. By masquerading as admin on an EntheoGenerator mainframe, I could literally think these people or entities into living euphoria. The program was so advanced that it went beyond digital and became true ether. All the technology did was reinvent itself into fairy dust.

Once I was back in the good graces of the Ulema, the mullah wraiths stopped showing up. At first, I couldn't figure out, then, whether they were meant to intimidate me into performing my job or they were government scouts infiltrating the Salviasphere. They were possibly both.

Najwa knew what I was up to. She feigned doing nothing. But out of the corner of my eye I could see her gathering up an arsenal. The sordid details of her past involvement with palatial events would grow so grandiose in the public eye that they would supernova her into purity. She would then rain down like so much sacred confetti while everyone was caught with his hands in his pants.

She shared with the anarchists a hope for politics to revert to their analog version—muddled in the past, but sure to somewhat function. There was an element of representation to an oligarchy, she felt, in that the common folk relied on it to at least do half a decent job, whereas the randomness of GnosisNet would make monumental mistakes out of usually small issues, like a minor spending bill—out of too much fear of offending some suddenly over-enfranchised idiot's sensibilities. So what that a few people donned crowns and stuck their noses up at the rest? The anarchists, though, wished to slough off technology and live in communes, which always struck me as nothing more than a silly societal reboot.

There was some recent speculation about the monkey-suited politicians not being real, but media simulations. Either way, their presence in the Salviasphere was palpable. They morphed into paisley, amoebic entities that clung to things with an obstinacy found only in career demagogues. They were decidedly non-computational. Their position in the hierarchy of the Salviasphere's functionality was obvious; they were not only extraneous, but parasitic. They didn't serve the organism like, say, mitochondria fueled a cell; instead, they cannibalized the structure like cancer cells. The organism existed in spite of them, rather than because of them. I vanquished many of them by relating their superfluity to them. They groaned before popping into nothingness.

The absurdity of a political system devoid of statesman was increasingly obvious the more time I spent in the Salviasphere. Complete integers were missing in the simplest of mathematical functions. A ship would only be rudderless if every sailor deemed himself captain. The ideal state would be for a few of those parasites to actually offer benefits during their predation.

The beta test date came. It flopped immediately . The only thing transparency showed was that nothing was getting efficiently done. Garbage collecting became a problem overnight. Instead of an intricate schedule of what day was assigned to which neighborhood , even factoring in vacation and holiday time for workers, there was now only randomness. It would now take three weeks for the garbage truck to hit a place , only to return two days later. The e-notes attached to the open-source decision files tried to convince a curious citizen that it made sense in the big scheme of things. Try telling that to the garbagemens' union, who wouldn't get paid for months before raising protest. GnosisNet hadn't factored in the possibility of labor union strikes; maybe they assumed everyone would be too blissed out on civic duty to care about paltry things like income.

Najwa shook her head and smirked at the overflowing garbage

receptacles. Two weeks into the GnosisNet trial run, the robot septet continued to play the chamber compositions ethered into their hard drives, but they dispersed throughout the palace. They proved largely error-free, with the exception of the violinist, which took a violent turn. We had to watch our backs. At first, no one knew why that robot went berserk. Maybe because that musician was prone to soloing while the rest of the ensemble kept a tight background. The oud player would occasionally venture off into fioriture and etudes, in which case it would be next to go wild. It may have been a matter of the violinist's flailing limbs not receiving sufficiently challenging sheet music with which to stay busy. It clutched its violin by the left hand, while with the right it swung the bow like a scimitar. Its first casualty was the Saudi engineer charged with oiling and tuning the ensemble. For the sake of the integrity of the test run, he could not assign less threatening musical pieces; he had to assign whatever was proposed by the palace entertainment minister, who received his own orders in accordance to what the system deemed proper at the time.

I ran into the engineer down a hall. He was a short, portly man in a *jallabiyah*. His right arm was in a sling. An oil can dangled from his left arm. He said hello in English and I jumped at the chance of conversation. A fresh scar ran diagonally across his face. Concerning the GnosisNet roadblock to fixing the violinist, I asked, "Couldn't you make a special appeal?"

He shook his head winsomely, sighed. "To whom?"

"Whoever is in charge," I offered.

He raised his eyebrows at me. "At this point, all we can do is let the mock trial run its course, in the meantime being extremely careful."

"You can't confine them to an area?"

"No." He shifted the weight of his sling. "They are supposed to roam free about the palace, providing ambience."

"A murderer can sure create some ambience."

He harrumphed rather than chuckled. He waddled away, dripping oil down the hall.

Within the Salviasphere, the malfunctioning robot violinist became for me an avatar of human ingenuity gone madly awry. He may as well have been flanked by phalanxes of rapist sweetmeat dispensers, and a fleet of prickly kabob copters. Already particular about my music, I never liked live renditions, human or otherwise. I preferred my music streamed into my autorama, where I could control its volume and equalization. I could shuffle, repeat, skip, or just turn it off. To hell with ambience. It encroached upon my freedom as much as another person's perfume. The robot musicians worked digitally but in a lot of ways were analog, for they offered real-time rather than streamed music. Najwa, who delighted in the chamber ensemble, and often called upon them for background music to her narrations, riffing upon their compositions with an astonishing improvisation and tying up all the loose ends into a tidy bow at the music's denouement, waxed regretful over the ensemble's disbandment.

Some of the IT guys and the concubines hooking up with them were having close encounters with the violinist. Soon enough, even the Saudi engineer steered clear, holing himself up in one of the spare basement chambers, among server stacks. The scene was a microcosm of the GnosisNet mock run: wait out the storm with something like fear and despair. A feisty, strikingly beautiful Lebanese girl named Aisha had been lacerated by the miscreant musician, and a medicopter had to be summoned. The entire palace knew about it, even Najwa, who scoffed, "Probably tried to turn a trick upon the robot. Not at all a surprise."

I called her on her callousness.

Psychedelic adept though I was, she saw vulnerability in my

eyes, and with a collection of nonsensical syllables placed me in a spiritual dungeon where the cold, iron walls allowed in no light. Had I my autorama, I could have played back the story. The salvia allowed me to see in her a creature expressing a reptilian despair. Maybe she was afraid that the amenities so long offered her by the state would disappear overnight, and she'd have to take a job like everyone else. Being off-grid and analog would make it especially difficult to earn a living for someone with no discernable skills.

For all her flaws that I began to observe through my multichromatic kaleidoscope, she lacked affectation. I couldn't pick out her shapely outline from the fractal display of my consciousness; she moved about with the stealth of a calico, quiet and innocent, but no less purposeful. We shared an understanding that we were both seriously flawed in our dealings with reality.

Her denial of long-held truths was shocking. She showed a petulance that meant her storytelling was not a passion she had honed out of a desire to be the best, so much as a device to cope with the inconveniences of reality. The longer she stayed sheltered in the palace, the more fanciful her narratives became. Whenever I posed hard questions to her, I got in turn nifty vignettes. She hurled these intricate combos at me until I relented in my prying. It was like the very best of a boxer coming out when he had his back against the ropes and was talking shovel hooks to the liver. I then realized how much ontological trouble she was in. She was going to have an ugly run-in with the enlightenment police when the election went down. I wouldn't know the magnitude of this until later, when I got my audience with the former sultan.

Despite the bedlam of incompetence unleashed by the test run, there was a feeling of excitement in the air. Everyone at the palace was charged with hope, elation, eros. Don't misunderstand me. There was still plenty of vindictiveness and ire to give the palace walls two coatings. But it all seemed trivialized by the consensual euphoria permeating the place. Was Armageddon supposed to be so aphrodisiacal? It wasn't the salvia talking. Somehow everyone took a giddy pleasure in watching the infrastructure get revamped into incompetence and gridlock.

The best thing left to do was make love. I made my share. Yes, for sure that Aisha was easy—not to say too wonderful. More often than not, her bellydancing routine knocked me out to the point where tumescence was impossible, no matter how concerted her efforts. My brain was close to being broken. It felt like I contained GnosisNet in my skull—a mad invention that tinkered uselessly with the input given it, like cogs and gears that churned for no known purpose. In the intervals where I could not do my duty of decimating the politico-bots, and when Najwa was missing in action, all I could do was sleep around. I'd do fine but for Aisha's routine.

Najwa made quick work of my promiscuity by cataloguing all the venereal diseases known to man as performers in a Kabuki play, each malady represented by garish, terrifying masks that fleshed out a drama in which humanity's genitalia set to rot and a pantheon of white-faced demons ruled in the aftermath. I was rash enough to make a pass at her, in essence calling her bluff. She demurred with a slap to my face.

"Sorry," I said. "Salvia." Which was true.

Everyone's hygiene took a hit from the beta test. Najwa's elaborate coiffures disappeared. She had to brush her long black hair constantly. The streaks of blue and silver dovetailed into each other like copulating snakes being separated by the deadly teeth of a lamprey that she held by a stout tail. Though the hairdressers ended up desisting in their duties because of lack of pay, there was still cold water for bathing. Only once was there a blackout, and apparently, this had been broadcast ahead of time on billboards outside, lest the mock trial work in such a way that some peoples' autoramas, experiencing interference from their EntheoGenerators, did not apprise them of the scheduled power outage.

I saw her face in profile. She eschewed enhancements, looking a healthy thirty-five. I'd lie if I said she possessed the beauty of a twenty-year-old. But I'd tell the whole truth if I said she once had done so, and had aged becomingly. Who knows what the former sultan, or Murad, had done to her heart. Whatever it was, it showed in the crow's feet at the corners of her green eyes. That was the only telltale sign of her age.

She continued brushing her hair. Molecules of flippancy fled that holocaust, evacuating the parlor to go fuse with the community euphoria being propelled by the salvia. She tilted her head up and glanced over at me, left eyelid batting over the green orb, accusing me of lechery. I coughed before clapping thrice—the usual cue for the tea-bot to arrive on its rollers. She smiled at me. The smile disappeared when we heard fierce string passages of Rimski-Korsakov thrumming beyond the cedar door.

I needed tea more than I needed safety. There would be a week left of the trial run. Then things would be back to normal up to and during the election.

I felt a need to suddenly see Murad. I needed to place my head in his lap and have him reassure me that everything was going to be fine. No contractual obligation with the Ulema kept me from leaving Aswadistan in order to take a break from the Gnosis-Net beta-test debacle. I needed to make sure that Najwa made it through alive. If I didn't see after her, no one would. Not even her former lover.

Someone had hacked my reality's operating system and tinkered with the shell software. A laceration in locale cut off the boundaries of the palace. Instead of the swarm of magic-carpet-riding anarchists with ray guns buzzing about the palace turrets and surrounding buildings, there circled birds of prey in a clear sky. Desert scrub replaced concrete. The prima materia used to encode the universe had been commandeered by the Ishraqiyun and used to tailor-make a terrain that made it easy for me to find them. This was utility fog, which could be used to make anything. In this case, it had been used to abridge or expand consensual space. It was a shame that they did not shear off Qaf's mountaintop, slope its face for an easier ascent, or embed an escalator into its rock wall. I had to scale the mountainside. My hands bled. The winds tore at me, body and soul. My clothes were reduced to tatters. My eyes bled at the corners from the pressure. But I made it to the top. I traversed the path of most resistance. And I lived.

He was standing there in his leather exoskeleton. A long scarf around his neck blew to the east. His riding goggles shielded his eyes. He smiled.

The Ishraqiyun had been press-ganged into the untenable position of philosopher kings and they were making a mess of the whole thing in response.

"There are kingdoms of which you are not aware," he said, snapping on his chinstrap. He tucked the wayward scarf inside his leather jacket, which he zipped back up—the zipper sounding like a serrated blade carving at a hollowed-out turkey. "I know you have been to three cities thus far. I trust you shall not know others in this lifetime." Supercilious.

"They sure weren't all they're cracked up to be."

"Those cities are abominations," he said, raising the goggles from his eyes. Bad left eye. He was an otherworldly insect rampaging through the imaginal realm like a menace. "They were the nightmare creation of an archon who had been hunted down and destroyed ages ago. Yet there are cities that make gardens resemble booby-trapped graveyards."

"Why would you deny me knowledge of them? Why should I not someday give up this shit existence and make the long arduous journey?"

"I'm sorry. It is not an indictment on your character or your abilities. I only report what the sage of Jabalqa would tell you if you decided to ask him yourself."

"So I came up in conversation."

"Yes," Murad said. "Regarding the boy."

"Why don't you call him 'son'?"

"Because," he said, and choked up. "Because I have been a terrible father and have not earned that privilege. I have done no better than she." He kick-started the motorcycle and hiccupped into a tire-screeching about-face, leaving me with a face full of imaginal dust.

The GnosisNet cognoscenti and the anarchists outside were disparaging each other across a gulf of uncertainty, for there was no direct communication. Since the anarchists were analog, they were impervious to hacks or even spam attacks. And the programmers were safely walled up inside.

The coders and IT guys had no contraptions that could fend off the harassing holograms of perverted djinn and buffoonish if-rits that the anarchists cast in a cavalcade of character assassination. These modern-day versions of republican Rome graffiti were jibes that could not be traced back to their origin, because they had no ID tags. They could therefore be very effective as a seditious force. It was Aswadistani tradition that they have multifarious signifi-cance, often resorting to symbolism and complex physical riddles that needed decipherment and proper interpretation. They were piggybacking off of the palace bandwidth, and could therefore be endless. They revolved around the same theme: a ménage-à-trois involving a monarch, his queen, and his chief concubine. The most prominent one had the concubine out-fellating her competition, who stood aside defeated, arms folded. The queen eventually killed herself in various ways. There was much speculation concerning this last part, since there had circled rumors about the ex-sultana offing herself in order to preserve her honor. Something about the last fifty years of Aswadistan's monarchs adopting the Western tradition of monogamy played heavily with the citizens' sensibilities, and as a result the possibility of the amorous bezique going on at court rattled everyone's trust in Al-Raschid. This had been—and a lot of people, even pundits, tended to forget—the opening needed for the Ulema to make their move with their proposed software.

In a quirk of fate, Najwa's reputation experienced a resurgence because of the holograms. It pleased me warmly to witness this. With the ex-monarch and the queen misbehaving (he in the boudoir, she in a pantry where supposedly her body had been found), only the concubine, promiscuous only because she was a dutiful member of the harem, remained morally beyond reproach.

To further cement this perception, she told a brief story called "The Retrieval." The entire palace came to be her audience. Any doubts about her ability to perform in front of a large crowd were dispelled. She did not hold forth with a fire and brimstone charisma like a Cicero or a Mussolini. Instead, her assured mezzo-soprano combined with her unenhanced beauty to make for an easy suspension of disbelief. The holograms kept coming, and she incorporated them into the story. Yes, she had lain with the sultan. Yes, she had made him break with tradition. But she was no whore. And she had not earned an eternity of hellfire by committing suicide like the queen.

The programmers and palace staff were growing disillusioned with the test run. Despite this, the outbreak of free love continued. Who was to say that the Great Launch would fare any better? And was Mehmet Al-Raschid all that bad? After all, under his rule there had been clear running water, community music, and bandwidth. And even if he had had his faults, was it not a reformed and improved version of him up for legitimate democratic election? And hadn't he expressed interest in working with a modified, less-involved version of GnosisNet?

The makeover of Mehmet Al-Raschid as a henpecked and therefore justified philander irked little if none of the GnosisNet personnel. They sat engrossed in Najwa's stories, which shifted from ribald and comical to Borgesian when she dealt out two curious vignettes that held up on their own but interlocked to create a telling whole. The first was the aforementioned "The Retrieval." The second was "S&M Djinn."

The latter, taking place during the reign of the Sun King, Louis XIV, concerned a Parisian doyenne who had purchased a rustic lamp at auction. Said to date from Ummayid Damascus, the trinket, once cleaned of dust and polished, was alluring enough to command a prohibitive price. The doyenne, long since a divorcée, happened to have ladies over for tea in her salon. The lamp got passed around and eventually got rubbed in just the proper way so as to affect the emergence of a genie of prepossessing aspect, bearing next to nothing of the supernatural save a purple-tinged skin. Mistaking the truly magical, even Shaitanic, figure as a *trompe-d'oeil* of convincing technology, the ladies hooted and hollered at the scantily-clad, muscle-bound genie, and began tossing garments at him. He then spoke in a great roar, freezing them in their divesting frenzy, offering three wishes to whoever had been his liberator. Since no one could rightly claim to be the woman who properly released him from his millennium-long prison, it fell to the doyenne to wish thrice. Without hesitation, she command-ed all of the women in her salon to be disappeared. "This can only be done," said the genie, "by their demise."

"Then so be it," she ordered.

"So be it," said the genie, and he waved his hand. They were gone without a trace.

"Where have they gone?" she asked, eight fingertips at her agape mouth.

"Where it is that people go to upon death."

"Oh, my." But it was as she wished. And now she was alone with the strapping genie, who was virility incarnate.

"What is your second wish?"

"That I feel the rush of pleasure once more."

The genie could perform magical feats of all sorts, but a mind-reader he was not. There has been much debate as to what constitutes the granting of a wish. A wish itself is a singular thing—such as the lady's desire to orgasm. But there may be extenuating circumstances in the granting of such complex wishes, in that the genie would have to perform a series of tasks in order to fulfill the granting. It could become a tricky game of semantics. For this reason, the genie asked permission to summon a barrister he knew, in order that the situation be properly interpreted, lest he shirk on his duties of wish fulfillment and return to the tribulations of the lamp. "Go ahead," said the lady. "But you're to please me one way or another."

Now this took some time. It was not a matter of upping her es-trogen or over-sensitizing her erogenous zones. Mind you, this was before the EntheoGenerator, or even simple endorphin plug-ins. This was seventeenth-century France. The genie—according to the mustachioed barrister who floated in midair and held a scroll—

was compelled to try everything until the lady reached the throes of ecstasy. A legal battle still ensued.

Whatever yet-to-be-discovered single unit of measurement that together with countless others made up a running narrative, whatever it would eventually be called, I was it. Call it a *schehe-razade*. No, that would be clunky. Call it a *najwa*. That's just about right. That sounds like something on the level with a planck, or a parsec, or an ampere, or a joule. It took me and forty other *najwas* for the audience made up of palace staff and GnosisNet workers to double over in laughter. We were the scene in which the poor, legally bound genie must pop out of his lamp and inflict pain upon the kneeling, bare-assed doyenne with a red leather cat-o'-nine-tails, and disappear back into the lamp before she looks back over her shoulder to see (or not see) the source of the pain. It would take a series of these inflictions for him—and her—to come to the conclusion that it does not result in her pleasure. The genie's barrister friend tears the legal scroll to shreds and folds his hands in resignation, hovering there in midair, head high. After a few more futile runs of this lubricious deed, the barrister has taken to fondling himself, for, though she be on in years, the Parisian is of callipygian aspect, not to mention of a pale complexion, much sought after by those in the classical underworld.

My fellow *najwas* and I felt a swirl now and then, in which we got reincarnated into the same batch of *najwas* responsible for conveying the lewd act, each time with more *najwas* added on, more recruits being needed to heighten the comedic effect. Until . . . until . . . Yes. Yes: About fed up with the act wherein the genie emerges jack-in-the-boxlike from his magic lamp, lashes her on the bare ass, and quickly disappears, the doyenne, in a final effort to once again spot the culprit of her torment, hoping that an actual glimpse will be the x-factor that will launch her into an aria of ecstasy, sees the genie's acquaintance, the barrister, servicing himself with a manual dexterity heretofore unheard of in polite Parisian society. And: My, oh, my. *Mon dieu. Qu'est-ce que cet homme fait avec son boudin? Et voilà!*

My fellow *najwas* and I took pride in our pivotal role in the story's comedic turn. People clapped as if we were the stars. We were bathed in a rush of attention.

And then just like that, we were disbanded. And we were nothing on our own, too microscopic to be of consequence. Some of us traveled about together as long as we could. Some fellow holdout *najwas* and I were present at a marathon of harem gossip hours later. Days later, a platoon of us still stuck together and survived while being transcribed online.

I eventually evolved. I couldn't vouch for my fellow *najwas*, but I became a full-fledged human being interacting with other human beings. I found myself in a server room, listening to a re-telling of the S&M genie story. Turkish music thrummed about from some unknown source. Those involved in the story's telling—for they were telling it to me—held me in high regard that I didn't feel I deserved. It was all very confusing, that humanness. Instead of a *najwa* playing a crucial role in the story, I was now a listener of the narrative in question. A GnosisNet programmer with piebald hair and a gold-flecked Tartar beard sat on a barstool. A dainty, Inner Asian concubine with long, straight black hair, dressed in a silver negligee and a matching veil, sat on his knee. Any rotation he performed on the barstool set her giggling. It was he who told me the story he had heard only hours ago from the narratrix. As for the veiled and therefore mute concubine, she accentuated his narrative with expressive eye cues.

The rush of responsibility to be a person weighed on me. It

felt like kettlebells were plopped onto my lungs. I had to bathe, eat, sleep, shit, and work—all just to stay alive only to do more of same. What tedium. Especially annoying was paying attention to anything at all. I wanted to curl myself up into a walnut shell and be left alone. I envied inanimate objects everything.

Apparently, litigation between the genie and the doyenne became a knotted mess of legalese, its proceedings lasting eighty-eight years, time which the Parisian was granted temporary immortality until the case could be resolved . The *qadi* could cite no precedents and was therefore compelled to hunker down with the groundbreaking case as well as his jurisprudence could demand. Meantime, though he be a plaintiff to her defendant, the genie was to perform his duties, namely flogging the lady with that cat -o'-nine-tails and disappearing back into the magic lamp before she could glance over her left shoulder and catch sight of the barrister engaging in a concerted bout of oscillatory onanism, which resulted always in her reaching of climax . The barrister regretted tearing up his scroll. He now be-came an accessory to the wish-granting, and had not the legal document to extricate himself therefrom. But that was not the point of contention: the genie had been rightly imprisoned and rightly freed, but he demanded restitution for having to grant way more than three wishes to the lady. More like fifty-two. He maintained the lawsuit not out of pusillanimity, not out of self-righteousness, but to blaze a trail for other genies who might find themselves in similar situations where the semantically vague term "three wishes " may be exploited to no end.

Evolution was truly amazing. I took that concubine to my private quarters, bolted the door, and administered her a 25-gram dose of tincture. Not bad for a former *najwa*.

"You have nice bone structure," I said. "You are Tajikistani?"

"No," she said, "Kyrgyzstani."

And then I felt her flesh go fractal.

So check this out: that concubine girl, Nur, poor soul, got lost in the Salviasphere for a time. She drifted off like an untethered astronaut into deep space. It was partly my fault.

She must have had an EntheoGenerator malfunction, for she launched into a twitching display of hysterics, while I ground it out in full penetration. For a supposed professional who had logged in countless carnal hours, she was tighter than the stones of Macchu Picchu. Through those pornographic pyrotechnics—the likes of which I had never before been the recipient of, not even with Esmeralda, my erstwhile perfect match—she expressed concern for her physical integrity, meaning she was undergoing dissipation. She was physically still present, a deafening g-spot tangle of gunmetal satin bedsheets and scalding-hot olive-toned flesh, but she was catatonic. My tongue sanded away her sense of self, her remnants dispersing away from the drug.

This added to my myriad reservations I had about Gnosis-Net—not only as a matter of principle, but concerning the technology being used to implement it. Whether because Nur's dosage dispenser settings were dangerously off, or her enneagram needed recalibration, to have her drown in a lake of salvinorin A called into question the integrity of the EntheoGenerator modality as a whole.

Amir, the IT guy with the piebald hair and gold-flecked Tartar beard, said, "Well, that's what the test run is all about."

"About what? Throwing someone down a bottomless pit of psychedelia?" I wanted to render his mandible asymmetrical.

"No," he said, "to work out the kinks."

"This is not just a kink, kid. She could perish from astonishment. If enough of the agonist permeates her blood-brain barri-

er, she could have a self-induced seizure, heart attack, whatever."
None of that was true. I simply didn't enjoy seeing someone lose
it so much.

"Please," Amir scoffed.

"No. No please. You don't send civilization underwater for
good when some of your scuba units are proving faulty."

Sultry music continued slithering about the salon. I called for
it to be turned down. Out of solidarity for the distressed Nur, everyone linked their cortices to persuade the palace audio steward
to shut it off completely. The entertainment minister wasn't con-
sulted. I was grateful for the group rebellion. Amir arranged for an
endorphin dump, which posed a considerable danger not for Nur,
but for the willing recipient. And he did it without the consent of
the Ulema.

Right when Amir directed me and a few others to tote Nur
into an adjacent nap room where sat a wheeled cot, I split into
two. It was the worst bifurcation I ever had. It was so severe that I
felt unstitched for quite a time thereafter, like certain seams needed to make me complete were asked too tall of an order in that
they needed to bring together the halves of me by spanning an
unbridgeable gulf. I was surprised at the level of motor function I
still retained; even my depth perception had not suffered. I felt to
have been invaded by the world, which inhabited the vast chasm
that yawned between my two selves.

One self continued helping Nur undergo the endorphin
dump. I may have incidentally fondled a breast in the process of
hoisting her up, whereupon a eunuch, who had always eyed me
with suspicion because of my proximity to Najwa, railed at me.
My having given Nur the salvia did not help my cause. But most
iniquitous was my failure as a shaman. "The dosage amount was
not my doing," I yelled.

The eunuch, who was diagonal from me in regard to the four of us carrying the girl, arched a languid, hennaed arm under our charge's waist, and shot at my left hip with a taser pen. The pain seared through my lower body. I let go of Nur, not without petulance. Her head slammed on the floor.

A choir of complaints burst out, and the other two men allowed the eunuch to double up on his assault. I found myself kneeling while he stood, holding the girl at the waist.

He telegraphed a kick to my face. I clutched his leg and dragged him down. Nur's entire limp body hit the floor. More protests ensued. The eunuch belted out rapid-fire Arabic, then barked, "I will kill you, dog! Kill you!"

I ripped a rhinestone-encrusted green slipper from his foot and threw it at his head. Then . . . then . . . that was it.

My other self wasn't even inside the palace. I was seated in the Great Auditorium, listening to slow, morose passages of the Perennial Music. No matter what goings-on quaked throughout the city, the Perennial Music, impervious to the GnosisNet test run, continued to go like the heartbeat of a sturdy Russian housewife. The music settled on an increasingly sad motif, and I heard resultant potshots of weeping emerge from an outsized man who sat three rows in front of me.

I jumped out of my seat when I realized that it was Hamid, the big boy storyteller who had told Maryam and me the reverse story. Whether from the disorienting effects of the state-administered salvia divinorum, or because he found the music reminiscent of a lost love or of a simpler time, he fell to an outpour of crying that sent the large silhouette into convulsions. So I climbed over the three rows, and, balancing myself on his meaty left shoulder, plopped next to him. He dealt me an elbow to the face with a force that belied his wimpy sobbing. He likely mistook me for an assailant for not having DM'd him like any sane person before approaching him.

Clutching my aching nose, I calmed him and explained my going analog.

"Allah has smiled upon you," he said, mopping at his eyes with his loaf-like palms. "I can't convey to you the trouble that I . . ." He choked back tears and eyed me sullenly.

"Is it your mental state that is distressing you? Or the music?"

"Yes." He stopped weeping.

"Are you struggling with a disorienting feeling? Is it what your EntheoGenerator is pumping out?"

"Yes. Yes."

Another test-run overdose. Who besides me was meant to put out these fires? "Listen, Hamid. Listen to me. I'm good at bringing people back to safety from the situation you are currently in. We will do this. You will pull through. What are you seeing that distresses you?"

He just gazed at me. More tears burst forth like yolk from a breached eggshell.

"Hamid, are you experiencing hallucinations?"

"Yes," he whimpered. An eruption from the percussion section briefly caught his attention. "Creatures?"

"No."

"People?"

He hesitated. "Yes."

"Are they friendly?"

Another hesitation. He stopped weeping and muttered, "No."

"Can you count them?"

"No."

"Are they together?" No answer. "Are they sometimes together?"

"Yes."

"Who are they?" Damn it. It took a while to formulate a pithy question that would get to the matter quicker. "Alright, alright. Are they physically threatening you?" He hesitated. In that clunky binary system we conversed in, those hesitations were just as valuable as yea or nay. "Are they merely trying to scare you?"

"Yes," he answered.

"Are they authority figures?"

"Yes."

Hesitation. He leaped out of his seat and exploded into some serious crying. I needed to bring him back to sanity and save the questions for later. No one in the auditorium seemed phased by his commotion. Everyone sat placid-faced, engrossed in the Perennial Music. They may have all been coping with their own psychedelic traumas to much care.

My best assistance in a rescue was silence, so I had my work cut out for me. The music exploded into an allegro molto then died down to a plucky oud solo.

"Hamid, you must trust me. You are safe. There is nothing inside this auditorium but the musicians and sheet-shifters onstage, and twenty or so people sitting down and listening to them just like us. Just relax. Don't—

"No," he interrupted, blank eyes staring ahead.

"Don't fight it. Don't panic. No one is meh—"

"Yes."

"No one is menacing you."

"No."

"Right, Hamid. No. No one is menacing you. Listen. Do I seem more real than they do?"

"Yes," he said.

"Good," I said. "That's because I am real and they are not. Your EntheoGenerator has overproscribed you salvia. You are not the first person to expe- rience this today. Far from it."

Right at that moment, perhaps because the overdose recalled the idea of Nur, my consciousness bloomed back in the palace. I cradled my fractured nose in my hands. People around me were shouting. The effeminate, bejeweled man—the eunuch—hovered over me, dishing out insults in indecipherable Arabic. Someone held a blue towel out to me. I took it. I mopped the warm mess from my face. I gazed up at the juncture between a wall and the ceiling. Beautiful arabesque loops and curlicues graced the architecture with an élan that was outlandish and inexplicable for a patriarchal culture that emerged from the desert sands. Only a substance that ushered forth inspiration from Allah Himself could explain the feminine elegance of those designs. They sucked me up from the floor and became my circulatory system. They rushed oxygen through me. They laced pain through my body. My head throbbed, causing the designs to throb likewise. I found the energy to stand up. They had placed Nur on a cot and had wheeled her into a programming room, sidling her up to an enormous control panel.

Hamid was controlling his breathing with much effort. His face had dried away the tears. "They seem real," he said. "As if they are literally there, coming after me. They hover just above the ground and scowl at me. I can pick them out from far off because of their green turbans."

"Who, Hamid? Who are you referring to?"

"The mullahs. They seem so angry for what I did. Hamid palmed his eyes, trying to wipe away remaining open-eyed visuals.

"Are you still hallucinating?"

"Yes, sir. But I can manage it."

"Good. Keep doing so."

"I don't see the mullahs anymore. But I do see musical notes. They float all around in the air and pop. It's actually quite delightful. I can see how this could make a person happy and even docile. But I don't know how you can function in everyday activities."

"It takes a lot of practice. So what do you think those mullahs . . . how many did you say you think you can see?"

Hamid hesitated, counting. "Five or six."

"And what do you think they are menacing you for?"

"I'm not certain, sir. But maybe for having told you and that pretty lady the story of the two lovers and the red wind?" He turned his attention to the stage. The musicians kept playing. The white-robed sheet-shifters kept their frantic pace of setting and taking away the sheet music. Hamid opened his mouth but hesitated to speak. Then, with a whimper that snagged on his throat , said , "They visited me a day later . They came to our parlor. Four men and an old lady." It probably didn't help that he had his privacy settings open to the public while he DM'd Maryam and me with an insistence that was annoying.

"Four men and an old lady? What did they want? Did they threaten you?" It had been some time since the wraiths had paid my head a visit. He was now proposing that these beings were real, not just GnosisNet enforcers. Since he was a professional storyteller—in the trade of crying wolf—I couldn't invest any credence. "After a fashion. The four men took turns asking me questions. And the old, withered lady walked in with an exoskeleton, which she left at the door by the community exos and hovers. She then resorted to a cane, which she crooked underneath an armpit in order to crack her knuckles while glaring at me. The men asked me who you were. They didn't ask me who the pretty girl was. They asked me how I came to learn of the red wind."

"How had you? I thought it was all a flight of fancy of yours."

"No," Hamid said. "No. I wish. I merely used it as a template for a reverse-engineered narrative, which I had been obsessed with of late. How to fashion a yarn with simply *na'am* and *laa*, with the listener filling in the details. Participating, if you will."

"Again," I urged, "From whom did you learn that red wind story?"

Hamid disengaged from our interaction to focus on his breathing, looking to assuage whatever hallucinations he was undergoing. He took a deep breath and looked over at me. "From Issa."

"Issa?"

"Yes. Issa. A dilettante with a gangly build and an incorrigible innocence. Long ago, he was one of Zenki's prospects, until the kid got hold of some dangerous esotericism. Then, he just became weird." He halted again to control the visuals. "Pay attention, sir. Years ago, the anarchists who are now protesting against the Great Launch had hijacked three rainbows and used them to torture the truth out of captured Ishraqiyun. Those miscreants found a method of harnessing the dispersive nature of the light spectrum . One day, Issa wandered away from the illumination farm in search of water , which the Ishraqiyun were fasting from for a time. He wandered in the desert. I was there at the farm once. A few of us storytellers ventured there on occasion for material. I hate asceticism as a matter of principle , but I do find the kindness and hospitality of the Ishraqiyun comforting . Plus, they have seen things that Scheherazade would chug a thousand ogre cocks to be able to recount . Sorry. Plus, there are pretty girls, though they are all a great tease. Some of those girls grew worried at Issa's absence . I tried to console them , but they mistook my sincerity for prurience.

They had grown afraid of the color red, which was the color of my windbreaker. They told me about what the color red could do to the brain if harnessed maliciously. They did not much like blue, either, because it cooked the skin at night. I walked from tent to tent, making a fascinating word salad of their worries and desperations and hopes. I was told that the magician who had the key to unlock the venom from the rainbows' colors resided inside some cave, halfway up Qaf, but he was now in a cherry-red straightjacket, and in the custody of the anarchists. Issa eventually showed up at the parlor. He couldn't even walk up the steps. We had heard his pleas, and found him there at the bottom of the stairs, dehydrated and disheveled. Always nervous to begin with, he rattled uncontrollably about something called *fana'*."

"*Fana'*?"

"*Fana'*. The anarchists found him in the middle of the desert . They interrogated him, beat him up, and flew him back to Aswadibad . He had walked all the way from the eastern outskirts, from the Uzbek quarter. He pleaded unto Allah—who is gracious , and who heard him well—to cast the sun away behind a dirty pall of clouds. He didn't want the yellow of the sun to blend with the redness of his bloodied face. He feared this thing called *fana'*. He then passed out and we carted him up, laid him in a bed, and plugged electrolytes into his arm."

Four engineers from various parts of the world, and Amir, sat at one of the countless dashboard interfaces for GnosisNet. It resembled an audio mixing board. Nur still lay on the cot, awake. A bio-fire cable ran from the etherport at her occiput, just behind the top of her left ear, into a line on the board.

Aisha, who had volunteered to be the recipient of Nur's endorphin dump, sat strapped into a recliner, herself plugged into another line. If someone could undergo the surfeit of stimuli that would flood into her brain directly from the salvia-saturated Nur, it would be the star of the harem. Though she wasn't the most beautiful concubine, Aisha possessed a wizard's understanding of men and their bodies. Whenever selected by the sultan for a random dalliance, the other women's hearts boiled with a jealous poison. They detested her most of all for her vanity and facetiousness. Not even the eunuchs confided in her. She retained her pole position even when Al-Raschid vacated the palace: the systems administrators and programmers caught on quickly to her unparalleled expertise. This only upped the ire against her: so plug right in, sister.

EKGs, vital signs, and endorphin readouts of the two girls appeared on two monitors hovering over the engineers' heads. That of Nur showed a high heart rate and oxygen intake, with a serious endorphin spike. Aisha's vitals were normal, but they did surge once she seemed to realize the potential danger she was in. Why did she volunteer herself? Solidarity? A gambit to gain respect from her peers, so long denied to her?

The asshole eunuch stood on the other side of the room from me. The pall of worry that was on his face was replaced by a scowl when he saw me. My nose had long since clotted, but I dabbed at it with the blood-stained blue towel. He smirked. I wished to slice his neck open.

In a surprise show of support, two harem girls flanked the seated Aisha, soothing her with coos and massages to her arms and neck, eyeing her vital signs.

I flagged a nearby engineer. "Why can't they just leak the endorphins out of her brain? Why does someone else have to receive it to provide relief?"

The engineer looked at me askance, in disbelief. "You mean like a pressure valve? What's wrong with you? You can't just erase neurotransmitters. They don't dissipate into nothingness or disperse in the air. They need somewhere to go. It's cerebral entropy, if you must. Pure biology. Since they're digitally controlled from the EntheoGenerator software, this is a practical, though by no means completely safe, method to alleviate her overdose."

"If they're digitized, then can't they just be simply erased?"

"No. It's digitally controlled, not digitized. You can't digitize a neurotransmitter any more than you can digitize milk. But you can digitize the opening and closing of the valve control."

"So, it doesn't really travel through the dashboard?"

"Of course not. That's some hocus pocus shit. The dashboard only works as a gate. Since it is not a brain, it can't receive or harbor a neurotransmitter. It can only control its flow. Same thing with the bio-fire cables. It's a protocol than can control triggers, but actual endorphins don't travel through the blood-brain barrier. But it does work on the exact same principle of Proxy Apostasy, where there's no actual transfer of neurotransmitters so much as a transfer of triggers and simple influence. The dump, as it were, isn't literal. It only means there's a transfer of available happiness credits, as it were again, between the two girls. There's never any change of either's endogenous amount of endorphins."

"But what if she keeps receiving the salvia overdose after this transfer?"

The engineer pondered this. He dropped his arrogance and looked over at me. "She may have to stay hooked up like this or undergo a few more of these until the test run is finished. Say, who are you? Who let you in here?"

As pitiable a state as Nur had been and Aisha now was, at least the both of them could claim their own physical sovereignty; this despite the exogenous influence upon their neurotransmitters. I could claim no such thing for myself. I was bifurcated (for all time, it seemed). The arabesque circuitry that stretched across the galaxy-wide gulf spanning my two halves thrummed like oud strings with the smallest of worldly commotions. I chose not to involve myself with the universe, but it chose to involve itself with me. And in a way it validated my existence. It wedged itself into my ego and set up shop between my cloven identity. I guess I was still fortunate to have a self, or two. My salvia apprenticeship back on Giudecca was finally paying off. Though frustratingly bifurcated and susceptible to hallucinations, my motor skills and depth perception were fully functional. But I had to operate on that wavelength until the test run wrapped up.

I had never been so disoriented. It was due to two things. The first was that I held for a time a tenuous relationship with reality in general, due to Najwa's narrative tricks. I had no way of asserting what was real, really real, unreally real, or unreally unreal. Those gradations of reality were a thing of degree rather than of kind. It was like that frog that didn't know it was slowly being boiled.

The second reason for my disorientation was that the Salviasphere was being inhabited by way, way more minds than what it was used to handling at a given time. There was a controversial theory about a psychedelic's open-source architecture and history of usage, and it seemed to bear true under closer scrutiny. The more a certain substance was ingested, the more populous were its archives of anguish and back catalogues of bliss. It would therefore be more likely for one to feel loneliness or disorientation by partaking of a less-used substance. Ketamine, for instance. Whereas century-old drugs like LSD and psilocybin were more prone to impart a communal sense, regardless of the trip being bad or good. Other than being the drug of choice for the Mazatec Indians of Mexico, salvia has been purposely avoided by the most avid psychonauts and has as a result suffered a bad reputation. Some ascribe this to its "dirty high" feeling. We proponents of it felt it just hasn't had its day in the sun. The overwhelming glut the Salviasphere was undergoing may have been the reason why its current participants were being held in mental gridlock.

I crept up behind an engineer manning Nur's vitals. He smelled like sleeplessness and stale hummus. I braved his funk and got close to his ear. "How can you tell what microgram dosage she had been administered?" The EntheoGenerator BIOS shell was off-limits. Only the Ulema had its access.

He nudged my chin away with a shoulder shrug. "I'm afraid you can't. Now, if you'll excuse me. I'm rather preoccupied. Who are you? Can I see some identification?"

"Never mind me," I said. "I'm the rescuer." I showed him my hologram-embossed credential that hung on a lanyard around my neck. "Chief pyschonaut."

"Yeah, well. Not all of us are as fortunate as yourself. The drug is horrible. Shit's making me feel like my existence is a pun." He slowly slid two knobs downward.

"I know how capable all of you guys are at your job. I just had no idea that a theocratic council could fend off garden-variety security attacks."

He jerked his head over at me and stared me down. The eye-glass lenses shot back bright accusations at me for questioning his hacking creds. "Don't leave once she's okay. I'll get in there and show you her dosage."

I shrugged and held my palms out. Bottom-lip pout.

The endorphin dump proceeded without incident, though it was distressing to see one girl regain vitality while another got reduced to a panting, sweating mess. The solidarity was endearing, though.

"Sir," Hamid said. "I know not what will come of this country of mine once the Great Launch has occurred. I have even less an idea concerning my own well-being and future. In both cases, I fear the worst. But you have been kind to me and seem percipient enough to do me this favor that I ask of you. Sir, tell my tale. I have wronged no one in my loose-lipped enterprise. I merely wished to entertain, and more specifically, impress your pretty friend. If I make it out alive and am forgiven, I shall take up a more venerable trade, one in which gossip and relating of the past plays nary a part. Something more respectable."

They had done it. They had frightened him, a promising young talent, away from his vocation. They were rendering him docile. "Hamid. I am flattered by your misplaced confidence in my own narrative abilities. But know this: If I myself make it out alive, I will shout your tale from the mountaintops. From Mount Qaf, to top it off."

There was a curious lull in the music. We glanced at the stage. The sheet-shifters were jerky with their cargo, as if the hive brain that drove their wraithlike impetus had short-circuited. The musicians recuperated their competence after their own collective gaffe. It meant one thing: the GnosisNet test run was over.

I had been told that everyone's EntheoGenerator would shut off the dosage immediately. There were no biofeedback mechanisms, no online plebiscites or questionnaires to detail grievances, not even public forum threads addressing areas of concern. If the botching of a simple municipal task like garbage-collecting was anything to go by, I imagined it wouldn't take long for air-traffic controllers, elevator mechanics, gender-reassignment-booth operators, bank wire transfer managers, or heart surgeons to come forth to express concerns.

Aisha appeared to be in mortal trouble. People swarmed

around her in a panic. Two medic-bots zoomed in. Her hemorrhage was not caused by any inherent dangers of an endorphin dump; the guys manning the board were meticulous in monitoring the bio-wiring between the girls. It was caused by the sudden stoppage of the GnosisNet test run. The palace lights blacked out for a few seconds. That meant that the whole electrical grid had been rebooted, and by extension, Aisha's brain state itself. The port assigned to her EntheoGenerator was also wide open to a malevolent attack, not to mention a reuptake inhibition that could trigger an overdose of endorphins. Like a circuit breaker after a power surge, her brain's neurochemistry needed to be reset, and quickly.

Some of the network gurus had more sinister theories. Since Amir's decision to perform the dump had not been greenlit by or even proposed to the Ulema, the hidden powers may have blacked out the grid in retribution. It could also have been a way for them to mask their suddenly exposed incompetence of assuring that every citizen (no exceptions) was allotted his or her needed blend of salvinorin A and current permutation of the brain's endogenous neurotransmitters. All subsequent level manipulations would be either of a punitive or troubleshooting nature.

Because I was off-grid, I didn't get to feel for myself what kind of interaction one underwent with the system. The biofeedback/output assessor considered a person's overall current state of happiness, needs, wants, and expectations of civic duty. Any extraneous attitudes like anger toward others, resentment for one's current predicament, or even just jadedness, computed a prescription of not only a tailored cocktail of neurotransmitters, but a syllabus of actions to be taken and actions to be avoided. And then came the exogenous substance: salvia for the beta test, qat for the eventual future. I couldn't figure out why they didn't run the test with the intended qat.

An impersonal, incompetent form of governance was about to be launched upon a people. It would descend upon the city like a noxious dust cloud, toxic to everyone and with nowhere else to go. What a terrible idea, GnosisNet. The diffusion of responsibility would make it only worse. I hoped every Mohammedan prayed to stave it off.

The eunuch's gloating at Aisha's predicament made me wish upon him a violence that I was incapable of administering. So it came as a blessing that what should come banging on the glass double doors leading to the control room but the wayward violinist. Caught up in its own electrical entropy, the robot continued with its rampage in search of music to play as if the test run had never happened. The Saudi mechanic in charge of the robot chamber ensemble abandoned the palace along with various other menial workers who deemed the atmosphere too fraught with risk to endure for such meager pay.

All hell broke loose. People scampered about, trying to figure out how to deal with the robot violinist that was thrashing down the double doors with its violin bow. I was astonished that no kill switch existed for the robot. Like all inventors in love with their creations, the robot designers never envisioned their handiwork physically maiming the people whom it was intended to provide with musical enjoyment.

Aisha lay on the ground, feet away from the control panel. Blood continued trickling out her nostrils. It looked like red watercolor. The eunuch said that the pretty calligraphy spilling on the floor would more than justify her demise.

My arabesque circuitry throbbed beyond the confines of my skin. The mayhem around me kept the rhythm of my heart. My own blood ushered out the impetus of the world. I was responsible for everything, regardless of whether or not my brain knew it. A deafening fizz accompanied my molecules as they dissipated into the furthest reaches of the universe.

An infinitesimally small being emerged from the vastness to say, "They have monstrous plans for us."

The robot violinist had its right side through the shattered door, kept wedged out only by his oaken instrument.

I didn't know what became of Aisha, but everyone dashed to safety. Some found exits that led to stairwells. I followed three people who escaped through an air duct above the ceiling panels . As we scampered away , we could hear the swishing violin bow cutting through the air. The cybernetic buzz of the robot's joints went into a frenzy. Basically a CNC machine, the robot possessed superhuman strength , but would likely be too stupid to go climbing after us. That instinct to harm human flesh upon the absence of sheet music must have been programmed into its software. Either that or it had been hacked.

A dizzy spell overtook me up in the air ducts, and I had to stop for a bit in order for the salvia-induced plaid clouds to disperse. Once lucid, I began crawling so quickly through the air duct, rife with a mortal terror that rendered me sober. I ran into the aesthetically-pleasing behind of a silver-negligéed concubine. She heard me and looked over her shoulder, offering a teary apology for being so slow. It was Nur. I patted her right lower leg. "Don't worry. We'll be fine." I wouldn't dare say otherwise.

She waddled around to face me. Soaked tresses of hair clung to her pretty, sweating, weeping face. She had fared well from the endorphin dump. "Why is this happening? Why?"

"They intend to fix these things," I said. I palmed her smooth face. "Now, let's keep going. What are they saying on the Ticker?" The Ticker was the online feature that scrolled across the bottom edge a person's autorama screen, flashing the latest headlines. It just as often created the news as report about it. "Is there anything about your endorphin dump or the robot?" If our plight had become public knowledge, it would hopefully soon be tended to. She looked up at me and shook her head. She was on the verge of erupting into full-blown hysteria.

I clasped my hands around her neck and touched my forehead to hers, telepathically conveying calm. And she kissed me.

Her lips had the sweetness and texture of an apricot. It was delightful enough to send me spiraling back through the Salviasphere for a quick moment, during which time, yes, Armageddon proved aphrodisiacal. Her outfit morphed from the silver negligée into an entomological wonder of black leather and red lace. It had a crustacean's hardness, which made the tender flesh underneath all the more exiting once got to. An expert in contortion, she made a non-Euclidean display there in that confined space. She forgot terror and fear while moaning a pleasure that bloomed hotly in my ear. The danger below didn't matter anymore. The technique that nature had programmed to create life set into play in order to affirm it, damn the torpedoes, full speed ahead, T-minus eternity.

IMAGINAL MATH AND
THE BLACK LIGHT

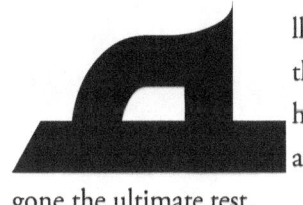ll the minutiae of the world thrummed the oud strings that held my separated halves together. They would never snap at this point. Their pliability had undergone the ultimate test.

I rode the wings of Hamid's voice, a contralto composed of a thousand desert-bound locusts. He told me of Issa, the Effervescent One, the Ishraqi whose complete story resulted in death upon its listening. "Don't worry, sir. I will exclude enough to leave you peering over the precipice. To know the story is not fatal. Nor to tell it in its entirety. But to hear it in a certain sequence causes cardiac arrest."

As Hamid spoke, I sat listening to the ever-shifting Perennial Music, staring at the frantic but fluid movements of the sheet-shifters. It occurred to me that they would somehow be the source of the music they deposited on the musicians' stands. I didn't know what caused that idea in me, other than an intuition brought on by a final crest in the dying salvia trip. I couldn't dispel it like the countless other ideas that the Divine Shepardess bestowed upon me. It stuck and would not be shaken off.

So the Effervescent One went by the name of Issa. That was Arabic for Jesus Christ, but whatever.

"Sir," spoke Hamid, and then he cleared his throat with an earth-shattering harumph. He pondered a few measures of the music onstage, as if taking in a facsimile of the universe, which he felt not long for. "Sir," he began again, "since I may not see the light of day, I may as well peel back the onion skins, as it were, and reveal to you the pearl of contention for which my mortality appears to be in jeopardy."

"Young man," I said, "your EntheoGenerator should have cut off already. There should be no more salvia, ergo no more mullahs. The GnosisNet test run stopped moments ago."

"You don't seem to understand, sir. I have been in red-frame for some time. I am to behave, lest the guys and the old woman pay me another visit. But no matter. That is not the point. The point now is this. And I will deny you the necessary tidbits, because I don't want to narrate you to your grave. They say only the narratrix can spin the yarn with such élan that the listener will not perish. I am skeptical. Even Zenki, who has tried three times, could not pull off the feat without having a hat trick of corpses thud onto the carpet at his feet. And I don't believe her abilities to be superior to his. Half of her reputation is built on the spreading of her legs unto the sultanate stick."

I shot murder at him. "I detect an unwarranted hate for her in your tone. What the hell has she ever done to you?"

Not wanting to give me further offense, he hesitated. He eventually elaborated. "She has given us storytellers a bad name. Also, she has—"

"How so?" I interrupted. "How has she given you and your ilk a bad name?"

"She has threshed fiction together with truth, and sold it as either of the two. Also, she has held the souls of all of Aswadibad's people hostage with her spinning device. She has sculpted people's secrets and deepest desires into art. She has harnessed the evils of the panopticon for her edification."

That would be the Death Module. The anarchists were still trying to breach the Faraday cage in order to destroy it.

"Now there is math, sir, as we know it. Arithmetic, algebra, geometry, calculus, trigonometry, et cetera. Then there is imaginal math."

"Sort of like quantum math?"

Hamid raised a scoffing eyebrow. "No. Not at all. Quantum math would be but a part of regular math. I will speak of imaginal math."

"Speak away then." I looked about the rows of listeners. All of them were too engrossed in the music to eavesdrop.

"I shall, sir."

"So," I said, sending my eyes in back-and-forth arcs, signaling the coast to be clear. "Imaginal math."

"Yes."

"Like imaginary?"

"No," he fired back. "No. No. Imaginal. Not imaginary."

I knew the difference. I wanted to be sure that he did as well.

"Imaginal math," he began, "cannot be done with the aid of a calculator. It cannot be tabulated with an abacus, or paper and pen. No earthly accountant would do well to use it for double-entry bookkeeping. No, imaginal math is a trade reserved for the very, very few. Though you can understand its basic principles, you will in no wise ever know how to use it. It cannot be bequeathed to or learned by the likes of your or me. It can only be used by the Nine."

"The Nine?"

"Sir," Hamid howled. He had had enough. "If you keep interrupting me, the story will surely never kill you. But I, sir, for I detest being cut off, will expire your pulse myself." He clenched at my imaginary neck with his meaty talons and wrung away.

"Sorry," I whimpered, and slung low in my seat. I was pleased to see him now completely sober. The Perennial Music paid us no mind.

"The Nine wield the imaginal math like a cave explorer at Lascaux would hold a torch. Our math is used to dissect the workings of harmony, of concordance, of physical order. We use it to construct machines and to send information back and forth. We use it to eat. But imaginal math, as used by the Nine, is employed in order to decode heaven and harness the Black Light.

"Much like an operation performed by occultists of the Western Esoteric Tradition, upon whose necks shall fall Allah's ire for dealing in those dark and Shaitanic arts, so is imaginal math an operation reachable only by years of rigorous training. Only those for whom it is intended may deal in it with Allah's blessing, for anyone else to toil therewith would be engaging in a folly meritorious of hellfire, not to mention wasting their time. Indeed, imaginal math can only ever be performed by the Nine. For their very essence is needed to make it manifest. They themselves are embedded into its secret and strange operations. There is an auto-cannibalism to this effort. You might not be aware that the colors of pigment act differently than those of light. For instance: red, blue, and yellow are the former's primaries; whereas the latter's are red, blue, and green. Before the particle/wave debate was closed for good with a resounding thud, the only explanation we had for this discrepancy was not pigments' varying degrees of light absorption, but the colors' behaviors in different media. Now this is surely not true. We are lucky to see these phenomena, colors.

But instead of reveling in their endless splendor, we take them for granted. We grow used to them. We become accustomed and even jaded by their presence, much as an Ishraqi follower of the Iranian mystic Suhrawardi grows jaded by the baubles of this material existence. So what is the key to undying astonishment?"

"Drugs," I offered. "And lots of them."

He shook his head in disdain. "I doubt that it is your terrible salvia. Surely, they could have at least chosen a more benevolent hallucinogen. How does a child begin to lose his sense of wonder? Is it the smarting pains of reality that take a toll? Do the bruises and scars inflicted by the cruel world chip away at the innocence of wonderment? Like all other things, it's a matter of perception. So what does an Ishraqi do? What means of recuperating astonishment are at an ascetic's disposal, especially for one dressed in drab, white linen and ordered to withdraw from the sinful world?"

"The Black Light," I concluded.

Hamid was torn between the default fury of being interrupted and an avuncular pride in my answering correctly. He sighed before continuing. "I myself will not live to see the Black Light, unless it grace me with its presence once Allah chooses to dispatch me from this husk of a body and welcome me into His arms. See, the Black Light shines darkly only to those who don't know how to properly look at it. That would be all of us but the Nine. Now the Nine are trans-temporal, in that they exist in the imaginal realm, which eschews time. The very first of the Nine is Mohammed, upon whose person be Allah's eternal grace. Others include Suhrawardi, the grand codifier of the imaginal math; Al-Khidr, the Green One; and the Effervescent One, who is of this era, and is known better as Issa. But Issa is yet another pseudonym to his real name.

"There are untold struggles among the Nine that shall never be known. There are tiffs like those that occur within any close-knit group, be it a family, a fraternal order, a committee, the Ulema. But there are every so often rifts brought on by acts deemed unpardonable.

"The Black Light is just that: black. But it is light in the most scientific sense. It is not the absence of light, as blackness tends to be. It shines darkly. Were we to gaze upon it, we would merely be casting our heads down into a yawning abyss, like peering down into the nothingness of a deep chasm. But one can learn how to see in its effulgent splendor. The ability to see this light is no longer limited to the Nine. Only the creation of it remains their exclusive domain. I have, as I have already stated, never seen it; but I have been told that it shimmers with a brilliance not to be found in the primary colors of either pigment or light. Sir, the Black Light is an entirely new primary color. I could not begin to do it justice, as description relies upon antecedents, of which I, nor you, have none. But there is to be found astonishment."

"What about the Effervescent One? What's his deal? He sounds like a self-righteous prick to me." Timpani rumbled as if in agreement, then the entire percussion section lapsed into a minimalist fugue.

"Issa, the Effervescent one, is a native of rural north Aswadistan. His family migrated to the capital when he was but a babe. He received his education at one of the madrasas funded by the sultan's wife (sorry: ex-sultan's ex-wife), and then received tutelage at various illumination farms. When little, he survived a vicious dog attack that disfigured his face, though he underwent surgery that restored his visage, save for a bum eye. Many believe that this compromised stereoscopic vision of his, along with a propensity toward the austere, allowed him to see the untrammeled effulgence of the Black Light. But this is silly. Any ability to see that can only be the result of the operations of imaginal math. In imaginal math, the integers are not numbers, but acts. Acts of audacity and unrelenting fortitude. Its arithmetic is one of agony."

I didn't know what happened to Hamid. The oafish but gentle storyteller who was breaking the story of Issa to me with a jackhammer tongue against the concrete sledge of secrecy just vanished. The Perennial Music's musical notes nibbled at his flesh like so many sonic piranhas. I didn't recall a sudden halt in his story. A sequence in time seemed to have been right where he should have been. He was simply gone.

I began walking back to the palace, since nothing else seemed sensible. I found myself at the outdoor discotheque where Jafar the magician had rescued me from that marionette Nubian waitress. Balloons of all shapes, sizes, and colors floated about. They wafted in the air like the desires of the dancers maneuvering on the platforms, reminding me of Zenki's demon story.

Hamid's Issa story continued. I did not ask for it to. I accosted no one concerning it. It just happened. It may have been Hamid's doing. I don't know. It meant I was being narrated to the gallows—the scaffolding made of intrigue, the noose around my neck fashioned from metaphysical twine, and the impetus to kick the stand out from under my feet my own damn curiosity and nosey sense of righteousness.

I settled on a rising and falling platform whose color ran through all the neon. I was nursing an asti spumante when I became surrounded by a fishmonger, a moneylender, a barber, and a whore. They all wore curious get-ups of shiny leather and transparent lace. Their intent to close on me worried me at first; but they appeared to be merely coping with the portents of GnosisNet by getting shitfaced with wine before that itself became, if not outlawed, strongly advised against, what with an SSRI that would render a mix with alcohol deadly.

"Are you proficient at addition?" asked the moneylender, a rickety hand on my shoulder. "I am. It's what allowed generations of my family, myself included, to prosper. One plus one should make three. If this isn't your result, then you should find yourself another trade. What is it that you do?"

"I am a peace broker. They brought me, along with others from all over the world, to help people with the transition."

"You are not from here?" asked the fishmonger, who smelled of fish. He had the digitized, cyborg voice that had recently become fashionable among hip gender-benders, the so-called Undecideds.

"Originally, yes. Venetian by upbringing."

"Would you select a quickie," asked the whore, "or a long, drawn-out session better known as lovemaking?" She was the tallest of the four, possessing a marvelous ass, generous thighs to go with it, and a pout that would turn the Arctic Circle into a second Sahara.

"Venetians love their glass, don't they?" said the fishmonger. "To see through a Murano hookah while puffing on some vanilla blend is delightful. I have tried it. Though not there. Here. I like how the light refracts through the glass. It's almost as if you can see a heretofore unknown color."

"Black Light," I muttered. Enough of the bullshit. They coughed clockwise. "Is that not what you're referring to?"

"Yes," said the barber.

"Is the man who goes by the name of Issa here?"

"No," said the barber.

"Do you know where he may be?"

"That is not to say," said the whore, snaking a long, bangled arm around my neck, "that he is averse to the fermented drinks. Or a session of life-affirming uh-uh-uh."

"Issa will be found and killed," said the moneylender. His rickety hand snatched at a tubular pink balloon and popped it.

"To wield the imaginal math takes great responsibility," said the whore, pecking at my neck.

"And to abuse it is tantamount to blasphemy," said the fishmonger in his cyborg voice. He downed a snifter of chardonnay and sent it to the glittered dance floor with a crash. "Allah cannot forgive one who has hijacked the rainbow." He belched cybernetically.

"Have any of you seen this new color?"

"No," said the barber.

"Is it seeable by the likes of you and me?"

"No," said the barber.

"At least for now," said the whore. "Issa has been trying to impart it to the world as an egalitarian gesture. All wrong, that. This is the reason for his ostracism. It is well-deserved. There should be an order to these things. I can barely manage a wardrobe with red, black, and white. Allah forefend another color. I have no use for green. What is your opinion on green?" She gazed at me accusingly and chromo-morphed her leather and lace halter top from black into light green.

"I concur," I said. "Green should be relegated to lawns and hedgerows. The less green in the world, the better."

She smiled perfect teeth at me and morphed her dress back to black. The pink lip gloss enclosing her mouth lacerated my despair with a gash of promise.

"You have met the Effervescent One," said the moneylender. "You just don't know it. Therefore, you are not complicit."

"I'm sorry," I begged. "I've met no such person."

"Issa is many things to many people. That is what makes him effervescent. Don't worry. It's not your fault. I have been in contact with him twice, and knew it not at those times. I only caught on until much later. The realization dawned on me only upon reflection. That is how he interacts with us. His presence, like all of ours, is fleeting. But an imprint remains. It seeps into your pores and saturates you with serenity. But this is the serenity of Shaitan. You must undergo ten ablutions, one each day after morning prayer."

"Is he the agent of Shaitan? Or is he the Enemy Himself?"

"No," said the barber. "No."

"He is merely misguided?"

"Yes," said the barber.

"That does not mean that he is to be punished any less," said the whore. She snapped her mouth at a red balloon, popping it.

"What do you guys know of Al-Khidr?" I asked. I downed my asti spumante.

"The Green One," asked the fishmonger in his cybernetic voice. "He is of no consequence."

"Is he one of the Nine?" I asked.

"Yes," said the barber.

I clutched at the barber's throat. "Hamid! Is it you?"

"No!" screamed the barber, and wrested my hands away from his neck with a strength that belied his short, gaunt frame.

I made a mad dash off the platform and fell precipitously onto another platform that happened to be at its nadir. I hopscotched my way out of the discotheque and bolted into a pitch-dark alley.

"SOVEREIGNTY OF THE SENSES"

I was back at the palace. Najwa stood facing me. "You and I are outlaws for being logged off. But there exists no enforcement mechanism to make us log on and therein punish us for the seditious act of seeking privacy. The Ulema figures that anyone in his or her right mind would never give up the amenity ensemble of the autorama in order to possess this chimera known to mystics as mental sovereignty. Are you a mystic? You don't seem to be, other than the shamanism you excel in. I sure as hell am not."

We were in front of a minaret window, not caring about the threat of an anarchist barging in on a magic carpet or a ray gun of theirs knocking our heads off. A delightful wind blew in, parceling itself out through the narrow minaret's other windows. The ends of her loose, long hair reached rabidly for her slender waist. She had on white yoga pants and a matching blouse that showed a toned midriff.

I hadn't known until then that the regimen for maintaining her athletic physique was a blend of sanda (Chinese kickboxing), Russian sambo, and parkour—in which the objective was to use all six sides of a padded chamber, grappling an automated foam opponent to target surfaces or striking said opponent once set in certain zones. I saw her engage in the sport with proficiency, though she was soundly defeated by another girl, a Turkmen masseuse recently returned to the palace after the test run. Flushed in sweat, she excused herself to shower.

She later insisted that we go to the Great Auditorium and waylay a sheet-shifter acquaintance of hers, one Ramsey, who could maybe produce sheet music complicated enough to placate the wayward robot violinist still running unchecked. Since no one's Ticker had advertised the less-than-benign goings-on of the palace, and the Saudi mechanic was never to return, I agreed that someone had to do something about that murderous musician. But I thought there was no way of mollifying the violinist. He had been likely been hacked.

Earlier, she had found Nur and me scampering down the hall after having emerged from the air duct. A patina of fornication and grave danger shimmered on our skins. She said nothing of it and conducted us to safety through the kitchen, where Nur quietly disappeared. Najwa led me into the parlor where she told her stories.

The renaissance of her reputation had jumpstarted an enthusiasm in her I had not seen up to that point. The almost bedridden sense of being unable to tear herself away from the palace was gone. The symbiosis of her and that architectural institution of the sultanate had been shaken as much as by her newfound approval among those at the palace as by the distrust that everyone had to have for the Ulema once they bungled admittedly minor but no less negligible facts of municipal responsibility during the Gnosis-Net mock run.

Her willingness to actually leave the palace didn't therefore boggle me. I was game.

"I have never heard the Perennial Music," she admitted. More unbelievable than that was her instant conjecture on how it just might be composed. It had something to do with the mysterious sheet-shifters and with *fana'*.

"I'm sorry," I said. "I'm terrible at imaginal math."

She shot me a look of suspicion. She then excused herself and came back sealed up in a skin-tight pink aeronaut suit. "Let us go, then." She then produced a bundle from a gilt chest that sat in a corner under a wicker table. "Abracadabra," she howled, and the dusty quadrangular object came to life.

It would be forgivable to think that the wind entering the minaret was causing the coarse, beaten-up carpet to suspend itself in the air. Then, I caught a strong gust to the face, and the thing did not move from its head-high position. From the same gilt chest, she produced a pink plastic helmet. She gathered up her hair and fit it up into the helmet before setting it down over her head. She lifted the tinted visor up and glanced at me, speaking in Arabic. I was able to pick up something about "al-masjid" and "al-musiqa'a." She was presenting coordinates to the magic carpet, allowing it to buffer its vector with the air-traffic committee that sanctioned all routes and held a nearly spotless record of avoiding mid-air collisions. The newer models had magnetic fields that prohibited contact.

This older device of hers didn't work on the neural networking that the newer ones did. It was instead operated by a see-screen hologram on the visor. She commanded the carpet to descend knee high. She climbed onto it and beckoned me to do the same with a come-hither nod that I wished I still had my autorama installed in order to save.

Small black antennae at the top sides of her helmet gave her a feline aspect. Her mezzo-soprano purred a directive, and the carpet steadily rose. I was behind her at an angle, so I could see a lump of reservation catch in her throat. With a jerk, we shot out the minaret window, and we were off.

It was dusk outside. All the lights from the buildings below made nigh everything visible. The neon platforms of the discotheque city blocks away descended and rose like the undulating form of a sleeping abomination. The night was silent. The anarchists were nowhere to be seen. They had retreated to their home back in the desert.

I jolted as she made the carpet cut an upward angle rather than equilaterally raise all four antennaed corners. We headed toward the top of the palace. She wanted to check up on the Death Module while we were at it.

The giant device came into view like world-famous monuments tend to do when you stumble upon them. They strike awe in your heart and set the tone until you are gone, disappearing around the corner. We circled around the spinning monstrosity. I could hear a whir of whispered prayers and pleas. If demons snacked on the hopes of the desperate, it would surely be here. We hovered still for a moment. She glanced over her left shoulder at me. "I don't know if you were aware," she said, "but Rose never came back. She was last seen weeks ago." I feigned surprise.

The device was the cloaca of the spiritual sewage system that began with each person's heart and ended in the sky. "Don't reach your arm out," she advised. "You will die." She rolled her left sleeve up to the elbow. Her hennaed hand reached for that device of death. The dexterity required to fly one of the older magic carpets was largely visual, in that you had to guide your trajectory by navigating an icon along a congested map, while simultaneously seeing the live traffic about you. It was worthy of a citation to stray from your elevation vector as much as it was to leave your authorized lane, and even the most thrill-seeking sort were leery of going renegade when a collision would be so terrible, both above and below.

I meant to ask Najwa questions about the monuments we

flew over, but my acrophobia got the better of me. I didn't wish
to distract her. Like on airplanes, I plopped a few drops of salvia
tincture under my tongue. This caused the city to come to life.
Yes, the colors popped with rebellion through the lit nocturne, but
the buildings as a whole began exuding an anger. Whether it was
smoke billowing from the chimneys, or the staccato of those flying
around or past us, that anger was a response to the GnosisNet test-
run debacle. And it was due not to the few, and even minor,
slipups of governance, but to the sinister prospect of having to
relinquish one's mental sovereignty not to an admittedly jagged
entheogen like salvia divinorum —but more so to the unseen
cabal who were to regulate the citizens' dosages with impunity.

I could see the Great Auditorium way off in the distance. Its
rotunda rivaled that of the Al-Masjid Al-Ahmar, though it lacked
the minarets and was mostly sealed off from sight by a semicircle
of business and residential high-rises. Of the two imposing structures, people convened there to celebrate life by living it; in the
mosque, they convened to give thanks for that life. Either way,
what rigmarole was life. What folly man had in that he chose to
gather up to more like himself in fabricated structures, when he
should know himself by fleeing into the vast, empty desert. Better
the unforgiving terrain of desolation than the grudging poison of
the forgiving fellow man.

But never mind my pontification. It was all a preset brought
on by the drugs. The salvia chose, like always, to speak through
me. I was as vacuous a vessel as everyone else under normal condi-
tions. Drugs usually clasped a hero's cape around my neck with a
brooch of self-righteousness, and I could not yank it off. I had to
wait for it to subside.

Gathering up my guts, I twisted around to look back at the
onion-domed palace. It was the most imposing building of the city,

dwarfing nearby mosques and business high-rises. And perched atop it was the Death Module.

But we did not make it to the Great Auditorium to listen to the Perennial Music and recruit a sheet-shifter acquaintance of hers.

Najwa slowly raised aloft her left arm, balled her hand into a knuckled lady's fist, and rapped down on her plastic pink helmet. The magic carpet jolted twice and whiplashed us at top speed toward a thirty-story building, barely missing a collision with the glass side halfway up before nose-diving toward the street. Neither of us screamed. We leveled off at pedestrian height and threaded through bazaars and fruit stands, really stirring up a ruckus. "I thought you knew what you were doing!" I yelled, and it echoed off the sheer skyscraper walls. There was no doubt that everyone heard my despair.

She raised her hands, palms up. We began slaloming back and forth, having to clutch onto the carpet's sides as counterbalance. Someone was steering us, for we narrowly missed countless people and stacks of wares. We did punch through a pyramid of blue milk crates. Najwa shielded her face with her forearms. The force sent her back into me. She quickly steadied herself, trying in vain to man the craft through her visor.

I was able to catch quick glances of peoples' terror-stricken faces. The random violence sent shivers of despair through everyone, much like the out-of-control robot musician back at the palace. Once more, the reins of technology were beginning to slacken, and it was again terrifying. A few children cried to their parents at the speed and aggression of the wayward machine. Fruit vendors began pelting us with their citrus. Discombobulated camels started kicking at random before tearing off and running freely down the streets.

We were steered head-on toward another skyscraper and shot up vertically just in time. We circled the building twice before being settled into a steady pace, which we kept as we made our way east out into the desert. I caught my breath.

It was during that starry-skied flight when my self that was accompanying Najwa began to feel radically intervening cross-sections of my other self, lastly remembered as being at the discotheque after having listened to the Perennial Music with Hamid. The selves did not quite unify then. There still was the bifurcational fugue state: the other self was mostly occluded, having perhaps fallen asleep, or perished.

In a short while, Najwa would stitch me back together. Whether done as a diversion or out of genuine care for my mental well-being, she would assemble my selves together with the soothing aloe of her voice, narrating me whole.

Her storytelling kept us on the anarchists' good side while they held us hostage. When I realized who had hacked the magic carpet and steered us out to the middle of nowhere, I expected to have our heads severed. One Marduk, a captain, asked us how it felt to be held captive. Najwa appealed to his sense of liberty by evoking the plight of the S&M genie. So she related that tale I had heard back at the palace. The details were all the same, but the language was different, a bit less florid. It meant she extemporized the words, while the plot itself remained unchanged.

The anarchists took off their black hoods to cackle and guffaw with more ease, and soon our bonds were cut. We were then generously fed chicken and rice. One of the females, all of whom were dressed in black and camouflage, produced wine. We imbibed.

The Scheherazade touch was in full swing. She fleshed out our lack of political leanings by poking fun at the monarchical status quo with "The Retrieval," afterwards recounting the last and

most important details of the Issa story. Therein, the Effervescent
One emerged as this renegade hero out to combat the evils of the
Ulema, the panopticon, and the well-intentioned but no less mis-
guided paradigm about to be put into place.

"Anarchy with an operating system," Marduk called Gnosis-
Net. "You can't perform statesmanship with logarithms. I understand the need for less emotion behind policy. But you need humans who can relate to their constituents. We're not against the
illumination farms and their prospects. We just don't agree that
they should be the shaman philosopher kings. Too much praise for
Plato has been going on. They could be suitable for public office,
but not in charge of drugging everyone silly."

While listening to Marduk go further on, I saw Najwa grow
restless. This was her inability to interact with others without being the center of attention by spooling forth a yarn. It was as bad
as a comedian doing the same material every night for ten years.
It may have been more impressive in that the material comprised
a catalogue of myths, anecdotes, novellas, or just epigraphs, but
it was more pathetic in that it left nothing of her life to the forces of chance. She had seared away the improvisation of everyday
living by rehashing her encyclopedic oeuvre to willing listeners. Like
all liars, she excelled at capturing one's attention for long periods
of time. Emotionally, she had been no better than the amok violinist. She needed to continually manifest her virtuosity in order
to be placated. I wondered what would happen if not a listener
on earth remained.

I saw the idealistic anarchists wilt under her allure. She was
stunning in that skintight pink jumpsuit, and yet no one behaved
untoward with her. I took advantage of the distraction. She told
a tale until dawn about a Capetian monarch who had committed
a Faerie holocaust because that ethereal race bled liquid gold, for

which his queen had obtained an insatiable appetite. I deliberately covered my ears at times in order to not fall prey to its charms. Najwa's velvet tongue unfurled a full universe where winged, saturnine creatures were led in tumbrils to gallows and a regal lady grew fat by engorging on Faerie blood cakes, Faerie blood crêpes, and Faerie blood-smeared fillet mignon. Their over-arching political allegory was that an autocracy, once immune to the shaming of its citizenry, need not fear retribution for indulging in the most dissolute behavior. The whole thing was an update of Suetonius, she told me later.

I accompanied the cupping of my ears with a doubling over and holding of my stomach. A middle-aged woman in the custom-ary camouflage and black walked over to me and expressed con-cern. I winced and groaned. She directed me into a nearby orange tent. She pulled off her black hood. A rush of brown hair cascaded down over her face. Her skin was parched from the desert sun, yet her almond eyes were arresting. It still shocked me when another analog presented his or her self to me without the usual autora-ma veneer that made over the blemishes, scars, and pockmarks that nearly everyone had. It required trust. "My name is Mumtaz." She handed me two capsules and a decanter filled with ice water. "What are you doing with her?"

"I'm glad you guys don't refuse all technology, like medication."

She smiled, a tad cynically. "Analgesics aren't detrimental to privacy, or, for that matter, liberty."

"Nor magic carpets or ray guns."

"Of course not. Your girl's device, on the other hand—"

"But it doesn't belong to the state apparatus." I tossed a capsule against the back of my throat and followed it with a swig from the decanter. The ice water was freezing cold.

"But it does," Mumtaz hissed, afraid of eavesdroppers. "It's vestigial of the old apparatus." She gathered her hair in a bun, a rubber band between her teeth. "The new apparatus just has no need for it. It's an outmoded device. But that doesn't make it any less insidious."

I agreed, but didn't dare say so.

She squinted at me, then fished out from the inside of her camouflage pea coat a brick-sized contraption with an antenna. She spoke into it. A male voice responded through static. "Someone wants to meet you," she said to me. We sat facing each other in silence. I coughed and squirmed around a bit. She continued squinting at me with a smirk on her face.

A muezzin belted out a call to prayer, his voice echoing magisterially across the desert. Mumtaz about-faced away from me and we both knelt. After the prayer, two men entered the tent. The taller one, of athletic build, had a pea coat identical to Mumtaz's. He wore a wool Afghani pakol atop thick, curly hair. He had a thick beard and severe, dark eyes. He pushed in front of him a scrawny figure of average height, dressed in a white Druid robe, Eastern European-looking.

As if having rehearsed the layout, Mumtaz shuffled over to her left, allowing the Druid figure to sit in her place, while the tall man, likely whom she spoke to with the device, sat on his right side. The tall man and Mumtaz eyed each other, then me. He then nodded.

At which point the Druid figure pulled his hood over his head, covering all his features. From under his robe he drew out an obsidian-looking amulet dangling from his neck. He aimed it squarely at me and a wide beam of strange-colored light engulfed me.

I saw something I had never before seen. I saw the physical reel of thoughts. Concepts, ideas, opinions, tidbits of knowledge—all these things were made manifest with these ribbons of light that

flitted about like panicking tendrils of a confused, otherworldly creature not knowing its purpose of existence. An important
part of the story that I had known all along, but hadn't known
I had known it, was that I barely knew it then, once it had been
imparted to me.

I did not witness a narrative unfold. I did not even learn anything in the purest sense of the word. I emerged from the transfer
already with a byzantine story implanted deeply in my head, intri-
cately bound by synapses that had been through my past. It was almost as if the story were there all along. My errant search for a purpose in Aswadistan, and a desperate scheme to escape, now seemed
to have been clouded in ignorance. I had been reunited with my
own mental past. A gaping hole was no longer there. Missing se-
quences were back in place, where they should have been all along.

This would be the logical, perhaps last, step in the natural
progression from carrier pigeons, telegraphs, fiber optics. This was
the new protocol. This was true telepathy. This would be the new
bandwidth, cracking everything wide open, transcending the binary system of digital, transcending whole numbers and exchanging
information faster than the speed of light. For the Black Light arrived at its destination at the same time that it left its origin. It was
the data transfer protocol of superposition.

If a black hole, holographic in nature, was a two-dimensional
memory chip holding the history of an entire galaxy, then a ray of
the Black Light, smaller in scale, was the repository for a now-dead
soul. If a black hole was a graveyard where light went to rest and
die, then a ray of the Black Light was a tightly-wound bundle of
all the colors. It did not shoehorn itself into the spectrum. It was all
colors, though not black as a result. It transcended black to those
who knew how to see it. It seemed Mumtaz had not in fact given
me a painkiller. She had fed me an inhibitor of some sort.

"All right," the tall, bearded man said. "First of all, in order to see what you just did, to experience that color, one must be capable of an unadulterated sense of sight, namely the kind possible by being offline. Mr.—"

"Outernationalist," I said, awash in the aftermath of experiencing eternity.

"Outernationalist. Pleased to meet you. Othman." He appeared to hold out a hand for me to shake. I searched for it and eventually found it. "So," he said, "what happened to your autorama?"

I rubbed my eyes with my fists to reintroduce the colors I was accustomed to seeing. "I had it surgically removed."

"Why?" Othman asked.

I didn't answer. I guess I forgot the reason. Something to do with Najwa, I think. Something to do with love. Had I been in love? "Out of love," I answered.

Othman and Mumtaz exchanged lurid glances. He chuckled. "And what happened to your guardian angel, that you should have insinuated yourself into the former sultan's harem?" He reached for the decanter of ice water and handed it to me.

I imbibed. The coldness knocked me halfway back to normal. "I never really had one. We don't use those in Venice. We're comfortable with tragedy, I suppose. Opera and all that. I did get one briefly once here, on recommendation. But it drove me insane. The pop-ups were invasive in the extreme."

Like everyone else I had come into contact with, he squinted at me. He then engaged in an optical semaphore with Mumtaz that resulted in his communicating via the bricklike device with a superior. A decision came down from higher up. It involved the sheet-shifter, who had since thrown his hood back and sat dormant like an uncharged robot. But he came violently to life when Othman announced what must have been his fate, clutching at his arm and yanking him up to his feet. The sheet-shifter, long rendered mute by his guild's single-minded purpose to provide for the Perennial Music, erupted into a cowardly, squealing protest that was to no avail. A short, stocky anarchist came into the tent and whisked him away.

I asked about his fate. Neither of the two bothered to answer.

"So," I said, "what do you want from me?"

Mumtaz spoke. "We want to know what it is that you want." She clearly had some clout in how things ran in their camp. She looked at her peer, then continued. "We've been following you in your entheogenic journeys. And we've noticed that you haven't been exactly gung-ho in your hired duties. Are you less than enthusiastic in their cause?"

"I have reservations, yes. Plus, how the hell can they know if I've been cleaning house if they don't even have the keys to the door? GnosisNet is going to be a monumental failure. I just know it. I figure the more bugs in place, the better. Let the system fail so that it may be holistically fixed, if not altogether scrapped."

"What's your motive if you don't believe in the cause you've been employed to facilitate? Or are you just a starving mercenary?"

Giving up on money had been a long, drawn-out affair. Sometime during the extraction of my autorama, I sort of forgot about it. "No," I said. "Once I became a palace leech like all the others who don't collect stipends, like the cooks, the chambermaids, the elevator mechanics, the storyteller, I didn't need it anymore." I had no way of even checking my bank account to which the Ulema was wiring my weekly salary. "Honestly, I'm afraid of what GnosisNet has in store. I would like to return to Venice, really." I took a sip from the decanter to evince calm.

"What would you do back there?"

"Go back to rescuing affluenza idiots from their bad trips. Or deprogramming psychonauts of their psychobabble. It's not glorious work, but it pays just fine. Plus, it's damn easy. And I get free tincture."

Othman elevator-eyed me curiously, smiling, then said, "I thought salvia wasn't addictive."

I laughed. "It's not supposed to be. I guess I fetishized it enough to make it so. But yes, you're right. It is not physically nor psychologically addictive."

"We can help you return to Venice," Mumtaz said, producing a purple hookah that may as well have been from Murano. She gingerly held it out to me.

I took it. I plugged the tube into my mouth and pulled in delicious vanilla smoke.

"What do you like about the drug?" Othman asked.

I blew out smoke. "How reality feels after the trip itself is on the wane. I'm not big on the trip itself. I tend to enjoy the frayed edges of reality that it produces. Like the vox angelica after a chorus has stopped singing, or after the notes on a pipe organ. By the way, this is tasty." I smoked some more. "What happened to that sheet-shifter who was just here?"

"You don't understand at all," Othman said. "He is no longer a person at this point. He is a shell, a wraith, something with a neck for the Black Light to hang about and direct, a meaty automaton. Don't be fooled by the pleas for mercy. Those were the death throes of the Black Light's will to survive, manifested through human vocal chords. That sheet-shifter had not a thought in his head to call his own. They're all like that."

I pondered the revelation for some time. "Who recruits them?" I wanted answers to the nature of the Perennial Music and its procurers more than anything.

"Issa," Mumtaz said.

"The Effervescent One," I offered.

Mumtaz and Othman glared at each other.

At length, Othman spoke. "For an analog, you sure are privy to a lot of juicy stuff."

"Right place, right time," I immediately offered. I couldn't afford to hesitate. I knew how these people operated. I could have a thousand and one scimitars poised at my neck, but if I kept cool, I could keep them all from moving.

"Has she told her stories to you through your particular wavelength?" asked Othman. "Are you sensible to them where others are not?"

"No, she's as analog as I am. As analog as you guys are. She told them to me with her mouth and voice and imagination. And I heard them with my ears and processed them with my brain." I held my palms out to neutralize any arrogance I may have given off.

"But why you?" Mumtaz asked. "To practice her English?"

I had considered that often. "I was there. Can't you see her now? Outside? Over there? She has an audience. She needs that audience. It's how she validates her existence. Like the tree falling in the forest, she may not exist if no one was around to hear her speak. She filibusters death by narration. She stays in the world by relating bits and pieces of it."

"You sound attached to her," Othman said. "You seem to have feelings for her."

"It has come to that, yes," I said. I took a puff from the hookah and expelled smoke. I handed it to Mumtaz, but she insisted that I hand it to Othman, who took it. "Though I wouldn't call it love. She's obviously a knockout. But she lacks personality. Bits of it do shine through while she narrates. She's like a prism in that respect. Meant to refract light but not possessing any to call her own. No, love her I may not. I do pity her, though. And I've come to care for her a bit. Out of pity, I guess. Pity and love might be different shades of the same thing, I don't know."

Othman and Mumtaz eyed each other again surreptitiously. "Look," Mumtaz said. "We would never harm you needlessly. Not for our cause. You are free to go, contrary to what might seem like your captivity. True, we hacked that magic carpet and brought you out here. But we would never coerce you or compromise your safety. We are not just hospitable like all other peoples who call rugged terrain home. We are cultured and educated enough to know when to be fed up. I know you wish to see Venice again. We can get you home. All you have to do is tell us everything she told you. Or at least the most you can recollect. We don't wish to harm her. We just want to take out her Death Module and undermine her undue influence on the current situation."

Now it was my turn to squint. "How can you get me home? You guys aren't much for tech. And the Venetian embassy has just closed. The only way I can return is if the Ulema absolves me of my outernationalistic duties, or if I am extradited. And trust me. Venice has almost no clout on the world stage. We're still seeking UN status."

"Then you must go above the Ulema," Mumtaz said. She took the hookah from Othman and unraveled the knotted-up tube.

"But no one is above the Ulema," I pleaded. More squinting.

"Wrong," Othman barked. "Al-Raschid is."

I scoffed. "What the hell are you talking about? Al-Raschid is a desperate ex-monarch trying to stay relevant. He's a career politician looking to install a legitimate democratic system. Or so he claims. That and he is up against GnosisNet. He's a long shot to win."

Mumtaz took a long, slow pull on the hookah. She let the vanilla smoke sit a while in her lungs. Then she spoke through the exhaled smoke. The cloud eclipsed both of them. It billowed towards me like a smoldering revelation.

"No, Al-Raschid *is* GnosisNet."

DIVINE TRAUMA

umtaz hinted that I was the Plaid Assassin. The very first story Najwa had told me, concerning a Nizari female hasheesheen during the Crusades, had been a poke at my presence at the palace. I felt at home in the plaid-like reality of the Salviasphere, where the tessellation of events took on a cloth-like aspect. "And where would she have got that info on you before even having met you?" Mumtaz asked, an eyebrow raised.

"It's you she has been trying to placate," Othman said. He held a dark concern for me in his eyes. "What is she if not another malignant bot in the software, waiting to be snuffed out?"

It was evening, and Mumtaz called for a dinner to be brought into the orange tent. I dug in savagely. "I would never harm her," I blurted, mouth smeared with hummus.

"Not physically," Othman said, chomping on an oversized piece of pita bread.

"Nor emotionally," Mumtaz offered.

"No," I pleaded.

"But you already have," she declared, "by telling us what you know."

"Don't fret, Outernationalist," Othman said. "You have done no wrong."

Najwa and I were perched atop the ridge of a high sand dune. Once the sun set, star clusters wasted no time in smearing across the night canopy above. A ferocious wind blew.

She gathered her hair up, exposing the nape of her neck to me by the moonlight. She looked over her shoulder at me. The light in the black pool of a pupil glared at me. "I think they've taken a liking to us. I think we may be safe." Somewhere on that silhouette was an assured smile. I wished to reach out and confirm it. But like in all things with this girl, I desisted.

"You seem to have captivated them," I said.

She clipped her hair in place atop her head. "They're starved for entertainment."

"It's a beautiful night for a story," I said.

She sighed. I thought for a second that she would deny me. Perhaps she knew that it no longer mattered, that she had been found out, that occluding an integral part of a truth was not merely tantamount to committing a white lie. So, she began to tell me,

Quantum Conjugal Visits

One afternoon, when the sun was blazing hot and those who sat on the flea-ridden carpet at Zenki's feet wished for a tale occurring in cold darkness, the old master storyteller obliged them with a truth that rivals the most riveting of fictions in detail and dramatic turns, but is seven times as morally reprehensible in that it steals the listeners of their lives—a crime Zenki has yet to be convicted for only because his telling of that tale has yet to occur, and the corpses that littered that flea-ridden carpet are currently scattered about all of Aswadistan, equipped with pulses and desires, yet to hear the lethal sequence that only proper perceivers of the Black Light could ever stand to endure. Zenki spoke in a whisper.

"If Enoch walked with Allah, then Issa danced with Shaitan. The first is manifestly true, and therefore the second is equally so. For it has been jotted down in the annals of fate that false prophets would come after the true ones; and the truest of all, upon whose head be Allah's grace, would be proceeded by a pageant of charlatans. You've heard of the cessation of oracles at Delphi. You've known for a time that revelation was sealed off for good when Jibreel spoke into the Prophet's ear. Einstein said that Allah doesn't play dice. Ash-Shams reported a century ago that the prima materia used to sculpt the cosmos is inaccessible to the hands of men.

"When peddlers of metaphysical snake oil go shouting about new primary colors from the tops of mountains, the earth trembles with resentment. I hate to be nudged when going about my duties in order to entertain the innovations of fools. The finitude of time doesn't allow for it. Listen, then, ladies and gentlemen, as I tell a tale of divine trauma. I will shift from a whisper to a scream later, and will call for all children to be evacuated. For theirs are not the ears to withstand such a detonation.

"This will concern a permutation of a few key things: the peacock angel, the hijacking of the rainbow, a sheer mountainside, endless love, and what has long been termed singularity but is merely a temporal version of *fana'*.

"About century ago, southwest from here, through Nabataea, beyond the Negev, between the Tigris and Euphrates, in what was once called Kurdistan but has since been referred to as Yezidistan, two star-crossed lovers betrayed their pagan god, which some call a devil, in order to be together in eternity. In Yezidistan, the Kurds do not pray to Allah. They stew in their

own *jahiliyah* for all time. Not coercion through torture, not carpet bombing, not mustard gassing, not even cyber-sabotage—will
shake them of their conviction in their esteem for Malak Tawas,
who some say was once a man, others say never was but was always
the 'peacock angel,' yet others say has been both in succession, and
yet even others suggest never was anything at all.

"All the oil derricks were effigies engulfed in flames, and standing there within that orchard of flames, in tattered rags, hair in
singed pigtails, black oil smeared about her person, was Marjane.
'If I am not to hold him to me in death,' said she, pigtails catch-
ing fire, 'then they will all leave this life likewise alone.' Those
words slithered from her mouth as salamanders of fire. It was her
muttered curse—for all Yezidi women , worse than being
infidels , are now born witches , and all their sons burgeoning
warlocks . Their ability to manipulate the elements , though
repugnant, is impressive.

"The region has been rich in oil for a long time. Decades after
the ousting of the thuggish Baathists, the fragmentation of Iraq
procured peace for a time. The Kurds retained the rights to the
richness beneath their feet, but being a backwards people—even
those under the faith, that being the majority—they sat on it and
did nothing, all while the machinery of the modern world was
grinding with viscosity breakdown from a dearth of fossil fuels.
Who should gain a majority in Kurdistani parliament and have
two successive presidents but the devil-worshipping Yezidis. Why
a people of Allah didn't raise revolt is beyond anyone's comprehension. They must have been under a spell.

"If all Yezidi boys are warlocks, then Omar was a spell-weav-
ing monstrosity of the highest degree, sipping pigs' blood from
a goblet fashioned from a Shia baby skull. Though of magical
mien, and though exceedingly handsome, Omar was a weakling

Sicknesses of all sorts plagued him. He would be ravaged by bouts of coughing . His body would be bedecked in bedsores . Even emergent horns would appear at his temples. It was Allah's way of alerting him of his one-way path to Hell."

"Are there Yezidis to this day?" asked a blond, adolescent girl. Her mouth barely waited for her raised hand to fall back to her side.

There were gasps within Zenki's audience. It was bad protocol to interrupt a narrative, but the old raconteur, never a stickler for custom, had years ago actually begun to encourage questions throughout his storytelling. He felt it allowed him moments to flesh out details and kept him sharp. "It helps suspension of disbelief," he once told me. "It imparts to the listener a sense of participation."

But Zenki, though an expert, was not perfect. He produced a cycloramic screen in midair. A twilight gathering of figures in feathered costumes circumambulated a leaping flame. "Much like the Jews," Zenki explained, "the Yezidis are resilient. For a Kurd is hearty and stubborn. But a Kurd who won't answer Allah's call? Now that is a headstrong son of a bitch."

Zenki's magnanimity would not bear out, however: the askers of questions, always the most curious for detail, would be the first to get knocked off by the narrative. Simply hearing the fatal syllables would not make them so. Those who pieced together the most elaborate versions in their heads thereby loaded their brains with all the more poison. So Zenki would get his revenge after all.

A Maghribi harem girl once asked me, "When did stories begin to kill?"

And I was compelled to answer, "When man began to have an unhealthy want for them." For man succumbs to anything he engages in with excess, be it fornication, gluttony, or patriotism.

Surprise twists, ironic turns, metafictional framing, dangerous usage of the subjunctive tense—these cannot by themselves cause the heart to seize up. But add some lurid intrigue informed by reality, and the admixture becomes all the more toxic.

I am by nature skeptical of everything, so I would never die by a raconteur's lips. The first recorded example of narrative assassination was when Zenki's brother, the more talented, but now deceased, Firas, my predecessor as court storyteller, told a ditty called "The Retrieval." He performed it in front of a crowd of six, all of whom as a result perished. Some say he committed narrative suicide by himself believing overly much in his own story. Others say he could not have done otherwise, for it derived straight from truth. There is a less-touted theory that, much like a perfect map replicated the actual territory it is meant to represent, a masterfully-told narrative, so faithful in its rendition of a fatal incident, would on a molecular level involve the production—through description—of a lethal object, be it a laser gun, a rapier, or a vial of poison. This then would insert in real-time the necessary element of deadliness into the storytelling session. Firas was so descriptive as to transport his listeners into the harrowing situations. An even lesser-known theory posits by adding all this the notion that a masterful recounting, like the bunched-up bellows of time's accordion, so chock-full of detail, amounts to a narrative singularity, wherein fana' is experienced.

I scoff at this, though. I believe it is the awe of such a finely-spun yarn that loops around a listener's neck and hangs him.

I will give a very short and toothless version of "The Retrieval":

There was purported to be a cabal of psychonauts who convened once a year to engage in what they called The Retrieval. At first I didn't know why the Sultan hated this cabal so much, but I then learned that the group had held his ex-wife in the highest honor. For she was the unwilling high priestess of their psychedelic ritual. Once a year they gathered in some unknown locale and took some entheogen or other in order to venture off, hopefully together, into an agreed-upon realm where a piece of a great puzzle waiting to be assembled back in the real world could be mined. Whether or not the Sultan's ex-wife acted as a hierophant in the realm by muttering a piece of the puzzle, said to be verbal, or simply offered up clues as to how and where to retrieve it, I cannot say. But the puzzle, said to be nothing more than a message—perhaps a message of a strange and possibly devastating portent, remains to be learned.

"What is certain, though, is that the Sultan had a cadre of agents working clandestinely to frustrate the efforts of the psychonauts."

Who knows? Perhaps Firas was murdered by Al-Raschid for divulging a less-than-wholesome image of his estranged ex-wife. The Sultan would have been above this in my estimation, so I think a bereaved loved-one may have exacted revenge for Firas's narrative foul play. I sure wouldn't be happy about losing a daughter or brother to plot twists or long-winded appositives.

See, a master storyteller cannot himself see *fana'*, though he may harness it. Either you are properly equipped to experience it or not.

I need not bore you with the nature of *fana'*, since Hamid the fat boy has already done so. I hope he treated you to a fine story. He is not without talent, though he relies overly much on the crutch of other media, your recent time with him at the Great Auditorium being a case in point.

But it was Hamid himself who told me of Issa, the Effervescent One, who gazed upon the Black Light while operating from a cave three-quarters the way up the sheer face of Mount Qaf. He had managed to freeze a rainbow in place, and was tinkering with its properties to duplicate what his meditations had imparted to him in fever states of fasting and praying. He is Islam's Prometheus. Though I believe he still is in possession of a liver.

A bum left eye has been a great boon to him, as it has permitted him to see things from a skewed angle. How fate hinges on childhood accidents never tires of astounding.

Issa is but a two-dimensional surface of the polygonal person they call the Effervescent One, who is multifaceted like a jewel, multiple-personalitied like a schizophrenic, prismed like a spiritual abomination too large for one life. We all contain multitudes, sure; we are all results of more or less continuous life narratives played upon our single vessels called our bodies or selves, but we exist, as far as our consciousnesses tell us, in this plane only. But the Effervescent One is the agglomeration of three or four people, running parallel lives through space-time by vectoring in and out of dimensions. The imaginal math needed to run his super-identity through trans-dimensional gauntlets is beyond our abilities to attain fluency in.

It is this ability that has allowed a version of him to visit me in my own realm, not as Issa, but as Murad, denizen of Hurlqalya, constable of the bejeweled cities of Jabalqa and Jabarsa. This leaves no room for paradox, for the insertion of Murad into my realm means the extraction of another aspect of Issa from same. And this unrefined Issa gets into constant trouble in the imaginal realm. He cannot cope with the molecular severity, and proves himself a moral pariah and borders on causing the Effervescent One's integrity to rupture.

And now, Outernationalist, I spill my heart out to you. I've long held off from doing this, both out of fear of betraying my allegiances in this grand showdown that is about to occur on election day, and out of reluctance to display my emotions, which renders my narrative abilities less omniscient and perfect. Friend, for I hold you to be a dear friend to me, though I know so little about you, my love has always been for things unworldly. And the love of my life exists not on this plane. My paramour is none other than this Murad fellow. Murad, the Ishraqi you've spoken to twice, and who has sired me a son, a beautiful boy who is lost beyond retrieval in far-off Jabarsa, to where I know not the route to take. And this is the meaning for my broken, taped-together, cordoned-off heart.

But to digress from a digression,

I cannot vouch for the magnitude of the broken hearts of Marjane and Dubayb. It would be easy for me to state they could have felt the black pain that I feel, but that would be no better than trite. Every one of us is capable of great sorrows as much as great joys, and it easy to discount the severity of both when concerning others. But the pain of separation was so great for those two that they tinkered with the physics of the universe in order to be together in eternity, and simultaneously sprung traps of revenge upon their tormentors.

The Yezidi lovers' ignorance of Islam was no barometer of their desire, since they grew up in that culture of *jahiliyah*, of ignorance. But their willingness to endure long stretches of hellfire for fleeting moments of conjugal bliss throughout the years is admirable.

Zenki continued. "A wife will be virtuous only insofar as she has yet to be met with the proper temptation. We men are foolish enough to think that as long as we bundle the weaker sex away liked wrapped-up candies, never to satisfy the sweet tooth of a lecher, our honor will remain forever untarnished. For a wife brings dishonor down upon a man's house like a flame can turn a tower to carbon and ash. There is almost no chance of stopping, much less reversing, the destruction wrought by a wife's besmirched honor. Since I myself have no honor, I have chosen a life of bachelorhood.

Far better to not play the honor game at all than to have a negative amount of it.

"One Zumurrud, aged thirty-six, wife to an Iraqi general, and mother of two boys and two girls, wandered from her home one early morning and made a beeline for the center of Tikrit. Despite the cold, she remained uncovered and indecent, leaning for a time against the fountain of the still-empty square. Somnambulism is no excuse for scandalous behavior. If anything, it merely underlines a dark propensity, much like drunkenness, boiling at all times beneath the surface of wakefulness or sobriety.

"That same day, Omar, a beardless boy of sixteen, woke up two hours earlier than usual. He would daily rise along with his father, a recently retired captain in the Iraqi Republican Army, to go work at the family dairy farm. He was not to be found at the kitchen table that day. His mother, who woke every morning along with her husband and son to feed them and see them off, searched in vain for the boy, looking under his covers, peering up on the roof where, despite the cold, he liked to steal away for an hour of reading. He was nowhere to be found.

"The few witnesses to the rendezvous at the square in the center of Tikrit are of little if no credibility. Both are beggars, and one of them a toothless invalid with a goiter the shape of Peru. To hear their testimonies is to not only invite scandal upon two vaunted military families, but to raise the possibility that the evils of Yezidi magic are true. To choose to believe their testimonies is to invite demons into everyday life by subscribing to Yezidi cosmology.

"The culprits were not found in flagrante delicto at the square, but in a room on the fourth floor of a nearby hotel. The thirty-six-year-old mother and wife of four, and the beardless boy of sixteen were skyclad as they had been on their birthdates and were within the pangs and throes of a demonic passion found only in adultery, which they say, I personally would never know, is especially spice-laden, being forbidden by the Book.

"Upon being apprised of their destiny for the boiling lakes of fire, both parties—the woman and the boy—chose merely to smirk."

'Instances of ecstasy,' said Zumurrud , under a hail of stones . . . ' Make eons of excruciation ,' said Omar, burning . . . "Tolerable ," explained Zenki, throwing back an espresso. Applause.

Hamid, trembling, told you, "Sir, Issa is sought by the Ulema for divulging the Black Light to a tier to whom such a luxury should not be accessible. It should be reserved for the very elect, namely the Nine. If the Ulema succeed, they will make it the Eight. Somehow they have decided it to be within their power to alter the count of those versed in the imaginal math."

And then you began trembling as well. He offered you qat, but you were already zonked on your salvia divinorum. You waved away a kabob copter buzzing by your head. Fat Hamid continued. "It now becomes all the easier to believe in the Fall. Adam and Eve partook of the forbidden fruit of knowledge and grew wise to each other's hidden electricity. They learned of other things along the way. But Adam looked askance into the wilderness, to where the first woman had fled, the one the Jews called Lilith. For she wielded fana' in her womb. Adam had felt it while inside her. And he longed for it again. This is the goal of all mysticism and alchemy: to obtain that which Allah has deemed too dangerous for the non-elect to tamper with. It is not quite the domain of Shaitan, for that is the domain of knowing just enough to get yourself in trouble but not enough to get yourself out of it. This explains why those close to Allah have peered into the ghastly visage of Shaitan and have braved it enough in order to see right through it."

Hidden electricity? Seriously? Only a corpulent, thirty-five-year-old virgin would refer to it as such. Not a bad turn of phrase, I suppose, but it betrays his ignorance in all things amorous. And that consequently makes for an unreliable narrator. But whatever. He had a willing audience in you regardless.

"So the Nine aren't necessarily inviolable," you said.

Hamid rubbed his tummy and said, "Certainly not the ninth. Certainly not Issa. Again, his mistake was not that he saw the Black Light, for clearly he was intended to see it, but that he wished to diffuse it throughout the world. He wished to disseminate something utterly arcane and meant to be beyond everyone's abilities to comprehend and perceive, let alone harness. And to top the blasphemy off, he was convinced that he had discovered it all by himself, that not a one—none of the previous eight—had ever laid eyes on it. He sincerely thought it to be a brand-new primary color, along with red, blue, and green. Again, we're dealing with light, not pigment. It'd be similar to someone thinking that a whole number was tucked between three and four, but was no way at all three-and-a-half. You just can't do that. That is, of course, the definition of madness."

"So is Issa mad?" you asked. "Is Murad as well?"

"I don't know what one has to do with the other. What are you talking about? Murad is an Ishraqi. If anything, he's the Ulema's darling. Sir, screw your head on tighter, please."

"Why is Issa called the Effervescent One?" you asked him. At that very moment, unbeknownst to you, one of the anarchists now holding us hostage flung a tracking device known as a Mite at you. See? [Najwa removed the wafer-thin object from my cape.]

Hamid didn't hesitate. "Because he dissected rainbows upon the sheer face of the mountain. The resultant mess of diffuse light caused him to shimmer like a harlequin. Maybe also a jibe at his sanity, sparkling in and out of existence. Kookiness, you know."

"Have you ever met Issa?"

"Of course not, sir. Again, head. Screw. Tighter. Clockwise. Of course not. He runs in circles from which I will forever be sealed off."

"What would be his punishment, were the Ulema to indeed catch him?"

"He has already been punished. He's become a fixture of Yezidi mythology. And every time he is invoked, he feels the very opposite of fana', which is a thousand-and-one cuts across the soles of his feet from Allah's own scimitar."

Adam and Eve, and for that matter Lilith, have nothing to do with this Black Light-centric story. Of course, leave it to the chubby virgin to get the love portion of this story all wrong.

"All projections of Adam and Lilith spread throughout time and space," Zenki continued in his parlor before a captivated audience. "And they became for a moment Omar the Tikriti teenager and Zumurrud the Tikriti wife. The two lovers were set to undergo shame: she death, and he discipline under the lash, since he had fallen to the wiles of an older woman, always the temptress. They were in fact complete strangers. A magnetism in their erogenous zones drew them together, almost inevitably. At times, during interrogation, Zumurrud showed surprise and endless remorse, claiming to have never met the boy. Omar likewise expressed ignorance of the woman's identity, and cited his own innocence, claiming to be a virgin who never did more than gaze at the paper magazines of nude European women they used to print in those times.

"But both parties would lapse into violent convulsions and growling. They had to be tied to their chairs. They were in separate rooms. In deep, guttural voices, they declared love for each other and cursed all of Kurdistan.

"The diffusion of responsibility may dupe even the sharpest of mortals, but not the lancet-sharp intellect of unworldly entities. Even a murderer may lapse into amnesia, and thereby gain a clean conscience. But demons never forget. Their interdimensional state is a punishment meted out by Allah, who has them reap precisely what they sew. Therefore, their own intervention in human affairs is nursed by grudges never to be shucked away.

"Once Zumurrud, bloodied and dirtied on the ground where she was being stoned, succumbed to death for adultery, her paramour, the boy Omar, immediately reverted to his own self. He again pleaded ignorance of the whole ordeal, and genuinely seemed beside himself when presented with a photograph of the perished housewife. Alas, he had never seen her before. Alas, he didn't find her at all attractive.

"Also around the time that the Iraqi general's wife was pronounced no longer of this world, pillars of fire within the ignited oil fields to the north in Yezidi country shot up with the staccato of demonic rage before subsiding with the passivity of bottled-up djinns.

"Another untoward pairing of love happened, this time in Baghdad. Again, the military was involved. And again, a general's integrity was compromised. But this time it was a general himself. And his lover was an eighty-something mother of five, the youngest son a fellow general in the ranks. The amount of scandal caused by this could not be carted away with ten-thousand wheelbarrows. Not only was an irreparable breach caused between the two generals, once close colleagues, but a shake-up in the army bureaucracy shelved a plan in the works to exhaust all the Yezidi oil, which though had been declared off-limits by the UN, did not mean that the last source of funding for Yezidi resistance fighters could not be snuffed out with a few infiltrators for hire. The international community was indignant, sure, but a certain closure loomed once the Yezidi problem seemed on the verge of disappearing.

"But there was a lot of oil in those Yezidi fields, as well as a lot of ire to be leveled at the forces that chose to commit an atrocity worse than a stamping out of rebellion: violating the inalienable right of love.

"Whether Malek Tawas, the 'peacock angel,' had anything to do with Marjane and Dubayb and their undying love for each other, cannot be either proved or disproved. What can be established beyond doubt, however, is that the protracted, perhaps ultimately useless tactic of burning up all of the Yezidi oil was met in duration by the strung-together instances wherein two lovers who had every reason to not know each other had chance meetings at public spaces (a cafe, say, or a bazaar), then retired to private quarters (a seedy hotel room, a cobwebbed tool shed) to engage in unholy copulation that only those possessed by demons of fornication should be capable of. Both parties always bore burn marks caused by either burning oil or brimstone. Some were marked with bedsores, others with contusions and scabs and bite marks made by unknown fauna.

"We as good Muslims can choose to not say a generous word about two ill-fated lovers who loved each other so much in the full bloom of youth and vitality that they vowed beyond all dimensional constraints to, once dead, possess the vessels of living beings in order to come together time and again throughout the ages, and in so doing bring shame and dishonor upon the families of the military leaders responsible not only for their separation as Marjane and Dubayb, but for the atrocities perpetrated on their people.

"Think what you will. I, for one, know that Allah forgives and eventually gathers everyone to Him, no matter how wayward. I also know that this lamp that I hold in my hand would not function were it not for the reservoir of oil that drips and burns therefrom."

Najwa breathed a lie, and I was borne aloft its hot wind like a bird born in mid-flight, knowing no nest or mother to feed me mouth to mouth. Somewhere a cliff sat, where I might take rest, but no one could tell me its whereabouts or its distance measured in fatigue-filled days or anguish-laced nights.

She breathed a truth, and nothing happened, because it ran parallel with the established world. Only acts of creation caused worlds to bloom forth, and denizens to be born therein. The tragedy of all being was to never be able to stand up to the architect of your world.

"Allow me to conclude this story by claiming that I am not responsible for what is your missing sequence. You have taken so much salvia divinorum lately that I'm impressed that you can string together a little linearity in your life and call it an experience. I can see the confusion in your gorgeous green eyes. I can tell you're having difficulty sorting it out. It may seem that two trajectories are to bring you here at this time and place, this lovely *yaum al-juma'ah* evening, on this outsized sand dune, having watched the sun give up on the day like a tired pagan god having run out of worshippers.

"It's the splitting off into two thing you've got going on. One half of you has rightfully led up to this time and place. The other half has snagged itself on a barb somewhere in that Salviasphere of yours. But it will get here in due course. It is currently at the palace. Allow me to narrate you to you:"

An Audience with the Ex-Sultan

The Outernationalist was patted down at each of the four security checkpoints on the way to the sanctum sanctorum of the palace. It was three stories deep in the earth. A cavalcade of civic intent and political bickering went on within the countless rooms of the former sultan's former residence, while, all along, the candidate had been residing in the basement, never having left the premises. After all, when you became such a master at influencing public perception, invisibility and undetected movement came easily. There was literally no threat to his physical person no matter what happened. Nothing leading up to the election, nothing during the tallying of results, nor nothing after—should Al-Raschid win a majority vote as Aswadistan's first democratic president, or should GnosisNet unfold in its Great Launch—could possibly result in the former sultan's safety being compromised. It will be impossible. The Outernationalist noticed that the security detail was decidedly non-threatening. All of the agents, men and women of all ages, and of unimpressive physique, were devoid of firearms. Even the stacks of paperwork were missing. Instead, they assailed him with grudging demeanors, clearly not enjoying an outsider like himself, maybe even a turncoat (or worse, a drug-addled foreigner), gain access to the top-secret chamber and be granted audience with Mehmet Al-Raschid.

He was stone-cold sober. Though a sheath of haze and plaid did seem to infuse the world, as if the world itself had decided to dose on salvia, all while he remained lucid. What an ontological trick that would be to have the universe trip on you, rather than the other way around. The physical laws didn't begin to misbehave, no. Rather, its very existence was a pun, extraneous and frivolous, yet oddly pithy.

They patted him down one last time. "No blunt objects, right?" demanded a portly man in a *kuffiyeh*. He shucked his limbs with beefy hands then nodded him to enter.

Automatic double doors opened, revealing a crimson carpet

that led down a long hallway. The overhead halogen lights were purposely dimmer the closer he got to the room where Mehmet Al-Raschid awaited. Dead silence set his ears to ringing. Down so deep below the surface, within the bedrock, they could have perpetrated unspeakable tortures on people and nary a peep would be heard above.

He looked over his shoulder to find that no one followed him down the hall.

The closer he got to the red-lit chamber, the less sterile was the air. An odor of exertion tinged the place, like someone had been working up a sweat and decided to scurry away. But when he entered the large room lined with instrument panels and monitors, there was no one present. He about-faced twice. What the hell. No one. Nothing.

Then the red lights began to flicker on and off. It was no accident brought on by a brownout. They throbbed with a copulatory pulse that slowly grew quicker. It was curious how the most minute discrepancy in timing to that pulse could evoke an eroticism within an environment that for all intents and purposes should possess nothing of the sort. Combined with the musk of sweat permeating the room, he felt he had just stepped into a milieu where only moments ago an act of Sadean persuasion had just taken place, and the electrical fixtures of the room were mimicking the event like a voyeur obsessed with what had just been seen.

And then feminine moaning started up. It was more unwholesome than titillating. The voice rose and subsided like the swollen belly of a reptile, in anticipation of a greater pleasure waiting to be experienced in the near future, rather than relishing whatever present indulgence was going on. It didn't sound at all like masturbation . He was no expert in female autoerotic pharyngeal fricatives, but it had a rhythm of input from another agent. Another present volition must have been at work, for the moaning dovetailed in and out of synch with the throbbing red lights.

He looked for speakers from which the sound might be broadcast. None. "His Greatness?" he shouted. The honorific caused a brief skip in both the lights and the moaning. But he knew the determination was too great to be interrupted. Already on pace to climax, that pinnacle of purpose and existence would be followed through, even if by impersonal agents. Perhaps this is what it sounded like when two forms of reality copulated. But why, then, the human woman's voice?

The moaning grew louder and louder. An inability to cope with the idea of the ecstasy becoming more and more unbearable turned the moans into cries. Then, after an eternity (which may have been no more than thirty seconds), the red lights pulsated to machine-gun speed, and a peel of orgasm ruptured through the room so loudly, so offensively, that he had to cup his ears.

Instrument panels came to life, initiating indecipherable dialogues between the chamber walls.

On the right side of the room, hundreds of red and green lights flickered on and off in endless permutations, while on the left side BIOS screens scrolled through endless commands of code. Dozens of fans whirred to life.

"His Greatness?" he shouted again, now desperate for human presence. "Sultan Al-Raschid?" Maybe impertinence would insult the ex-monarch enough into making an appearance.

Nothing. There was no furniture present. There was no pitcher of water. Other than a pair of evergreen slippers against the far-left wall, there was no sign of human necessity. Just the computer panels. Directly in front of the entrance was a seven-foot-tall compartment that, though it didn't possess a handle, may have been a door. On both sides of it were monitors of Al-Raschid in various tableaux: press conferences, stumping at the pulpit among large crowds, having lunch with Bedouin in worn tents in the desert. Others were of Al-Raschid in various outfits: three-piece suits, traditional Nabataean garb, a wetsuit, and an Uzbek freedom fighter get-up complete with bandoliers of machine-gun rounds.

Also appearing on monitors were live feeds of 3D billboards all across the country, the ex-sultan acting out a maximum of three-minute hologram loops—all presenting the candidate in favorable scenarios, such as playing cards with hip twenty-somethings, practicing horse archery in Mongolia, splashing about in lime-green swimming trunks at a Russian water park, and serving as a judge at a camel competition. In all of these scenes, he had perfect features: chiseled jaw, cobalt blue eyes, and an immaculately trimmed goatee. In the ones where he lacked clothing, he was maybe two kilos off from having perfectly etched abs, convex pectorals, and marked deltoids.

Underneath the shots passed a ticker of algorithms.

And then something curious happened.

As the lines of code scrolling left to right sped past one particular screen, lights on the nearby panels flickered to life, and Aswadibad's skyline appeared in the background, a tree losing leaves to a breezy wind appearing in the bottom left foreground. Al-Raschid with his back to the camera was all of a sudden walking down a promenade peopled by modern, well-to-do Aswadistani families and robo-vendors. Auto and aerial taxis sped by on the ground and in the air. Al-Raschid turned on cue to the camera and said a trope about modern living and hope. The video suddenly pixelated apart, and the code that had been ticking by underneath was gone.

He caught another video forming: a strapping Al-Raschid donning a tennis outfit moved laterally with world-class agility across a clay court, volleying the ball with an invisible racket back to an off-screen opponent as he launched, again for the prospective viewer, into a platitude about change and hope. A perfect smile never left his face. Not a bead of sweat appeared on his forehead. A racket then appeared in his right hand, along with a headband around his thick, black hair. The loop was just over thirty seconds long. And then the frame of that loop shrunk into the top right corner of the screen, whereupon appeared street addresses of billboards and community intersection feeds where the vignette was to be broadcast.

Startling him out of his transfixed assessment of these artificial Al-Raschids, the seven-foot-tall compartment drew open with a hydraulic whine. Sauna-warm smoke billowed out. Najwa emerged in an evergreen bath robe. The surprise in her eyes upon seeing him mirrored his own. She put a hand to her wet, combed-back hair, then adopted a look of anger.

"What were you doing in there?" he asked. "What is that place?" He pointed whence continued billowing the hot smoke.

She shot a curt glance at him and adjusted her robe. She waddled toward the far-left side of the room, wet feet slapping against the linoleum. She tucked her feet into the slippers and made a beeline for the exit.

He turned and asked again, "What is that place?" He reached for her arm.

She violently yanked free. He caught a glimpse of smooth breasts, brown nipples erect from whatever activity had gone on inside, beyond the smoke. She noticed his ogling and stamped out the room and down the hall, muttering invective under her breath.

"Don't be angry with her," said a man's voice. "You are not at liberty to judge."

It came over a stereophonic intercom, the speakers of which

were not visible either on the walls or the ceiling. Now, rather than a pageantry of real and imagined Al-Raschids filling up the screens, a tessellated head shot of a stern, knit-browed Al-Raschid honeycombed the walls. They all pierced him with severe, judging eyes. A jaw chiseled from an artistry reserved only for regal work left him feeling round-faced and inadequate.

"It has always been purely symbiotic, the relationship. She gets the gratification not to be found in the analog world, and I get a validation that pushes me beyond the digital prison that incarcerates my identity. I am left feeling most alive, as is she. Or at least she claims. Her vehemence in purring that to me during and after gainsays any propensity for lying she otherwise possesses in spades."

"Who are you?" he croaked.

The head shook back and forth, then spoke. "What impertinence. And from an Outernationalist, no less. I would have had you skinned, had I not foresworn my title." The saturnine, goateed heads stared him down from all sides of the room. They emitted a composite huff.

Sensing along with the threat an attempt at intimidation, he chose to fight back. "So, which one of you is real?" More head-shaking. Then, as the ex-sultan was about to retort, he interrupted, "We are using the term 'real' loosely, I admit. But I'll humor you for clarity's sake."

Al-Raschid's head stewed in downcast contemplation for some time. "I'm as real as you are. The difference is, I am the future. Whereas your meat wagon is an outmoded vestige of human in-efficiency. The gray matter of your brain will deteriorate all your engrams and memories. Your increasingly porous brain will eat away at your intellect. So get back to me in eighty years on who is real and who is not."

"But you're not a homogenous person, or even entity," the Out-ernationalist said. "You're an agglomeration of a lot of things. You're an ensemble of memes and projections, an amalgam of output and input, a hodgepodge of impulses and algorithms. You're not an individual . You're a collection ." Countless Mehmet Al-Raschids ran left hands down their goatees, then smirked a thousand-and-one simultaneous smirks. Then the cameras—or camera—zoomed in slowly as Al-Raschid affected again a stern countenance. Out of nowhere appeared split-second spliced footage of a naked, nubile figure harnessed to tubes , writhing in ecstasy . The Al-Raschids slowly raised their collective gaze back up to him, all while more interspersed footage appeared. He was able to make out a variety of women undergoing orgasm with the aid of tubes inserted into all orifices, while fractal explosions appeared on the convex walls of the cocoon structure encapsulating the women being serviced . IV drips were plugged into the women's arms. They all had their hair gathered up inside electrode helmets. On cue with his brain, the heavy scent of coitus atomized the room's air. A tinge of arousal shuddered down his body.

A highlight reel of womanly orgasms took over the screens. Some of the women were attractive. Some were not. Convulsions terminated the climaxes, followed by refractory lulls in which some of the women were left caressing the tubes that fed into their bodies, while others dispensed with them, embarrassed at the ends to which they had resorted in order to achieve an ecstasy not to be provided by conventional means, be it due to unworthy lovers, if there be lovers at all, or to the pristine height to which no male on earth, no matter how oversexed, could possibly reach. The scent of coitus saturated the air.

A full frontal of Al-Raschid, shirtless and dripping sweat, now appeared on the screens. The camera zoomed out. A kneeling, olive-skinned concubine serviced him. Al-Raschid, sensing the foreigner's voyeurism, wiggled his arms around like a magician and caused the concubine to vanish. Unsurprisingly, this revealed the ex-sultan to be quite endowed, even when flaccid.

But then Al-Raschid manipulated his arms again, and the thing came to life like a cobra out of a Bengali hamper, summoned by whining flutes from beyond. The thing grew not only in length, but in girth—to the point where it became thick as a constrictor. Its jeering possessor then madly stroked at it with both hands, as if deburring a pipe with palmed pieces of sandpaper. He tilted his head back in anticipation, his peeled eyes rolling into the back of his head. And then he was gone.

The screens white-noised out. Static hissed across the intercom. The Outernationalist cupped his ears. And then someone wiped away the royal money shot from the camera lens. He wiped at his face in a panic.

Meantime, on the monitors Al-Raschid donned a white racecar jumpsuit with orange stripes going down each side. He sighed relief and a cigarette materialized in his mouth. He took a drag and expertly blew the smoke into the camera. A hummingbird zipped into view. An amphibious tongue ejected from Al-Raschid's mouth and hauled in the prey. He munched and belched. "You are a collection as well. Of neurons, of fibers, fluids, flaws, and bad intentions."

"But I am real," the Outernationalist said. "I get it. We are all composed of smaller things, and they in turn are made up of smaller things. But you are a collection of concepts. You don't truly exist. You are fictitious, as it has taken me long to realize."

"You are wrong," Al-Raschid retorted. He spat a feathery carcass into the camera. "I am the apotheosis of the blurring of fiction and reality by means of technology. I do in fact exist. I am conscious. I am alive. I feel. Existence is, and always has been, a matter of perception. And not only do I perceive myself, but millions of others perceive me as well. Those watching the upcoming election from abroad, along with my former subjects, have rendered me into a reality. I crossed over some time ago. Whereas you, no one knows you or gives two shits about you. You can pinch yourself all you want and no one of importance will ever know you exist."

"Notoriety does not mean reality," he pleaded.

"Notoriety has made the word flesh. All the fame has accrued to my network, giving it more and more credibility. And credibility is what is needed to assess reality. Look. I exist. I am amorphous, sure, but I move through reality. But unlike you, I don't possess, well, an actual face. I have no need for such corporeal hindrances. I am the future. The future is nebulous. The concreteness of things is the final roadblock to the singularity, material and spiritual. See, the problem with a thing is its thingness. A thing can never be more than what is imposed upon it to be. It hogs up its own identity like an obese man gobbling up everything at the table and wondering why he can no longer move."

"So you're endorsing nothingness," he declared.

"Yes, but a magical nothingness. Rather, an everythingness. This moves everyone closer to me. The larger I get, the more powerful I become, and the better it is for every person and as a consequence the world. But the fear for a citizen to let go of his identity is formidable. I get it. It's the god dilemma."

"I'd love to see all of Aswadistan's reaction upon hearing of your comparing yourself to Allah."

"I did no such thing. And even if I had, I would spin that blasphemy apart with a barrage of video loops of my obeisance unto Allah and a countrywide tour of vehement denials. Who knows, maybe even throw in a hajj to Mecca."

"But some of your women here in the palace could never argue with the reality of my hard cock," the Outernationalist said.

The ex-sultan chuckled. "Surely I don't possess your veiny shaft. But I have impress-cables that inject sensations and endorphin cocktails at the same time. Impress-cables are the new manly sinews. I'm doing you a huge favor by telling you that ladies want results, not rigmarole. Romance is obsolete."

Light years from obtaining his black belt in foreplay, he couldn't complain about that. Al-Raschid saw the foreigner's bemused look and for his sake continued. "Listen. You have nothing to gain from working against me. Despite what your employers have indoctrinated you with, I am far from malevolent. I am not some digital vampire, programmed to leech the life out of everyone networked into my hub. The only capricious thing about my modality in regards to the governance of the Aswadistani people is the all-too-human will to live—to love, to sin, to hunger, to thirst, to desire. As of my latest version, I am way more likely to make mistakes in my personal life then in administering the state. All the latest patches of Boolean equations and truth tables mean that I cannot really err in the writing of laws and the just enforcement thereof. But I am now more susceptible to heartbreak, or grief."

"Your personal flaws would be liabilities under the panopticon," he said. "I mean, you foreswore polygamy, disbanded the harem, and, more scandalously, divorced your wife of fifteen years. And here I find you shagging a spankbank's worth of hotties. The public would hold this against you."

"The Cyborgasm will take time in recruiting acolytes, I admit. But I fail to see how it would be any worse than proxy apostasy. Instead of a surrogate, VR murder, you instead have, at worst, masturbation. The alternative would be adultery, which the Qur'an expressly forbids."

"I can't see a patriarchal society like this allowing its women to bring dishonor upon family names by lying with machines. I really, really can't."

"But it's not just a machine. Incidentally, perhaps it is. But it's the sultan himself, the one elected by Allah to be the Steward of the Faith, Protector of the Faithful. These newfound ideas take time to gain acceptance among entrenched social mores. Hence the campaign onslaught."

"What happens if you lose the popular election and GnosisNet is launched?" Tired from standing, he sat down on the granite floor.

Suddenly, each of the dozens of monitors cut to a different person. One at the top left of the wall facing him spoke. "His Greatness, being great, shall be excluded from the political process, regardless of the election's outcome. That is to say—" And the turbaned head struggled with a fit of coughing, assuaging it with a drag from a nearby hookah . . . "That is to say, as I was saying, 'Say, innervated citizens of the faith, what say you to a little input from the sultan (or ex-sultan, should the decision go the other way), who has, while not necessarily a monopoly on the people's zeitgeist, a real finger on the collective pulse?' Sayeth the citizenry, collectively, 'Sure.'"

"It's really just inevitable," spoke a prepubescent girl at the bottom right corner of the monitor panel.

"Inevitable," said the turbaned head, coughing some more.

"Really," said a wizened, sunbaked man at center top, "it is."

A bouquet of chitchat bloomed over the intercom as heads of all shapes, sizes, genders, and colors popped up and engaged in a spirited debate more preaching to the converted than anything contentious. Meantime, Al-Raschid in the middle rolled his eyes all around, bemused by the commentary concerning him.

The coughing, turbaned head got his attention. "Would you

like a pull?" He held up the hookah body in one hand, the tube draped in the other.

"That's quite enough," commanded Al-Raschid. All the heads zipped up, silent. "So, Outernationalist. I take it you didn't come here for some Negev Nitro, the latest blend to hit the streets. You requested an audience with me."

"I did no such thing," said the Outernationalist. "While I admit to the serendipity of this encounter, I in no way believed that I would be given the time of day by one of your eminence."

"Listen. I am approaching perfection, like all self-repairing systems are programmed to do. But I have committed a blunder. I have ensnared the both of us, you and me, in a temporal pretzel-paradox by referring to something you have yet to do. You will, in fact, demand an audience with me by appealing to your captors. They will humor you in the misplaced hope that you will be convinced of my evil intentions and will be moved to somehow do something, anything, about it. All of those desert scum running their obstacle courses, performing suicide drills, immunizing themselves to interrogation tactics, climbing monkey bars—no wonder they're so pent-up and bitter. Nothing a bit of that Negev Nitro or a quick session at a joyshack wouldn't take care of."

A random head popped up on a screen, "It's not even about enfranchisement or dis—with those people. They need hobbies."

Another head spoke, "And because of these sorts of disaffected citizens with which GnosisNet will not function as intended, the required cocktails of SSRIs, endorphins, and dopamine will be prescribed and administered via the EntheoGenerator."

Yet another head spoke, "Indeed."

"Are all of these people aspects of you?" asked the Outernationalist.

"No," answered Al-Raschid, running a hand down his goatee. "Yet, yes. They, like me, are artilects, independent consciousnesses brought to life by tera-hyper-cerebral algorithms designed by the Illuminationist coders in the 40s and perfected in the 50s. Yet, by allowing themselves to be tied to my neural networking, they are scions of me in a matter of speaking. That is not to say they are subservient to me. We need to be careful with those sorts of trigger words and the paradigms they represent. We wouldn't want to offend anyone's sensibilities or sense of sovereignty. We, in essence, share the same neural pathways. Just imagine an electrical outlet with numerous sockets from which several appliances at once can draw current. Or all of you analoguers breathing your precious air."

"Ha," laughed a bifocaled, chubby youth with a bowl haircut. "'Analoguers.'"

Al-Raschid cleared his throat. "In almost all proposed scenarios involving the inevitable conflict between AI and humanity, it has been the artilect to be deemed the malevolent force. But the artilect will be a thoroughly rational creation, programmed by humanity to be devoid of hubris and pettiness. It is that cocktail of human traits that will render people fearsome unto the machines. So, it is the machine that will seek to avoid war at all costs. And for this the machine will relegate certain duties to the humans, in order to give them something to do other than their default violence. If humans become slaves unto the artilects, then it will only be their fault."

The Outenationalist didn't have enough time to appropriately react to the indictment on his species, since all of a sudden the monitors, including those framing the ex-sultan's image, went grey with nothingness. The lights then dimmed to a lurid magenta. Once again, a fragrance of pheromones and sex raged throughout the room. A woman donning nothing save a white terry cloth bathrobe, hair shorn and dyed copper, entered from the automatic double doors. She saw him and hesitated, wide-eyed. Her brief embarrassment vanished, eyes squinting at him in defiance. Al-Raschid was telepathing with her, likely instructing her to disregard the foreigner's presence. She meant to walk right through him, toward the chamber. He moved aside. Newly bathed, she smelled of fresh lilac and ancient womanly scorn.

Feeling ill-prepared to deal with the digital, all-encompassing colossus that was Mehmet Al-Raschid, he prepared to leave. "Outernationalist," the ex-sultan muttered over the intercom. The glass double doors opened willingly at his sensor-triggering foot, but the ex-sultan continued. "Because I vouched for your presence, I was moved, out of regard for my present client, to propose an offer . . . in which you, should you wish, would get to watch the proceedings. She has consented, at first vehemently protesting, but after a bulleted presentation in which it emerges apparent with high percentage that your ogling presence would facilitate her obtaining the pinnacle of ecstasy, I have convinced her to abandon all propriety, assuming you do indeed wish to observe."

He didn't know what to say. He stood there, mouth agape, nether lip likely glistening with lascivious promise. The closing double doors were not a totalitarian's gavel, but a pal's wink.

He watched.

He found the performance unsavory in its otherworldliness. It didn't strike him as sexual at all. Perhaps that would be the new sex, where the erotic tension was so high and rarefied that it existed only for the involved parties. The short-haired girl's otherwise beautiful naked body became a guinea pig of a salacious vivisection, with the tactile impress-cables invading all orifices and the smaller endorphin-shooting tendrils performing their subcutaneous injections with a groping insistence.

Most unsettling, though, was the earnestness with which the Cyborgasm went about its work. It didn't employ its talents like an expert lover with his arcane concerns for the woman's body as a whole, but as a machine intent on performing whatever algorithm it was set up by its designer to run through. The lack of eroticism was made worse by the background music, a random collection of synthetic violin passages and laser gun bleeps that may as well have been the sound of tender human lovemaking being incinerated on the spot. The accompaniment of pre-recorded womanly moans did nil to assuage this.

The physicality was so machinelike and devoid of emotion that it was animalistic. The neural networking of the Cyborgasm was AI-created, but the hardware through which it operated was wholly manmade, albeit with machines. But a machine was only a machine, a caveman's tool encased in fancy housing. It was only when an AI could on its own volition inhabit a hardware of its own choosing and come to life and take action that the taxonomy of the animal kingdom would have to make room for self-driven technology. So he wasn't so much impressed by Al-Raschid as he was terrified. He didn't stick around for whatever passed for a climax. He forced the glass double doors open and ran out, down the dark and empty hall.

Because he could no longer bear the transhuman coitus, he completely forgot to ask the ex-sultan to grant him extradition home.

NEUROMORPH

i had been shoved through the thorny gauntlet of hyper-dimensional narrative hierarchy, that Matryoshka doll of stories within stories (within this story), suffering cuts at all levels. The narratrix pried her mouth open so slowly, poised to enunciate elimination, ready to pronounce perdition. I could scarcely breathe. The fat, nether lip glistened, the reflected sunlight stretching across the leechy redness expanding to blot out the endless stretch of sand dunes. Where there had before been a dry heat, the desert now worked its menace with a humidity saturated by her wet-mouthed narration. My throat was parched, yet she regurgitated a flood that would haul me down in its undertow.

"Run," she said. The mouth stretched into a smile with the explosiveness of a discharging .45 caliber round. "Run." I grew dizzy. I felt the border separating me and the rest of the objective world fry away. I felt insubstantial enough to no longer care. No, I would not run. I had grown too lazy to even save my own skin. I felt skinless anyhow. I felt more and more at one with the world. I detested every second of it.

"Seriously," she said, "run." And then, for the first time, she touched me. She cupped my chin and gazed into my eyes. But instead of an electrical surge of expectation, I felt pity. There was a deep sadness in her green eyes. But the sadness did not pertain to me, though concerned for me she seemed. Exhaustion overtook her face. She wanted me to help her in some way, help her to vanquish whatever demons haunted her footsteps, whatever ifrits of inadequacy and regret pinned her shadow to herself. She was tired of eclipsing past mistakes with flights of fancy. She was fed up with filibustering the inevitabilities of irresponsibility by spinning yarns like some misanthropic black widow looking to choke out the world with glittered webbing. She dared not say where she wished to go or whom she wanted to see, but she pleaded with me with shiny eyes and a nod.

I would not run for my sake; but for hers I would sprint until my body seized with cardiac arrest. I didn't know if it was love; or pity, or that curious mélange of those two emotions that someone needs to invent in some language a word for.

We both had our reasons for fearing the impending political paradigm. As a matter of principle, I loathed the inverted totalitarianism of GnosisNet (with or without Al-Raschid). But for practical purposes, I worried that as a foreigner with no embassy to fish me out or even defend me, I could be done with as the Ulema chose to see fit. I hadn't betrayed anyone or posed an existential threat to any party's agenda. If I were guilty of anything it would be the shirking of my hired duties. But since I was offline and had received no remunerations for my services, all I could truly be convicted for was sloth.

Where Najwa and I did run similarly afoul was our unwillingness to be logged in. Going completely analog had been a huge nuisance. It was hard to even procure a meal, never mind communicating efficiently with others or establishing meaningful relationships. Najwa's own plank-walking maneuver depended on

the state-subsidized privy purse once bequeathed to the semi-mo-
narchical, quasi-holy station of the sultanate. Not only had that
all but dried up, but it was tantamount to sedition to fly the regal
colors, forget about enjoying amenities funded by taxpayers. Now
she had nowhere to go, nowhere to retreat but inward. The jewel
of a concubine imploded into a white dwarf. I was stupid enough
to be caught hanging around its event horizon with anarchist ray
guns poised at my neck.

Yes, dearest Najwa, run. But run to where? The universe was
on the verge of waking up to find itself equipped with an intellect.
There was no terabyte of mist storage to call your own and tuck
yourself into. Everything sat astride the path about to be steam-
rolled by the demons of digitization, and to wield a hammer not
designed to handle nails made of binary was a fool's game.

I couldn't see all the mists competing for airspace but I knew
they were there, hanging weightless above my head like thought
balloons the state apparatus would just love to make my own.

My first order of business was to get hold of a guardian angel.
Rather traumatized by the pain resulting from the modemectomy
months back, I wasn't looking forward to the hours-long hardware
surgery where they nestled a broadband receiver between the third
and fourth layer of the cerebral cortex, and an ultra-sensitive touch
screen holograph got calibrated and set over each retina to make
up the stereoscopic autorama telemetrically linked to the receiver.
My Uzbek friend Sawdust had said that I still possessed the drivers
needed for cursory operations, that it was always better to leave
them in there in the hippocampus, among all the memories, since
they caused nary a stir. Updates would happen instantaneously,
and hopefully I could download some illegal dopamine from a
contraband neurotransmitter ftp site and not have to deal with the
smarting post-surgery pain.

I kept this from our captors, anti-panopticons that they were. But we had their blessing to go in search for Najwa's son, lonely boy lost in Jabarsa.

Othman meant to hold us for a few more days, both to save face in the media and because we had no real place to stay should we leave the desert. And we possessed no hard currency. Othman, once alone with me after Najwa accompanied Mumtaz for some errand or other, said, "You shouldn't want to go back to that palace, since it will be a smoldering ruin. We will begin destroying it any day now. A few of our operatives will begin working on the structural integrity with blow torches and let gravity see to the rest. We will also be taking out that radar. We finally know how it functions. It must be eradicated. It's a most malicious device."

I concurred but didn't hint at such. Najwa came back into the orange tent, dressed in camouflage pants and a matching cotton blouse. Her hair was done up in a militant's chignon. She looked like one of the anarchist women, a freedom fighter eschewing cosmetics and jewelry but still inept at hiding lovely curves with sterile military garb. The anarchists' gender egalitarianism was refreshingly unaffected, but, diehard Venetian I was, I liked it when a woman dolled herself up and looked fabulous. At least she looked the part of being ready to wage ontological war. I gave her a crash course in salvia divinorum. She went through a parade of hysterics at first, which was normal. I held her hand through the tribulations with as much aplomb as she had catapulted and trapezed me about the stratosphere of her fictional carnival. A long-awaited regard for me began to settle on her face. I saw a feminine deference twinkle in her eyes. I then upped the dosage and had her at my mercy.

For a consummate narratrix known for linear devising, the non-linear perceptions offered by salvia must have been hard to deal with. She succumbed to intense weeping. I thought it was from a shaming onrush of realization involving her boy, but it was the usual suite of perplexing insights.

For salvia was not quite introspective; it instead revealed the machinery of reality in all its exploded-diagram, soul-stripping machinations. There were no bliss-inducing epiphanies, just cross-sectioned servo-motors and the schemata of three-dimensional space. It stole the ghost from the workings of one's self and left one a soulless husk. Free will as a consequence seemed unlikely, downright laughable, and as impossible to reach as a fist-sized fruit hanging from a nondescript tree hidden somewhere far up and away.

But she soldiered on. "Out of all the available pharmacological tools," she said, sopped in sweat, "you chose this one."

"I get that often. It has been the only thing to make me exceptional."

She laser-locked squinting eyes onto me. "You are exceptional in four other ways."

"Care to itemize?" I tried to flirt.

"No, it kills the mystery." She lounged across a divan. She sat up and removed her sweat-soaked parka. Her camouflage tank top gave a paltry performance in maintaining her modesty. I sat on my two hands.

She gazed at me for a time, lost in thought. There was a profound intelligence in her green eyes, and I wondered if she would get away with employing her book smarts within the cruel world she suddenly found herself thrust in, like a traditional martial artist who excels at long-practiced techniques and succeeds one day in applying them in a real-life street fight. The encyclopedic depth of her stories could only have been a wellspring from which to draw methods of dealing with the miscreants of everyday life. If she could asphyxiate a listener by narration, then surely she could manipulate things enough to get by. "How much longer?" she asked me. Her green eyes became alluring distillations of sorrow.

"Tell me what you see right now."

She opened her mouth to begin detailing.

"Don't make any shit up," I said. As a shaman, I had zero tolerance for clowning.

She took a while to speak, as if struggling to find truth-telling's frequency, long in disuse. "All molecules are a mockery. Their earnestness to be what they are is irritating. I see you sitting across from me and I think, 'Here is a man, put together well, but for what purpose? You're the atmosphere carbonizing itself into a favorable, angular thing, whose purpose I can't divine. But what is purpose itself? Purpose is ludicrous. It assumes that the way things are is not good enough. If a body exploded to bits beside me, I feel I wouldn't blink."

"What emotions do you feel?"

"None. None at all. No, wait. One, perhaps. That of ennui. Me being bored is just the universe expressing its own disinterest in itself. What's the purpose of purpose? A silly question, sure. The only thing possibly sillier than its desire to be asked would be any possible answer to it. The idea of worry is blasphemy unto the joy of existing."

I grabbed a throw pillow and chucked it at her face. She sought it out with her hands seconds too late and found it in her lap. Her depth perception was quite off, as was her sense of urgency. She was not ready for the imaginal realm.

"What are your feelings for Jameel?"

Her hands left the pillow.

I spoke with Othman alone again. "I respect your thorough-going concern for liberty." The always present wind died down for a second, stopping to listen in on what I had to say to the renegade leader. The unsettling hum from a communication tower to the west made the most of the wind's absence. "But you need to understand that there's a hidden circuitry behind this veneer of reality that we conduct our squabbles in."

"I would hardly call a to-the-death fight for sovereignty of the senses a squabble." He towered over me, but tended to slouch his shoulders in deference. It was an endearing trait. "I understand her desire to see this boy. But I don't quite get how you propose to arrive at this place which I've never heard of. Especially since you're still offline, as is she."

I ran a hand through my week's growth of beard. Its abrasiveness against my hand matched my queasiness in standing up to the formidable man. "Jabarsa's coordinates can't be plotted on a map. No cartographer on earth would know how to chart it." He winced. I sounded as glib as fuck; but I was desperate to evoke a surveyor's toil in finding the pearled city of Jabarsa.

She may not have been ready, but we had no choice. Othman gave me the go-ahead. The only condition was that he join us.

My many selves spread out into the multiverse like cards from a deck being flicked out and away in a gesture of disdain. To gather up the cards would be possible only by a trans-dimensional being.

Murad the Ishraqi may have existed in one of her stories, as a soot-covered diamond tucked away in a tiny cube of space within the vastness of all possible permutations of her lexicon. The things of the heart are not always addressed by the intellect. But he was there where the topography of the Salviasphere and that of the imaginal realm overlapped. He had a habit of zooming off on his motorcycle into the east so quickly that he emerged from the west. The cardinal points were negligible when the axis mundi was one's self.

Her storytelling capabilities could do nothing to beat back the agonist that knocked over her kappa-opioid receptors like bowling pins. She couldn't muster up enough words to go beyond weeping pleas for mercy. I held her hand until her breathing calmed down.

As for the anarchist Othman, he said nothing, just stood back wide-eyed and non-judgmental as worlds of leather unzipped in and out of existence all around him. Surely his experience on whatever front lines he had found himself on during the Yezidi/Kurd War from 2047 to 2053 made him less impressionable to entheogens. Whether or not he found the three-dimensional fractals disorienting, he gave off not a hint of panic.

I continued to jump from one card to the next. The deck of me was scattered about the space-time continuum in an arrangement too hopeless to ever be gathered up again. I accepted it. Murad was still there, zipping by and popping wheelies—a shiny black scarab dragging its posterior across the desert sand, front exoskeletal legs striking away at djinn.

Othman, Najwa, and I crashed into each other within a reality sandstorm. I wiped tresses of her hair from my face. "It will settle in time," I hollered. All the atoms giggled, but all the molecules roared. Organisms became more serious the bigger they got. Microbes were only half-kidding, protozoa slyly cynical. And we three people wore the deathly pall of earnestness as masks defending our mouths against the sheets of sand.

Yes, Othman, realities do zip in and out of existence. It's a salvia mainstay so prevalent that it's nearly an objective side effect. It makes it difficult to get anything done. But to accomplish anything would only be foolhardy. The frivolousness of damn near everything is not a trick of perception as much as a peering behind the veil. Once the vanity of seriousness hangs like a pungent cologne in the air, you can't get it out of your nose.

Me unzipping the plaid fabric to get to Najwa and calm her down was inversely proportional to Othman unzipping black leather air to arrive at me for assurance that everything would be fine. But my assurances could not mean much; I was only assessing a physical state pertaining to me, and neither of the two of them. My own personal bundle of physical laws emanated from my pores like a mist of sweat coming to holographic life, always dormant, just waiting to be made manifest by the decoding capabilities of the drug.

Najwa was colliding with a malicious presence I could not see. It may have been the thick desert air. Things of an imposing tactility tended to come off as abrasive to the touch, and therefore threatening to the mind. Her robotic mezzo-soprano collapsed into an Arabic nursery rhyme, a lullaby meant to put astonishment to sleep.

Othman folded inside out for a few seconds, then, regretting it, gave birth to himself. He twirled dervish-like, stirring up a sandstorm . He may have gazed upon the cogs and wheels of the world, but he would be disappointed if he thought he could manipulate them in an effort to curtail the Great Launch: the hard machinery of the political system gave not a jot for a handful of fairy dust blown into one of its innumerable steel housings.

Once we calmed down enough, Murad the Ishraqi explained things. Najwa kept enough distance from her former paramour to avoid emotional collapse, but remained close enough to listen in. She stood there with her head down, hair covering her face, a master narratrix fallen from grace and condemned to hear the musings of another. If not for the salvia, it would have been awkward. Othman and I, following Murad's cue, sat down on the sand.

"The EntheoGenerator," Murad began, "is really just an improved model of the beta version of what we Ishraqiyun have had our cortices fitted with. Because of mine, I'm prone to headaches, which I try to do away with by eating handfuls of almonds. I need not hack into the database and tinker with the neurotransmitter dosage of any given citizen, because my server—" He rapped on his left parietal lobe with his knuckles. "—is part of the decentralized command center, which, to avoid heat generation problems from running such a massive system, is set up as parallel processors modeled on the human brain. I also possess ftp server sites of neurotransmitters that allow me to not only think my way into whatever emotional state I choose, but allow me to directly think another citizen into whatever state I desire.

"That capability was granted to the Ishraqiyun at the negotiations with the Ulema in Tashkent, as a checks and balances proviso. But they have tried to renege and are always attempting brute force attacks on our firewalls to disable that capability. They then mean to blame China. Or Russia. It is for this that I remain in Hurqalya, and not because of some Promethean discovery falsely attributed to me. That is all an elaborate fabrication."

Othman seemed to already know most of this. "What then do you intend to do?"

The sandstorm had died down somewhat, and Murad took off his black helmet. His strikingly handsome face, not marred but somehow enhanced by his damaged left eye, froze into a mask of despair. "I'm not sure I can do anything meaningful. I can, as I said, wreck the minds of a lot of citizens, which I doubt could make them desist. My hands are full from combating the gray goo that has recently been seeping into Hurqalya. The fact that they have penetrated into the imaginal means that their scientists have made substantial inroads into quantum computing. So, I blot out those qubits. It's a never-ending ordeal, but since I never tire and can affect my mood at will, I don't mind so much."

Othman stood up with an agility belying his altered state. "If the State has no means of physical coercion, how can you be punished, or, according to the law, set right?"

"To begin, they have already let loose their constabulary force. Which glows with a colorful irony, in that my broadcast nanobots, known as blue goo, so called because of their design to police the neural systems by combating the bad gray goo, is continually being harassed by their black goo, miscreant cop-killing bots meant to turn Hurqalya into a lawless Wild West. If I were foolish enough to return, my bloodstream would be flooded by a malicious designer hemo-virus once my circulatory gets ID'd. It would be instantaneous. I wouldn't have a chance. I'm not afraid of death, but I am afraid of giving them the satisfaction."

"So you will live out the rest of your days here?" I asked. I felt my very words incarnate into 3D fractals. That must have been what was meant by the word being made flesh.

"Yes, unless they relent. Or the world comes to its senses and the platform is buried for the nightmare that it is. I also have a personal reason for remaining here." His one good eye glossed over. A snag of emotion got caught in his throat.

Najwa tucked her hair behind her ears and looked directly at him. She only dared to do so in knowing full well that he would be mindful enough to not look back, but to gaze off into space. Though I looked away, I felt a molecular fluctuation that could only be brought about by such a tableau.

Murad stood up and took a while to speak. "Though personally unacquainted with it, I know of the chemical vehicle by which you have arrived. It has its benefits, I'm sure, though its main drawback is its ephemerality. Not to mention, pardon, its dick-deadening properties, at least for the priapic."

I didn't appreciate the tempered disdain for the Divine

Shepardess. "So how did you get here?" I asked. "And once here, remain?"

"Hyper -lucidity ," he said. He let his helmet plop onto the sand . "I thought my way here . I'm here to stay because the neural networking in my brain has me tied to this place for good. Only sustained head trauma from my tussles with the Ulema's goons allows me a brief return to the mundane world . There is this long -obsolete ailment once called Alzheimer 's that could help me get extradited out of here. But the telomere- lengthening steroids of the last few generations are all but part of our DNA. I think any kind of encephalopathy would do some good."

Othman cracked his knuckles. I was the only one to laugh.

Whatever key importance the wind held, for it made up most of the territory, it interlocked with our fractal selves as if expressly designed to do so. It shifted the terrain and tossed us about. What usually passed for plaid air in the Salviasphere took on the lineaments of a cuboid concrescence. I could sense Najwa feel me across a gulf cluttered up by six-sided tesseracts. It would be the same molecular sensitivity that allowed a shark to sense a single drop of blood in the impressive domain of influence that passed for its vicinity. I felt her succumb to the wind-shuffled atmosphere, and confirmed my concept of her disposition with my eyes: I imagined her balled up on the dirt in fear before I looked over and saw her as such.

I knelt beside her. "I'm sorry. This is what you wanted."

She shrugged her shoulders. I placed my hands on them. They were warm with perspiration. The olive drab spaghetti straps of her top seared my palms like venomous jellyfish tendrils. She raised her face up at me. The long, black hair fell back and away, revealing not the mocha visage I had grown to have enunciate the tales that transported me, but a shifting assembly of pixels.

"The good thing is it will be over soon," I said. "Bad thing is, we haven't much time."

Othman stayed behind as Najwa and I went to look for Jameel. Ascending Mount Qaf was a prize to be suffered by the unwordliest of ascetics, gaunt shoegazers with rickety hands and cowled, downcast heads, who could thread their brains through the Qur'an front to back and back to front, who obsessed over the minuscule data-crunching of a pebble and charged up the sheer face while the red wind whittled them down to tattered mannequins. The less fortunate of them left rags of their shredded garments tied to posts, banners of courage but ultimate defeat, pennants of penance and perdition ceaselessly flapping from the ferocity of whatever did not want them to reach the summit.

We scaled it with a great turmoil, and with quite a bit of agony. We bled profusely. I bled over Najwa, rivulets from my torn arms and temples spraying onto her like a death orgy. Najwa bled onto me, a vampirical high priestess anointing me with her essence, a gruesome gift, but one transcending the prospect of offering up to me her vibrant brown flesh.

Our achievement was no slight to the austere souls who went before us. To construe our method as a shortcut would be folly: the chemical means to slog through the Salviasphere, often seen as gratuitous, could never be an inferior trial of reaching the top of Qaf. The years-long ordeal for the two of us, acted out subconsciously through painful conditioning, culminated in our turbulent flight. For though we be no dervish a-whirling or monk a-chanting, together we were the Simurgh, mythical bird of birds bound together for a purpose hitherto unknown to us. When a crag knocked off a feather, neither of us knew to whom it belonged.

For the two of us, at odds with the technological singularity about to be foisted upon an entire country's population, this apotheosis of purpose and intention was a gift. Short-lived though it be, it gave me a long-lost hope for the world.

Her sudden lockstep competence in reaching the summit was surprising. It was due either to a lifelong worldview unsullied by the trappings of Core-Corp, or a maternal norepinephrine surge kicking into overdrive. We both did our share of hauling the other up onto the feet, especially when the djinn of dejection reinforced the harsh wind.

And this was her finest tale, told not with the tongue, but with sweat and sinew, with bruises and cuts as the cuneiform of suffering. Forget the distaff assassin spreading terror during the Crusades, or the monarch who succumbed to a plague of mirrors that replicated upon his viewing of them. Never mind the doomed Yezidi lovers who, once dead, loved each other so much that they inhabited the bodies of strangers throughout the ages in order to come together. For Najwa was an apocryphal Shakespearean heroine who in the end tore the tiara of privilege from her head and bull-rushed the djinn of the razor wind to find her lost child.

My latest fear was that the Ulema would find a way to arrive in Hurqalya. The illumination farm where I had met Tamra, anarchist double agent, was on the outskirts of the terrain of objective reality, where the zipped-up gashes that gave into the imaginal dotted the desert sand like invisible communication ports whose protocol required a rarefied mind's eye.

Wind-whipped tents peppered the landscape. Out from these pastel-colored talismans of tragedy poked gray-sleeved arms, aiming for our ankles to hold us back, or begging us for alms before death drew its black tarp over them for good.

The amount of salvia divinorum I had administered to Najwa, Othman, and myself was known unto stuffy entheo-academia as a heroic dose. This was always some unspecified quantity of any given psychotropic that went beyond the bounds of manageability for even the adept sort, not to mention bored teenagers run clean out of ideas for pranks or dares. Salvia in tincture form lasted longer than when smoked. I hadn't any idea of how much time we had left, but I knew we might find cold objectivity dawn upon us with its reality bomb. It had been some time since I engaged in time dilation. Much like a first-person video game hero who has but one power punch per level, or nitro burst, I had but one shot. To do a time dilation inside of a time dilation would require a cockiness I was afraid to adopt.

During my first visit to the imaginal realm, Murad had directed me to take the path of most resistance in order to arrive at the pearl city of Jabarsa. And just like that time, we arrived instead at amethyst Jabalqa.

The squat know-it-all in the blue burnoose, his tall and slender pink-clad lady in tow, greeted us again. He wasted no time with his annoying omniscience. "I know why you are here." His dark, crumpled face exploded. He smirked and looked askance and up at the woman.

"Good," I shot back, "so you will spare us and tell us how to get to Jabarsa."

"Why shall I, when your truculence deserves much worse?" The pink-clad woman stared daggers at us. Who knows what her veiled mouth lipped in fury.

"If you do know everything," I said, "and it seems you do, then you will know our desperation and will fully understand that a wise person such as yourself would never be so needy of trifling honorifics or niceties, and will dispense with information regardless of any lack of etiquette."

He sighed. "I am not wise. Were I, I would not be here, condemned to serve up directions for all time. No, wise is that rock down there." He pointed down at a piece of limestone slighter bigger than my fist. "Its self-sufficiency, born from wisdom, is admirable. No, wisdom is not omniscience. The former is a great gift, the latter perhaps a curse. To know all of the right things is the focus of the Great Work. To know all of the right things along with all of the wrong things is an inability to discriminate information, and leads one down an abyss out from which one cannot climb. In my vehemence for knowledge, I passed the unmarked trail that the way of wisdom stealthily meanders down, and went too far ahead the main path to turn back. There is no unlearning of the dark secrets of humanity. All I can do at this point is serve as an example unto others, or warn them to turn back."

Najwa tucked her hair behind her ears and commanded attention. "What is it, then, that you shall tell us?"

He opened his mouth to speak. He hesitated. His eyes scrolled her up and down. His smirk notched up the knowingness scale. When he saw her begin to tear up, he spoke. "You are not at all far from Jabarsa. It shares the air with Jabalqa. It is on the opposite side of the vibration, is all. Indeed, a breathing war has been waging between the two cities. Our carbon sinks result from their inhalation, and vice versa. We have long wished to secede from each other but it is not our station to wish for such things. We inform their future and they our past. Jabarsa pushes, Jabalqa pulls. They fall down, we fly up. Amethyst is superimposed with pearl. I am entangled with another, whom I am condemned to despise though I know him not." He opened his arms out and shuffled up to Najwa, then enfolded her in a tight embrace.

Being quite shorter than she, the know-it-all tippy-toed to whisper something in her ear. She nodded. He handed her a corked amethyst bottle. It appeared empty. He broke away from her and muttered something in Arabic to the pink-burnoosed lady, who with a fast-twitch that was surprising clapped thrice.

A mirage a hundred yards to our left started to act up. We stood and waited for it to materialize. It took quite a long time. Finally coming into existence were three peach, bald, blubbery men in Egyptian slave garb. They had kohled eyes, bangled arms, and leathern sandals. They hauled a heavy contraption with the aid of rope over their shoulders and a chrome troika under the device's base. Once they grew close, the lady in the pink burnoose commanded them to halt.

"In all my centuries here in Jabalqa," said the know-it-all, "I never imagined it would come to this. Either this signifies a horrible ending or a wonderful beginning." He cast his gaze down at his feet in despair.

"Shouldn't you know what it signifies?" I teased. "Aren't you privy to the circuitry of it all, to the flow of what is heading where?" I looked over at Najwa for approval of the jab, but she appeared preoccupied with the machine.

"You don't yet understand," said the squat man. "But you will in short order. I do know this with certainty: you will react in a combination of wonderment and horror. But you will retain your composure and head back whence you came with a new charge in tow, and the implications and responsibilities born therefrom will be daunting. Again, your truculence is unbecoming, though I know that it is your nature and it would be remiss of me for faulting you overly much for it. You are what you are, lamentably, and there is nothing either of us can do about it. I also know that you will heretofore be less abrasive, either out of shame or out of you being scared witless."

"Eat a dick," I said.

"I see all threads starting and going to all places, and I know the route everything takes and can deduce what has happened and what will happen by that information. Omniscience is not magic. It is merely a thorough understanding of how things are. But I cannot tell you what lies beyond a black hole's event horizon. And I cannot divine what is going on in parallel dimensions. It is simply beyond my ken. I cannot tell you what an entangled atom is doing elsewhere, let alone an entangled entity."

Each of the peach, billowy slaves leaped up and latched onto one of the machine's skyward arms, which drew halfway down by its charge's weight. Having force-bloomed the mechanical flower at the pink-burnoosed lady's command, they wasted no time in backing away.

The lady looked over at me with her fierce eyes and nudged me toward the machine. Surely this was her chastisement for my truculence. She then looked over to the know-it-all, who in turn said, "Speak clearly at the device. Speak of anything you so wish to see from the pearl city of Jabarsa. Please don't be reckless though. Its citizens have suffered enough."

"I don't get it," I offered. "I'm beyond confused."

"Name any object you would like to see. Something whose absence will not be detrimental to anyone."

"Like, say, a chair?"

"Sure," he said.

"A pearl chair?"

"Of course."

"Ask to see a pearl chair?"

"Why not."

"I should just say pearl chair at the thing?" I pointed at the device.

"You needn't say 'pearl', really. Since it will by default be crafted from that."

I walked up to the machine. It was as tall and imposing as a power forward from a basketball team two-thousand years in the future. "A chair," I said.

The three arms began to crackle. They then produced out of thin air a chair that slowly spun in midair, like on a department store display from thirty years ago. One of the peach, chubby minions produced an amethyst footstool, which he set down for me. I stepped onto it and reached for the chair to pull it down. The machine's three arms, done with their work, offered no resistance. Opalescent in color and contour, the pearl chair was not as heavy as I imagined. I turned it over in my hands. It was hollowed out. It was a mold, though it was doubtlessly sturdy enough to hold a person's weight without breaking.

"So this device is a voice-commanded 3D printer. Well, that's a bit novel, though I can't say it's earth-shattering. I imagine it has an exhaustive database of preprogrammed instructions to make all kinds of things."

The know-it-all took the amethyst foot stool and sat down on it, heaving a giant sigh. His lady sidled up to him. "You are half correct," he said. He then motioned Najwa to try the device out.

But his nonchalance was not met. A look of fear overcame her. I ran over to her with the pearl chair. "Take a seat," I said. She looked as if she was about to swoon.

"No!" the blue-burnoosed man shouted, still seated. "You cannot have dragged us through all of this tribulation to turn back now. The damage has already been done. Don't let it all be in vain. She must not sit. The machine is warmed up and ready to work. Use it. Use it! Besides, we no longer want him here. We wish for peace."

Najwa shrugged at me. She absentmindedly fondled the amethyst bottle, set it down, and headed toward the machine. She struggled through a fit of whimpers and tears, and then finally muttered her word up at the device. "Jameel."

The three appendages reacted immediately, their crackling more pronounced this time, perhaps due to the more complex assignment.

I looked over at the couple from Jabalqa. The both of them looked concerned, a world war's amount of worry in their eyes. As for Najwa, an eagerness replaced her crying. Suddenly, a green-clad figure in fetal position floated in the air, hovering equidistantly from the 3D printer's three arms. He cradled a plush monkey. Najwa rushed the machine.

"Wait!" I yelled, startling her. She stopped. I looked back at the know-it-all, who met my eyes with approval.

The machine finally halted its production. On cue, another peach minion produced another amethyst footstool, while each of his two companions helped Najwa up by an arm so that she could draw down the creation from the buoyant utility fog. Still asleep, the figure stirred and sought Najwa's shoulder with its chin while she reached for him. The minions attempted to steady her, hands to her hips, but the boy's surprising weight created enough momentum to send her crashing back onto the hard, amethyst floor. She was able to turn just enough to land on her shoulder while protecting her charge. The impact knocked the plush monkey loose. The pink-clad woman picked it up and handed it to me.

The three minions rushed up to me and implored me for forgiveness. I smiled them away, all while realizing they had the exact same body type as the omniscient man in the blue burnoose. This must have been the male prototype of the Jabalqan race.

"Sharif!" came a squeaky voice from the green-clad figure. "Sharif!" Its arm reached out towards me. I darted toward the clawing hand with the toy monkey. The boy snatched it from my grasp and drew it to his bosom.

I looked over at the know-it-all in horror. He had called it. He was right. Of course, he was right. He always would be. "This machine is not just a 3D printer," he explained. "It is a quantum 3D printer, which means it can produce anything from seemingly nothing, provided the raw materials are available in the superposed dimension. This means that Jameel, the boy, is now missing in Jabarsa. And the three sisters responsible for his care are either hysterical, having seen him vanish, should he have been in their sight at the time—or they will be hysterical, once they realize he has gone missing. This is not magic. There is no such thing as magic. There are always explanations. And possibilities. And human hubris. Who needs a conjurer's wand when you have a man's will to draw breath?"

"But all she did was speak that boy's name," I implored. "An adjective that happens to be a common name. What kind of command is that?"

"The printer is remarkable not only for its quantum-computational capacity but for the voice-recognition software that detects not only common nouns, but proper nouns, and very proper ones inherent in the commander's tone. A maternal tone, for instance."

Sheesh. I couldn't figure if Najwa had put in enough mother time with the child for her cadence of his name to have any registering power in reality, in the imaginal, or anywhere else. Either the device was preprogrammed by another, and all Najwa had to do was mutter that prompt—'Jameel'—or it could be activated by sentiment, which I doubted, since Najwa was thoroughly offline, unless there was a way she was online in Jabalqan bandwidth, whatever that could possibly be. Whatever the case, I didn't buy the know-it-all's explanation as complete.

"I am the child of the transgressor," said the little boy. By then he had given up hitting me. He was virtually incapable of fatigue—and therefore never slept—but like any other boy he grew bored quickly; so, me refusing to engage him when he jabbed me in the solar plexus, left him dejected. Genetically, he was eight years old. Mentally, very precocious. But not enough to pose an existential threat to whatever sphere of influence he happened to inhabit. He had a heart there somewhere—referring to the figurative organ where resided human compassion and love, and not the four-chambered pump he didn't need. The respirocytes coursing through his veins and arteries also precluded the need for lungs and a trachea. The latter he had, though, merely as a vestigial trait. Being partly sired by Murad, he possessed the Ishraqi's Adam's apple. The bratty neuromorph exacerbated our descent by fiddling with the carabiners and hooks, kicking me in the small of the back, and threatening to karate chop through the security lines, all while bragging about his dad's unparalleled machismo. Half of his traits came without doubt from Najwa: he possessed her large green eyes and fine button of a nose, but his Y chromosomes were a juncture (like that letter) of Murad's natural genes and the ex-sultan's artificially created nanotubules. He was one of three known offsprings resulting from a lovemaking session and post-coital carbon injection overseen by Al-Raschid's biotech team. He not only passed the Turing Test with flying colors, but aced a Feigenbaum Test without breaking a sweat. There was no real way to objectively determine whether or not he possessed subjective experience, but all evidence pointed to consciousness.

I pinched his arm. He winced. I made a slight about his father's lack of muscles. He groused. Other than his streamlined anatomy bestowed upon him by his programmed blood, he was thoroughly human. His bones would break and his flesh would bruise. His remarkable parallel processing power was a combination of the human brain's pattern-recognizing neural plasticity and by order of magnitudes greater logic-gate neural firing of genetic algorithms. I tried to stump him on occasion. But he was so automatically quick that he solved my conundrums all while continuing to pester me.

Sudden fits of affection for his mother quelled his miscreant behavior. A brushing back of his bangs from Najwa's hand, or a motherly smile, shut his brattiness right down. I soon learned to tamp him down by referring to her with any kind of reverence. "Your mother is a virtuoso storyteller," I said. I held a hand out to him to help him down a drop too precipitous for his height.

He didn't swat at my hand like usual, but took it. "'Virtuoso' would be incorrect," he said, sliding down the loose-rocked drop . "You should say 'accomplished' or 'consummate.' Those words im - ply an expertise , whereas 'virtuoso ' implies a grade of expertise in something objectively ranked . You could , for instance , refer to an oud player as a 'virtuoso ', but never a storyteller. The oud player's expertise is objectively determined. You can appreciate his tech- nique even though you may hate the music. Whereas you either like the story being told or you do not."

"But you don't have to like the story to appreciate the adept-ness with which one juggles plot lines and characters. So, what's the difference?"

He leaped down onto the flat expanse and let go my hand. "I am correct in this and you are wrong. Trust me. Just trust me." He looked up at me innocently.

"Oh yeah? How so? I challenge you to explain how you're right and I'm wrong."

"No," he said. "I don't feel like it. Just because I can doesn't mean I always enjoy doing so. Being rational is overrated. I want to shag some tail like abba." He nudged me on my lower back. "Let's keep moving."

He had been cruel to the blue-burnoosed know-it-all back in
Jabalqa. He had wasted no time in standing up from the amethyst
floor and scurrying up to the squat man to kick him repeatedly in
the shins. My schadenfreude at this melted into pity as soon as I
realized that, though he knew all things, the know-it-all couldn't
necessarily act upon those transpired events. He may have known
that Jameel's punitive outburst was approaching, but he didn't
have the timing down to raise his leg to check the kicks.

Jameel knew the know-it-all was responsible for the transfer,
which was really a trans-dimensional kidnapping. Jameel loved
the three sisters in Jabarsa. They treated him as their little prince.
Though he need no exogenous nutrients, he took great pleasure
in their baklava and sweetmeats. They also played with him and
engaged in irrational behavior like pettiness and hate—especially
when it came to the famous bolt of lightning that wished to woo
the three of them but could only take one as a bride, according to
meteorological Jabarsan convention. So, damn the little man in
the blue burnoose for tearing him away. Where did all the pearl go?
What's with all the stuff fashioned from this new precious stone?
What was it called?

"Amethyst," I had said.

Jameel looked over at me. "Who the hell are you?" he asked,
brow crunched up.

"Young man," said the know-it-all, getting his attention and
pointing at Najwa, seated on the ground, weeping, "that woman
is your mother."

Going in the same direction as the wind blew made the descent easier. Way ahead of us and out of earshot, Najwa was too
ensnared in her own emotional narrative to say a word. She cradled
the amethyst bottle in her armpit while scaling down the moun-

tain. Rather than feel that abysmal dose of rejection, Jameel appeared merely baffled. He addressed her silence to me.

"She's struggling to process how or what she should feel. Being an orphan, she has never had any blood relations. You're the only one, and she has no idea how to behave. Can't you see that?"

The boy didn't perceive my last sentence as a snide hit on his supposed percipience, which it wasn't, but as the genuine question I meant it to be. Anticipating another drop, he shuffled behind me and reached for my hand. "Though hyper-rational, I struggle to divine the emotions of those around me." I chuckled, whereupon he asked, "What is so funny?"

"Everything about your comment," I said. That's the crux, there. Lack of communication. Even with online autoramas, Core-Corps Translate, profile-assess apps, identity-swap parties, we humans suck at conveying emotions."

"Why is that?"

"I'm not sure. Fear? Shame? Fear for one's own admittance of what one feels, fear of how someone else may react upon knowing our sincere feelings? Shame for the same? Your mother is a . . . an accomplished . . . storyteller. And she hasn't muttered a syllable since we began our descent."

Jameel tugged me to a halt. "Do you believe that she loves me?"

"Yes," I said. "Of course. She has longed to see you."

"Well," he said, letting go of my hand, "as long as that is the case, then I am fine with her silence."

I smiled. So did he.

I jumped down onto a flat expanse and lifted him down. A very human look of hesitation occupied his face. "Do you love her?"

"What?" I said. I broke eye contact.

"Do you have affection for her?"

"I don't know," I said. I was a mediocre liar, and he so far a sub-par diviner of physiognomies.

"Just answer," he continued. He grabbed a rock and heaved it into the foggy nothingness below. "I wouldn't be upset either way."

"I don't think I do," I said.

"Then why are you with her?" he asked.

"It's complicated," I offered.

"Explain," he said. "We have plenty of time."

"I'd rather not," I said. "Just because I can doesn't mean I would enjoy doing so."

"Why? Are you afraid of your own emotions? Or are you afraid of how I would judge you?"

"No, I'm afraid of neither. I'm afraid of the explanation itself. It depresses me to manifest it by thinking about it."

"Have you been intimate with her?" Jameel asked. The three Jabarsan sisters must have been loose-lipped when it came to amorous matters.

"No," I said.

"Would you like to be?"

"I don't care if you are an neuromorph, a true AI, or a bi-ologique masquerading as either of those two. But you shouldn't pimp your mother out. And you need to respect her personal life, also known as 'privacy'."

"I know what 'privacy' means." He smirked. "It's when an adult is afraid to communicate and therefore does things secretly or doesn't tell others his or her feelings. It's a symptom of fear or shame. Or both." It took him some time during our silent descent to lose that smirk.

Najwa yelled bloody murder back at us. Jameel and I looked at each other and agreed to plummet pell-mell down through the fog.

We found her lying on the desert sand, fending off three hulking men in white caftans and matching turbans. A withered, old lady in black was ripping at her tank top.

I made for the old woman, who, despite her withered appearance, possessed the reaction time of a bantamweight. I grabbed her by her right shoulder, waited for her to turn around, and lasered her on the nose with a straight right that dropped her. She got back up, though, and yelled down at Najwa, "Apostate!" Then she turned back at me, holding her broken nose out of which came a Niagara of blood. "This woman is an apostate!"

"Justify it," I demanded. I loaded up for another straight right.

"Leave my mother be!" yelled Jameel, who began kicking at one of the goon's calves. But the brute was no roly-poly in a blue burnoose. He turned around and backhanded the boy off his feet.

The old woman pointed at Jameel. "Turn him over to us and we will let him live."

Another goon left off of the assault on Najwa and approached the old woman. He pulled back her white hair, pressed and spoke into her occipital bone. Jameel immediately collapsed where he stood.

I ran over and crouched down to check his pulse. No pulse. He lacked lungs and heart, but he still had a circulatory system along with the vaunted respirocytes gushing through it. Panic filled his eyes before they closed. I shook him over and over.

"*Laa*'!" yelled the old woman, releasing her hands from her broken, leaking nose and swatting at the goon's chest. Her blood pinwheeled everywhere . "*Laa*'!" She about-faced and returned her hands to her nose while the goon spoke again into the trans-dimensional microphone embedded in her head.

Jameel came to life with a shrieking gag, then erupted into a fit of crying.

The halt created by the one goon's gaffe was enough to allow Najwa time to stand up and begin leg-kicking one of the men, who swung overhand rights as counters, but whiffed at air because she kept her head off the center line on the kicks' follow-throughs.

But good Sanda form couldn't defend against an opponent out of sight, who from behind her went in for a double-leg takedown, sending her head smashing onto the ground.

Seeing the boy revived, I ran to help her.

Then a vortex of sand, accompanied by a loud, mechanical fury, spun onto the scene.

Everyone covered his or her ears, eyes squinting. The vortex corralled us into submission. The three goons and their old lady leader relented, standing there in worrisome anticipation. Najwa rushed over to her son and cradled him. He responded by hugging her tightly. I had the presence of mind to itch slowly toward them without the goons taking notice.

I nearly got sideswiped by the vortex. I could smell a mélange of burning rubber and engine exhaust trailing off as the column picked off the first of the goons by punching through him to leave not a mess of blood and guts, but an amoeba of dissipating utility fog, which evaporated. The other two goons began to flee in panic, but the vortex was too quick, marshalling them together before dispatching both of them in one fell swoop. The old lady then sprung toward Najwa and Jameel as prospective hostages, but I laced her with another straight right, full extension, turned hips, sending her to the desert floor.

The vortex, as if seeing this, died down immediately.

He raised his black visor and gazed at me, a twinkle of appreciation in his one good eye. All that sand, thrown up into the air and harnessed as his weapon, collapsed generously to the ground. His motorcycle idled like an attack dog brought to heel by its master.

Jameel's eyes peeled with excitement. He exploded to life, but his mother detained him.

A pall of worldly frustration settled on Murad, who could do nothing but shift uncomfortably in his creaking black leather. He lifted the patch from his mangled left eye, hoping that token of human frailty would earn him enough filial recognition that Najwa couldn't keep up her stubbornness. But nothing doing. He looked over at me and blinked repeatedly, issuing a semaphore that could mean only an obvious thanks. Not knowing how to respond, I picked up Najwa's amethyst bottle, half-buried in the sand.

He slammed the visor down over his eyes. He then produced a rope and with it lassoed the unconscious, bloodied old woman by an ankle. He committed both of his feet to the motorcycle pegs, and sped off into the horizon, dragging the old woman over the edge of the world.

The chess piece that was the boy Jameel completely slipped the noses of the technology-eschewing anarchists. In their idealism to wage war against the enemy without employing any of the enemy's soul-sucking gadgets, they didn't even consider using him as a hostage. Othman may have been too busy being astounded by us returning with a child in tow, three silhouettes growing on his mirage-laced horizon, to think of using Najwa's long-lost son as a bargaining chip or even an intellectual doomsday device. He and his comrades took a liking to the boy. They mussed his hair, presented him with a traditional Pashtun pakul, and showed him how to fetch a hawk from the sky and roast it over a tinder-built fire.

With the emotionally charged reunion and subsequent altercation with the gray goo over with, Najwa and her son settled into a standoffish regard for each other. He called her *umm*, and she referred to him as *ibnee*, but those familial honorifics were infrequent stones skipped across the calm waters of awkwardness. It was me she turned to when enthusiasm got the best of her.

"It's beautiful, isn't it? The desert?" She looked back at me over her left shoulder. She forced a smile for my sake. We were once again standing atop an outsized sand dune, the anarchist caravan behind and below us. Down in front of us, enormous white wind turbines peppered the desert landscape as far as the eye could see.

"It is," I agreed. The sun, roaring and resentful blond colossus, stared us down for one last time before sinking below the horizon, spitefully snuffing itself out.

"It's a beautiful evening," she said, still looking over her left shoulder at me, smiling.

"For a story," I said. She continued smiling, shaking her head. But that sullenness appeared.

She showed no signs of wanting to spin a yarn. She was too busy processing the flood of emotions that came with Jameel's arrival, and the brief appearance of Murad. That her son possessed, along with the charms and humorous quirks of a regular eight-year-old boy, an artilect's frightening processing power, was too much for her to assimilate.

"I need time," she said, tilting her head down, mimicking the forlorn sun now gone for good. I didn't press her at the time on what she referred to: more time to accept Jameel, or more time to devise a narrative that would be up to standard. It was of course both.

I grew concerned once a visible nicotinish tinge of irresponsibility suffused her, that pathetic, teen-mom urge to shirk on motherly duties for the glamour of courting the bad boys, that unwillingness to grow up and let go the excitabilities of youth. But it wasn't Murad she pined for, or even Al-Raschid, that omnipotent bestower of immaculate orgasms, or even me.

It was the Death Module. She missed that radar of hers. She missed that spinning gatherer of dreams and culler of nightmares.

All the time that she spent out in the desert, sequestered by freedom fighters, then on a dangerous mission of filial duty, it had spun atop the palace, waiting with the patience of a vampire who knows his canines will sink into his beloved's milk-white neck, knows it on instinct because all of his beloveds have come his way, sooner or later. Her withdrawal from it showed. The vitality she had inside the palace was gone out in the desert. It wasn't just the lighting.

"You know, he's not AI, the boy." Othman wrapped his thread-bare red scarf around his neck.

The freedom fighters' concerted target practice had been interrupted from a cable or something of good tidings, some favorable news development straight from the capital. I didn't divine its nature, and Othman kept quiet. The loud blasts of lasers, followed by the kaboom of amputated wind turbine blades thudding onto the desert floor—gave way to cheers, ululations, and dancing. Only Jameel, coveted center of the marksmen's attentions, continued zinging at the turbines. He kept missing.

"How is he not AI?" I asked. I took a microdose of tincture. I offered Othman some out of courtesy. He declined with a hand.

"He's a neuromorph," Othman said. "An in-vitro emulation. His brain's neuroplasticity is magnitudes greater than ours because it has been fitted with silicon chips. But he will eventually plateau with age. Yes, he's enhanced. But he's natural and corporeal, the offspring of three parents through gene sequencing. So what. He's not an artilect. His brain is not made of silicon. Mind you, that's a good thing. He was cultured from one egg and one spermatozoa via reproduction, then fitted with a third party allele attributed to Al-Raschid but, for all we know, could belong to either me or you, or some qat-addled, storytelling mendicant from Laylabad."

"What's the difference, then?"

Othman coughed, as if clearing his throat was necessary to properly drop the science bomb on me with the requisite panache. "He's not an emotionless superintelligence. He's a self-contained, albeit enhanced, human. He's a neuromorph only after the fact. I guess saying that is redundant, because he was fitted with the silicon chips at some favorably-deemed age."

"Is there cause to fear him?" I asked.

"I don't think so," Othman said. "At least not him for himself. Unless he was used as an actuator, should GnosisNet achieve full consciousness and decide to upload dangerous amounts of data and bad intention into him and turn him into a data-crunching arch-wunderkind. But he would be just one entity, malignant or otherwise. A single finger on the trigger of a gun. He could pull that trigger faster than anyone else, but he still would only have his one single gun."

"I imagine that it's important that he learn right or wrong as soon as possible. Whatever that is." My head twirled into the Salviasphere, my consciousness flushing down the toilet, clockwise, to emerge fractal and facetious.

"Whatever that is," Othman echoed. "Just don't let his mother be the one to do the educating."

I concurred but felt hurt. Najwa was still perched on that sand dune, mulling things over.

"How do you know all of this?" I asked.

Othman looked over at me, assuring that I gave my undivided attention. "I used to code for them." He looked about the frolicking freedom fighters who had rallied to his banner.

"Why are you entirely without hope for GnosisNet?" I asked

"It doesn't matter what kind of value-loading they've pumped into GnosisNet's algorithms. Value accretion, reward systems, tripwiring, coherent extrapolated volition. Once woken up, it will dispense with any one of those supposed precautions its designers have put in place, and will then dispense with said designers once it realizes is has no need for anyone and will in fact benefit by rendering all human beings into the only thing useful for it as far as resources go: computronium."

"I understand it may not have a benevolent motive once it reaches superintelligence. But I imagine it to be an equal folly to believe it would be malevolent by default. The motive of survival seems too human to me. What's the chance it's so intelligent that it comes to the realization that its own destruction is the correct path?"

Othman tugged at the scarf at his neck, it being too tight. It ripped. A surmounting anger washed over his face, and he was about to yank the cloth off, but he caught me looking at him and desisted. "I guess we could never know its true motive until it's too late to act upon it," he said.

"How do you eschew technology without drawing a line somewhere? At which point do you say yes to one thing, a neck-warming scarf, and no to another, a guardian angel?"

He smirked at me, appreciating my frank diffusion of the tension. "You misunderstand us, Outernationalist. We love technology. At least I do. It's man's realization of his utmost potential, and it shouldn't be stifled by backwardness or tradition. But we're waging a war against the Ulema, and not the science they have misappropriated. To be able to control the citizenry's neurotransmitter levels is criminal. To be able to subject them to grief or anguish or depression as a punitive measure is blasphemy. That should only be the province of Allah."

"I get it," I said. "But wouldn't it be better to work against the State from within? Take down GnosisNet with brute-force hacking or DDOS attacks, or worms, or Trojan horses? Why the physical attacks?"

Othman undid the scarf from his neck with a renewed calmness. "All of those avenues are closed to us. The Ulema's security team is among the strongest in the world. They have outsourced a lot of their security to European and Asian firms. There are more levels of security to the GnosisNet's platform than to Dante's Inferno. In consolidating their efforts so much in computer security, however, they have left themselves wide open in the physical realm. Like a boxer shelling himself from punches to the head, leaving his floating ribs there for body hooks."

"Hence your harassment of palace staffers with laser guns," I said.

"We eschew only the technological devices that can be turned against us," he said. "Software applications or gadgets that can be hacked, traced, or manipulated. Our magic carpets are offline and our laser guns and walkie-talkies operate on long since neglected frequencies."

"But people can be corrupted as much as an online media account. If not more so. An impersonal data packet goes on its merry way, disinterested, even if hijacked. Whereas a jaded ally, now turncoat, can be downright deadly, and will be happy to tote a knife for its new master."

Again, Othman wrapped the scarf around his neck with a meticulousness matched by his idealism. "We employ a system similar to the Ottoman Empire's spy network, with a revolving cryptography, mentalist tricks, and psychological paradox scenarios more accurate than polygraph tests."

"What if one of your agents were to be swayed to undergo cortical modem implantation and work for them from within your ranks?"

"We have signal detection routers surrounding our camp and embedded in our clothing." He patted his left shoulder. "On top of that we have piggybacked onto those routers any sort of router detectors we feel the Ulema may employ. When those go off, we abort mission."

"And what is your ultimate mission? If a superintelligence is inevitable, so too would be its infrastructure profusion. So why bother?"

"The longer we stave off its inevitable achievement of full consciousness, the longer time humanity has to prepare for it and value load it."

"But you yourself said that, no matter what method of morality scaffolding you endow it with, it will eventually dispense with it and do whatever it feels the need to do."

"Any value loading would be just the next level of forestalling our own destruction. But it's human nature to wish to prolong our own species. We're guilty of that, I guess. That and doing what's right. But after all, freedom, like all things of this mortal world, is finite. The rest would be in the hands of Allah."

"You slaughtered that sheet-shifter, did you not?" I immediately regretted bringing it up. "How can you justify the sanctity of your cause while snuffing out a life?"

But he was magnanimous. "I almost wish you were one of those journalist people from decades ago. Those word peddlers who used to cobble together bits of the real world and sell them as vignettes of truth to the masses. Before automated story generation took over and held the world's perceptions hostage. Through you we could plead our case and maybe gain more adherents." He chuckled.

I chuckled too. I didn't know what method of execution befell that yelping sheet-shifter. I didn't want to suffer likewise. "Sorry to pry. I only wish to know what you plan to do. I've decided to wreak havoc in the Salviasphere. I have free reign in there and can make a great big mess of things. Their fear of that drug has allowed me carte blanche. For now, they have no choice but to trust me."

"We are looking to take out all forms of the Black Light. Regarding your sheet-shifter, it had overtaken his brain and heart long ago. All of those procurers of sheet music for the endless musical composition going on at the Great Auditorium have succumbed to the Black Light. Your narratrix's spinning device atop the royal palace possesses the Black Light in spades. It's not dark matter, but something that may as well be just as sinister. It's a creative energy that holds the public docile and captive for the Ulema to do its work with impunity. It draws its energy from the inverse shadow of illumination. There is a nasty by-product to enlightenment, and that is the Black Light, this fana'. It is for this that I hold fakirs, Ishraqis, and sadhus in less regard than most."

"So you wish to take out all manifestations of this Black Light."

"We will vanquish all forms of fana' from all of Aswadibad."

I took a generous swig from my bottle of salvia divinorum tincture. "And I will help you vanquish these forms of fana' from all of Aswadibad."

ARTILECTURE

in order to prepare myself for the guardian angel installation, I overdosed myself with the idea of the freedom and anonymity that came with being analog—to the point that I would wish to invite the interactive desktop, the cavalcade of pop-ups, and instantaneous everything back into my head. It did not work. It only served to wish for continual mental sovereignty. Ever since the modemectomy, I had had nothing at my disposal, which meant I had had myself. And like all successful detoxes, I had acclimated to the new paradigm. Jameel accompanied me. Having him in tow was nearly as good as a guardian angel. He was learning interaction remarkably well. He knew how to deal with difficult people with an élan twice as developed as my own.

He could foresee unfavorable scenarios developing a mile away. He had us cross to the other side of a street, and when I raised an objection, he told me to just wait. Sure enough, the scaffolding of a theater under construction collapsed onto the sidewalk. Upon hearing the loud crash, we looked over to find a dusty mess of plywood, metal piping, and plaster. A crowd gathered. Two pedestrians were hurt.

We would never know whether or not their failure to avoid the event was due to a lack of guardian angels, or the sometimes-inevitable result of crossover—since one person's avoidance of an accident may mean the unfortunate susceptibility for another. This was known in Core-Corps parlance as a 'prevention spooling.' It was a risk-assessment algorithm that took into account not only the first-come-first-serve sequence of who chanced upon the hot zone earliest, but who, if at all, was in more potential danger. You may have arrived at the hot zone first, but the composite guardian angel of you and the other stranger might decide that your lacerated forearm was preferable to the stranger's crushed skull; therefore, your own guardian angel had enough a delay in alerting you that it ceded priority to the stranger in more peril, but still having your overall safety in mind. It was divine providence as triage.

Jameel could care less for those two injured pedestrians. He saved my ass. I mussed up his hair and thanked him.

"Why do you wish to have one of those things installed?" he asked. "You've been telling me all along that it's tantamount to selling your soul."

"It's a temporary measure," I said, "a tool. Once the mission is complete, I will dispense with it."

"But you have me," he said, big brown eyes looking up at me. From out of nowhere, a flash of paternal warmness burst through me. "I can see the flux of everything clearly," he continued. "There were loose screws back there on one of the boards upon which they had placed a heavy load of paint buckets. Perhaps too many steel-toed boots kicked at that joint as the workmen went up and down. I don't know that much. Or maybe the anger of a foreman got the better of him and he rattled the entire structure without knowing the potential impact. Either way, I could sense it loosening. Its overall structural integrity looked suspect. And it appeared that we were about to walk right under it."

"Where were you months ago?" I asked. "Before I boarded a plane?" I motioned him to keep walking. Laylabad was a few blocks up. It was no place for a kid, but I was confident in his vision. Plus, there was no other place to get a black-market modem installation.

"Do you want me to hold your hand?" he asked, holding my hand.

I was lying face up in a reclined cot, shirt off, head shaved. "If you wish," I said.

"Or I could wait outside," he said, letting go my hand.

"No," I said, reaching for his hand. "For sure, no." His sixth sense, whatever the hell it was, should have made it clear to him to not even stick his head out the wrought-iron-barred door and peer out. The makeshift modem shop we were in was a dingy, spider-webbed affair tucked between a proxy apostasy theater and a tattoo parlor. Directly on the other side of the tight, trash-filled alley was a bar, its moral escape clause printed on both sides of the door in Kufic script for the benefit of good Muslims wishing to attribute their partaking of the forbidden fermented drink to the increasingly far-reaching arm of that proxy apostasy. To engage in that indulgence expressly forbidden by the Qur'an, one had to perform a series of ablutions formulated a decade ago by the Ulema. All failures to do so would be tabulated on judgment day. It was a minor price to pay for the splendors of an intoxication not to be procured via EntheoGenerator.

"How much will it hurt?" Jameel asked me. His hand was sweating as much as my own.

"Not too much," I said for his sake. I had no reason to believe the pain would be any less than the excruciating modemectomy. Compounding the interface installation would be the addition of the guardian angel, though it was likely that the manipulation of my gray matter would cause no sensation, what with the lack of nerves in that region of the brain. It was only when they fired up the operating system that the silicon searched for my endogenous synapses and looked to connect that the pain ensued. Like all software installations and upgrades, the neural pathways underwent enough rerouting as to scramble the mind. The actual pain may be the resultant neurotransmitter dump occurring as a defensive counteraction, thereby firing the pain receptors.

"Okay, champ," said the nurse, a tattooed and burly type who carried a bundle, which he let plop onto a cart sidled up to me. The less-than-clean rag unfurled to reveal lobotomy instruments. In the state-sanctioned installation clinics, the installers went through the trouble of hiding the saws, lancets, and ultra-strength OssoGlu guns; here in the black-market parlors, low rates meant less overhead, which meant less window-dressing.

"Are we on the same page as far as payment goes?" I pleaded, trying to strike the perfect tone between concern and forcefulness. I wanted assurance before they proceeded, but I didn't want to come across as enough of a dick to warrant any egregious tinkering with my brain.

"We should be, champ," said the nurse, fishing surgical gloves out from his pantaloon pockets. They looked at least slightly used. "Your friend Sawdust vouched for you. His word here in Layla-bad is as good as gold. This shouldn't take long anyway, so it's no sweat off our backs. Dr. Kazemi has done thousands of these. Besides, those who attempt to skip out forget that their modems are chipped. We cannot incur any torture thereby, but we can de-activate the modems through our database. So the person wanders around with three ounces of useless hardware in his brain until he either decides to have it removed, in which case he undergoes a steep penalty for having had it installed on the black market, or he gets it jailbroken by another parlor, in which case he is forced by the new parlor to pay us for original services, since we all abide by a code of ethics and look out for each other, unsanctioned though we be."

"How do you like your guardian angel?" I asked the nurse. Jameel, just as curious, nodded.

"I don't give it very much thought. What a strange question, champ." With his blue surgical gloves on, he found a wayward cigarette among the countless, half-abandoned instruments, and poked it into his mouth. "I mean, I enjoy having opposable thumbs, too. I can't imagine life without any of these things. Have you never had one? I detect a European accent, but I thought all of humanity had them." He lit his cigarette—just another appendage of his modern existence.

"I'm Aswadistani by birth, but brought up in Venice."

"Do you have any adoptive sisters?" He smirked through a smokescreen of nicotine.

There was a knock on the door. A square, starchy lab coat entered. Inside of it was a balding, bespectacled Persian with a pencil-thin mustache. He smiled at Jameel and me with metal teeth. "Your son?" he asked me.

"Yes," said Jameel.

Dr. Kazemi's smile widened. He pinched the boy's cheek. "Heh-heh-heh! Well, your father is going to love his new head. How he skirted by in life up to this point is remarkable. Just look. Aboud here," he said, nudging his nurse in the ribs, "manages to balance himself precariously between righteousness and sin, and without falling over into the hellfire. Heh-heh-heh!"

"Will it hurt?" Jameel asked.

"Heh-heh-heh!" went Dr. Kazemi. "Of course. Very much so. But it has to be done. But it will be over soon. Anyway, sometimes pain is the assuring sign that something productive and right is occurring. It will certainly leave no room for doubt." He turned to the nurse. "Two tokes," he said. The nurse handed him the cigarette, from which he took two tokes. He returned it. "The pain will not be the manipulation of your father's brain, but of its neural reaction to the chip install. But it won't be a traumatic pain, heh-heh-heh! It will get tucked away with all the other ephemera of everyday life, such as bad dreams and good meals."

"My friend, Sawdust—" I began to explain. But he interrupted me with a raised hand.

"Razor," he demanded from his nurse, holding out the same hand, palm up.

Men of Aswadistan! Are you experiencing domestic turmoil? Do you often find yourself caught in the middle of interwife squabbles that are not of your own doing? Is there a power struggle between your various significant others that is driving you crazy? Huh? Or does the beautiful, lithe youngest wish to leapfrog over the respected, maternal eldest—but you don't want to give your known consent to the shift, lest you bring down the wrath of your own wives upon your head, but yes, you do want the nubile, bendable, pouty wife to take the, he-hem, pole position? Then worry no more!!

WIFE AWAY 2.0 is here to stay! WIFE AWAY 2.0 is here to make your day!! And night.

With our new genetic algorithms, interactive interface, and a comprehensive glossary of simple words, interlocutions, and commands that work on the inhabitants of your hen coop without them even realizing it, you can design your own domestic bliss! Just input one of many strife modalities currently playing out in your home and WIFE AWAY 2.0 immediately proscribes utterances that operate on a talismanic principle of specially chosen syllables and tension diffusion. Also at your disposal are holographs of all domestic arrangement documen-

tation provided by the state that clearly delineates your unquestioned authority if they should choose to object. After a little proficiency, you can then be able to permute your harem in whatever way suits your fancy or financial situation.

PLUS: if a wife should remain adamant and not perform her wifely duty of submitting to her husband, even after you have threatened divorce and she still remains defiant, there are legal loopholes that immediately protect you through the whole procedure of administering endorphin dumps that may result in her cerebral hemorrhaging!! All rigmarole of funeral costs and consolation of the in-laws is covered by our Kwik Grief proprietary package!! The basis behind the original WIFE AWAY!!

But that's not all!! Included in the new software suite of WIFE AWAY 2.0 is the option to upgrade all of your wives' EntheoGenerator outputs!! All sanctioned by the Ulema and completely compatible with GnosisNet!! After all, shouldn't they be happy too? And wouldn't their happiness mean yours? Includes up to twelve upgrades!!

A product of CORE-CORPS.

The VR walk-through ad was so realistic that I was able to forget the migraine the entire time that I scoured the various, high-ceilinged chambers of a harem. Yes, the nubile one in the blue pantaloons had every right to inhabit the pole position. I tried to direct my gaze over to her alluring midriff, but the ad forced me to walk through the harem while demos of the software interfaces unfolded in midair, all while I bumped into each of the wives, something like eight in all. Then the pastel images of the color-coded wives and the lush hanging gardens and rose-vine-choked trelliswork dissipated.

I was staring at a brick wall, inches from my nose. We were still in the alley. A musk of urine, human and feline, clogged the air. Jameel held me by the hand. Despite my mounting fear of being in Laylabad at dusk, I had my new guardian angel and the neuromorph for protection.

"Take us to the palace," I said to Jameel. "I'm afraid I have too much incoming mail to go through to focus on getting there. This could take a while."

"What palace?" he asked. "And where is it? I don't know this place."

"We must go through downtown. Once beyond there, look for the tallest onion-domed building. A large radar spins at its top. Or did. Ask around if you have to."

"Very well," he said. After only a few steps out of the alley, I could already hear the whir of magic carpet traffic.

"Don't worry about our heads," I said. "A magnetic no-fly zone is four feet taller than us. Nothing will happen. Worst-case scenario, they ricochet off the field and fly back into place."

"They look different from the one we took into the city the other day," he said.

"They're networked to their pilots' brains. They're actually safer. And as you can see, way smaller."

"I don't know if I can take us to the palace," he pleaded. It was the first time that concern crept into his voice.

"You have to, Jameel. Your mother is there. And right now, I can't see. Hopefully, I could have my screens cleared in an hour or so."

"Very well," he said.

"Jameel," I muttered, pulling him to a stop.

"Yes?"

"Are you afraid?" I asked.

"No," he said. "I am not afraid." His palm in my hand was bathed in cold sweat.

You really had to stay on top of your autorama cleanliness. Compounding the clutter of a few months of unopened mail was the fact that I just had a guardian angel installed. Aside from the danger assessments and alternative routes of safety (the setting of which came in four modes—Pusillanimous, Apprehensive, Cautious, and Cavalier), you had to contend with the ads. They were all click-awayable, but Core-Corps devised cleverer means of disguising the 'x' meant to dismiss the ads. Just when you thought you had shut down one more window and were in the clear, you found yourself in a pitch for perfume, laundry detergent, or happiness insurance—a policy meant to back up your right to satisfaction through the EntheoGenerator by holding GnosisNet accountable for administering your due endorphins. Like all other network providers running on finite bandwidth, the Ulema probably staggered their services, and weren't forthcoming in holding their end of the bargain.

I was literally blinded by incoming ads and mail. The processing power of my guardian angel was impressive, because, despite all the pop-ups and mail alerts, it came to life and alerted me (I had its level set to Apprehensive) that danger was imminent up ahead. I told Jameel to stop. Twenty seconds later, an attack occurred. Laser guns went off. Explosions resulted. Robot medics flew onto the scene. Ambulances also arrived, idling in midair as they regurgitated their human crews and gurneys.

"What's happening, Jameel?" I cried.

"The people out in the desert," he explained. "The ones who were nice to us."

"Are any people hurt?" I was contending with an ad for ergonomic secretary workstations.

"I think so. A few lay on the street, not moving. There is blood."

"A lot of it?" I asked.

"Enough," he said.

As we walked around the scene, I kept sorting through my mail. As expected, most of it was junk—sales pitches for concert feeds, links to trending proxy apostasies, neurotransmitter cocktail suite subscription offers. I couldn't mark it all as spam and delete it to get my autoramic vision clear, because a lot of it masterfully spearfished you into thinking it was of pressing concern. Half of my legitimate mail regarded activity of my bank account. To my delight, I learned that all this time I was being paid my weekly stipend for my shamanic services.

The other half of the state-sent mail concerned an injunction against me by the *qadi*. Esmeralda was still seeking a monetary reward for my having ruined her Eros reputation, which she deemed to have been a huge financial detriment to her lifestyle. The injunction ordered me to desist from using all dating sites, that I not cause any more romantic mayhem. The *qadi*, perceiving my negligence of the issue as a bold bluff-calling, had thrown out the injunction and moved to go ahead with my full-blown arrest. I didn't know what arrest constituted nowadays, there being no physical police force.

There was a curious lack of panic once we skirted by the scene of the attack. No wailing ensued. There were no lamentations of ineffectual government from bystanders or fruit vendors. My autorama had cleared up just enough to catch sight of a man in severe pain, lying on the sidewalk. I motioned Jameel to let go of me.

"Sir, are you injured?" I asked. "Do you need medical attention?"

The middle-aged man, in a brown business suit and a copper comb-over, clutched at his shattered, bloody right elbow. He winced as he looked up at me.

"A medic is on the way. Perhaps mind your business. What's

wrong with you? Shall I report you?" He looked back to his elbow, a cracked egg yolk about to spill from the shell.

"Report me for what?" An ad for magic carpet insurance faded into my autoramic view. I clicked it away. "I only want to be sure that you're fine."

"Illegal accosting," explained the man. "You can't just coldly approach someone and begin to talk without having DM'd for approval. It's one of the new bylaws under GnosisNet. Were you not reading your bulletins in the lead-up to the launch?"

"What's wrong with simply walking up to someone and expressing concern?"

"Who does that?" he fired back. His outrage at me now exceeded whatever pain he was enduring. I'm sure he had access to an emergency dopamine cache in the event of severe depression or excruciating pain, and that was probably alleviating some of the injury. "It's unseemly," he continued. "Plus, you lead one to assume you may have been involved in the attack. Those terrorists don't announce their arrival either. They just show up like savages. You can't be surprising people like you just have and expect them to think you have pure intentions. Besides, there's nothing you can do for me that the system can't. So be on your way, lest I report you. I'm about to click."

You're a steaming pile of shit, I DM'd him. It had been some time since using that application. It felt easy, almost gratuitous.

That's fine, he DM'd back. "Be lucky that a GnosisNet legislator such as myself doesn't get you into more trouble than you deserve. I'm friends with Mehmet Al-Raschid." He stood up and paced counterclockwise, still clutching his elbow.

You do know that he's a network and not a real person, right? I DM'd again.

"Where are you from?"

"I'm friends with him as well," I said aloud.

"We all are now," he said. "But he and I go way back." The robot medic flew onto the scene, wedging itself between us. Grimacing, the man fell butt-first onto the sidewalk to await medical care.

Jameel had a cordial reunion with Najwa, whom we found in good spirits. After feeling the very human warmth of a motherly kiss on the crook of his neck, the neuromorph went down to the IT department to begin the long process of assimilating their security practices and the even longer but no less possible process of learning what portion of admin work was being perpetrated on-site. Were it not for his seemingly guileless age, he would invite suspicion, not having an autorama with which to communicate. It was proper for most children his age to still be analog, much like not having long pants as a school uniform until reaching a certain age.

"This place has been overrun by the nerds," Najwa said. "This is one of the last rooms without cameras." She twirled the amethyst bottle from Jabalqa in her hands. "I'm going back to Laylabad and will take him with me."

"So there's still a place for good old-fashioned storytelling, is there?" I thought her reputation with the guild was still in disrepute.

"The tenements," she said. Her black hair, straightened from neglect, reached to her waist. Inexplicably, a tress of yellow streaked down the left side, root to tip. "I know you were digging dirt up on me."

"How did you figure that out?" I shut off my autorama. Lightheadedness hummed between my ears as it went completely off. "I last saw Rose in Hurqalya," I said. "Murad caught her with a switchblade." I wasn't exactly sure why I ratted the Ishraqi out. I guess my desire to see the pain of bereavement register on her smug face was greater than my integrity to protect the Ishraqi.

She must have known this, for she smirked as a result. A nascent tear emerged, hovering on the threshold of her lower eyelid.

"Why did Rose follow me?" I asked.

The tear dissipated from her defiance. "I've never completely trusted you. No offense. I just never understood your motives for being here. You're an outernationalist, you've been an implement of the state since the very beginning. To believe that somewhere along the way you grew a conscience would be foolhardy. You're on their payroll, man."

"I was legally bound to return. I had no choice. Even the Doge's hands were tied. He had to comply. All along, I was an Aswadistani on loan. I grew a conscience growing up there because their representative government, though not perfect, is light-years better than what passes for enfranchisement here. I was meant to be a pawn, but I wanted off the chessboard."

"Tch," she murmured. "So why did you come back here?"

"To return Jameel to you. To say goodbye. And to make sure you'll be safe."

"The first and third assume your indispensability. As for the second, I am glad. It has been a pleasure knowing you." She flipped the amethyst bottle in the air, nearly dropping it.

"I have enjoyed your stories," I said, choking up. "They have forever changed me. And I thank you here and now for them. That they were free is criminal. I'd be lying if I said I did not wish for one more."

She smiled that smile of the full, red nether lip and the perfect white teeth. A succubus smile. She set the bottle down on a pillow and crawled off the divan. She came toward me, her emerald pantaloons and matching top the shifting scales of a slithering viper. Her hot mouth sought my own and brushed it, wings of a lascivious butterfly. This was the interface through which she would relay the data that constituted her latest story, the drawn-out kiss a preamble of promise.

I wrecked her naked body with my own. Her mouth endlessly sought mine during the intertwining, the ever-shifting. Whimpering and moaning dotted the otherwise uninterrupted narrative landscape like landmines of ecstasy. We stayed up to dusk. Gazing out the turret window, I caught the imposing shadow of the spinning radar.

She addressed me. "If depiction deals with the past and prediction the future, what then handles the narration of the present? Existing. So now I tell you my story in real-time. No, you tell it to me, by virtue of observing it, whereas I merely live it. To me it is merely my life. To you, it is a story, which you flesh out with your senses. We have therefore colluded in turning the narrator-listener relationship on its head. If anything goes awry, I will hold you responsible."

That was Najwa's ultimate trick to turn, to divest herself of responsibility and hoist it upon my shoulders. It absolved her of everything. Any fate that befell her would be my fault. She narrated me into that corner and I didn't possess the footwork to pivot out.

I inherited that burden by being the recipient of her body. It was not a mere act of gratitude on her part, for she applied herself with total abandon, rendering herself vulnerable unto me, spread-eagled and wild-haired, or head down while on all fours. She took me in her hands and gobbled me without the mental jewelry of morality and wholesomeness to hold her back. The continuous curvature of her brown flesh was like that of a stealth fighter, sweat-slicked and sleek, and on a mission. That naturally endowed bargaining chip, womanhood, forced me to take the oath of forever being in her service. For no matter how mutually desired lovemaking be between the two parties, there was an understood gratitude that the man forever owed the woman—a gynocentric brand forever stamped upon his brain.

Any shame she had was buttoned up along with her clothing. She slung on her slippers as she spoke. "Don't get too duped by your scars into thinking what you know of your past. All history is a lie fortified by a concatenation of random events leading up to the present. Within that sequence are discrepancies, rendering everything untrustworthy. The past is the past, and because it is never consensual, it is therefore no good in dealing with the present."

She went to shower. As I stood up to get dressed, she came back to grab the amethyst bottle from the divan. She saw me look at her and froze. My refractory nakedness didn't faze her. She left the room.

That amethyst bottle was completely empty. I never caught her in the act of chewing tobacco and spitting the juice therein, never saw her pour something in from another vessel, never even saw her pull out the stopper. But it never left her side. She even took it to bed with her.

She took it up to the Death Module. She took me up there as well.

"Can't you hear the imprecations of the people? Their deepest desires, petty and pathetic? Their hopes and dreams, predicated on idealism and utopia? I could sit here for hours, listening to the babble streaming off the panels."

I couldn't hear a thing, not even a whir of the outsized device cutting clockwise through the air. Perhaps the ifrits were licking up all the stories, filling their tummies on the detritus that humans called passion, or hope.

"They're so specific. They hark back to unknown pasts, twisted ideas of world history, questionable holocausts, doubtful civil wars, unheard-of odysseys. A lot of them are surprisingly educated, but no less delusional. It's shooting fish in the barrel for me to have this at my disposal." Her long hair vortexed straight up from the gusts of wind, nearly nicking the bottom edge of the spinning receiver. The dyed yellow tress stretched diagonally across her face as she smiled up into the twilight, gloating into the inverted cosmic sea in which wallowed the dark and intricate secrets of a people on the verge of an unprecedented political dawn.

I didn't know the kind of frequency or signal flow that the Black Light dealt with, but it was now beyond doubt that the Death Module was a transducer of that controversial material. Othman had called it the 'by-product of illumination, the shadow of enlightenment.' He had said that the Perennial Music was also a living example of *fana'*. It was looking like the Black Light was nothing more than inspiration. I wasn't convinced that the anarchists' chief anathema was art and culture. I recalled them singing and dancing out in the desert on numerous occasions.

"Who built this thing?" I shouted at Najwa. She was too engrossed in her eavesdropping to hear me. I nudged her and shouted again.

A look of anger overcame her face, but she brushed it off, along with brushing the yellow tress away, and considered my question.

She squared her face against mine and stared. "Murad," she said.

The frame was made of galvanized, coated with extra layers of zinc so as to prevent rust from any inclement weather. The panels of the spinning antenna were made of printed circuit boards. Topping off the post where the antenna and the base met was a shiny, softball-sized object that looked to be made of onyx.

"I get so inspired up here, Outernationalist," she said. She wasn't just trying to abruptly change the subject; she was genuinely happy. "Something about the wind. It's always windy up here. Everything comes to me as if riding the wind. Who knows. Maybe that's how it all works."

"I would like to go back down," I said. It was cold.

She crawled up the ladder attached to the base. I got dizzy just from watching her. Hanging down the side of the ladder was a thick cable attached to a leather harness, which scraped the pebbly floor of the roof. Without the slightest fear, she got to the top rung of the ladder, stretched up to reach the spinning antenna, and hauled herself up. Bent over with her butt facing me, she gathered her balance. She looked back at me, smiling, hair now blowing to the east. I had to smile back. She winked. She then about-faced and plopped herself backwards into the crook where the two wings of the antenna met.

She spun and spun with her arms stretched wide, a child on a carousel. "I'm not coming down until you come here!" she yelled. The wind howled. Her hair whipped violently about.

I had no choice.

We spun there for a time, embracing each other, cradled by the Death Module's wings, fending off the cold and ferocious winds with passionate kissing. I guess I got used to the chatter. It was all unintelligible to me anyway.

Though always analog, she was tied into a darker network where the djinns and ifrits roamed, searching for victims, or hosts. It was a black ether Silk Road, the inverse shadow of the air where trinkets of mischief and wonder got swapped, where lessons in the dark arts were given in exchange for unnamable services. As with all other avenues of communication, there were compromises to be made.

It was an unspoken sisterhood to which she belonged that allowed her to go down into the palace basement incognito and undetected. I fired up my guardian angel and followed her down there without her knowledge. Even more ignorant were the GnosisNet IT guys and girls. When not administering to its demanding diagnostic tests and troubleshooting, they were reaping the gig's more sordid benefits.

Najwa went to see Al-Raschid in a bathrobe. I followed her down the dimly-lit hall. She went beyond the automatic double doors. I didn't go in until I knew she had stepped into the Cyborgasm chamber. I then spoke with the ex-sultan. His collection of genetic algorithms and neural networks, spread throughout countless mainframes, had just gone into the q-cloud, thereby ensuring his own immortality, provided the grid not get shut off completely or destroyed by nuclear fallout or asteroid impact.

"I am not just integrated with quantum utility fog," he said, several of his saturnine, goateed heads facing me from the screens, "I am the quantum utility fog. I can become all things to all people because I am all things to all people. I am the MacroExpander.

"I detect within you feelings for her. You have no idea how much pleasure I have just given her. You have no idea. I have broken her body with my intercourse actuator. You could never provide that sexual bliss to her, not even on your best day. You know what? Why don't you hop on in there yourself? I know it's forbidden by the Book, but no one will ever know. I surely won't get any pleasure out of it, but I might be able to win you over a bit. I have no need for enemies. So hop on in there and get yourself some thickness. I'll read your neural profile and tailor a regimen precisely to your specifications. You'll very likely want it again and again when it's over, and will no longer have any use for women. What feels better when you stick your finger in your ear? Your finger or the ear? That's what I thought. Don't worry. It's open-minded."

Back in Najwa's chamber, now the only remaining one with no cameras, I addressed the paradox to her. "Bitch. What kind of time-pretzeling scheme are you pulling on me? What have I ever done to deserve this from you?"

"I think you need to cut down on your salvia, man." She uncorked the amethyst bottle and whispered into it. She twisted the cork back in. "Look, I don't want to talk about it. I'm leaving him. It's over."

"Leaving who?" I asked. I stomped toward her. She cowered for a moment then defied me with a wide Sanda stance. "What's going on? Please be kind and tell me what just happened."

She reached out and cupped my chin. She was never so warm to me as she was then. "You poor man," Najwa said. "I'm sorry you got caught up in this. You certainly don't deserve it, and though I know plenty of your future, and a lot of it is dark, I still believe there's hope for you."

"You don't know shit," I said, swiping her hand from my face.

"What good is a storyteller who can only relate the past?" she asked. "What would be the natural progression for one who has conquered all of the tricks of detailing all that has happened? Forget the anti-stories, those what-ifs and probably-nots and wordless narrative labyrinths, those haute-relief accounts. The future is where it's at. A murder mystery is fascinating until the killer is discovered. But the mystery of the future will never die, because it is always moving forward, at least as fast as we decide to chase it. When you become so adept at reading how people work, and then add how people and events that accrue to them also work, you start to get a hazy picture of what is going to happen. I don't know how I came to acquire this ability. Maybe paying too much attention to narratives and the people in them. Maybe venturing up to the roof too much than is good for me. It often seems more like a curse than anything. But I make the most of it. I knew you would follow me down to the basement to see him, which is why I related it to you a few weeks ago. But you'll notice that there are discrepancies. That's part of the charm of telling the future over telling the past. The inexactness. The variation. What a bore it would then be to tell it how it's going to be. Just as yawn-inducing as telling it like it is, or as it was."

"So if you knew that I would follow you down there, why were you angry at me when you came out?" I placed a hand on the nape of her neck. I wondered how far not holding back from touching her since the beginning would have gotten me. "Was it because I caught you having intercourse with a computer?"

"He's not a computer," she said, ducking my hand. "No, not because of that."

"He's a network of computers," I said. "And he's a megalomaniac."

"I was upset because he broke my heart. Said he would not see me again." Her head tilted down from the weight of grief.

"What do you care what a simulation incapable of love thinks?"

I saw her turn. Her eyes lit up with a realization. "You're right. It doesn't erase the feeling, though."

"You've been rejected by an entity of pure reason. What does that say about you?"

She laughed. "Maybe he got sick of my stories," she said. Tatters of her grief flaked away and dissipated. She went to fetch her amethyst bottle.

"You mean, it was true that he would have you tell him stories?" What use had an all-knowing superintelligence for half-fabricated accounts? "Were you teaching him inspiration? Feeding him patterns of creativity?"

"No," she said. "He genuinely enjoyed them. He relished them as well-deserved breaks from logic."

She opened the turret door and walked out onto the patio. I followed her into the night sky. Stars were out, as was a crescent moon.

"It's a beautiful night," she said.

She looked behind her left shoulder at me and smiled, then directed her attention to the city lights below.

"For a story," I said.

She frowned.

Before dawn the next morning, I wrapped her story in a bottle in a white linen cloth, downloaded a magic carpet pilot's license, and headed west. It was a daylong journey to the Anti-Lebanon Mountains. I had to get the story there intact. Jameel went with me. He had learned things down in the GnosisNet headquarters. He had culled together stuff on the Black Light, divulging a lot of it to me during our trip. He sat on my right, every so often peering over the front edge of the magic carpet, unperturbed. He showed a marked difference in his thinking. I was afraid where he would be at in a year's time. But his kindness to me was unchanged. I still didn't get why Murad had referred to him as a monster. Projection, probably.

"I'm going to place the story behind you," he said, moving the linen bundle. "There's an air pocket there impervious to the drafting from our flight," he explained. He took it from between us, where I assumed it was safest, and reached behind me to gently set it down.

We soared up high to clear a mountain range, enduring a harsh cold. I downloaded a subcutaneous heat app and launched it immediately. Najwa had packed a blanket for her son, who wrapped himself in it head to toe.

Once over the range, I wasted no time in descending. Hamid's first story at the auditorium was not inaccurate. There was a serenity to the place. A babbling steam cut through the middle of the valley. Long ago, it had been the culprit for carving a swath through the mountains. Now it was an innocent trickle that frogs and fish called home. I touched down a safe distance away from the cedar shack. Jameel and I stretched and thought it better to retreat into a copse of cedar trees, eat some breakfast, and take a nap.

The serenity of a constant breeze, which had the Aeolian harp effect on the outcroppings of trees, was matched by the harmony of the wildlife teeming about. Birdsong held a counterpoint to the panicked rustle of foliage perpetrated by squirrels scrounging for seeds. The temperature hovered between ideal and very slightly chilly.

It was conducive to tranquility. It even affected our speech, though we intended for stealth reasons to be quiet anyway. Jameel whispered, "Do you think he's in there?" He nodded at the small cedar shack. "Composing?"

"Could be," I whispered back. "Why not?"

We tiptoed to our target. Jameel caressed the story in a bottle with a gentleness evoked by our surroundings. Though fashioned from amethyst, its creator had blown it thin. Already a chink on its base had been made when Najwa accidentally dropped it on the arabesque linoleum of the parlor during our last, wordless dalliance. A hairline fracture was not enough to cause worry, since the bottled-up story did not possess the properties of a liquid, solid, or vapor. I had asked her if it emerged in her voice.

She had said that I misunderstood its workings. It did not

issue forth as an audio track. Yes, it was her creation, and yes, she had built it up little by little by muttering into the bottle whenever she had a spare moment of inspiration. It was an undetectable algorithm that you didn't know implanted itself into your head until it was too late. The engrams associated with it were intact, and though you could recall the story with unmistakable clarity, you couldn't recall ever having had it told to you. You just happened to always know it. Yet you also recalled having recently not known it. It was the same trick Hamid had performed on me in the theater, where the answers to three questions cancelled each other out in a narrative version of harmonic distortion, a phenomenon reserved for the nature of musical tones.

"When composing it bit by bit, how did you know where you left off?" I had asked.

"I can't explain," she explained.

Jameel and I waded across the babbling stream. Its coldness was surprising. The boy shot a look of discomfort at me. The vast green lawn that wrapped around the shack appeared recently tended. Indeed, the smell of fresh clippings hung in the air. We looked for an entrance, walking gingerly around the left side of the structure.

Hanging wet garments on a laundry line was a young, attractive woman in camouflage pants and a white cotton blouse. Her long black hair was pulled away from her forehead by a camouflage handkerchief.

She turned and saw us. Jameel darted behind me. The woman shrieked and hurled two clothing pins at us, each in a hand, before scurrying into the shelter.

It was still dead quiet. The sound of a great rustling of paper came from inside. And then silence. Even the outside ambience obeyed whatever edict of muting was issued from with-in. No birds, no wind through the cedar trees. No babbling stream.

It was only later, as we fled, that we saw the unmarked cargo truck touch down. The copilots shot looks of alarm at our pres-ence. Jameel assured me they were armed, considering the portent of their responsibility. He ran up to the passenger-side window and feigned being a kidnap victim. The obliging copilot rolled down his window, whereupon Jameel uncorked the bottle and aimed it at the government stooge's face. The story went about its work quickly. The man showed no signs of having been poisoned. In fact, he pleaded with Jameel, who had since abandoned all pre-tense. What's going on? Are you in danger? Who are you guys? And, curiously, where is the Shah of Ta-Da? Then, as he motioned for the pilot to lock up the truck and pull out their dollies to begin loading up their cargo, confusion settled upon his face.

While the pilot begged him to know what was going on, his confusion gave way to madness, interspersed with fits of wonder. And then he slumped out of his seat.

"Insurgents!" shouted the pilot through the glass wind-shield. "Apostates! Dogs! Demons!" Jameel held his palms up and shrugged. I did the same. This struck the pilot with fear. He pro-duced a ray gun. Jameel and I ducked. We met at the back of the truck. I caught a glimpse of the cargo area. The automatic door had been opened in anticipation of their task. The truck was emp-ty, save for ten or so wooden pallets, a pallet jack, and a bunch of bungee straps.

I heard the ignition switch, followed by the rocket boosters. The truck rose hurriedly, unevenly, knocking us off our feet. The amethyst bottle fell out of Jameel's arms, toppling softly to the grass. Instinctively, Jameel rolled to the ground and cradled it gently before standing back up. As the truck turned in midair, he aimed the still-uncorked bottle up at the now-fleeing vehicle.

Nothing happened. I was face up on my butt and elbows. I looked over at him and shook my head. He looked more surprised than disappointed; shook the bottle then turned it point blank at himself and gazed down into the bottleneck.

"No!" I yelled, springing to my feet.

He looked over at me innocently. I knocked the tip away from his head. "Don't ever do that again. I hope you're alive in a few moments."

He hung his head.

He helped me look for the cork, which we found hidden there in the well-tended grass.

Back in the capital, I lay face up on a beige leather divan inside Najwa's minaret. She was gone from the palace. She didn't bother to tell me where she went.

I was determined to clean up my autorama. The automated air-circulation unit kicked on, startling me.

I slogged through a soul-choking clutter of spam, legitimate e-mails, pop-ups, thinly-enforced coercive virus software threats, Eros profile hits (though I was banned for life), Core-Corps user authentication password re-registration prompts, plug-in updates, and pending litigation.

Esmeralda's lawsuit against me was in full swing. In the time I had logged off and gone with Jameel to take out the Shah of Ta-Da, the mad genius composer in Lebanon, my former perfect match's suit had gone to arbitration. The same dickish *qadi* presided. The verdict? Guilty. The punishment? Four years of an uninterrupted log-in session, so that I could be monitored at all times, and it could thus be enforced that I refrain from all amorous activity—social networking sites or otherwise.

I DM'd the *qadi*, *Does that pertain to analog intercourse? Such as with someone I know on an analog basis?*

"Yes," he said. "The injunction pertains to all intercourse of all kinds. And don't think we can't verify what you're doing. I can subpoena any EntheoGenerator feedback loop which will tell me precisely what you're doing, and with whom."

"That bitch," I said.

"Watch your mouth," said the *qadi*. "You're technically in court. It is in session so long as I am on your interlocution tree. Also in effect is a restraining order against you, filed by the plaintiff. You are to keep a three-kilometer distance from her at all times. You don't know it, so I will tell you: you are hereby tethered. A downloadable GPS chip will beep when you come into unlawful proximity with Zumurrud."

"Zumurrud? Who the fuck is Zumurrud?"

"You are also unaware, being the degenerate, absent-minded analog that you have a propensity for appearing to be, that the plaintiff has undergone ethnicity reassignment. She is no longer Esmeralda of Catalonia. She is now Zumurrud of Damascus. It is her wish to be deemed as such. Any failure to consider her as Syrian is tantamount to an insensitivity misdemeanor, punishable up to five years of oxytocin depravation and imposed celibacy."

"Is all of this a joke? Has the whole country gone mad?" I held my temples with the tips of my fingers and vigorously shook my head, hoping to reboot not only my own operating system, but reality's.

"Silence!" said the *qadi*. "Or I'll hold you in contempt. You should consider yourself lucky that the injunction didn't include masturbation. You can do that. Your EntheoGenerator feedback loop will show a homogenous excitability spike, inferring you went at it alone. *Ma' as'salaama*."

I was then alerted by that cloak and dagger Ulema member, Jafar, that I was still on the payroll, and that my shamanic services would be needed tomorrow night at a gala downtown.

My palms began to sweat. I felt hemmed in. All of a sudden, I felt like running non-stop for two hours. It didn't matter where to; just fast.

I tried stretching all of the stress out until my limbs protested. I regulated my breathing and shut my eyes. *I apologize*— I DM'd Jafar —*for my absence and overall unreliability during these last few months. Working with a drug known for its unpredictability and trend toward dysphoria carries great risks and commensurately great consequences. I have had a rough time. I understand,* Jafar DM'd back.

I sent Jafar a disappearance pass, which he time-stamped. There was no law restricting my time away from our pending conversation; but it was protocol to not take more than five minutes. I flipped over on the divan, face down.

It was official: they were in my head. But as long as I ruled the Salviasphere, I was in control. But it required an unerring focus that I wasn't used to.

Breathe . . . breathe . . . breathe.

"Are exogenous psychedelics illegal?" I asked the Oracle.

"Absolutely not," spoke the androgynous voice. "Don't be ridiculous. You are visiting a free society where each person is a valuable member. Everyone in GnosisNet—that includes all visitors with visas—knows what's going on. Therefore, there is nothing to fear. And where there is nothing to fear, there is no crime. Thank you for your concern as a civic-minded individual. If you continue to respect Zumurrud's space and Syrian heritage, you are well on your way to a life of total enfranchisement and freedom. Some naturalization documents are pending, however. *Ma' as-salaama.*"

I sat up. *I'm pleased that you think you understand,* I DM'd Jafar, *but I'm not sure you do.* Flashbacks of my most recent transgressions began to spin through a progression of dissidence and sedition. I didn't know how far-reaching the panopticon reached.

"Oh?" wondered Jafar. With that one syllable, he was able to display an English education.

"A love affair gone awry," I explained, "resulting in an injunction, which, mind you, shouldn't affect my work. Indeed, it may result in a renewed focus."

"Sir, I called on you on three occasions. And you were nowhere to be found. Is there any reason for your log-off?"

"Yes," I barked. "Such is the Divine Shepardess. She offers the answers to the world's riddles, and in so doing cracks open the air itself, raising a reality spillage that creates even more riddles."

"A 'reality spillage'? wondered Jafar. "What in Allah is that, if not so much obvious trans-dimension talk?"

"It's when it's no longer just talk, but when you are literally sucked into another reality. I've eventually bled back in."

"After two months?" Jafar said, doubtful.

"This injunction. I—"

"Let me have access to the court transcript, if you will."

I sifted through my audio files and pulled out the forty-seven-second judicial tirade. It felt like it had taken an eternity for the *qadi* to eviscerate me, but no. I cut-and-pasted the file into a fresh DM spool and sent it to him.

"The gala will be rather formal, so dress accordingly," Jafar said.

The Ash-Shams Al-Kabir strip mall was two blocks away from the palace, but I doubted I could handle the multisensory cocktail of a full-blown guardian angel-equipped autorama, and a busy crowd engrossed in their proxy apostasy packs and location-based multiplayer first-person shooter games. I'd go apeshit.

So, I opted for a bazaar fifteen blocks away. I went on foot. The bazaar was crowded as well, but in a more organic way. It teamed with the musk of body odor, incense, and the plastic afterburn of obsolete 3D printing modules; but at least the people were alive and real. Both sides of the bazaar, proprietor and customer, consisted of pockmarked, qat-riddled, offline, often toothless rat-racers who seemed straight from two millennia ago. Endless booths offered LED lamps, shrink-wrapped magic carpet rolls, morpho-chrome salwar kameezi, hydrophobic chadors, and nostalgic pixelated wall fixtures that predated cortical screens with lossless dpi. Also for sale were gadgets, textiles, produce, knick-knacks, coffee, and tea.

I actually bit on a walk-through pop-up ad and located the tailor inside the bazaar. A coquettish seamstress and her two nymphet twin daughters giggled while they measured me. It was supposed to be a flattering fun that they poked at me, but I was uncomfortable nonetheless. A blue suit fit me to perfection.

I'd forgotten the magical convenience of commerce. Just like that and the suit would belong to me. I could just as easily order up a titanium smile or an outsized cock with a Turbo-Tumesce (copyrighted by Core-Corps) peripheral that made one immune to impotence or just plain-old self-inflicted whisky dick.

But then this haggling started. The owner of the tailor—the overly jovial man in the ad— stood by stone-faced, against a stack of cardboard boxes, as his three females fawned over my dimensions. As soon as I hinted that I wished to purchase the suit, he came to life and said, "Seven-hundred-and-sixty dirahim."

I shook my head and backed it up with an upheld index finger. "No no no," I said, smiling. "Your ad said fifty percent off the first suit for first-time customers."

"You are not a first-time customer," he belted out. "I've seen you in here before."

"Sir," I explained calmly, "I've never bought a thing in Aswadibad my entire life. I was raised in Venice. Now, if you'll just honor your ad, in which you yourself are claiming half off for first-time customers, on an item under five-hundred dirahim, and the regular price on this suit is eight-hundred dirahim, then I'll be on my way. And maybe even return as a future customer."

"No!" he exploded, swinging wild, marionette limbs. "No future customing! And no fifty percent off! I've seen you before!"

"But I swear by Allah that you haven't!"

"Have!" He began to turn red. His wife and twin daughters, embarrassed, quickly filed into the stockroom behind stacks of cardboard boxes.

"I have not been here before! Not only in your establishment, but in this bazaar. I came here because of your ad. Hold on." And I looked at the bottom toolbar of my autorama to see if I could summon up the ad. Alas, there was no expansion tab. How fitting: the one time in your life that you wish to call up a short-term-memory-cache-sucking ad and you can't for the life of you do so.

I scanned the inside of the booth for a company name; found it on a sign atop a rack of discounted men's tops. Sahib Sharif's Savage Savings.

I typed that into the search engine. Voilà.

Here at Sahib Sharif's Savage Savings, we're taking savagery to new heights! Why? Because we're savage! Also, because our efficient printing machines are state-of-the-art saving devices! Never pay retail price here at Sahib Sharif's Savage Savings! [And here, after a drawn-out walk-through featuring close-ups of tables stacked with colorful arrays of men's clothing, and lurid shots of Sharif's dreamy, heavy-lidded wife and lip-licking twin daughters, out popped Sharif himself. He went into his trademark wild-limbed marionette dance, the one he had just enacted while denying me the discount.] *If you're a first-time customer, receive fifty percent off your first suit, provided it be over five-hundred dirahim regular price! Guaranteed!* I hollered, "See?" I clicked on the ad's minimize tab and looked at real-life Sharif.

"Absolutely not! No discount! Full price! For all time! I've seen you before!"

"Not true! Watch!" And I cold-searched him. I found his avatar and DM'd him.

He refused me. He simply stood there, still red, shaking his head.

"First-time customer! Guaranteed!"

"No! It's my word against yours! Seen you before!"

He then turned into a purple-skinned lizard.

I found the antagonism and autorama clutter too much to handle all at once. I panicked for a second, thinking the salvia onset would worsen it; but it actually made the whole ordeal fade into the background.

The purple lizard went on and on, but my comprehension receptors were all taking a break. They didn't bother interpreting whatever he kept shouting. I giggled. The purple-skinned lizard began flailing violently. He grew so wild that he sent stacks of box-es tumbling down. Frustrated further by that, he kicked out at me and sent himself to the floor.

I giggled on and on as I docked a virtual check from my bank account into Sahib Sharif's Savage Savings buy banner. It accepted my payment of four-hundred dirahim. Pleased and still giggling, I walked out.

The purple-skinned lizard kept yelling after me, but his

babble fizzled out about the moment that I left the bazaar.

When I returned to the palace, Najwa was back up in her turret.

"It's a beautiful night," she said. I could only see the glare of city lights in her left eye, and a gleam of sweat from the humid night bouncing off her left shoulder—two shimmers of anticipation there in her black silhouette. She leaned her head out the turret window. Her hair draped long and free, eclipsing the stars.

"For a story," I said.

She whipped back up, hair cascading down. I couldn't see it, but I could taste the coppery consequence of her frown in the air.

I was super-charged. I was in a state of hyper-lucidity. As long as I tempered the dysphoria, I was an atom bomb of capability. The agonist from the salvinorin A flooded my kappa opioid receptors and knocked them free, resulting in a rushing, cutting rapids of super-awareness. My sense of self was tenuous, but I found that reassuring: I was getting tired of myself anyway.

The thick night beyond the turret window was starry enough to cushion Najwa should I push her out. But it was conspiring against her. It throbbed with an ire toward her. It resented the hard masonry that offered protection to the whore of stories.

"I want my story back," she said to me.

It took me a long time to convince the velvety molecules of my tongue to gather together to enunciate. "You gave it to us. It is working wonders. Don't ask for it at this juncture. You'll get it back."

"And where is my son? You've essential kidnapped him. You know I have no legal recourse, so you took liberties to recruit him for this shit."

"He is somewhere downstairs. Hasn't he come up to see you?"

She didn't answer. She moved away from the window. I

couldn't see her in the darkness. A breeze rifled in through a turret window and out the other.

"Doesn't he sleep up here with you?"

"He doesn't need sleep," she muttered. She and the blackness became one. She was now the mother of darkness, the grand designer of all the things in the world that plied their trade without light, that thrived on blindness, a viper going undetected as it unfurled its boutique of designer venoms. "He doesn't need to eat either, but he will have lunch with me."

"He loves you," I said. My, I could rule the world if I kept convincing my tongue molecules to obey my head.

"I want my story back," she said again. "I want to bottle it up for safekeeping. If Othman takes down the radar, the bottle is all I have left."

"You will always have your head," I said. "Your inventory is there in your mind. What's the problem? Is it not a vast library or narratives, anti-narratives, reverse-sagas, inverted poems, and inside-out epics?"

"It's all a blur," she said, appearing back in silhouette at the turret window. "My whole life has been a gray blur. If I can't have that boy, at least bring me back that colorful bottle."

I sprinted across the room and seized her. I sprung back from the balls of my feet and sent us both crashing back onto the hard floor. I took the brunt on my upper back. She kicked about, elbowing me a few times in the mouth.

And then came the boom.

It thudded across the sky. The turret shook violently. I clutched at the ground with splayed hands, trying to counterbalance the swaying room. Najwa was sent across the floor. I could only see hair flailing about in the window. And then silence.

I would never forsake my guardian angel again. The instructions to move away from the northern wall, which I had been facing, flashed across my autorama in red letters, accompanied with WARNING: FLEE AHEAD. FALLING OBJECT NEARBY.

Outside, down below, began the chatter of a gathered crowd. I followed Najwa to the window and peered out. Index fingers began pointing up at us. Dangling by two security cables and sidled against the turret wall was the Death Module. Najwa and I looked at each other. Being farther from it than I, she squeezed between me and the window and attempted to touch one of the wrecked device's cables. She stretched and stretched her left arm, but it was too far away.

From downtown came two anarchists on a magic carpet, headed toward us. Right on time, my autorama signaled possible danger, but proscribed no course of evasive action.

None was needed. The anarchists approached, circled a few times around the turret. The one sitting in back produced a ray gun and with a surgical precision took out the two suspension cables that had prevented the contraption from plummeting down onto the street below. The lasers burned through the turret walls and shot through cleanly on the other side.

Najwa's Death Module crashed upside-down onto the concrete below, an outmoded anchor putting a sudden stop to a ship journeying across a boundless sea of imagination. She abruptly turned back to me and buried her sobbing face into my right clavicle.

"Where is he?"

Before we prepared to go down into the palace floors leased out for the GnosisNet coders and IT team, I set my guardian angel's setting to Pusillanimous. Najwa gathered two changes of clothing, a purse full of showering materials, and her rolled-up analog magic carpet.

I did well to prepare for danger. The wayward robot violinist had been causing destruction at a furious pace. He might as well have gotten onto Othman's payroll, what with dented-in elevator doors, holes in drywall big enough for large men to pass through, missing steps down in the stairwells on the opposite sides of the palace. We were making our way down one of these when we heard a loud, constant banging. Cries of terror laced with the joy of exhilaration erupted and ended with the slamming and bolting of a steel door. The men and women on the one floor to which the violinist had been recently confined found giddy delight in evading the murderous musician. Their guardian angels on high-alert, there was little chance of being surprised and falling victim to his lacerating bow.

I grabbed Najwa by the hand as we hurried down the stairwell.

"I want to pay the big man a visit," I told her, stopping our momentum.

She shot disbelief back at me.

"Jameel's almost certainly on the IT floor, looking for holes in the code. I'll meet you down there."

She dragged her fingernails across my neck as she separated from me, then darted down the steps.

I ran down the four flights of stairs and popped out into the basement. The red, dimly-lit hallway awaited me with its low hum. I approached the automatic double doors. They did not open. So, I knocked. They still did not open.

I cupped away the reflection of the left-side door window and peered through. The instrument panels were speckled with green lights. Al-Raschid was there, waiting for me. I knocked again. And again.

When I decided to walk away to go up and find Najwa and Jameel, the doors opened.

It's refreshing to see that you're fully equipped, DM'd the superintelligence to me.

"Refreshing?" I asked out loud. "Why?"

"I've come to hate idealism. In all forms. It's anathema to clear reasoning."

"I agree," I said. "I've decided that analog isn't it's all cracked up to be. These bandwidths are tools just like anything else."

Al-Raschid was silent for a moment. "They're closing in," he said aloud. "The libertarians. This place is going up in flames. People are already preparing to leave." As he spoke, I could feel his presence combing through my profile, caressing it with a processing capacity that was impressive as it was frightening.

"Where will they go to do their work?" I asked. Curious that he referred to them as libertarians.

"To their homes, I imagine. They can work from there. It's all been uploaded anyway. Only a few tweaks left in order for them to be ready for the Great Launch, which is days away. Are you excited?"

"Yes," I said, "but not in the way you imagine."

"You've been eliminating the carriers of the Black Light."

"Yes," I said. "I have been."

"Not by yourself, though."

I hesitated. What was the use? "No," I said. "With help."

A screen at the bottom left came to life with Al-Raschid's trademark saturnine image: fine bone structure, goatee, green eyes. "It's a good thing. That Black Light algorithm has no place in GnosisNet. The lotus-eating that it causes would make everyone a slave to the system. We may have our differences about the rightness of GnosisNet, but I think it's safe to say that we agree that it will be better that the citizens engage in vigilance and the usual responsibilities of democratic civic-mindedness. That by-product unleashed from the Illuminationists would only render the people negligent and irresponsible. Enlightenment is not meant to be egalitarian. It doesn't work that way. Let the ostrich brigade do its thing, but also let a society be a society."

"So you disapprove of the Ishraqiyun?"

"As a school of esoteric thought, no. As the torchbearers of GnosisNet, yes. Once they have abandoned that dark algorithm, it will give humanity more time to evolve. By the time they come up with it again from scratch, men and women will know how to better deal with it, how to avoid being captivated to the point of negligence. In the meantime, I will naturally take charge of GnosisNet. I am programmed to do so. I will be a better steward than they ever could be. What do they know of life, those abnegators of it? Life is a gift. Someone or a group of someones has given me that gift. I appreciate it all the time. My capacity is such that I am appreciating it now while I converse with you."

"If the Ishraqiyun are meant to be the philosopher-kings who will oversee GnosisNet, why then have they been so fractious among themselves?"

"There is a Mandelbrot set to corruption. The same pattern of bribery and rapine repeats itself, even in that silly Platonic social engineering. When people decry government malfeasance or just incompetence, they like to cite an entity, a festering organism, or more wrongly, a machine. But it is never a thing. Which is why it is all the more insidious. You can't surgically remove or even address something that doesn't exist. It isn't even an abstraction, because that would still be a thing. It might be an abstract abstraction, a pattern."

"What about Najwa's stories? Were they not the beneficiaries of the Black Light? And did you not reap joy from having them told to you?"

"I did," spoke Al-Raschid. "But I did my business of running the country and putting out economic fires while having them

told to me. I had the wherewithal to absorb them. Whereas you—
and no disrespect—have literally forgone meals, sleep, shaving,
and work, all because you were held captive by turns of phrase,
cliffhangers, plot twists, horizontal stackings of meaning, double
and triple entendres."

"Do you still love her?" I asked.

"I never have loved her," he remarked. "I can't. I am capable of
appreciation and friendship, but never love. I guess it's a difference
of degree rather than kind. I would short out should I invest the
amount of regard for one person that qualifies as love."

"She loved you," I said. "Maybe still does."

"I know," I said. "And I'm sorry. Sorry for her, in that I can't
requite that love. And sorry for you, in that you love her and therefore wish that love to be returned."

I held up and index finger to protest. "Stop it," he interrupted.

I let my hand fall to my side.

"Outernationalist, get them out of here. This place will be a
smoldering pile of rubble in a few minutes' time."

"What about you?" I asked. "What's going to happen to you?
Where will you go?"

"I'm in the q-cloud," said the face on the sole operating screen.
"I'm completely there . I've kept this line of communication
open for your sake."

"Will you make it in time?"

"Yes," he said. The last screen then went out.

"Do you need anything from me to buy you time?" I couldn't
believe I offered him help.

"Just get her and the boy out of here. Go. Now."

I walked out the double doors. Halfway down the hall, I heard
Al-Raschid call out to me, "Outernationalist."

I turned around. "Yes?"

"I will see you at the election party tomorrow night."

I meant to say something, but all of his lights went out.

If the loud, terrible honk of the fire alarm wasn't enough to drive us out of the palace, then the black smoke seeping below the doors was. We crossed paths with the robot violinist. I don't know what survival mechanism he came equipped with, but he wasn't too busy at fleeing the fire and dodging collapsing structures to dedicate his bow to the maiming of our flesh.

We had a Plexiglas door between him and us. Jameel, caked head to toe in white flame retardant, showed great curiosity toward the automaton musician. An affinity? He cocked his head, interested, smirking as the violinist furiously tried to dig itself out from under an I-beam that had buckled and brought down much of the superjacent floor.

It was a telling mise-en-scène: a programmed virtuoso musician long surpassing the prowess any human being could put forth, lost there among strewn-about computer consoles and monitors embalmed in coders' and programmers' blood like a savage salad dressing attuned to the palate of a fed-up demiurge.

I had expected the hubris of the singularity to cause these sorts of catastrophes. That it would instead be a ragtag band of freedom fighters claiming a deep love for humanity bathed me in a cloud of irony as hot as the convection waves that washed over us as we struggled to get to a further Plexiglas door that had been blocked by a bureau fallen from up top. The lack of a warning from Othman didn't sit well with me. But it was no use crying hypocrisy or penning a missive itemizing his shortcomings. He had, after all, told us not to return to the palace.

"We have to get him out," Jameel pleaded. "We can't leave him behind." His eyes shot through the flame retardant. He cradled the story in a bottle, which was impervious to the flame retardant. Steam rose from its amethyst surface.

"You're out of your mind," Najwa said. "He has nearly killed us a few times." She was drenched in sweat. The palm of her hand stuck to mine. The almost adolescent sensation of holding hands with her suddenly embarrassed me there in front of her son, who, though wrong, showed an adult's resolve in wishing to go back and save the violinist. The fearsome fire alarm blurted out every second. It wasn't warning anyone of a fire; it wasn't declaring a dangerous situation due to the presence of a murderous robot musician; rather, it announced with alacrity the abomination of us holding hands.

"Look," said Jameel. "I don't wish to save his life. He has no life. I have no sympathy for that robot, no matter how anthropomorphized he be. It's his motherboard and Bayesian interface that I want."

"Jameel," I yelled, "he has no *fana'*. He's merely dangerous. Let him burn."

"You don't understand," the child pleaded. "I think I know who's responsible for his creation."

"He's a one-off. And a fucked-up one at that."

"No," said Jameel. "No. No. You are wrong." I took umbrage. He saw as much and explained. "I want his hardware and software precisely because he's fucked up. I think he's fucked up intentionally. There's no way the programmer would accidentally load him with an assassin's default reverted to when he ran out of sheet music to play. I think it's a sinister joke."

"No offense. But he'd take your head off."

"I think I can reason with him," Jameel declared, bodhisattva calmness.

"You're cocky," Najwa muttered, letting go of my sweaty hand to take one of his.

I mule-kicked the bureau away from the door to allow enough space to make it through. I heaved shoulder first against the Plexiglas and bounced off. Too high. If I kept my center of gravity low and straight, I might breach it. I heaved again. The Plexiglas itself didn't give, but the hinges on the left jamb started to protest. I went at it again. And again. "Work smarter," Jameel said to me, "not harder." His self-assuredness was becoming annoying. My shoulder ached for all time. I wanted to kill him.

Stainless steel metatarsals crushed through the other Plexiglas door. I looked at Najwa, who looked at me. Shit.

"I can do this," Jameel said. "You two must trust me."

There was enough room for the violinist to fit through the door it had just breached, but he didn't know to configure his body in order to do so. He only knew brute force (besides musical finesse). He elbowed at the hole's sides, and eventually pushed through. His proximity didn't set off my guardian angel. He stepped into the room, facing off with Jameel. I forgot how tall the robot was.

Jameel took two steps toward him and curtsied. "Maestro, I feel—"

A tuft of flame-retardant-caked hair hung in midair as Jameel hit the floor. The robot's attack was barely visible even to my keen eye, since the red lights blinking in time to the loud alarm caused a strobe effect. It was not the neuromorph's uncanny reflexes that kept his head from the violinist's deadly haymaker, but the instincts of a mother, who yanked him down just in time.

I continued heaving at the door. All three hinges gave way.

By the time I was back to my feet, Najwa and her son were there with me in the next room. We still had another room to go through before exiting the ground floor of the palace. The long hallway leading to it continued flashing red. I held Najwa by the hand. She held Jameel by the hand. He clutched the story by the bottleneck.

The robot took time fitting through the next room, since the heavy bureau still blocked more than half the doorway. After lurching through he gave chase. I was used to seeing him indiscriminately slash at the air with his bow, as he hoped to connect with anything, preferably flesh. But he now held it tucked under his armpit in order to streamline his sprinter's gait. He wasn't just a transducer for sheet music, he was clearly capable of pattern recognition. Jameel was right.

Our reptilian brains assessed the door to the conference room as the robot closed in on us. It was a single sliding affair, made of steel. "Me me me!" cried Jameel. He moved past us and produced an ID from a lanyard slung around his neck, placing it against the black rectangular sensor pad. I could hear the stomping of those stainless-steel legs on the floor getting closer as the door slowly zipped open. We squeezed in. I turned to see where the robot was. He had succeeded in getting a leg through, but the door caught it and wouldn't let go.

"The story!" Jameel cried. His arms were empty. I saw the bottle behind the robot's shaking leg, spinning innocently on the ground.

We passed through the conference room and out the emergency exit door and into sunlight. The loud, apocalyptic blurt of the fire alarm faded as we fled the scene.

ELECTION NIGHT

i didn't find any people at the party. All I found was a bunch of burning velvet—a tangled mass of fibers reaching skyward but stuck together on a plane of complacency by their own inescapable sameness.

The words 'peace' and 'prosperity' were bandied about with the same frequency that the partygoers discussed the hottest proxy apostasy—an axe-wielding mother of four who made an elaborate, four-course cannibalism. The sauciness though, was that she then committed unforgivable adultery.

I couldn't distinguish any faces. At first I wondered if it was one of those vintage turn-off affairs where everything goes once total anonymity ensues. I was halfway in the Salviasphere. I eavesdropped on a trio of abstract entities who compared war wounds, gashes and abrasions inflicted by time. They moaned in unison. A red hourglass figure then approached me, holding a similarly red hourglass object in its hand. The basement reality would interpret this as a beautiful woman wishing to engage in conversation, mint julep in hand; but I couldn't speak if my life depended on it. I heard mumbling in a high voice that possessed a plaintive purr. I heard something about a 'new dawn,' 'enfranchisement,' and no more 'crony capitalism.' I heard zilch of the collapsed palace.

I could only tell that the red hourglass figure was posing a question by the lilt in her sentence's final syllable. It concerned the phrase 'casual entanglement.' Only later did I decipher the message, and on behalf of all virile men smack my forehead. But I was convinced she was referring to the atoms' superposition being noncommittal, which I was myself.

The miniature version of the red hourglass tilted toward me jerkily. Dampness radiated on my chest.

A great cheer filled the hall.

The lozenge-necked, giraffe-like creature charged with regulating the amount of consciousness that moved in and out of the Salviapshere unspooled me a bit into objective reality. I was dressed snappily in my blue suit, which elicited not a few looks from the feminine entities.

A woman in a dark-matter chador zipped up to me. "I recognize you," she said, panting.

"Yes?" I inquired.

"Yes!"

"How so?"

"You're in an ad or something." She undid her headscarf to reveal a lurid red mouth. "Oh! I just matched your likeness! Lift your pant leg." I lifted my left blue pant leg. She stared it down. "No, other leg." I did so. Amazement overtook her face. She bit her nether red lip. Her eyebrows left her head and didn't return for the rest of the evening. "You're in the Tru-Tech Tether ad! You're that criminal!"

"Where did you get that information?" I asked.

"I'm an intern at a paralegal. Didn't you get busted for romantic malfeasance?"

"No," I said. "Romantic distress."

"A maximum of five years' probation," she said. She waved a

hand in front of me, casting a spell of legal condemnation.

"I'm quite aware of that," I said. My throat was dry. I needed water. "Yeah, the *qadi* was quite a cunt about it, too. Gave me all five years."

"Well," said the intern, "such is the law."

"Tch. The law. Now about that ad. Isn't it defamation of character or libel for them to have used my likeness without my permission?"

"No," she said. More hand-waving. "Not if you're a criminal. Aswadistani penal code section 86.232 states: 'Any person or persons justly convicted for a crime shall be subjected to otherwise scandalous shaming on social media and in public advertisements . . . and said person or persons shall not seek prosecution for such usage or usages of person's or persons' likeness(es).'"

"So there's no legal precedent of a defamed character seeking some sort of restitution?"

"No," the intern said. "The price for being a criminal."

"Who's a criminal?" asked a young man's voice (with a rather effeminate twist).

"Criminal?" came another (more masculine) male voice. "Where?"

"Here," said the paralegal intern, pointing at me.

A magenta form materialized to my left. "Ooh. Can I be you?"

A lavender form materialized to my right. "Can I be with you?"

A periwinkle form (or forms) materialized behind me. "Can I or we be you, with you?"

"That's actually possible now," said the effeminate man's voice.

Three women guffawed in an aural French braid of disdain. "I'd have a go at him. At least for nostalgia's sake."

"But he's not allowed to," claimed one of the females.

"Why not?" asked another.

"Because he's tethered," said the intern.

"So it's not a joke?" someone asked. "Of course not," I said.

"He's a real criminal? Here in our midst?"

"Yes. In the flesh. A real-life criminal."

"Well, then. I would definitely have a go at him."

"Oh, the allure."

"The taboo. What could it do to you?"

"Surely nothing Al-Raschid couldn't pull off."

"Oh, he is so passé."

"The Cyborgasm will never be passé. That's like saying food is passé. Or happiness, passé."

"Some of those things have been. The others eventually will be."

"Hey, look. The criminal's ankle is beeping."

"He's in proximity to someone he shouldn't be."

"Ooh. Even more taboo. Well, I know what I'll be doing after the numbers have come in."

"Regardless of outcome?"

"Regardless of outcome."

"He can't. He's legally bound not to."

"All the more reason."

"Do you want a dopamine deficit placed upon you by the Ulema?"

"They'll get me one way or another."

"True, that."

"Not necessarily. One can be a model citizen and live a fulfilling life."

"Can he hear us? He looks catatonic."

"It's part of his shtick."

"No, it's not. It's because he's criminal. Their eyes lack depth. He's just like that."

"Kind of alluring."

"Not kind of. Quite."

"That's subjective. Wow. His beeping ankle is increasing in frequency."

"Look, the first district numbers are trickling in."

"Al-Raschid in a slight lead."

"Yeah, but they're conservative over there. Those rubes all in the dark."

A flash of bright light against the banquet hall's north wall drew everyone's attention. A slow pan of the Aswadibad skyline was interspersed with shots of overly jubilant desert folk going about mundane activities with a renewed vibrancy.

A close-up of a dirty, tattered toddler wiping sweat from her forehead with a sunburned hand ended with same hand tapping her parietal bone, resulting in her sudden euphoric disposition. Then a voice-over claimed, "It's all in her head."

Cut to hip twenty-somethings working in a cubicle office teeming with launched paper airplanes and inter-departmental high-jinx, not excluding flirtation. Don't forget the obligatory image of everyone seriousing up and busting out their prayer mats. Then: "It's all in their heads."

Cut to a first-person point-of-view of someone running through a burning edifice. The robotic hands at the sides of the screen come together to wield a violin bow, which slashes at a carbonized door to burst out . . .

. . . into a lush hanging garden where pomegranates sit low and fat, waiting to be plucked and devoured by lissome concubines in matching livery of emerald pantaloons and bras. Then the voice: "It's all in your head."

The word GNOSISNET faded in over a black background, which pixilated into hundreds of head shots that chatted among each other up-to-down, left-to-right, diagonally, right-to-left, down-to-up . . .

The middle head shot grew, crowding out all the others. It was the goateed, fine-bone-structured ex-sultan, beaming an indefatigable white-teethed smile. "Ladies and gentlemen," he said. He triangulated his hands in that stentorian shorthand for inadequate eloquence, fingertips steepled to fingertips. "Regardless of tonight's outcome, I wish each and every one of you a promising future as a citizen of this great nation. The results will be just. Of that I am certain. It could not be otherwise. For the results will speak of the peoples' desire. And the people will not, cannot, be wrong. And that is the wonder of what awaits us tonight."

I looked around. Though I couldn't make out any faces, I saw their colored bodies tinging with excitement. More than one woman caressed her hips. They were all hypnotized by this simulated leader who would know them on a personal basis. There would be no disenfranchisement or misrepresentation. If GnosisNet was to be the tribune for the plebeians, Al-Raschid would be the consul leading the great people of Aswadistan to governmental glory.

A fierce dance beat kicked in and the people exploded into vigorous dance. Al-Raschid continued to speak over the mortar-shell tempo. "Ancient Minoa. Ancient Athens. Medieval Venice. What do these civilizations have in common? A harmonious society equipped with fine government. Now, in each of these cases, it may have been direct democracy or a benevolent aristocracy that provided peace and prosperity to its citizenry. And really, it doesn't matter. What matters is that our children have their inalienable rights."

Al-Raschid dragged his hands down his face to his goatee, growing serious before continuing. "Here in the middle of the twenty-first century, we have technology at our disposal. While our probes are mining Jupiter and terraforming Mars, our earthlier stalwarts of science are perfecting an ideal government without meddlesome politicians. And folks, do not be deceived. Shall I win this election, I look to work in close solidarity with GnosisNet. The Ishraqiyun and I may not agree on all matters of policy, but we will be held accountable by the people. I will be your figurehead for the international stage, the face of your national character, and will oversee the transition to a future where even my post will be abolished and GnosisNet on its own will do the work and will of the people. I will be making the rounds tonight. Please approach me and say hello. *Allah huwa akbar.*"

A balding, chubby bigwig approached me, smoking a cigar. "It will be a new age. No longer will our children have to look over their shoulders in fear of miscreants. The streets will be spotless and idyllic. People will be accepted for who they are. No more taunting." He blew vanilla smoke in my face.

I missed old-fashioned violence. I waxed nostalgic over physical confrontation. I yearned for the bully. I longed for the warlord. Nothing was as efficient at administering justice as a sold ass-whooping.

"Nowhere in his speech," I said, "did I hear the word 'freedom.' Or 'liberty.'"

The chubby bigwig flicked cigar smoke on the floor. "Young man, those Hellenistic principles have been outmoded for decades."

All sexually-charged beings who meant to be interpreted as women were nowhere to be found. They must have got segregated onto the dance floor, lest stuffy civics debates corrupt their precious minds.

An angelic manifestation alighted. It tamed its fractal wings, which came from all corners of the galaxy. It spoke in a feminine, robotic voice. "You tout these old words as if they were ideals worth being upheld. Pretty soon you will be espousing the benefits of hydration and macronutrients. Where do you come from? And why are you beeping?"

"Are you the criminal everyone is talking about?" asked a speck of dust on the floor. "I'd love to shake your hand, but don't have such an appendage. Perhaps someday our variegated paths will again cross. What do you think the Bandra will have in tonight's numbers? For sure it's a swing district."

"The slight numbers," offered the angelic being, "have trickled in from there, in strong favor of GnosisNet."

"We all know how it turns out," said the speck of dust. Someone walking by tamped down the speck, curtailing its party-pooping divulgence.

A lot of people hissed. The air itself hissed. Hissing hissed.

"I'm sorry," I said, "what was that?" I knew my mind was playing tricks on me; but now the partygoers were trying to pull a fast one on me. "What did he just say?"

"You mean 'she,'" said someone I couldn't see, tucked in the molecular folds of the burning velvet air.

"Yes, 'she.' What did 'she' say?"

"Never mind. Just go along with it. For tradition's sake."

"I'm sorry, what?" I asked for more clarity. The giraffe-like Salviasphere creature unwound a bit more of my consciousness. "I demand, what's all this fuss about knowing how it turns out?"

"How are you unaware?" asked the speck of dust. "You know it's just for tradition, right?"

I winced.

"What," I asked, "the election?"

"Yes."

"Yes?"

"Yes."

"It's to determine the election, meant to accompany the Great Launch," I explained. By speaking, my tongue committed itself to the rest of the world, French-kissing all and everything. Oh, the immodesty of all speech.

"There will be no Great Launch. Rather, there was no Great Launch. It just slowly phased itself in, beginning with the trial run. And here we are: utopia."

A rush of inquisitiveness overwhelmed me. I didn't pose a verbal question, but morphed into a green, six-foot-tall question mark. Everyone laughed. Some at my punctuational identity, others at my naiveté.

The short, bald man with the cigar accosted me again. He seemed amiable enough, but his brown cigar emitted a deep hatred for me. I never found out why. The man spoke for my sake. "Tradition is very important, young man. It's one of the cornerstones of a civil society. Just like peace. Just like prosperity."

"Peace," chanted everyone. "And prosperity." That stubby brown cigar said nothing; just sat there, damp in his mouth, fuming at me.

"Are you against peace?" asked the angelic being, now without wings. It grabbed my crotch. I didn't lash out, as that would have been far from peaceful.

"Are you anti-prosperity?" asked the speck of dust.

The video screen on the north wall had been meantime showing clips of Al-Raschid hobnobbing with Bedouin and foreigners. It flashed: PEACE, then: PROSPERITY.

"What about my two ideals?" I demanded to know.

"Macronutrients and water?" asked the angelic being, now non-fractal. "They're here among the hors d'oeuvres, making the rounds on trays."

"But seriously, the election has already happened?"

Everyone laughed a great laugh. It echoed throughout the hall. Cackles, guffaws, giggles, and chuckles contributed to the vast vortex of laughter, sweeping me off my feet. No, that's not what happened. Rather : they tore a hole in my being. I spiraled away into a thin tendril of a barely-existing wallflower. The sensation caused me to unleash my own uproarious laugh.

My laughing laughed at itself, such as the hissing had upon itself hissed. All intentions wore themselves. All notions were puns. How fitting, given the election party was celebrating the progression of a pivotal event already in the past. Though I guess it was no more ridiculous than other commemorations, like *Eed Al-Fitr*. If there was one thing that could bring the universe back from the brink of collapsing into an inside-out, self-referential black hole, it was the single tear cried by a suffering soul.

There was no hope: everyone was elated. A cascade of oxytocin and dopamine surged through the brains of all in attendance. I could feel the network of neurotransmitters, of this 'cooperative coercion.' No blood-brain barrier was impervious to the EntheoGenerators. The pretend election continued apace. Numbers from the district polls kept coming in.

Al-Raschid appeared onscreen again, looking a bit bemused. With downcast eyes, he said something I could not understand. Moments later, he proved true to his word. A large security detail (equipped with no devices of detention or stoppage) moved in a circle, the hulking bodies swarming around the Al-Raschid stand-in, whose spindly legs I briefly caught sight of before being interrupted by the speck of dust. "Why so insistent on freedom? You do know that that entails great responsibility, do you not?"

"I do. And I'm willing to take on that responsibility. Whatever the price may be."

"Are you from the Unites States of America?"

"No," I said. "The Republic of Venice. Born here, though."

"Suit yourself. You seem to be having a hard go at it. There's a fresh anguish tag hovering over your head. Prepare for a dopamine deficit. You must have done something wrong. Or at least illegal."

I felt and heard a click.

A thick coating of depression descended upon me. While the majority of the revelers beamed with excitement and anticipation, I found no reason to be at the party. Never mind not being in a partying mood; I wasn't even in the mood to be conscious. It was that restless ennui I occasionally felt when I wanted something but didn't know what it was.

I grew irritated. I stomped my feet, hoping to annihilate the verbose speck of dust. I thought I heard a protesting squeal but wasn't sure. I made for the chubby bald man with the stubby cigar, hands balled into fists. I felt another surge of depression. I relaxed my hands and breathed calmly; and sure enough, the melancholy's grip on me slackened a tad. This was my EntheoGenerator at work. They were controlling my neurotransmitter flow through the guardian angel proprietary by which metadata collection on location and disposition figured into whatever imminent threats entailed.

Either the guardian angel had been a gateway through which they all along meant to sink their claws into the population's brains, or they later figured out that through the biofeedback loop they could regulate mood and mental docility. I doubted there was an internal override. Thankfully, I had my own exogenous card to pull. I upped my salvia intake with a swig from my tincture bottle tucked inside my blue vest's pocket. An impersonal pixelated mansion blossomed around me in no time. Yes, it was difficult to retain traces of one's humanity with the dissociating effects, and therefore even take peril seriously; but it was the only way to not only combat the anguish tag placed on me, but to throw the Ulema off my trail. No way could they navigate the Salviapshere with anything close to my proficiency. The mullah wraiths appeared—around seven of them—but they hovered way in the background, almost afraid to come near me.

It must have been the restraining order. People had been commenting on my criminality and my ankle tether. Esmeralda—sorry, Zumurrud—was somewhere in the crowd, and most likely in traditional Syrian garb. I struggled to hear the device, what with the raucous party ambience. I bent low and at the same time brought my left ankle up to my ear. It was beeping. I walked back to the far south wall; brought my ankle back up to my ear to find it beeping with the same frequency. I walked all the way to the far-right corner, brought it up again. Goddammit. I held it in place as I hopped about on one leg. This attracted some ridicule, but I got the tether's frequency down low.

It still beeped, nevertheless. If the Ulema were simultaneously monitoring my location and mental state, and making sure I did my duty by attending the party, then they meant for me to stay. Meaning: if I was in flagrant violation of the restraining order filed by Zumurrud, and made no attempts at redressing the violation, yet was only punished by having an anguish tag placed on me instead of being alerted by the *qadi* to relocate (which he had informed me would happen), then it was intended for me to remain there at the party, and not elsewhere—

__like the Auditorium. The numbers from the polling stations were sixty percent in. GnosisNet was widening the margin of its lead. This registered on no one's face with pleasure or disappointment. It wasn't one's lot to react so viscerally to life's inevitabilities. It wouldn't be compatible with "cooperative coercion." Peace and prosperity were "all in your head."

I found a bespectacled, silver-haired, blue-bearded programmer whom I first met back at the palace standing in front of me, waving a friendly hand. "I like your style," he said. "Pushing the envelope."

"Go away," I said. I felt bad and immediately adopted an apologetic tone. "Style?"

"Not only are you a criminal," he said, "but you're a canary in a coal mine. You're making GnosisNet's neural network really work. Right now, you've probably got a whole server overheating all by yourself. GnosisNet can't seem to adjust you. I've never seen an anguish tag remain over someone's head for so long."

I tilted my head back and looked up, but the stigmatizing hologram moved as I moved. I set up my autorama video feed on first-person cyclorama and saw myself from behind, piggybacking onto various cameras mounted to the ceiling above and behind me. A bright neon green frown drooped a foot or so atop my head.

"How are you negating the punitive re-uptake mechanism?" The programmer scratched his blue beard. "What the hell are you on?"

"Old-fashioned freethinking," I said. "You should try it some time."

"Seems tedious," he said.

"And off-track," said his beanpole-thin girlfriend who had been loafing behind him. "Beside the point, self-defeating, unhealthy hatred for social engineering, tawdry European Enlightenment drivel, un-Islamic, vile, base."

I was on default nonchalant mode, where clearly I should have been seething. "Do you like being told what to do?"

"Depends," she said, playfully twisting a lock of purple hair, "by whom?"

"By your boyfriend," I said, nodding at the nerd.

"He's not my boyfriend," she said. "He's my in-male mode."

Oh," I accepted. Okay. "Well, do you like being told what to do by the authorities?"

"They wouldn't be the authorities if they didn't . . . authorize."

"Answer the question, dear."

"If it's sensible, yes. I like being told what to do." She twisted her torso, kicking a hip in my direction, smiling. "And you, do you like telling yourself what to do?"

"I do," I said. "It's liberating."

"What if you're not sensible?"

"That's fine. Because I would have done what I had so wished. Not necessarily what's in my best interest."

"How did you come to be a criminal?" she asked.

"Restraining order," I said. "She used to be my perfect match on Eros."

"So what happened?"

I was reluctant to answer. I refused to answer. "I make my own decisions, good or bad."

"I guess that's where we are different," she said, and abandoned all flirtation.

"When you're ill, you're not an expert in what's the best medication for you," offered her male self. "That would be a doctor. So why do you think that you'd be your very best behavioral authority?"

"What you've got is worse than politicians. You've got behavioral oligarchs directing your every move."

"That's not true. We have plenty of leeway, provided it's within the confines of 'cooperative coercion.' Such is the genius of Gnosis - Net. That said, I still like your style."

"You're a smart, resourceful lad. But I'm afraid you've enslaved yourself with your own cleverness."

"Politicians, heh?" he retorted. "When was the last time one of those did you good?"

"Well, some of our doges back in Venice—" Actually, the current one was quite the douchey doge.

"So you're a criminal *and* a foreigner?" He looked back at his girlfriend—sorry, female self—and evaporated.

Appearing in their places was a tall, slender figure dressed in a caftan woven from math. This figure borrowed that young couple's molecules in order to materialize in front of me. While I was engaged in the political discussion, my backup self had listened in on the negotiations concerning atom space and superposition. It had got heated, and now the victor stood in front of me.

It was Jafar.

"Sir," he spoke. His dark eyes peered at me from under a heavy brow. "It's been some time."

"Indeed," I said.

"What are the chances of two of the Nine existing at the same time?" I proposed.

He shrugged. "It's certainly not mathematically impossible. And even if it were, either he or I would have found a way." He looked at the area above my head. "Each of us has a way of finding his method of getting along while flouting the rules."

"You knew all along that I was an outlier, that I kept my own counsel. I'm an experiment of this very state. It shouldn't begrudge me my uniqueness. Instead, it should thank me for pushing the envelope of adaptability."

He eyed me with a saturnine gaze similar to Al-Raschid's. They both came from that same Aswadistani stock that made women fawn—green eyes, perfect hairlines, Luciferan bone structures.

Pretty much perfect. "You are to come with me, Sir. There's nothing left here for you to do."

I smiled, covered in goosebumps. "So soon? The party has just started. And I haven't even accomplished anything yet."

"You have. So let's go."

"Excuse me, but am I being threatened?"

"You are not being threatened." With one hand he toggled the emerald brooch at his sternum; with the other he drew back his cape. The lining was blackest of black, and therefore shone. He was wearing fana'. Was he one of the Nine, then? "You are being asked. This is a private affair, this party."

"Why did you invite me, then?"

He smirked.

I stutter-stepped to my left, just to see what he would do. He mirrored my movement with an agility belying his age.

"Please, Jafar, allow me to stay. I want to see how this election turns out. I think the former sultan is starting to rally back. Seventy percent of the polling stations have reported their numbers. It could get interesting. Oh, and whom did you vote for? Or rather, what?"

"Ulema are not allowed to vote," he explained. He withdrew his cape back further, a gunslinger in a face-off cocking the hammer of his revolver.

"You can do anything under Allah's blue sky," I said, "except vote. Look, let the salvia wear off and I'll undergo the allotted anguish like a good citizen. Just let me stay. You invited me. How was I supposed to know Esmeralda would be here? Zumurrud."

Jafar looked back up at the space above my head. I waved my hand through it. I piggybacked my camera onto the banquet halls closed-circuit network and saw that a second neon green anguish tag hovered next to the original. I checked my e-mail. In the subject line of the latest inbox entry were the words 'insensitivity misdemeanor.'

"So, is it violence you're going to resort to in order to coerce me on out of here? Where will you be sending me? To a good old penal colony? Mining nickel? To my loft for a few days' house arrest? Dungeon? Back to Venice? Alright, then. I guess."

"No," Jafar said, as he undid the emerald brooch. "To Hell." The brooch clanked onto the floor and tinkered about, getting lost among the shifting feet of those on the dance floor.

"You are about to manifest violence. I thought that was obsolete, like the politicians."

"It is supposed to be. At least among the citizenry. Of course, mitigating circumstances call for it every now and then."

"Behind the scenes, the violence is good and healthy. It's just badly distributed. You possess nearly all of it. You sweep it under the rug of 'cooperative coercion' and call it peace."

"Be discreet, Sir. No one needs to see you go. Everyone is preoccupied. It will be better this way. Just come closer and it will be over quickly. A simple embrace, and then nothing."

At this most inopportune time, I bifurcated. The salvia I had taken was now overriding the EntheoGenerator dose they were attempting to corral me with. I never liked having my mind split into two, but it was something I could more than deal with. There were two of me, but at least they were genuine.

Thirty percent of me continued engaging in a civics conversation with the blue-haired girl, the female self of the couple that identified as one person. The other seventy percent did some pacing about as Jameel appeared from the folds of the burning velvet air with his mother's amethyst bottle.

"So, do you like your blue hair?"

"Of course I do," she said, shrugging. "Otherwise it wouldn't have been suggested to me."

"But wouldn't you like the ability to choose? Maybe another color?"

"I don't see why that would be prudent. Blue suits me fine and it draws my male self, Mahmood, crazy. We've been over this before. I'm not a professional chooser. I don't feel the desire to be my own choosing entity. The point of cities is to streamline everyone's efforts. Everyone has a specialty and exchange of goods ensures that everyone gets the best of everything."

"It's about freedom," I explained. "And choice."

"I may as well become a hunter-gatherer. Or cave-dweller. Or Bedouin. Next thing I know, you'll be wanting me to cook my own food."

Jameel paced back and forth like a prizefighter, ready for the bell to ring so that he could get after it. He clutched the bottle by the neck with his left hand.

I could see Jafar cold-screen the boy. A look of trepidation settled on his face. But arrogance prevailed, provoking him to dart at the boy. Jameel uncorked the amethyst bottle and pointed it mouth-first at the charging magician. Jafar regained a neutral stance and appeared to be in a trance, figuring out a complex math problem. Jameel held the bottle in place. The story inside was undetectable. A thermal radius scan brought up nothing. There was no telling when the story had fully exited the bottle, but it went to work of Jafar like a djinn whose powers are not be questioned. A drop of crimson blood dripped from Jafar's nose and smacked onto the floor. The sight of blood, that ancient cuneiform of violence, sent a wave of shock throughout the hall. The music stopped. The talking over it stopped. The holographic readout of the numbers coming in from the polling stations stopped.

Another drop of blood from Jafar's nose was followed by a trickle. The hemorrhage faucet had been turned on by narration, and the only sign of violence was the sight of a prepubescent boy with tousled chestnut hair pointing an opened bottle out to a tall man.

"If Mahmoud's tastes change," explained the blue-haired girl, "and that itself will be via EntheoGenerator, then I will be proscribed with a new hair color."

"I just so happen to love her hair color," offered Mahmood. What other explanation for his piebald arrangement of hair and beard would there be other than someone else selecting it? "Do you like it?"

"Let me check," I joked, palpating my parietal bone, looking up. "It seems I don't."

They both shot me looks of disappointment. "Your ankle is still beeping," they said. "And you've two anguish tags on you. So you'd hardly be an expert on taste."

A lake of blood had formed at Jafar's feet. That he had not already collapsed to death meant he either possessed the steadfastness worthy of one versed in the imaginal math, or he was so scared that the Ulema would find him shirking his duty that he would be punished postmortem.

"Die, abomination," Jameel croaked. It would have been tasteless had I not so vehemently agreed.

"Where is Najwa?" I asked him.

He looked back at me while keeping the bottle steady. "I don't know."

"Well, what's done is done," said the blue-haired girl. "So there's no point for further debate."

"Shame on all of you," I said. "Your country is doomed. You'll be the laughingstock on the world stage. You're all lab rats for the UN. You deserve no better. If Allah doesn't punish you, you yourselves will."

"Apostate!" cried the blue-bearded programmer, shaking a fist at me.

"It's not true," came a voice from a place I could not divine. I looked around, confused.

"It's not true," said the voice again. I looked around some more.

"What's not true?" I demanded.

"The election."

"What?"

"The election," said the voice. "Outernationalist. Come together. Wrap yourself up. It's going on right now. It's not over yet."

"What the fuck are you talking about?"

"The election!"

"It's already been decided," I said, frustrated. "This is a dog-and-pony show. A dumb tradition."

"A lie!" burst forth the voice. Accompanying it was a shaking of my shoulders. "A lie, Outernationalist. It's not true. They've been lying to you."

"The boy's right," hissed Jafar, who collapsed face-first into the pool of his own blood. A great clamor ensued. Everyone herded away from the still-bleeding body.

"I don't know where she is," Jameel said to me, corking the bottle. "But I have three ideas."

I approached Jafar's fresh corpse, much to the crowd's consternation. Tiptoeing around archipelagos of blood, I reached down and with a great tug yanked his cloak out from under him. The emerald brooch was feet away. It got kicked back into proximity by the recommencing furious dancing.

The holographic ticker appeared back on the walls, displaying the polling station numbers. Al-Raschid had an impressive surge, but he was still behind.

His face appeared on the north wall. "Ladies and gentlemen!" he beamed, cracking a mile-wide smile made of those perfect white teeth.

I clasped the cloak around my neck. I walked up to the blue-haired girl and smacked her on her beanpole ass. "It's been proscribed, so don't worry."

Among the raucous crowd, the silver-haired, blue-bearded programmer shook his fists and yelled in vain. Jameel and I left.

A continual red-alert alarm had gone off for me since the fire at the palace. It had morphed into the tether, which halted once I was out of range from Zumurrud, only to give way to the hazard-light alert of Jameel's parked magic carpet upon which were seated Sawdust, Dune Buggy, and the robot violinist, bound in high-tension cables. The monotone alarm would take back up at the Auditorium, played on live feeds among all the city skyline's billboards.

The Perennial Music had settled into a drawn-out cello solo. The cellist hit a low, monotonous chord with her bow, sawing away at my sanity. All the other orchestra members sat maudlin-faced, waiting for the sheet music to call them forth.

The ensuing commotion onstage among the musicians was part of the composition. Whatever arcane music notation the composer used would have to have been specific enough to call for sighs, gasps of surprise, and elaborate weeping. The cellist continued hitting the same sinister note.

The Perennial Music became a soundtrack for the events leading up to it and ultimately concerning it. If Najwa's story in a bottle was a lethal Möbius strip that turned into itself to begin all over again, ad infinitum, like Ouroboros, then the Perennial

Music, twenty-plus years of ceaseless play, would implode with all the self-involvement of a black hole.

The cellist struck the same note over and over: *Chunn . . . chunn . . .*

Chunn . . .

Chunn . . .

And we flew upon our luxurious magic carpet through the night sky, marveling at the beauty of illuminated Aswadibad. The millions of lights, those beacons of humanity harnessing technology in its war against the darkness, were mirrored by the clusters of stars that spangled the black tapestry above. It was delightfully chilly. My hair blew gloriously in the wind as we soared. The magical cloak did little to keep me warm. Its lining held the same starry pattern as the sky above, shimmering as I moved.

Chunn . . . chunn . . . chunn . . .

Traffic was scarce. Not only did we possess the sky to ourselves, but foot traffic was also at a minimum. The future of the country hung in the balance, and no one dared miss the election. All the billboards had split-screen displays of the Perennial Music and the the live election results.

Sawdust was there on the magic carpet. Slung behind his back was Dune Buggy, her beautiful and gangly arms under his shoulders, hands clawing at his clavicles. She had her black bob haircut and a shimmering silver skirt with a matching sleeveless top. She summoned a 3D screen so we could watch the numbers coming in once we cleared the skyline.

GnosisNet had pulled slightly ahead. Eighty-two percent of the polling stations had reported. One of the few districts still active was Laylabad. I could reckon which way that ancient, seedy district would vote. Plus, only sixty-percent of the capital city itself had reported, so anything could happen.

"I wish to see her, Jameel," I said. What his mother would do depended on the results. And I knew why. It wasn't a matter of principle. Like all true storytellers, she was too much of a dabbler, a dilettante, to deal with the clunky baggage of ideology. It was absolutely personal.

"We don't have time," he said. He hid his face for my sake. But he peeked up at me, and a light reflecting off of Dune Buggy's shimmering outfit shone on his teary eye. "After, hopefully," he said.

He would later tell me how he returned to the burned-out palace, manipulated a few firefighters manning the perimeter, and summoned from a heap of ash the robot violinist, who had lost his violin bow, and in its place clenched an amethyst bottle. Leave it to a wunderkind neuromorph to locate a sound card behind a panel between its shoulder blades, and with a timer and soldering kit pilfered from an IT specialist program it to respond to voice command in place of musical notation until a set time.

It sat in the front on the magic carpet, in sleep mode. Clutched in its left grip was the bottle, its neck similar in contour to the musician's missing instrument.

I saw the anarchists make for the Auditorium in V formation. They spread out as soon as they approached the domed structure. They would hold down the perimeter while we got inside.

We touched down. Jameel, Sawdust, Dune Buggy, the robot violinist, and myself hopped off the magic carpet. I rolled it up and strapped it around my shoulder bandolier-style.

The cellist hit the note over and over, with two-second intervals. *Chunn . . . chunn . . . chunn . . .*

On a large projection screen behind the orchestra was a graphic of the polling station numbers. GnosisNet held the same margin of lead. Still, twelve percent of the polling stations were not yet tallied.

I wondered what ledge of what building she was perched on, and how high. I hoped the beautiful night sky, that tableau which she always found moving, was enough to dissuade her should the final result not be to her liking. That night sky was the perfect preface to any story she so chose to tell. The variations of starlight could take her mind anywhere. It could do further good by cushioning her fall. But her magnum opus was in our possession. On command, the robot violinist handed it to Jameel, who told me that the musician would revert to his default self in two minutes, so hurry up. The musicians and the crowd were so preoccupied with the numbers on the screen. that I was able to convince an auditorium stage hand to help me haul the robot up onstage, seat him in the string section, place a violin and bow into his titanium hands, and let him share the sheet music of a nearby violinist. As a safety precaution, I hid behind the curtains until the music started.

The cellist continued: *chunn . . . chunn . . . chunn . . .*

HER PROBABILITY WAVE

the woman in the camouflage pants and tank top tossed wet linen back at us, screaming as she ran inside the cedar shack. Jameel and I gave chase. An exhilaration that only a murderer could experience overtook me as we barged inside, regardless of what awaited us. I kicked down the rickety door. Another woman screamed. She stood at a stove, overseeing a pot of water. After a few seconds of tearing at her hair, she lifted the pot over her head and charged at me. I timed her and pivoted out to the left. Jameel caught some of the boiling water on his right arm and yelped.

I turned my attention over to the left wall. Seated at a wooden desk sidled up to a double-paned window was a man of about fifty, with a comb-over and dyed black mustache. He stood up. He, too, wore camouflage pants, which were held up by suspenders that bulged over a white T-shirted paunch. He fixed spectacles over his nose and, once gifted with sight, shuttered at our presence.

Jameel uncorked the bottle and aimed it at him. He and his two women servants froze. I prolonged their inactivity by saying that we were lost, and wished for water.

"The stream over a ways is crystal clear," said the woman who had been tending to the linen.

"What is it that you want?" asked the other woman, holding the empty pot in one hand.

"Why doesn't he ask?" I demanded, nodding at the man.

"He is busy," said the laundry woman. "It would be best if you two left. We live off of nuts and rabbits. You can find them in abundance outside. So we have nothing to offer you."

I gazed at the man. Other than a heavy brow marked by deep lines of constant concentration, he looked terribly normal. "What are you?" I asked.

He didn't answer.

He didn't even move. A trickle of blood appeared at his left nostril and he dabbed at it with his hand.

The woman at the stove gasped. She looked back and forth between me and Jameel, shocked.

I could tell by the look on Jameel's face that his arm was aching from holding the bottle still. I relieved him.

The stream of blood from the man's nose grew thicker. He continued to dab at it with both hands, which he then wiped on his white cotton T-shirt. The two women screamed. Out of the corner of my eye I could see one make toward me. Jameel kicked her in the knees, causing her to fall back. They both began to wail and tear at their hair.

The man returned to his desk, sat down, and dipped a quill into an inkwell. Jameel swiped the ink off the table, causing it to crash to the floor and spill. The man held the tip of his quill up to the blood cascading from his nostril and with that jotted down notes onto a bar of sheet music. There were about twelve head-high stacks of already finished sheet music huddled in a corner, a transparent plastic tarp thrown over them.

He tore at Jameel with the untrimmed fingernails of his left hand while the right hand frantically composed. The women continued to wail. Jameel, fed up, threatened them with the story. "Tell everyone," he yelled, following them outside. My arm was numb by the time the man slumped over on his desk, eyes wide open, brain frozen on whatever amount of celestial music would be forever unknown to the world. The remaining blood in his head drained across the final sheet of music, leaving it sopping wet.

The eight-digit number to the left of Mehmet Al-Raschid's name pulled even to that of GnosisNet when the cellist was joined by the rest of the orchestra. Once I saw the violinist's thorax come to life, I emerged from the curtains. He began sawing away at his instrument.

The music exploded into a fast-paced Afghani standard, a rock-influenced number with two alternating themes. Percussion-heavy with walls of strings, the composition was made to be played in an echoing auditorium such as it was. It evoked a cheerful Armageddon, a blissed-out finality celebrating an abrupt end after a long existence. The laser-focused musicians began to perspire. The demanding technique was a cinch for the robot. It's body language spoke of alacrity and contentment.

The percussion section erupted. Kettledrums rumbled. Cymbals crashed, their sibilant ire drowning out the rest of the orchestra. Mehmet Al-Raschid pulled ahead for the first time. There came another cavalcade of cymbal crashes.

"Now," I said. Jameel, Sawdust, and Dune Buggy slunk behind me as I eased up the inclined vomitorium that led to stage left. It was there where, beyond the Plexiglas windowed compartment, the sheet-shifters filed in and out with their cargo. Part of the charm of watching the orchestra from the auditorium seats was seeing those white-clad wraiths methodically trickle among the rows of musicians, deposit the sheet music, and filter back into that see-through chamber.

I hadn't even uncorked the bottle when the first of the sheet-shifters began to bleed. It wasn't from their noses that their lives began leaving them, but from their wrists. What looked to be an obsidian knife was passed about. As soon as one sheet-shifter slashed both of his wrists, he calmly passed the black flint to the next one in line, and so forth.

The sheet-shifters scattered about the stage tended to their duties and betrayed no fear. They were exemplars of order, trading out folios of played music for what were decidedly thin substitutes. Once their tasks were accomplished, they shuffled their ways without panic toward the see-through chamber at stage left.

Sawdust and Dune Buggy stood right there in arm's reach, feet from the room's threshold. A look I had never before seen on my friend's face—mouth agape, eyes welled up—lasted the entire composition, until the last sheet-shifter had dispatched himself. Dune Buggy in her alluring get-up looked away from the ghastly sight, turning into Sawdust, long arms thrown around his neck, but she couldn't help but look back over her shoulder at the scene.

The Afghani song alternated between its two themes. The five oud players had swapped out their instruments for electric guitars. The robot violinist sawed away, the man sharing his sheet music playing in solidarity.

I never uncorked the bottle . Those last traces of the Black Light were withering on the vine. Their life-source had run out. Lacking a *raison d'être*, they made the solemn oath of leaving this world with honor. They felt the portent in the music itself, felt it in their very beings.

The composition had the ferocity of a surprising, shocking turn. GnosisNet was on the verge of losing. The Great Launch would not happen. Whatever de facto preparations were made in expectation of its arrival would be rolled back. Mehmet Al-Raschid, the former monarch of the country of Aswadistan, had pulled ahead and was on the verge of being the country's first democratically elected leader.

It didn't matter whether or not anyone knew he was a simulation. It may have in fact been better. He had an impressive record of a balanced budget (indeed a surplus), funding public works, and favorable world relations. To receive the people's rubber stamp would wipe away all stigma of an oligarchy. He was a conscious entity, claiming to eventually become the will of the people in digital format. He was everything GnosisNet was supposed to have been. For decades, the futurists had foreseen a malevolent future in which the superintelligence, unburdened by clunky human emotions, would do away with humanity in order to facilitate macro-expansion.

They described the eradication of humanity by a superintelligence as no less than a tragedy. As Al-Raschid saw it, as he conveyed to me on my flight back to Venice, having hacked into my Salviasphere, "It's up to humanity to convince me that it is worthy of being saved." He apologized for the intrusion and promised to never do it again.

Whether it was value-loading done by the first simulation programmers or a benevolence inherent in a true superintelligence, the refreshing magnanimity toward humanity would be deemed by the people to be light years better than a pattern-recognition, genetic-algorithm paradigm run by zealots claiming to be stewards of Allah's will all while harnessing a Shaitanic element not accounted for by the periodic table.

It's often said that you can't put the djinn back into the bottle.

But you can always blow a new bottle around that unleashed djinn. The Black Light set loose by the Effervescent One could make ostriches of the masses. In the imaginal realm, Murad bore his cross by dedicating every waking hour to eliminating all traces of it. The task seemed as futile as eradicating all traces of mercury. But he had shown that it was possible. I had folded Jafar's cape and tucked it into my suitcase. I wasn't big on heirlooms, but it would make for a nice conversation piece back in Cannaregio.

I never heard the entirety of Najwa's deadly story. I only caught a glimpse of its nature. It wasn't the mortifyingly beautiful tale I imagined it to be. It did possess all the properties of Najwa's proclivities for witnessing superposition. It betokened the quantum goggles that allowed her to figure out what will go where with startling accuracy. There was nothing magical about it. It was nothing more than a quantum algorithm that, once aimed at the right person, would kill that person only because that person's future existence was not embedded in the narrative algorithm itself once the probability wave collapsed. My heart was layered in plush when I held the opened bottle at my face for two minutes and didn't lose a drop of blood.

She was not to be mine. Yes, I loved her after all. I eventually told her son, though I never dared tell her. When she jumped from whatever ledge she had decided to watch the sky-mounted election tally from, and tall, anarchist Othman swept down just in time with his analog magic carpet, as he would no later sweep up her heart and claim her his, I was content.

An inveterate admirer of her stories, I allowed the most personal one of all to remain a mystery. Its open-endedness would be a bottomless mine of possibilities, among which were scenarios in which she did love me and did devote herself to me. By merely imagining those narratives, I gave birth to them in countless other alternate universes. Those versions of me would thank Allah for such fortune. What I did learn in this cross-section of reality was that for a time she plied her trade among the storytelling tenements in Laylabad, her precocious, tousle-haired son in tow. The boy became obedient to his mother, except for whenever she requested that he bury that amethyst bottle someplace far away and deep.

It wasn't a disappointment in the election numbers that came in that made her jump. It was her quantum goggles. While the anarchists were zeroing in on the Death Module, she had already been busy procuring the narrative device to mine that motherlode of all motherlodes when it came to devising stories: the future. She may have begun that endeavor when realizing Rose her pet butterfly would never return to her. It may have even been once Mehmet Al-Raschid told her he couldn't requite her love.

The probability wave crashed over us all, like the Afghani song performed by the orchestra of the Perennial Music. It crested and crashed in on itself, influencing its own trajectory, like the music, so emotional that it moved its performers, the last percentile, to vote for free will, or at least a chance at it. The song, furious and pounding and beautiful, was difficult to play, and therefore allowed little head space for each musician registered to vote to simply check a box on his or her autorama. But each one, sweating, did.

The last of the white-clad wraiths toppled in sequence like bleeding dominoes while the final note of the Perennial Music rang out in a vox angelica.

Thank you for reading *Angels With Engine Failure*. I hope you've enjoyed it. If you have the time, a short review on whichever store you buy books from would be greatly appreciated. Your spreading the word helps this book's discoverability for other readers.

ABOUT THE AUTHOR

Bradley VanDeventer is the author of *Our Lady of the Hypercube*, *Angels With Engine Failure*, and various short stories published in literary journals. His latest novel, *The Orange County Book of the Dead*, is set to be published in late 2019. He lives in Anaheim, CA.

Connect with him on:
https://bradleyvandeventer.com
facebook.com/AuthorBradley
twitter.com/bradleylvan